CONDITIONS

"You will all know my name," he said. He had a strong accent, but Stella had no difficulty understanding his words. "You will all fear my name." He seemed to be looking through the camera, right into Stella's eyes; she felt exposed for a moment, even though she knew he could not possibly see her. He had to have personality mods, to convey that much command presence in a recording. "I am Gammis Turek," he said. He paused. His mellow voice, perfectly modulated to convey strength, determination, menace, was far more frightening than the harsh bellow of a thriller actor.

"You must understand this," he said. "I can isolate your world at any moment. My fleets control the spaceways; my forces can disrupt ansible communications whenever I wish. I have many allies; their forces, too, are at my command. I have more ships than any system militia and weapons that can turn your home worlds into cinders." A carefully measured pause. "If you force me to use them against you, I will have no mercy. You and th_____ _____ thing you have wo_____

By Elizabeth Moon

The Serrano Legacy
Hunting Party
Sporting Chance
Winning Colours
Once a Hero
Rules of Engagement
Change of Command
Against the Odds

The Serrano Legacy: Omnibus One
The Serrano Connection: Omnibus Two
The Serrano Succession: Omnibus Three

The Legacy of Gird
Surrender None
Liar's Oath

The Deed of Paksenarrion
Sheepfarmer's Daughter
Divided Allegiance
Oath of Gold

The Deed of Paksenarrion Omnibus

Paladin's Legacy
Oath of Fealty

Remnant Population

Speed of Dark

The Vatta's War Series
Trading in Danger
Moving Target
Engaging the Enemy
Command Decision
Victory Conditions

with *Anne McCaffrey*
Sassinak (The Planet Pirates Volume 1)
Generation Warriors (The Planet Pirates Volume 3)

VICTORY CONDITIONS

ELIZABETH MOON

www.orbitbooks.net

ORBIT

First published in the United States in 2008 by Del Rey Books
an imprint of the Random House Publishing Group,
a division of Random House, Inc.
First published in Great Britain in 2008 by Orbit
Reprinted 2008 (three times), 2010

A CIP catalogue record for this book
is available from the British Library.

ISBN 978-1-84149-598-9

Typeset by Palimpsest Book Production Limited,
Polmont, Stirlingshire
Printed in the UK by CPI Mackays, Chatham ME5 8TD

Papers used by Orbit are natural, renewable and
recyclable products sourced from well-managed forests and certified
in accordance with the rules of the Forest Stewardship Council.

Mixed Sources
Product group from well-managed
forests and other controlled sources
www.fsc.org Cert no. SGS-COC-004081
© 1996 Forest Stewardship Council

Orbit
An imprint of
Little, Brown Book Group
100 Victoria Embankment
London EC4Y 0DY

An Hachette UK Company
www.hachette.co.uk

www.orbitbooks.net

For Anne McCaffrey

Acknowledgments

A final volume in a series should really list everyone who helped, but that would be far too long in this case. For this volume alone, the Usual Suspects offered frequent support, encouragement, and included Richard Moon, David Watson, Allen Sikes, Beth Sikes, and members of the fencing group and the choir of St. David's Episcopal Church. The concom, other guests, and members of SwanCon in Perth, Western Australia, were also helpful (some without knowing it), including the gentleman who confirmed my suspicions about the relationship that might exist between secret agents in different political entities. Regular posters on my newsgroup were helpful in pulling up details from previous books that would have taken me hours to dig out even if I'd been home to look them up. My agent, Joshua Bilmes, keeps me focused on the job at hand when my attention wanders.

Special mention goes to Mel Tatum and her husband, Chris Merle, who let me use their house as my private office space between Conestoga and NASFiC, so that I got the revisions done on time, and to Mel and Alexis Latner for their timely critiques as I worked in "Writers' Camp."

Finally, it's time and more than time to thank all the editors who've helped me with this series: Shelly Shapiro, who got it off to a good start, Jim Minz, who came in midway and did a superb job, and finally Liz Scheier, who took over for this last volume. I'm indebted to all three; they made all five books better than they would have been otherwise.

VICTORY
CONDITIONS

ONE

Ky Vatta glanced around the table at the captains crowded into her office. It still felt a little unreal, but here they were, all waiting for her to say something: Argelos and Pettygrew, there from the beginning; Yamini, who had been Argelos' military adviser and who now captained the stealth observer they'd captured from the pirates; Ransome and Baskerville, the two surviving captains of Ransome's Rangers; Major Douglas of Mackensee Military Assistance Corporation, assigned as MMAC's liaison to her. His assistant, Master Sergeant Cally Pitt, seemed quite at ease standing in a corner.

"Our main problem, as I see it, is that we're always reacting to Turek," Ky said. "We don't know much about him, what his goals are—besides killing people and getting power—and we can't understand any of the transmissions we've overheard. We've got to find a way to get better intel."

"Mackensee might share data with you," Major Douglas said. "If you don't mind me butting in." He smiled at Ky.

"I don't mind," Ky said. "Before we go into jump, would you like to ask them about that?"

"You particularly want information about their language, any history anyone can dig up, is that right?"

"Oh, I wouldn't mind knowing where they are right now, where they're going next, and in what force," Ky said, grinning.

"If we knew that, we'd be hauling mass," Douglas said. "All of us. But I can ask if any of our linguists know the language. You gave them copies of the transmissions, right?"

"I did, yes," Ky said. "And another thing . . . I know I need a staff structure. We talked about that before, but with over forty ships to command, I need something now, before we get to Cascadia."

"Think any of those privateers will give you trouble?" Argelos asked. Ky was mildly amused to find that the former privateer no longer considered himself one of them.

"I doubt it," Ky said. "Aunt Grace sent them; she'd have checked them out."

"You don't just need a staff," Douglas said. "You need a combat control center. You can't command forty ships from the bridge on this one—it's too crowded, and it doesn't have the right communications setup. Your shipboard ansibles are an incredible advance, but they can't do everything and they are bulky."

"My office—"

"Isn't adequate," Captain Yamini said. "I agree with Major Douglas. Running the additional communications cables in here would be next to impossible, and they must be shielded cables. You're talking over forty ships now, and maybe more if the Moscoe Confederation sends ships from Cascadia. That's a lot of equipment, not just for communications but also for scan, if you're to have the data you need during a battle. I don't know how you'd get one in this ship—you'd have to practically rebuild it, I'd think—but then you've told us it needs serious work anyway."

"On our ships, the CCC is built in when the hulls are laid," Douglas put in. "But I understand that some systems have modular CCCs that can be retrofitted to vessels. We don't, but maybe they can do that at Cascadia."

"Before we go FTL, we should ask Stella that," Ky said, adding another line to the list in her implant. A long list, now, since she had heard about the Slotter Key privateers on their way to Cascadia, turned down Mackensee's offer of a commission, and accepted the suggestion of a liaison to travel with her. In a few short hours, her little group would leave the Mackensee headquarters world and head for Cascadia Station . . . and she would have to be ready, when they arrived, to take charge in reality as the commander she had hoped to become.

"We'll have two jump transitions on the way," Argelos said. "Do you want communication there, or not?"

"They're both just waypoints, aren't they? Uninhabited systems?"

"Yes. But the ansibles are up in both right now. We might find out what's going on—"

"Good idea," Ky said. "We don't want to delay more than we have to, but stripping bulletins from ansibles doesn't take long. Everyone should do it, so you can each run your own analysis and we can share. Intership communication only by onboard ansibles, no matter how close we are."

Her deskcom chimed; Hugh Pritang's code. "Yes, Hugh?" Ky said.

"Last load's coming aboard here, Captain. Last for *Sharra's Gift* is a half hour out. *Bassoon*'s complete. Mackensee's Traffic Control officer has given us a priority departure slot in two point five hours. Next after that's at three point five. Thought you'd want to know."

"Thanks, Hugh," Ky said. To the others, she said, "We'd

better get with it, hadn't we? I'd like to take that early slot, so this meeting will have to be short."

For another hour, they hammered out the organization of skeleton staff, to be filled out once they arrived at Cascadia, then dispersed to their various ships. Ky made the calls courtesy required to the Mackensee officers who had assisted them, sent databurst messages to Stella, Grace, and Rafe, and then went to the bridge as they undocked and headed out toward the jump point.

Nexus II, Headquarters of InterStellar Communications

Rafe Dunbarger, acting CEO of InterStellar Communications, looked at the monitor in the central control room of ISC's detention center. The man in the security cell looked older than his official years and very tired. All the gloss of wealth and power had leached away, leaving his face exposed, the dissatisfaction and ambition clear to see.

"You sure you've got everything?" Rafe asked his new internal security chief.

"As sure as we can be. His implant was coded to self-destruct if removed, of course, but we were able to block that and examine it. Downloaded everything we could. And before we took his implant, we'd done a full panel, 'cept what you'd told us not to." Faint regret colored his tone.

"I have my reasons," Rafe said.

"I'm sure, Ser Dunbarger. Not arguing, just saying."

Rafe watched the man on the monitor shift his weight on the narrow bed. Now came the question, the final question at the end of all the data collection. What to do with the man who had destroyed his childhood and much of his adulthood, who had separated him from his father, who had schemed and plotted and finally attacked his own mentor, Rafe's father? Who had contrived the killing of Rafe's sisters, the death of his surviving sister's husband and child? He surely deserved death, but . . . what death could encompass his crimes? And what about legal procedures?

He'd made discreet inquiries, and the answer came back that it was ISC's problem. The government didn't want a noisy, embarrassing, expensive trial any more than he did. They wanted the problem removed.

"He's a hundred percent liability," he'd been told. But he'd been told that about himself, when it wasn't true. Was it ever true? The man had intelligence, talents, charisma . . . he had earned the trust of the Board, of Rafe's father . . . could he have been, in some way, as misunderstood, or at least as complex, as Rafe?

"Would've been easier to kill him that first day," Gary said.

"True." Rafe sighed. No matter what he did, leaving Lewis Parmina alive would be too dangerous. The man was a threat, not only to him and his family but also to ISC, Nexus, and the new alliance. In the heat of his early rage, he could have enjoyed killing the man himself . . . but now his stomach churned at the thought.

"You going to tell him?"

"He expects it," Rafe said. "He's not stupid."

"They always hope," Gary said.

"I'll speak to him," Rafe said. He wasn't sure why he felt that he must, but he knew if he didn't he would regret it forever.

"Not without a guard," Gary said.

"No," Rafe said. "I'm not stupid, either." Gary grunted, and Rafe grinned at him. "And not you—I'll take whoever's on duty in the section."

It was only a short walk to the guard station at the

entrance to the block of cells. He let the guard open the cell, and then followed him in. The guard stepped to one side, stun-rod ready.

"Enjoying yourself, aren't you?" Lew Parmina said. His gaze flicked to the guard and back to Rafe's face. His smile widened. "Still the scared little boy, are we?"

"Cautious," Rafe said, keeping the edge out of his voice. Mild interest, no more. "You might take it as a sign of respect."

"Not from me," Lew said. He put his hands behind his head; the guard shifted slightly, watchful. "Having fun with the company? I left you a few surprises . . ."

"As much as possible," Rafe said.

"My family?" Judging by the sneer on his face, he didn't really care about them.

"Are fine," Rafe said. He waited a predictable two beats.

"No conjugal visit before the end?"

"She refused," Rafe said. Parmina's wife had done more than refuse; she had gone into hysterics at the mention of that possibility.

"Ah. Well, then, I presume this is the obligatory so long, farewell, see-you-in-hell session? Or are you going to go all mushy and ask why I betrayed your father's trust?"

"I have no interest in why you did it," Rafe said.

Lew shrugged. "Well, then. Get it over with. Unless you're planning to drag it out with torture or something. I know you—you can't pretend you don't enjoy killing."

Rafe smiled down at him, holding Parmina's gaze until the man had to look down. "I ration myself," he said then. He nodded to the guard, who opened the door and turned to leave.

"You coward!" Lew screamed, and lurched forward. Even as Rafe spun, drawing his own weapon, the guard's stunner struck Lew; he collapsed, clawing at his neck.

"Go on, ser; I'll take care of this," the guard said.

"Quickly," Rafe said. He holstered his pistol. "No play-time."

"Absolutely," the guard said.

Rafe waited in the corridor outside. After a moment the guard emerged.

"Autopsy?"

"No," Rafe said. "The family has requested no autopsy and no funeral. I'd say dispose of the body to medical research, except that he might have hidden something else nasty internally. If you can remove the implant in a secure facility, do that. Direct cremation's safest. Be sure to fill out the paperwork."

Back in his office, Rafe made the necessary calls. Lew's wife cried, more with relief than sorrow, but he still felt compelled to comfort her. The daughter Lew had abused listened stony-faced, and said only "Good." Rafe's sister Penny nodded once, then burst into tears—clearly relief, this time—and his mother, on the com, did the same. Official reaction was subdued but clearly glad that ISC had handled ISC's problem.

He felt none of the exultation he had felt before . . . only a peculiar sense of loss that he finally identified as grief. Lew Parmina was dead, and deservedly so, but he had been as human as Rafe himself. He thought suddenly of Ky, and her moment of compassion for the spy they had caught on her ship . . . she would have understood this. How could someone have gone so wrong?

He informed the Board that afternoon, at their regular meeting. "Lew Parmina is dead," he said. "He tried to attack me, in the cell; a guard killed him. The death was reported to all the proper authorities; the family declined to receive the remains or hold a funeral; they asked that ISC dispose of them. He was cremated immediately."

"About time," Vaclav Box said. He had urged the need for Parmina's death more than once. "Poisonous creature." Others murmured agreement. No one wanted to be seen as defending Parmina.

"Next," Rafe said, "the latest medical report on my father." At first they had demanded such reports almost daily, but lately he had noticed more time between questions, and less apparent interest. "His speech has improved, though slowly. His doctors, however, hold out no hope that he will be able to take up his duties as CEO even part-time within the next four months . . . and they do not think he will ever be able to use an internal implant."

"Not even on the other side?" Vaclav Box asked.

"Apparently not," Rafe said. "Because of the existing damage, they're concerned that any manipulation to create the pocket could cause seizures—or worse. An external device might be possible, but . . . he had had a right-sided implant his whole life." He looked down for a moment, imagining what it must be like without an implant, without that reassuring presence. "We had all hoped, of course, that the neural regeneration would proceed more swiftly." Then he could have gotten back to his own life, though he had no idea what that life might be.

Glances passed back and forth across the table; for a long moment no one said anything.

Finally, Box cleared his throat. "About your father . . ."

"Yes?"

"You know I've talked to him. So have some of the others. I'm certainly aware he's not what he was. And— for the most part—we don't want him back." Box paused a moment, clearly trying to gauge Rafe's reaction. Rafe felt as if a load of rock had dropped on his head; he couldn't think of anything to say. "I'm one of his oldest friends; I still consider him a friend. But he got us into this whole mess; his judgment was faulty long before his injury. Or perhaps it had been tampered with, but that doesn't really matter."

"You've canvassed the Board?" Rafe found his voice at last, looking around at them all.

"Informally, yes."

"You can't blame everything on him. It was Lew—"

"He was fooled by Parmina, to the point of repudiating his own son." Box went on, enumerating the same things Rafe had struggled not to see. "The policies he approved led directly to the mess we're in now—the erosion of our ability to protect our monopoly, the failure to gain control of new technology, the theft of our intellectual property . . . Parmina may have been the mastermind, but your father did not see the dangers."

Neither had the Board, Rafe thought. They had all been fooled just as much as his father. Had they ever done anything more than nod yes and take their compensation? "Then . . . if you don't want my father, you won't want me," he said. He felt letdown and relief at the same moment.

"Not at all, Rafe. You did see the problems; you've clarified them for all of us; you've started turning the corporation around. We need you and we want you. Now and for the foreseeable future. I don't believe—and I am sure the Board concurs—that there is anyone else who could possibly save as much of what we had."

The others nodded. The weight fell back on his shoulders. He wanted to yell at them, insist he was not the one for the job, but he knew . . . he knew he was.

"The only problem," Box said slowly, "is this thing with the Vatta family and your relationship with them. On this I stand with your father, and I think I speak for most of the Board. There are reasons to be concerned; they are involved in too many of the things that have gone wrong, that have cost us."

"You can't seriously believe . . ." Rafe stopped, faced with that double row of stony faces. They did believe it. He would have to change that—they would have to understand that their future lay with a Vatta alliance.

Moscoe Confederation, Cascadia Station

Stella Vatta, acting CEO of Vatta Transport, watched a crawler line move across the screen of her deskcomp— silenced, as she liked it—and flicked for full download. The columns of figures she'd been working on faded; the screen showed a newsman from Central Cascadian News Service standing in front of another screen, which showed an explosion repeating, over and over.

"—just in, a vid apparently sent by ansible to at least a dozen system governments. We're not sure of the source, but analysis suggests that it is, as it claims, an actual unedited vid. The person you will see identifies himself as Gammis Turek and claims to represent a large force— I must warn you, this vid contains disturbing images and language, unsuitable for children. But we feel it is urgent—"

Stella felt cold to her bones. Gammis Turek. The man Ky insisted had been connected to Osman Vatta and the attack on their family . . . and behind the disruption of the ansible network, and the conquest of systems like Bissonet and Polson.

The screen changed, so the explosion filled it. This time, it did not repeat, but changed to a man in a dark-red-and-black uniform, standing against a background of a night sky, arms folded across his chest. He seemed tall, though without any background clues it was impossible to say how tall: dark-haired, dark-eyed, a strong-boned face that might have been attractive if not for the expression.

"You will all know my name," he said. He had a strong accent, but Stella had no difficulty understanding his words. "You will all fear my name." He seemed to be looking through the camera, right into Stella's eyes; she felt exposed for a moment, even though she knew he could not possibly see her. He had to have personality mods, to convey that much command presence in a recording. "I am Gammis Turek," he said. He paused. His mellow voice, perfectly modulated to convey strength, determination, menace, was far more frightening than the harsh bellow of a thriller actor.

"You must understand this," he said. "I can isolate your world at any moment. My fleets control the spaceways; my forces can disrupt ansible communications whenever I wish. I have many allies; their forces, too, are at my command. I have more ships than any system militia and weapons that can turn your home worlds into cinders." A carefully measured pause. "If you force me to use them against you, I will have no mercy. You and those you love, everything you have worked for, will die in an instant. Here is one proof of it."

Now the scene showed an expansive office, where well-dressed civilians, all clearly humods, backed away from armed men wearing Turek's maroon and black colors.

"They argued with my commands," Turek said. The troops fired, in short bursts, and people fell, some screaming at first, until at last the room fell silent. "They did not obey," Turek said in a voice-over, as the scene shifted to a brief battle between a rock-throwing mob and the soldiers. "That was Polson," Turek said. "I own it now.

I own its jump points. I own its ansibles. Only my people live on the world once called Polson. And it is not the only one." The scene changed to a ruined city, smoke rising from shattered buildings. "Here someone killed one of my men. Just one. Hundreds died here, maybe thousands. It doesn't matter to me. I do not tolerate disobedience." He did not sound angry, but like someone stating an undeniable fact.

The scene shifted again, this time to an image of an ansible platform exploding, then again to Turek standing as before.

"Do not make the mistake of thinking this an idle boast. Or that you can save yourselves by banding together. It is too late for that. My agents are everywhere: those of you who conspire against me will regret it." He smiled, a chilling smile that was at the same time alluring. Stella remembered from her brief bad affair what strings were being pulled here. "Remember my name. Expect me. I am coming."

The announcer reappeared. "We have no way of knowing whether this is some kind of scam, or whether this person really exists and actually is behind the recent disturbing events we reported some time ago—the apparent overthrow of the governments of Bissonet and Polson by a foreign force. But we felt this was important enough to bring to the public. We have already sent this vid to the Moscoe Confederation Defense Department, who are now analyzing it further. We will keep you informed."

Stella tabbed back to the spreadsheet she'd been working on. Cascadia felt a lot less safe than it had a few minutes ago; she had been so sure that nothing would happen here until Ky reappeared, and then Ky would take care of it—or someone would—and she could go on leading Vatta Enterprises and Vatta Transport. And there was nothing she could do, really, except make sure that new onboard ansibles came off the production line as fast as possible. One production line might not be enough; she might as well work on costing a proposal.

Ten minutes later, her implant scheduler reminded her that her ward Toby would be back soon from school; foreign crisis or no foreign crisis, she could not put off any longer a serious talk about a purely personal matter.

She waited until Toby had engulfed his usual after-school snack before broaching the topic she knew would upset him.

"Toby, I need to speak to you about your friendship with Zori."

"Why?" From his expression he suspected the reason.

"Her family isn't happy with it, for one thing. If you were both older, that wouldn't matter . . . well, it wouldn't matter on Slotter Key; I'm not sure what the courtship rituals are on such a courteous place as this. But you're not older, and her family has a right to influence her choices."

"She likes me." Toby's face settled into a stubborn expression. Zori was his first girlfriend, and he had fallen as hard as a boy his age could fall.

"Yes, so I gather from her mother. But their concern is twofold: we are not an old Cascadian famly, and we are the wrong religion."

"We can't help it that we just got here," Toby said. "It's not like we're criminals or anything."

"No. But—" Stella sighed. This was a part of the caution common to prominent families that she had not understood herself, at Toby's age, and her own stubbornness had caused no end of trouble. "They're just being careful of her, Toby. They think—right or wrong doesn't matter—that she will be happier with someone of her own kind—someone whose family they know."

"She doesn't care about those boys," Toby said. "She cares about me."

"That may be, but it doesn't change the fact that her family would prefer she not care about you that much."

"We're not *doing* anything," Toby said, flushing in a way that suggested they probably were, though Stella hoped not as much as she herself had. "All we did was— kind of—you know—I mean, I touched her hair."

Stella knew, to the marrow of her bones, what Toby was feeling, and also what magnitude of trouble that could cause.

"They're her parents. You don't want to get her in trouble—"

"No, of course not. But they—"

"Are her parents," Stella repeated. "Look, I've had two long talks with her mother. Explained—" Stella caught herself. Telling Toby she'd told Zori's mother that the two were in no danger, that it was their first attraction, that they'd get out of it faster if the parents stayed calm, would only make Toby determined to prove how serious they were and how permanent their affection. "I explained that we were a respectable, even prominent family on Slotter Key, that you were a responsible young man. They're not accusing you or her of anything . . . wrong. They agree that you're intelligent and well mannered. But they're adamant that she quit visiting here unless I guarantee adult supervision. And even then, not more than twice a week."

"Here? But it's our office! It's—it's a public place. It doesn't even have a bed!" Though not because he hadn't asked for one, so he could stay overnight working on his projects. Stella forbore to remind him of that.

"Toby, this isn't about you, specifically. It's their culture, their family, their daughter."

He had hardened his jaw, but now he nodded slowly.

"I suppose . . . I should be glad that they didn't forbid her to visit at all."

"You're right. And they want to meet both of us. Two meetings: one with me alone, and one just you and her parents."

"Zori didn't say anything—"

"She may not know yet, and for this meeting she won't be coming. Her mother suggested lunch at a nice restaurant, and I agreed. Her father may or may not make it."

"So when—"

"Tomorrow."

"Can I tell—?"

"I see no reason why you can't tell Zori today that I'm meeting her mother for lunch tomorrow. But if I were you, I would not be too specific about why. Her parents have a right to tell her what they want her to know."

"It's not fair to keep things from people—" Toby began.

"It's also not fair to start trouble between members of another family," Stella said.

"Liking someone isn't starting trouble," Toby said.

"It can be," Stella said, with a rush of all-too-vivid memories.

Stella arrived at The Glade, the restaurant Zori's mother had suggested, a few minutes early; her security team ran its usual check, and she signed them in with the maître d'. "Ser and Sera Louarri aren't here yet," he said. "If the sera would like to wait in the lounge?"

"Thank you," Stella said, glad of a few quiet moments alone to collect herself. The morning had been a chaotic scramble as worried officials demanded to know when ansibles on order could be delivered and where Ky was and when the promised Slotter Key ships would arrive. News outlets had played Turek's speech over and over;

normally courteous Cascadians were even snapping at one another and at Stella. The familiar dance of family relationships could not be as stressful as her morning, even if it turned out badly for Toby.

The lounge extended the Cascadian theme of forest design to include a floor covering that looked, felt, and smelled like a carpet of real moss, a sound system projecting the rustle of leaves in the breeze and birdsong, and visuals that produced moving shadows and lights on the surfaces, as if sun glimmered through leaves. Stella appreciated the artistry, but wished some decorator would choose another theme . . . a beach, perhaps, or a mountain lake, or a meadow full of bright flowers. Surely the planet wasn't all forested.

"Ah, Sera Vatta!" The woman who came into the lounge was older and had once been in Stella's class of beauty, but dark-haired, like Zori. Now she had the thin, brittle look of someone fighting a long illness or under great stress. Her ice-green suit fit perfectly; her jewelry was obviously expensive but not flashy.

"Sera Louarri, what a pleasure!" Stella said. She knew she was being examined and evaluated in the same way she looked at Zori's mother. Hair, manicure, makeup, clothes, jewelry, shoes . . . she had correctly guessed the right level, and Sera Louarri acknowledged that with the briefest change in expression. As far as fashion went, they were equals.

"I'm not sure if my husband will make it," Sera Louarri said; her voice was tense, as if expecting Stella to complain. "He sent me a message; something at work had come up—"

"I quite understand," Stella said. "Should we wait, in case—?"

"A few minutes only, if you don't mind," Sera Louarri

said. She sat upright on the edge of her chair. "He said if he was not here in ten minutes he would not be coming, but—"

"You have a charming daughter," Stella said, hoping to put her more at ease.

"I hope she hasn't been too forward," Sera Louarri said. "She's . . . she's vivacious sometimes, she speaks out. Her father—" She gulped. "Her father indulges her."

Stella wondered if the woman was ill, or if meeting her daughter's boyfriend's guardian was really such a strain. "Not at all forward," she said. "Very polite, I would think by the standards of your world as well as mine."

"Would you tell me something of your—and I assume Toby's—world?"

"I grew up onplanet," Stella said. "The main family house was in the country, though my father's business took him to the city much of the time—" She noticed that Sera Louarri's face relaxed. Was it the country, or the city? "Slotter Key has four main continents and a lot of good-sized islands. The family as a whole has tik plantations on several subtropical islands, but we lived in a temperate zone—stone fruits in our orchards, lovely in the spring. My cousin Ky—you have heard of her, I know—lived on one of the tropical islands, with reefs just offshore on the east side. We visited each other often."

"You could grow Old Earth stone fruits in quantity?"

"Oh, yes. Exported the fruit and nursery stock off-world—for some reason, the result of terraforming there worked for all the rose-family plants, and our family lands had varied terrain so we could grow just about all of them. The first time I went outsystem, I was amazed to find that not all planets could grow them, even after terra-forming."

"You must have traveled a lot," Sera Louarri said,

sounding wistful. "And so young. Did your family approve?"

Surely she had heard . . . Stella explained, as if no one could be expected to have done research. The family business, the habit of sending young people out to sample the universe.

"I also grew up onplanet," Sera Louarri said. "My family has—had—timberland. We export hardwoods, you know. The native vegetation, not Terran."

"But for food?"

"Oh, farmland's terraformed, of course. But not the forests; the native trees have incredible wood. My family were Firsters." She seemed more relaxed now, more confident. "We had a grant that covered all the ground from the coast to the inland range, for a thousand kilometers."

"We called them Chartered," Stella said, smiling. "The first colonists on Slotter Key. Vatta's Chartered."

"You are?" Sera Louarri peered at her a moment. "But that's the same—?"

"If I understand Firsters. Your family goes back to the colony foundation, and you were investors, right?"

"Right." Now Sera Louarri sat back a little, and her smile widened. "And your nephew, he grew up the same?"

"Not exactly. His parents live in another system, running a branch operation. I'm not really familiar with his home world."

"My husband's business also operates in multiple systems," Sera Louarri said. "But you—you're not married?"

"No," Stella said.

"And your family does not mind? They do not press you for an alliance with another?"

"My family," Stella said, carefully controlling her tone, "is mostly dead. But my father wanted me to have experience, he said, before I married. If I married."

"Zori is too young to marry."

Stella just managed not to laugh. "So is Toby, of course. But young people—they will form attachments."

Sera Louarri's gaze wandered away and back. "I think my husband is not coming, and we should go in to lunch."

Cascadian custom prohibited business discussion at most meals—certainly in a place like The Glade—and Stella wondered if the follies of youth were considered business. Through the appetizer, Sera Louarri said nothing of the youngsters, commenting only on the food.

With the next course, she made a few comments about Zori's upbringing, the importance of their traditional religious rites. "And your family?" she said.

"We are not of the same faith as you," Stella said. "But if I understand correctly, yours originated from the Modulan, did it not?"

Sera Louarri nodded. "Our beliefs are also descended from Modulans. So . . . you are opposed to unnecessary conflict? Our emphasis on courtesy and serenity does not seem excessive to you?"

"Not at all," Stella said.

Not until dessert came did Sera Louarri bring up the matter at hand. "I shouldn't be eating this," she said first, taking a small mouthful of berry pie. "My husband—and I do not wish to become plump, you understand."

Stella, already halfway through her own pie, thought Sera Louarri was already overthin. Did her husband like her that way? And what, in Cascadian custom, was the polite response?

Sera Louarri did not wait for a response. "I am re-assured by what you tell me of your family, and having met you, by you yourself. It did bother us that you were only Toby's guardian, not his mother. I understand the events that made that necessary. And I apologize for being influenced by the unfortunate revelations in that legal matter."

A tactful way of saying that Stella was a notorious criminal's bastard. Stella admired the woman's euphemistic skirting of brutal fact. "It certainly came as a surprise to me," she said.

"Of course. And your adoptive family was, both from what you say and by the evidence of your own behavior, what we could hope for in one of Zori's companions. I hope you do not find our concern too offensive."

"Not at all," Stella said. "Your daughter is a lovely girl, and any responsible parent would be concerned." Should she add that she was equally concerned that Zori be suitable for Toby? Probably not; it might be construed as an insufficiently veiled insult.

"We would very much like to have Toby visit us at home," Sera Louarri said. "When my husband is there, perhaps for lunch? Not a school day, of course."

"I'm sure he would be delighted," Stella said. Sera Louarri suggested the next nonschool day, and Stella accepted on Toby's behalf. She returned to the office refreshed; though there were monsters loose in the universe, boys and girls still fell in love, and parents and guardians still schemed to keep them safe.

TWO

Toby picked up slang as easily as any other information, and Zori Louarri, out of class, had a colorful collection of words that sounded like nothing else. "Bistim gai," she said, nudging him with an elbow and glancing at a schoolmate neither of them much liked. Bortan asked questions just to delay the class.

"Prot," Toby said. It was like a secret language, Zori's slang, a way around Cascadia's fussy formality. And so far no one had complained about it. Everyone had been on edge anyway, with more to worry about than adolescents using slang that might—if understood—be rude.

"E-prot," she said, grinning. It was rude, very rude indeed, but it was also funny. Toby grinned back. She switched to normal language. "My parents will be pleased to meet you, I'm sure. I know Mother has been——" She paused, clearly thinking how to say it; they both knew that her mother and Toby's aunt had locked horns with the utmost courtesy and determination. "——less than understanding of your family's position back home. Now that the Slotter Key ansible is back up——"

"They'll find out the family was nearly destroyed. That should definitely help." Toby felt worse the closer they got to Zori's parents. They lived in Cascadia Station's most exclusive neighborhood, The Cone, with live trees along both sides of the pedestrian-only street. Cone Park, outside the gates, was the station's largest, and held a small grove of pines. If Zori's parents wouldn't listen to Stella, why would they listen to a boy under legal age? He felt much older than his official age, but he knew that did not matter. He was Stella's ward, and too young to plead his own case.

"Something helped, or they wouldn't have invited you to meet them," Zori said. She glanced back over her shoulder. "Your cousin is still mistrustful, I see."

Toby could think of nothing polite to say. Stella had told him, over and over, why he must have security along on this social occasion. Clearly she did not trust either Station Security or Zori's parents, and that was a form of insult. But he was her ward; he had to do what she said.

Zori patted his arm. "Don't worry—I'm not upset with you. After what happened with your family, I can understand her feelings. But really—we're in the safest area of the station. You don't need your guards there, I promise."

"I know," Toby said. "I know that, but—she didn't just tell me; she told them. And they listen to her." He cleared his throat. "How angry will your parents be?"

"Kafadit," Zori said. "Tiagri banta zo. But she'll have told them, I'm sure, and they'll be upset with her, not you."

They were near the security gate now. Toby felt the prickle of sweat under his arms. "Kzuret," he said softly. "Zurinfar kzuret tsim."

She blushed. "Kzuret adin," she said. "But we had better not say that around my parents."

"I wish you knew what language it was," Toby said, as she punched in the code. "What root, anyway . . ."

"Commercial code, my father says," Zori said, as the

gate slid aside and she led him through. "Don't you Vattas have something similar?"

"Yes, but it's based on one of the Slotter Key languages, extinct now. Tam-something."

A yell from behind made him turn around. The gate had shut before his security could get through.

"What happened?" Toby said.

Zori scowled. "Your cousin must not have told my father that you were bringing them. The gate was set for only the two of us. Well, that's one way of getting rid of them—"

"I can't," Toby said. The two men were glaring at him through the gate. "Stella would—" He moderated his first thought, shaping it to Cascadian terms. "—be most upset."

Zori gave him a challenging look. "My parents were most upset about you, remember? And I faced them down. Are you that—" He could see the effort she made to frame it in courteous terms and then she shifted to their slang. "—that protvin?"

That stung. "It's not a matter of courage," he started; her brows went up, the expression on her face all scorn and utterly beautiful at once. Toby felt his heart turn over. *Kzuret adin*, she'd said. She loved him. He still didn't know why she loved him, but cowardice certainly wasn't the reason. He could still feel her warm breath on his ear when she'd said it; he could still smell her fragrance. "I have to explain to them," he said. "That's only polite." She nodded, her face relaxing now.

Toby walked the few steps back to the gate. "I'm sorry," he said. "But apparently Stella didn't tell Zori's father that I would have an escort. The gate's set for only two, and Zori doesn't have the right to let anyone else in. When I get to her place, I'll ask her parents to let you in, but really—you can see, you know, it's The Cone. Nothing bad happens here. I'll be fine."

"You should come out. You know that. Your cousin told you—"

Toby shrugged. "She wants me safe; I understand that. But I'm perfectly safe here. It's The Cone, after all."

"It's our job; we're supposed to be with you at all times—" And they had been, and he and Zori had not been able to do anything without those watchful and—he feared—amused adult gazes on them.

"I'm not coming out," Toby said. "I'm just going to meet Zori's parents, and it would be rude to be late. You can explain to Stella."

"We certainly will," said the elder.

A few minutes later, in the elegant salon of Zori's place, Toby returned the polite bow of the older man—Zori's father—whose perfectly tailored suit and polished shoes seemed impregnable as a suit of armor.

"And this is my wife, Zori's mother," he said, gesturing to a dark-haired woman in a gown of pale green. She had not risen from her chair. Like all the others in the room, it had thin curved legs and a narrow seat upholstered in stripes of green and cream.

Toby bowed again, this time more deeply as appropriate for a young man to an older woman. His voice broke on the formal phrase of greeting; he could feel the blood rushing to his face.

"It is our pleasure to welcome our daughter's school friend," Zori's mother said. Something in her voice reduced him to the level of grubby schoolboy, the age to have sweets stuck to his pocket linings. He was more than a school friend, he wanted to say, but he knew he could not.

"Toby's very bright, Mother," Zori said, breaking the awkward silence.

"So you have told us, Zori," her father said. He glanced

briefly at Toby, a glance like a knife blade. "It is the first time you have not headed the class, so he must be . . . remarkable."

"Do sit down," her mother said. "We have a little time until the meal is served."

Zori perched on the chair nearest her mother; Toby, following her glance, took one two seats away, across from her father, who now sat next to his wife.

"I understand," her mother said now, "that your family has had a great tragedy."

"Yes, sera," Toby said. He forced himself to speak calmly. "We were attacked, across many systems. I am fortunate to be alive."

"You yourself were attacked? A boy so young?"

"Yes, sera. If not for my cousin Stella, whom you've met—"

"I have not met her," Zori's father put in. "I have spoken with her, only."

"Spoken with," Toby said, wondering at the vehemence of that correction. "If not for her, I would be dead. She saved my life."

"And now you honor her," Zori's mother said. "How very appropriate." Her fingers twitched, pleating the fabric of her skirt. "I understand your family had extensive holdings on several planets—especially on Slotter Key. That you were in fact among the founding families there."

"Yes, sera," Toby said. He knew Stella must have told them this; why were they asking him?

"We value land, you see, not just wealth, as a sign of a family's . . . stability. Land stays; people wander. Those who have no roots in the land are . . . rootless. Do you not think that is so?"

"I suppose . . ." He had never thought of it that way; the Vatta family owned land, yes, and some of the family farmed or ranched, but the point was always trade and profit—selling the produce of the land, transporting it to market.

"Tell me, Toby," her father said. "Did you grow up on a planet or in space?"

"On a planet," Toby said. "My grandmother always said children need to get mud between their toes . . ." A quick glance passed between Zori's parents.

"How . . . quaint," Zori's mother said. "You did not wear shoes, then?"

"Not at the beach," Toby said. "Or at the lake." He had forgotten that Cascadians did not approve of bare feet . . . of course not, onstation, but what about onplanet? Did they not swim in their lakes and rivers and oceans?

"Ah." She smiled at him, and for a moment he saw in her face the similarity to Zori, until now concealed by age and dress and formality. Zori had her eyes, her cheekbones, but her father's chin. "Your culture's customs are less formal than ours, I believe?"

"Yes, sera," Toby said. He dared not say more; he'd put his foot in it already.

"Still, lands . . ." She glanced at her husband. "Formal or informal, there is more difference between landed families and those rootless, than between formal and informal."

Zori's father stirred, on his chair; it squeaked a little. Then he stood. "There is still time before our meal, Zorais," he said. "I will show your friend my collection of Cascadian curiosities. Come, Toby."

Zori flashed him a grin as he stood and followed her father out of the salon. Her father's office was almost as large, paneled in dark wood carved to represent vines with leaves and fruit, tree branches, even animals and birds. Translucent panels gave light that varied from green to gold, creating a forest-floor ambience. Pin-lights picked out some of the carvings, intensifying the illusion.

Two big display cases flanked the room, their contents carefully illuminated: shells, feathers, mineral specimens, tree cones.

"These are all from our estates downplanet," Zori's father said. "As you are planet-born, I thought you might like to see—I understand you have not been downplanet here yet?"

"No, ser," Toby said. "Not here."

"You know that we Cascadians revere trees—our family has over ten thousand hectares of primary forest, never terraformed, and five thousand terraformed, at Riverrunning, our primary home. The river provides fish, shellfish . . . see here . . ." He put an arm around Toby's shoulder and urged him toward one of the displays. Toby felt the strength in the man's arm, but it was not hostile . . . just vaguely uncomfortable.

The shells looked like shells from the lake at home; Toby said so.

"Yes. To our surprise—but I am not an ecologist, you understand—the native aquatic species build shells of calcium carbonate, and those shells are similar in shape to those of Old Earth organisms, I've been told. Here's something different."

Something different had had an exoskeleton with long, intricately branched spines. It was a little longer than Toby's hand.

"That was from your river?"

"No—that was a gift that's come down through the family. I don't know where it's from, but I find it beautiful. The spines are still toxic, however long ago the creature died."

Zori's father had moved his arm to gesture; Toby eased away to look more closely at the display.

"I'm sure you're wondering," the man said, "when I will remind you that Zori is my beloved daughter, and demand that your attentions be honorable. And in fact, I had planned to have that conversation. But I can see, from your demeanor, that you are an honorable young man, and that you care for her very much. I see no need to threaten you—"

"No, ser . . ." Toby began, but her father raised a finger for silence.

"I would merely remind you that you are both young, and it is too soon to make binding agreements. You love her, you think—and perhaps you do. She loves you, she thinks—and perhaps she does. But many young people are in love with the idea of love, and cannot yet distinguish that from the true and lasting affection that leads to a secure relationship. I believe I can trust you—" His gaze sharpened. "—not to do anything foolish. Can I not?"

"Yes, ser," Toby said, hating the blush that he could feel heating his face. "I will not do anything . . . like that."

"Zori has always been headstrong," her father said, looking away. "Like me, perhaps. Her mother is . . . more biddable." In that was something that chilled, though Toby did not know what. "You will need to be the man, Toby. Do not let her have her way, when it comes to . . . foolishness. Do you understand me?"

That much he understood. "I won't, Ser Louarri," he said formally.

"Excellent. Now tell me—I hear from Zori that you have not only good general intelligence, but outstanding ability in certain technical fields. I am aware of your cousin's patent application, and the contracts to manufacture this miraculous new device that will free ships from reliance on the ISC . . . it has already had an influence on the market. Is it true that this was your invention?"

Something—he would never be quite sure what—tied Toby's tongue for the merest instant, and Stella's advice flashed into his mind. "Not really, Ser Louarri. I just noodled around a bit—it was more accidental than anything else, and others refined it." At that moment, Toby remembered his security. But how—without extreme discourtesy—could he ask about that now?

"It would have been truly remarkable if a boy your age had invented it," her father said, smiling. "Well . . . I think perhaps we should join the ladies now. Lunch should be on the point of service." He reached out and ruffled Toby's hair, as if Toby were still a child.

Then he gave a sudden quick nod, like someone who had just taken a skullphone call. "Toby, your cousin is most insistent that your escort attend you at once—I am sorry she did not let me know they were coming; we would have prepared food for them, of course. They are on their way now. But have you felt at all anxious here? Other than the natural anxiety of a boy meeting a girl's parents for the first time?" His smile now was open and warm.

Toby smiled back. "No, ser, of course not. I thought Stella's precautions were excessive, and I'm sure they were not from distrust of you, but to teach me more caution."

"Your cousin is wise, Toby, and I have taken no offense. The young are often incautious. Had I known about your escort, I would have arranged for their entry, of course."

Lunch, after that, was marred only by the presence of his security, two stolid men standing against the wall, refusing to eat while Zori and her parents and Toby consumed four delicious courses and made small talk. Zori's mother had stories of her childhood on the planet—excursions into the country to boat or ride, parties and dances.

Her face came alive as she told them. Zori's father said little, but smiled fondly at Zori even when she tried to tease him into response.

After lunch, Toby hoped Zori would walk back with him, but she came only as far as the gate to The Cone. "I have to talk to them," she said. "But you did very well, Toby. I know they liked you."

"I was scared," Toby said. "Until I thought of you. But I can't—" He glanced around; the security men were there, as always. "Kzuret," he said. "Kzuret adin."

"Kzuret adin," she said. "See you tomorrow in class." Then she was gone, walking briskly back up the passage to her home, and he led his security back out into the public areas of the station.

When Toby got back to the Vatta offices, Stella called him in at once. "What did you mean, leaving your security behind?"

"I had to," he said. "It would have been rude to be late; I was going to ask Zori's father when I got there—"

"But you didn't," she said. "Did you?"

"I couldn't figure out how to do it without being rude," Toby said. "Besides, it was safe. I was in a private home, with friends—"

"Acquaintances," Stella said. "Just because they're respectable and rich doesn't make them friends."

Toby felt hot. "Zori—!" he said.

"Zori is *your* friend. Don't bristle at me; I like her, too. But she's not her parents. And it took her father a long time to unlock that gate for your security."

"He said if you'd only told him beforehand . . ." Toby's voice trailed away at Stella's expression.

"I did," she said. "Of course I did. He said it wasn't necessary; I said it was our policy. Think about that, Toby. Would people we want as friends lie to you?"

Toby wanted to argue with her—it couldn't be true, these were *Zori's* parents—but Stella would not lie to him. That much he knew.

"He must've had a good reason," he said, knowing it was a weak argument.

"I'm sure he did," Stella said. "Did he try to talk to you about your research?"

The uneasy feeling he'd had in the study with Zori's father returned. He couldn't define it; he didn't want it. "I need to work on my paper," Toby said without answering directly.

"Do that," Stella said. He could feel her gaze on his back as he went into the lab where he had left his schoolwork.

A couple of hours later, Stella called him. "Toby, do you have any linguistic analysis software that can make sense of this?" She held out an audio cube and a printout.

"What is it?" he asked.

"Ky sent it; it's a recording and phonetic transcript of transmission by pirate ships. Nobody in her group can understand it, and she sent it to me. Nobody I've talked to so far has a clue; I'll send a copy to some university language departments onplanet, but I don't expect much. Cascadians are pretty much monolingual, and even on the other worlds of the Confederation, they don't have much linguistic diversity."

Toby took the cube and printout and glanced at the latter. "That's odd," he said.

"What?" Stella was already back at her own desk.

"This word—*prot*—it's kind of slang."

"Kid slang?" Stella said. "I don't think the pirates would be using ordinary kid slang, and anyway others would recognize it."

"Zori said it meant—something rude." He was not

about to tell Stella exactly what. She had laid down her
rules about anatomical humor long before.

"Zori?" She turned to face him. "You learned that word
from Zori?"

"I don't know if it's the same word, exactly. It sounds
like it, but there could be words in different languages
that sound the same and mean something different. Vatta
code uses some that Standard—"

"I know that," Stella said. "But do you see anything
else you recognize?"

He and Zori just talked slang; they never wrote it down.
Toby worked his way along the page, sounding out the
words; the transcriber had used phonetic symbols he
wasn't entirely familiar with. "What's this thing with a
hook under it?"

"That's a *sk* sound," Stella said. "I think Ky's com officer
just ran this through a computer transliteration—it's all
in formal linguistic symbols. Let's see—that one there,
that's another consonant cluster, *kz*." She looked up at
him. "Do you recognize any of this?"

"I'm trying—wait—this one is like the word for 'far'
or 'farther.' This one is like 'profit,' with the suffix for 'no.'
And this is like 'out of here,' and there's a 'now' . . ."
Suddenly he felt chilled. "It's . . . it can't be . . . just coincidence. Not this many words. Can it?"

Hope died with Stella's expression. "You learned all
these from Zori?"

"It's . . . it's her family's private slang. Like our Vatta
trade-talk. That's how I know the word for 'profit.' "

"That's what she told you."

"Yes. She said she learned it from her father, her mother
doesn't use it so much. He told her not to use it in public,
that it was rude to talk in a language others didn't understand, but sometimes in trade, in business, it was neces-

sary. She wasn't supposed to teach me, but—" He looked at the page again. More words made sense now. "Ship" and "ships," a few numbers—he had learned the numbers up to twenty. "I'll have to ask Zori—"

"No." Stella's tone brooked no argument. "You will not ask Zori. You will not tell Zori about this message. And you will find a way to separate yourself from Zori and her family, without fuss—"

"I can't do that!" He felt panic and outrage together. "We just—her family gave permission; you said—"

"You must. Come on, Toby, you know what this means."

"I don't." But he did, and did not want to.

"She speaks—her family speak—a language unknown to anyone else I've asked, which just happens to be the same language the pirates speak. That Gammis Turek speaks. What does that tell you?"

"It doesn't tell me Zori's a pirate," Toby said, past the lump in his throat. Not Zori. Never Zori. "Maybe they—maybe somewhere back, somewhere along the way, like Osman, maybe one of their relatives went bad. Any family can have bad people in it—"

"Toby, I understand—"

"You *don't* understand!" Anger drove out grief; he pinned his mind firmly on Zori, unfairly accused. "Zori is not bad! She loves me, and I love her, and nothing you can say will change that." He could feel the heat in his face, hear the tremor in his voice. He could not stand it; he flung himself out of her office, grabbed his books from the lab, and bolted for the door, his security clumping along after.

Stella looked at the door Toby had tried to slam. There was something funny—or would be someday—about her, of all people, having this conversation with Toby. Did all young people use the exact same words to their parents and guardians when they were frantic about their first love? *Nothing you can say will stop me* . . . she remembered throwing that in her mother's face, then her father's . . . the father who was dead now, only he wasn't her real father, the mother who hadn't told her the truth. She pinched the bridge of her nose, hard, and called Toby's escort on her skullphone.

"Don't let him be alone with the Louarri girl," she said. "No matter what. Tackle him, if you have to."

"He's upset," one of them said.

"He's angry and hurt and scared and convinced she's the love of his life and I'm to blame for trying to separate them," Stella said. "You were young once, I assume."

"Yes," the man answered. "I was. We'll take care of him."

Toby had dropped the cube and printout from Ky; Stella picked them up. Pirate jargon? She found the words Toby had mentioned. Was that enough to go on? She wrote those out, in standard script, not trusting the computer at this point, security or no. Ky had recorded transmissions in a combat situation . . . surely from even a few words, someone could devise a translation . . . "ship" or "ships," "far" or "farther," "now," "profit," "out of here." No, "out of here now."

Stella looked at the rest of the page. What was that rude word Toby had mentioned? *Prot?* She looked through the rest of the printout. *Prot* appeared often . . . it was probably a cussword. Probably, from Toby's reaction, anatomical. That wasn't going to be very helpful.

When she got back to the apartment, Toby's security was outside. "He's studying, he says. He hasn't left the apartment; he hasn't made any calls."

"Thank you," Stella said. She dreaded going in, starting

the confrontation again, yet more than her comfort or Toby's rested on his ability to translate the pirate jargon. Had her parents ever dreaded talking to her? She'd never considered that possibility then. For the first time, it sank in that if she'd had that child, she would be a mother in fact, and the mother of a youngster not that much younger than Toby. At least she'd have more experience . . .

The apartment was silent; Toby's door was closed.

Stella moved into the kitchen and dialed a prepackaged meal. She had no doubt he would hear her moving around. As it heated, she tapped on his door. "Supper's almost ready."

"I'm not hungry."

She knew better than that; Toby was always hungry. "Toby, I expect you to come to supper whether you eat it or not."

A long moment, then he yanked the door open. His eyes were red, his hair disheveled. He looked down. "I won't eat."

"That's fine. I know you're working on a paper, Toby, but this translation thing is urgent. Ky needs it. Everyone needs it. Right now, no one can tell what the pirates are planning, even if they overhear them."

"She's not a pirate." Only one possible *she.*

"I didn't say she was . . . but we need to know what they're saying here, if you can figure it out."

"Ky's sure this was from pirates?"

"Yes."

"All right." He took the paper and cube. "You still want me at supper?"

"Yes."

As Stella expected, Toby started eating when she served his plate, his eyes darting now and then to the paper beside him. "Do we have any way to get this into standard script? I don't know all these symbols."

"Yes," Stella said. "I've got that in my implant, and it's on most computers, in the word processing section. You could upload it into yours, now that you've got the adult model. But don't use an outside source." She had given in to his request for the most advanced implant on the grounds that he really did need it to do the research he was doing, and she needed someone as backup for the Vatta command set.

"I don't know nearly as much as Zori," Toby said, shoveling in the last of a serving of rice with vegetables. His lack of appetite had already dealt with a double serving of cultured turkey with gravy. "I don't know all of the words I can even read."

"We can't ask Zori," Stella reminded him.

"Not even when it's this important?"

That was the sticking point. It was that important. If it came to it, if it meant life or death for Ky, or for planets, they would have to ask Zori—force Zori, if it came to it— to do the translation. Or her father.

"Any such request should come through official channels," Stella said. "I've already given a copy of this to the Cascadian government; it's their job to decide what to do with it. Though now that I know someone knows the language, or some of it, they need to know that."

"It'll get Zori in trouble," Toby said. "Maybe I can figure out more of it."

"I hope so," Stella said.

Toby tapped a stylus on his desk. Zori could not be a traitor: that was a given. Zori had, however, taught him some words that appeared in a pirate transmission. That was a fact. Now that Stella knew that Zori knew some words, Stella was half convinced of her guilt. Zori's father had taught Zori those words, and Zori's father gave him a sick feeling in his stomach. He'd assumed it was what any boy felt around the father of the girl he loved, but maybe not. Maybe the man was a traitor. That didn't mean Zori was. Zori's father could be a traitor—both her parents could be traitors—and Zori could still be innocent. Zori's father could have learned a few words—the ones he'd taught Zori—from someone else. Maybe he wasn't a traitor. But if Stella told the government about Zori, then nobody would believe her innocence. He had to find a way to save her from that.

The first step was to find out if she knew all the words in the transmission—because that would mean she could translate the transmissions. If they went to the government themselves, then she could be a hero who translated pirate lingo, not a suspect.

But Stella had forbidden him to show Zori the transcripts or tell her what was going on. And if—he didn't want to think this, but he could not help it—if she was guilty, if her father was a traitor and had raised her to be one, too, then showing her the transcripts would be as dangerous as Stella said. How could he find out if she knew more than the little she'd taught him, without breaking Stella's rule?

A flash of worry that Zori might not like what he was thinking of doing was easy to banish. He was doing it for her, to protect her, and unless she was a traitor (and she could not be a traitor; that was a given) she would understand and agree, if—when—she found out.

"My parents like you," Zori said before math the next day.

Toby couldn't answer; he just nodded.

"Is your cousin causing problems?"

"Not . . . exactly. She says she thought she told your father about my escort."

Zori gave him a look. "She thinks my father is lying? That's an insult—"

"She didn't say that." Actually she had said that, but Toby was not going to admit it.

Zori settled back, lips tight. Then she looked at Toby again. "I . . . need to talk to you."

"We can start this lesson when everyone is attentive." That was Ser Galvan. Toby looked up just in time to avoid a mark for discourtesy.

During break, Zori and Toby ignored the nudges and winks of the rest of their class and backed into a corner with their snacks. Toby's security were nearby, but in the noise of the break room, they could not be overheard. Probably.

"What?" Toby asked.

"My father says he likes you but sometimes . . . sometimes he's just a little sneaky."

"Sneaky?"

"I mean . . . yes it would be an insult if your cousin said he was lying about her having told him about your escort. And if she insults him, then he has a legal claim against her, and if he has a legal claim against her, then obviously he won't let me see you. He might even take me out of school."

"So . . . you think he li—he said that in order to find a way to break us up?"

"Maybe. It's not always discourteous to lie . . . it's wrong, but it's not against the courtesy code. Not if you're not under oath."

"Wait a minute . . . you mean, it's fine to lie, but wrong to complain that you've been lied to?"

"I wouldn't say fine . . . it's just not a discourtesy, whereas calling someone a liar is."

"But if they are lying, and you know it, how are you supposed to handle it?"

"You can ignore it, if it's not important, or you can

report it, if it's a criminal matter, or you can ask for a formal statement before a legal representative. That can be phrased without discourtesy."

"I'd think that would make it worse," Toby said. "If you ask for that, aren't you in effect calling someone a liar in front of others?"

"No . . . not in our society. But anyway, if your cousin ever needs to challenge my father she needs to do it properly. Get legal counsel."

"Mmm. And what do you think?"

"You're asking me to indict my own father?"

"No, I'm asking what you think."

"You don't understand. I can't answer that. It would be . . . it would be wrong. Worse than prot."

Toby sheared away from that. "Look . . . can we meet after school? You have a free period last, don't you?"

"Yes, but I can't meet you then. I promised my mother I'd go to some boring women's meeting with her. I can get out after dinner, though, as long as I'm home by nine. We could meet for ice cream or something."

Toby looked into her eyes. Zori was trustworthy; she had to be. She loved him. And it was important to get this translated. "I'm trying to write an adventure story in . . . whatever it is you've been teaching me."

"My family's secret language . . . why?"

"Someday it will be *our* language. The way we've been saying things, you know. You've been speaking it for years . . . I'm trying to learn it. You know I'm more visual than you are; it'll be easier for me if I write it down. And you said you didn't have any texts."

"I don't think anyone writes in it," Zori said. "It's just for chat."

"If your father uses it for business, maybe he writes memos in it."

"I suppose." She looked thoughtful. "But you're writing in it?"

"Trying to," Toby said. "I'm not very good at it. I thought it would be easier if I did it as a story. The dialogue so far sounds more like one of those adventure series for children. Well, except for the rude words. And I made up a bunch of words, too, because I don't know enough."

"Can I see it?"

"I guess." Toby had put together a mishmash of the words he knew, a few he remembered, a few that he had guessed, and some he made up. "It's a space battle: all this part is the bad guys. With the rude words you taught me, it's easier to do their side. And I'm not sure of the spelling in a lot of places . . ."

"You're making excuses. Let's see . . ." She looked at his handcomp. "Wow. You've learned a lot . . . I don't remember teaching you some of this—"

"It's mostly made up, where I didn't know the words," Toby said. He had inserted a few made-up words into the text Ky had sent; this was only about a page of a transmission, with interpolated plot.

"But this—" Zori pointed. "—this really is the word for 'ammunition.' Lucky guess, Toby!" She grinned, then went back to reading, while Toby's heart seemed to sink through his shoes. She knew more words. Why would her father teach her the word for 'ammunition,' anyway? " 'No profit in this, get out of here now' . . . I like that. So the pirates are running away from—who are the good guys?"

"Space rangers, of course. Who else?"

"This is wrong, this bit here. You made up *blaggorn*, didn't you?"

"Yes. It's supposed to mean 'defeat'—"

"No, that's *randik*. *Randik msendim* would be losing a bid to another bidder. This bit here means 'lost too many ships to that . . .' I didn't teach you that word!" Zori's cheeks reddened.

"Does it really mean anything?" Toby asked.

"A very bad word for a woman. Who is she supposed to be?"

"One of the good-guy captains," Toby said.

"Oh, then that's *kobi-parash*. Means 'one of our captains.' The other is just nasty."

The buzzer went off. Zori handed the handcomp back. "I hope my father doesn't find out you're writing stories in our trade tongue, Toby. Don't publish it. 'Specially not with all those really rude words."

"I wouldn't," Toby said. No doubt now that Zori's father's trade tongue was that used by the pirates. He could not doubt Zori . . . but her father? If Stella's father could turn out to be Osman Vatta . . . anyone's father might be an enemy.

THREE

Ky Vatta reset the controls in *Vanguard*'s fully programmable small-arms range and slipped another magazine into her Rossi-Smith. She fired at the lowest of the five targets, something with tentacles. A green light blinked. "Most of the pure target shooting I did was learning to shoot, from my parents." Another shot, at the next higher, something with teeth; another green light. "Then I did some hunting. Not a lot—and some of it was archery—" Another shot, this time an armored space suit. Another green light. Ky took out the last two targets. "Your turn, Major."

Major Douglas shook his head. "No thanks," he said. "I'm past my peak—another time."

Ky nodded, shut down the system, and reset the ventilation.

"But back to Turek," Douglas continued. "My guess is that he'll start going directly for ship manufacturers. He's got Bissonet; they made their own warships, but not very big ones, and their capacity for their largest ships was limited to only about five a year. You blew a year's production in one battle."

"So he'd be looking for facilities that manufacture large ships in quantity?"

"Yes. Not many planetary space forces need those. Smaller ships are sufficient for most insystem jobs, handling the kind of pirate incursions most of us saw before Turek. So there hasn't been a large market for them, and it's been saturated by just a few manufacturers. I strongly recommend contacting those entities when we come back out of FTL and seeing if they've had any thefts, attacks, or even large orders recently."

"And recently would be—"

"Within the past two to three standard years. The big ships take that long to complete."

"Some systems might order larger ships now that they've seen the menace," Ky said. "We need a better way of detecting the wrong kind of order, don't we?"

"My recommendation would be to see what orders have been made—quantities, payment sources, and so on—and then look for anomalies. The Moscoe Confederation may have useful data."

"At some point Turek is going to run out of his own resources. There can't be enough pirates in the universe to crew hundreds of ships, govern all the territory he's conquered, do all the mundane chores that a fleet needs done. Who would join forces with someone like that, if they weren't under direct threat?"

"A good question," Douglas said. "I would say criminal organizations, but they're a minority of the population. They are good at intimidating more people, though. Major political or religious movements?"

"There's the anti-humods," Pitt said.

"Like the people on Gretna," Ky said. "But I don't know how prevalent that view is—the militant side of it, I mean. The anti-humods I grew up with were harmless, just very earnest and ready to explain how the real human race was disappearing."

"We have some concerns," Douglas said, meaning Mackensee Military Assistance Corporation. "Our intel has been watching a couple of seriously anti-humod governments over the past ten years or so. They could be a source of funding, if Turek convinces them he's anti-humod and out to restore the position so-called real humans deserve. If any of the governments on our list are the ones ordering warships, I'd be concerned."

"Well, until we come out of FTL, we can't even ask the questions," Ky said. "Nor can I pick Captain Yamini's brains, since he's on another ship. So let me bounce another set of ideas off you, if you don't mind—and that's how best to use the slender tactical advantage we have of being able to tap Turek's transmissions and operate in channels he doesn't have. We hope."

"Downjump fifteen minutes . . . secure for down-jump . . ."

"Time flies," Ky said. "I cut it too close. I'll see you on the bridge." She was there with five minutes to spare. Nothing should be here; this was just a convenient mapped jump point far from anything habitable or worth mining; there should be an ansible, though, for the convenience of passing ships, like theirs.

Or the enemy's. As she'd ordered at the start of the voyage, weapons went live at T minus two. Ransome should be out now, advance scout for them. A minute crawled by, then another, then *Vanguard* lurched out of FTL into normal space, scan blurred by downjump turbulence.

"Nothing so far," came the cheerful hail from Teddy Ransome. "Empty as a beer bottle in the morning, and the ansible's live."

"That's good," Ky said.

Argelos, Yamini, Pettygrew, and Baskerville all reported in within fifteen seconds of their expected time. The three lighter ships microjumped out to keep watch. Ky had allotted two hours here, time to strip the news from the ansible, share it, even discuss it, but she didn't plan to have everyone clustered and vulnerable. The automated ansible had a minimal number of system boosters, but Ransome, reckless as always, microjumped within a quarter second of the ansible itself, stripped out the news bulletins, and shared them with the others immediately.

"That's Turek," Ky said, when the image of a man in crimson and black followed one of an explosion. "We've seen a picture of him before."

"Interesting choice of postures," Douglas said. "Notice—no podium, no column, the only scale to measure him is the sky and stars. The way he's folded his arms—it's like something off a poster, or a book cover. He's claiming authority—"

You will all know my name . . . You will all fear my name . . . I am Gammis Turek . . .

"Insanity," Hugh said. "Why would he send out something like this now?"

"To scare people," Douglas said. "Interesting voice, too. Either he's had voice training or he's using a modification."

"Let's listen," Ky said; they fell silent, and listened to the rest of it, watched the massacre of civilians, the town burning. Next came bulletins from different news services, commenting on Turek's speech.

"Save those," Ky said. "We don't have much time; let's consider Turek's own statement first. Why would he give his name now? Remember that spy with the suicide trigger, who died saying his name?"

"He's worried," Douglas said. "Something has shaken his confidence in his plan."

"I don't know why," Gordon Martin said. "We've bloodied his nose a couple of times, but no worse than that. So far he's won every system he's attacked."

"That we know of," Argelos said. "He might've been unsuccessful somewhere."

"I agree," Yamini said. "But even if he hasn't had a major loss, he would be running into some problems of scale by now. I don't care how many ships he's got, he's got to have crew for them—reliable crew, lots more than he started with—and he's got to have supplies for them, and munitions, or the ships are useless for war. That's a lot of resources. It isn't just the money; it's also the market—where's he have to go for resupply?"

"If he's got allies among the anti-humod systems," Douglas said, "that may be his funding source. They could also be hauling his supplies in commercial vessels."

"Geoffrey Baines' *Practical Tactics for Regional Conflicts,*" Yamini said. Ky stared at the screen, confused.

Douglas smacked his forehead. "Yes! That's what I was thinking of. That's his playbook; that's what he's been using. And that picture of Baines, the frontispiece, all dressed up in some kind of costume—"

"The Royal Irregulars," Yamini said. "Blue and yellow, instead of maroon and black."

"Explain, please," Ky said. "I don't remember that source in our tactical studies."

"You wouldn't," Yamini said, "because we didn't use it. Baines wasn't actually military; he was an enthusiast, an amateur historian. His tactical instincts were good but he didn't really understand modern space warfare."

"It's been effective for Turek so far," Ky pointed out.

"Yes, but Baines doesn't go beyond the elementary. Look, you've been able to defeat his people even when you were outnumbered," Yamini said. "You picked up his tactical approach right away; you were able to improvise something effective against him."

"Why didn't he use something else?"

"Maybe he doesn't know which to use. Most texts now assume a force with certain proportions of ship types he may not have. Or maybe he can't get his people to understand them—"

"Or he doesn't trust them," Douglas said. "He started with criminals, pirates and stationside both. People so unreliable he had to implant them with suicide triggers to be sure they wouldn't blab his name."

"He's got instant communication," Ky said. "And people he doesn't completely trust . . . that's going to constrain his tactics, isn't it?"

"Absolutely," Yamini said. "And inhibit his subordinates, and annoy them, too."

"Downjump turbulence!" Lee said from the pilot's seat.

Hugh turned to look at the screen himself as other ships reported the same. "Estimates?"

"By the turbulence, big and fast." He looked at Ky. Douglas, to one side, looked as though he wanted to speak but didn't.

"We run," Ky said. Hugh looked surprised, but Douglas gave a tiny nod. "Priority's getting to Cascadia." She spoke to all the ships. "Close formation, jump on my mark. Come out at the next jump point in the same formation as here, weapons hot, and immediately go into Yellow Three." She waited as they acknowledged and Teddy Ransome microjumped back to his place, then gave them the signal. The safe haven of FTL closed around *Vanguard* once again.

"What do you think that was?" Hugh asked.

"Worst case, pursuit," Ky said. "And maybe we just missed our chance to take out Turek . . . but I don't think so. I'm wondering if somebody found out where we were going, and that was a tight formation of his ships."

"You mean a leak from Mackensee?" Douglas asked, frowning.

"Not necessarily." Ky felt stupid for not having thought this through before. "Turek knew we left Boxtop with you—the logical destination was your home planet. He must know Stella's in Cascadia, and that I'd go there; this is on the logical route. All it would take is one person on your home world telling him when we left. Would you vouch for everyone in your system?" Ky asked.

"No," Douglas said. "But I don't like the idea that we might have a leak somewhere. Or that there was someone to intercept and act on it so quickly. If that was pursuit, they were within an hour of us. And they probably know where we're headed next."

"Or it could've been someone making a fast transit through because they were worried, having run into that broadcast somewhere else," Hugh said. "Have to say, I'm glad you decided to leave, though. Just in case."

"Let's look at the rest of what we pulled off the ansible," Ky said. "I'm sure the others are."

The first, time-stamped only shortly after Turek's broadcast, were simply comments on it, but down the stack came more disturbing reports. One of Sallyon's two manned ansible stations had been blown—apparently by local terrorists—with the loss of all its personnel. A second message from Turek made it clear that this was because they had "harbored" ships from Bissonet's militia, and that he would do worse to anyone who supported an allied force opposing him.

"They deserve it," Martin said. "After the way he treated you."

"Nobody deserves it," Ky said, "even when it makes a tidy picture."

"Notice this is the second time he's mentioned an allied force," Douglas said. "I think he's realized that potential because you've bested his people twice now. If he has agents on Slotter Key—and it would be smart to assume he does—he may know Slotter Key privateers have been ordered to Cascadia. Or agents at intermediate stops or on Cascadia may see a buildup."

Cascadia Station

Despite his conviction that Cascadia Station was safe, Toby had no intention of making Stella angry enough to forbid his going out at all. He told his escort where he was going, and did not object when they fell in behind him. Everyone knew the O'Keefe Ice Cream Palace. Everyone knew it was the place lots of students met in the evenings, just as they knew that *ice cream* had multiple meanings, not all related to frozen treats. He had been there before, many times.

Zori would be there at 1945, she'd said. He slid into a booth and ordered his usual, five variations on the theme of chocolate. She didn't expect him to wait for her; she'd order her own when she arrived. His two escorts watched the chaos with obvious disdain as he ate. He could imagine what they were thinking: kids, noise, silliness, stupidity, possible infractions of the code of courtesy. Gales of laughter from the other side of the room underlined that. Toby craned his neck, trying to see what it was.

"Not your crowd," one of his escort said. "Older kids." His voice carried the same message: *Stupid idiots making a disturbance.*

"Zori won't want to stay here if it's this noisy," Toby said.

"Her security—" Her parents insisted she have an escort in the evenings, though by day they let her travel alone.

Something crashed to the floor, just out of sight, sounds of metallic and glass breakage mingling with hoots of laughter and squeals of alarm. One of Toby's escorts stepped nearer to him; the other looked toward the entrance. One of the employees, an older man, bustled toward Toby.

"Excuse me—can you help, please? I've put in a call for help, but these ruffians—" Another crash, this time with less laughter and more sounds of alarm.

"We're on duty," one of the escorts said. They glanced at each other, then at Toby.

"I'll stay here," Toby said. "Promise."

"Do that," one escort said. "Do not leave this booth . . ." And they were off, wading into the thickening crowd. The noise level rose.

"A complimentary drink," a voice said. "With our thanks—"

Toby glanced up, started to say "Thanks, but—" and a fine spray tingled on his face. Down a lengthening dark tunnel he saw, very clearly, the tiny face of the man who had sprayed him.

Zori and her escort got to the O'Keefe Ice Cream Palace a few minutes late, thanks to the squad of station peace-keepers blocking the short route there. Zori led the way around, through a narrow passage, and emerged in the wider service passage as the back door opened and three men in white carried someone out on a litter.

Someone with Toby's hair, Toby's face—pale, but—

"Toby!" Zori said. The men glanced at her, put on speed, and hustled their burden into a utility vehicle with SANITATION DEPT stenciled on the side. "Wait!" Zori tried to run toward the vehicle as the men piled in, but her escort grabbed her arm and pulled her back. "Let me go!" Zori struggled, but could not get free before the vehicle hummed off down the service passage. "That was Toby, you idiot!" Zori said, putting enough distance between them that she could see her escort's face clearly. "I was meeting him here; you know that. Something happened— I have to find him—follow them—"

"You can't do that," her escort said. "I have my orders from your father. To O'Keefe's and back from O'Keefe's and nowhere else."

"But it was *Toby*! Someone took him! He was hurt, or dead, or—" She took a deep shaky breath. "I have to go see his cousin; she has to know."

"I'm sure if he has been injured, the receiving clinic will notify her. Do you want to go in, or shall we return home?"

"That wasn't an ambulance . . . you know that. Someone's snatched him. I'm going to call her—" Not for the first time, she wished her father had let her have a skullphone module in her implant. He'd always said there were enough phones around that she didn't need one.

"No." The man's expression hardened. "You're going home. Now."

Zori stared at him. Not since she'd been a small child had any of her escorts used that tone. She felt a shiver pass down her back, an icy current. The man's fingers twitched, moving toward a pocket in his jacket. Thoughts raced through her head, almost too fast to pick up, far too fast to analyze. Without letting her gaze waver from his face, she thought about options. The back door to O'Keefe's was only a few strides away and she was fast— but she'd have to turn. He was too big; she could not push past him to follow Toby. Sideways—along the passage they'd come . . . but it was narrow and had that sharp jink and if he caught her from behind . . .

"Pardon, please!" The breathless male voice from inside O'Keefe's took the escort's intent look off her for an instant. Zori slid one foot back, then the other. "Have you seen anything of a boy—about sixteen—coming this way?"

"No," her escort said, as Zori glanced, recognized Toby's escort, and said "Yes," in almost the same instant. From the corner of her eye, she saw her escort lunge toward her; she jumped back, whirled, and ran. She wanted to scream, but she couldn't scream and run. Toby's escort, startled, stepped out of her way and she plunged into the staff area of O'Keefe's, shoving her way through a crowd of people, some in waiters' aprons, some clearly curious and frightened customers. Someone had spilled pink ice cream on the floor; she slipped in it, fell against a worktable, and tripped over someone crouched there. She landed hard on one hip just as more noise broke out behind her. "Excuse me," she said to the person she'd fallen over—a younger girl, white-faced, her clothes smeared with pink and brown and yellow. "I'm so sorry . . ."

"No offense," the girl said; she was trembling. People near the door were yelling, anger and fear mingling; Zori couldn't make out all the words, but then came a series of dull thumps and screams. The little girl leaned into Zori and grabbed for her hand.

Zori looked around—nothing but legs in that direction. Under the worktable was a shelf partly filled with all-metal bowls and pots. Zori pushed some aside, making a space. A childhood memory nagged at her. "There. Get in there and stay there until you hear the station peacekeepers."

"Don't leave me," the girl whispered. "Please . . ."

Zori had never seen herself as the nurturing type, but

she could not unclench the child's fingers without hurting her. "We need to be careful, then," she said. "Let's just crawl."

"The floor's dirty," the girl said.

"We're already dirty," Zori said. "Come on . . . hold on to my sleeve, so I can crawl."

A short crawl brought them to a door at the far end of the kitchen. Zori put her shoulder to it; it didn't budge. When she looked up, she saw the touchpad of a security lock and the words PANTRY: EMPLOYEES ONLY. Back the way they'd come, the crowd heaved and struggled, the back of it retreating toward them. This end of the work space had no convenient gaps to hide in.

Memory burst on her. She had been in a kitchen, the kitchen of her childhood home, looking up from this angle. She wasn't supposed to be in there, but Estelle had been cross, pulling her hair as she combed it, and Cook, who didn't like Estelle, would probably let her sit on her lap, might even give her a cookie or jam roll. But Cook wasn't there. The child-Zori had the idea of hiding in the pantry, waiting for Cook to come back.

When footsteps came into the kitchen, she shrank back, leaving the pantry door open just a crack, in case it was Estelle and not Cook.

"You can't—!" Mama's voice, high and tense. "You can't stop me! I'll tell—!" Something that sounded like a book slammed onto a desk. A cry of pain.

"You!" Daddy's voice, menacing. "You'll tell no one."

"You hit me!"

A laugh, ugly and not funny at all. "That wasn't a hit. That was a promise. Remember what I told you."

"My family—" Mama's voice now was shaky, barely heard through sobs.

Another laugh. "Your family's a long way away. I'm here.

And if you leave—what do you think will happen to the child?"

Mama crying. Daddy angry. Child-Zori couldn't stand it. She'd opened the door; she'd said—something she couldn't remember. She'd seen her mother, hand pressed to her face, crying. Her father whirling around, his face shifting in an instant from a terrifying mask of rage to the familiar smile; his hand opening to lay something—she had not seen what—on the counter.

"Zori, you little minx! What are you doing in the kitchen at this hour?" His voice, warm and welcoming. He'd held out his arms; she'd run to him, already sobbing in fright and confusion. "What—did you want a cookie? Did Estelle scold you?"

She tucked her head into his shoulder. "Daddy—"

"Hush, child." He felt the same as always, the big warm shoulder, the broad strong hands gentle, comforting, as they supported her. She lifted her head, seeing through a blur of tears her mother's white face, a shaking hand pressed against one cheek. "Don't be scared, little bird. You're safe with me. Your mother's just upset." He turned to look at her, facing Zori away from her mother. "Now, my dear, don't you see you've scared the child?"

She relaxed into his arms. From behind her, her mother's voice, no longer high and tense, but once more the cool voice she expected, said, "Zori, I'm sorry if I scared you. Your father is quite right. But you should not be running to the kitchen for treats between meals. I'll speak to Estelle."

"Oh, let the child have a cookie," her father said. With his thumb, he gently lifted her chin, wiped away the last tears. "Cheer up, little bird. If I say you can have a cookie, even your mother has to agree."

"Of course," her mother said. "One of the plain—"

"Chocolate," her father said. "One of the special ones. This time."

The chocolate cookie had melted in her mouth, the flavor so rare and tantalizing that she had not noticed anything odd in the sleepy feeling, the softening of memory's sharp edges. Until now.

She could hardly breathe, as that and other memories long buried unfolded and changed her known past. "I'm scared," the girl said.

"I'm Zori," Zori said. "Hi, Scared." It was all she could think of, in the turmoil, but the girl's face relaxed for an instant and she giggled.

"That's silly . . . my name's Hordin. But I am scared. Why aren't the peacekeepers here?"

"I don't know," Zori said. "Maybe—"

At that moment, the loudhorns the peacekeepers used blared from near the back door. "Everyone: hands on your heads. Stand where you are. Do not attempt to run."

"We aren't standing," Hordin whispered. "Can I just hold your hand?"

Zori didn't want to be seen any sooner than necessary; this was as good an excuse as any. "Lie down," Zori said. "I'll lie down with you." With any luck, they'd think she was protecting the child, that both were hurt. Just how did someone feign unconsciousness, anyway? Her eyes kept opening as she heard the shuffle of feet, the voices demanding ID, the other voices trying to explain and being told to save it for the court. Customers and staff were being moved toward the front of the place, away from the back door.

Very shortly, she was looking up at three peacekeepers in full riot gear, their face shields pushed back. "Are you hurt?" one of them asked her.

"I—I fell," Zori said. *Always tell the truth when you can,* her father had said. "I think I'm just . . . just bumped around . . ." She pushed herself up to sitting, and shook her head when he offered her a hand up, turning instead to Hordin. "Can you stand up now, Hordin?"

"This your child?"

"No, ser. I fell over her; I was worried about her. I don't think she's badly hurt, though. We tried to crawl into a safe place, but there wasn't one . . ."

The one with more marks on his riot vest sighed. "These two aren't part of it, but we'll still have to take ID."

"My name is Hordin Amanuse, and we live at 342-A, branch 3, twig 27," the little girl said. She too was sitting up, her lower lip trembling. "I . . . I don't mean to be impolite . . ." Tears tracked down her face, through the dust and streaks of food from the floor.

Zori put an arm around her shoulders. "It's all right, Hordin. No one's blaming you."

"You know her, then?"

"No, ser. I fell over her, when I was trying to get away, and then I thought she might be hurt, so . . . we introduced ourselves."

"I said I was scared, and she said I'm Zori, hello Scared, and then I said that's silly and told her my name," Hordin said. Her hand in Zori's no longer trembled; her tears were drying. "She was nice to me. I didn't want her to leave and she held my hand."

"That's very good, serita. Can you stand if we help you?"

"I think so." With the peacekeepers' help, both of them stood.

Zori looked down at her clothes and shook her head. "What a mess. Hordin, we both need a change of clothes."

"And your name, sera?" The peacekeeper's tone was perfectly polite, but implacable.

"I'm Zori Louarri," Zori said. "And when you've found Hordin's parents or guardian, I need to talk to you."

He smiled down at her. "Surely you aren't going to tell me you started this riot . . ."

"No, ser. But I do know something which you should know, not for a child's ears."

"I'm not just a child," Hordin said, pulling her hand out of Zori's.

"Of course not," Zori said, in concert with the peacekeeper. She went on, looking directly at Hordin. "But you know there are things that must be confidential. It is that kind of thing. It would be rude to speak it here."

"Oh." Hordin looked thoughtful a moment, then nodded.

"Were you here alone, serita?" asked the peacekeeper.

"Yes, ser," Hordin said. "Mama let me come to get a soda but I was supposed to come home right away. Only there were grown-ups who got angry and started a fight, and the lady who brought my soda said come with her, and she brought me here and was going to call my family, only then all these people came in the kitchen . . ."

"We've contacted your family," the peacekeeper said, tapping his head to indicate a skullphone. "Your mother is on her way. If you'll just go out front with Willem . . . do you need Sera Louarri to come with you?"

"No, ser," Hordin said. "Peacekeepers are our friends." She smiled at Zori. "Thank you, sera, for letting me hold your hand when I got scared. My mama will want to thank you, too."

"It was my pleasure," Zori said. "Be well, Hordin."

The other peacekeeper took Hordin's hand and led her out of the kitchen.

"Well, sera?"

"I came here—with my family's permission and an

escort—to have an ice cream with a young man in my class at school," Zori said. "We were to meet at 1945. I was a few minutes late—there was congestion out front—so I came through the back way. Just as we came in sight of the back entrance, I saw three men carry out someone strapped to a litter. Unconscious. It was my friend. I tried to stop them but my escort pulled me back—for my safety, I thought, but then when I wanted to call my friend's guardian, he told me not to."

"I'm not sure what—"

"Ser, please. My friend should have had two escorts with him—his guardian insists, because they were attacked elsewhere. I saw his escorts come out, after the men who took him were out of sight—"

"Carrying him?"

"No. In a vehicle with a SANITATION logo on the side."

"You're sure it was your friend?"

"Of course I'm sure . . . ask his—where are his escorts? Didn't they speak to you?"

"What's his name, sera?"

"Toby Vatta. His guardian's Stella Vatta, of Vatta—"

"Yes, I know who Stella Vatta is. Sera, I think we'd better get you home; we can interview you later—"

"No." That came out louder than Zori intended; from his expression he found it rude. "Excuse me," she said. "I intend no discourtesy, but please, listen to me." He nodded. "My escort—my father insists on an escort in the evenings—there was something wrong about him. He didn't just stop me from intervening when those men took Toby. He told me I could not call Toby's cousin—Sera Vatta—and he reached for his weapon—"

"Your escort is dead," the man said. "He appears to have shot one of the boy's escorts, and then the other shot him. I cannot speak more about that; the survivor is being interrogated. I would have thought, though, that your escort thought he was protecting you—and even if he wasn't, your parents are still—"

"Please," Zori said. "Please forgive my interruption; no discourtesy was intended. I think—I think my father did it—had it done—"

"What did your father do?"

"Took Toby."

"You think your father had the boy kidnapped just because you and he are friends?"

"No. Because he invented the shipboard ansible that can communicate with system ansibles."

The man's expression hardened. "I think you had better speak to my supervisor."

"I'll be glad to," Zori said, though she was beginning to feel very shaky indeed.

He escorted her to the front door, provided a privacy hood, and handed her to another peacekeeper who opened the door of a squat vehicle. Inside, she joined four others, all shrouded in privacy hoods like hers, and in moments they were moving. No one spoke; Zori tried to use the time to sort her thoughts. What had really happened? What did she think it meant?

Did she really think her father was guilty of . . . whatever had happened to Toby? Just because the escort had made that move? Just because of that flash of memory in the kitchen?

And where was Toby? And what was happening to him? She felt her shoulders jerk and tried to still them. She couldn't help Toby directly . . . she had to wait, had to talk to the right person, say the right things.

Toby never quite lost consciousness and the long dark tunnel that engulfed him at O'Keefe's shortened and spat him out into awareness that he was swaddled in a wrap held tight by restraints. He tried to speak, but he could not move his jaw or his tongue. He could not even move his eyes; he stared almost straight up at the inside of a vehicle of some kind.

A face moved into his line of vision, a face he did not recognize. "Comin' to, are you? You'll find you can't move."

If he couldn't move, if they had paralyzed him, how was he breathing? All at once he was conscious of something in his throat, of pressure on his chest.

"You can't see it, but you're on a respirator," the man said. "Just keep that in mind, boy: if we turn it off, you die."

He wanted to say something, explain to someone that it wasn't his fault, that he had done everything he was supposed to . . . but he couldn't. Stella would be frantic. Did she even know? Where were his escorts? Where was Zori? Was Zori also a captive? Hurt? Would Stella blame Zori when she found out he was missing? He had to do something—he had to—

The vehicle he was in stopped with a jerk. The men—he could now see their bodies when they leaned over to unhook his stretcher from the vehicle—worked in silence, swiftly. One of them laid a jacket over his face, blinding him; he could just see light through the weave of the cloth. He told himself to think, to observe, but he heard nothing identifiable: the men's breathing, the steady rasp of his own breath forced in and out by the respirator, the softer friction of their clothing as they lifted him out of the vehicle. They carried him through a door—he heard it open and shut—and along what he thought was a narrow corridor, from the sound of their feet.

When the man pulled the jacket off his face, Toby saw a bright light directly overhead, painfully bright. The man leaned over him again and sprayed something on his eyes; his vision blurred, but that did not dim the light enough for comfort. "That gel protects your eyes from drying, if you're interested. The paralysis won't wear off for hours; you're safe enough here. When you move, the instruments will tell us, and we'll have a little chat . . . have a pleasant evening." His laugh was anything but pleasant; he moved out of Toby's view, and from the scuff of feet and the sound of the door closing, Toby assumed they'd left and locked him in.

He had a few moments of panic—what was going to happen to him? To Zori?—but with the suddenness of a switch being thrown, it vanished, replaced by the familiar alert concentration he felt when working on a new technical problem. Was it something in the drug they'd given him? Shouldn't he still be too scared to think? Rafe had said something about that, about the ability to wall off the fear and think through problems. Toby tested that with a math problem from that morning's class. Whatever this detachment was, it wasn't simply inability to think.

If he could think, he should be able to get himself out of this somehow. Would his skullphone work? Not without being able to use the tiny muscles in his throat. Could he detect surveillance in the room with his implant? He started testing that. Obligingly, his implant produced a wireframe display of the room, with little red dots where instruments were located. That included the surface on which he lay, a medical sensor pad measuring vital functions.

What was it telling them? His implant also monitored his vital functions. Respirations controlled at twelve per minute, heart rate eighty . . . faster than his own normal. Normal temperature, blood chemistry . . . Toby would have frowned in concentration if he'd been able to. Last semester's chemical database was still in his implant. It displayed the structure of the molecules that held him captive.

And how to break them apart, as well, in the implant's biochemical hierarchy. But the room's sensors would tell his captors if he moved. They would come back . . . that could be worse. Maybe patience would be the best tactic here. Stella would find him . . . someone had to know by now he was missing. He refused to think about the alternative, but he could not help thinking of Zori. Of course she wasn't—she hadn't—but the same men who had captured him might have captured her, and Stella wouldn't be as concerned about Zori. He had to get free and make sure Zori was safe.

Meanwhile the light boring into his helpless eyes hurt, hurt more and more with every boring minute. So did the tube in his throat.

Maybe his implant could at least fox the medical pad? His implant told him that the medpad's data report function was hard-cabled to some external location, with safeguard functions to detect RF interference in the usual ranges. Yet the data collection function needed RF sensitivity to the electrical emissions of his own body. He could interfere there, at the source, at least as long as his implant's transmissions matched the parameters the medpad had been programmed to pick up. He queried . . . feeding the merest trickle of power to the external channel . . . and the pad responded, reporting a fictional heartbeat. That worked; excitement made his heart speed up. He hoped his captors would think it was from fear and pain.

The light boring into his eyes, the choking feel of the tube in his throat, had to be fixed next. He had access to his implant's biocontrols. That meant access to conditioned sleep, pain management for both acute and chronic pain, even complete sensory decoupling. That came with major warning flags: not a good idea.

But interfering with pain signals from his eyes and throat seemed safe enough. Immediate relief. Toby felt a burst of confidence. Now what? Control the entire medpad output. If he could do that, then he could deconstruct the paralyzing drug most of the way without revealing changes in metabolism.

Toby defined the parameters and instructed his implant to insert them into the datastream. Then he damped his throat's sensitivity to the tube even further. If he could break down the paralyzing chemical, the first natural movement would be a gag reflex and a blink, something the video surveillance would pick up. He had to appear to be paralyzed right up to the moment he was ready to take on whatever came next.

Then he set to work on the chemical problem. Could the reaction products from breaking down the paralyzing drug counteract the effects of hours of immobilization? Strength, agility, what else? *Zori,* his emotions said.

"You what!" Stella felt a wash of icy terror and white-hot rage meet in the middle of her head; she wanted to fly into pieces. And she must not.

"He was abducted," the escort said. His voice was strained; he was a mass of bruises, scrapes, cuts. "And yes, sera, I know we have given you ample cause for anger; Duirman is dead, died in his defense, I hope you will remember—"

"When I have time to remember," Stella said, "I will honor his sacrifice. Right now Toby is in danger—"

"We are searching for him," the Station Security officer said. "We have a good description of the abductors and the vehicle from Zori Louarri—"

"Her!" Stella said. "I knew there was something—"

"Sera, she has been most helpful. She told us to contact you at once; she has refused to return to her parents' home and wishes to see you."

The last thing Stella wanted to see was a hysterical teenage girl in love, whether she was guilty of anything else or not. "I don't have time—" she said, but the man was already nodding at the door.

Zori rushed in. "I have to see you," she said to Stella. "You have his dog. You have to get his dog."

"Rascal? Why?"

Zori nodded. "He told me about it, about his dog at home, where he came from. It could follow scent; it could find anyone it knew. Rascal can follow his trail and find him. They won't think of that; we don't have any other dogs on the station."

Stella wondered for a moment if it could work, and then shook her head. "Zori, not all dogs can track. I don't think Rascal's that kind of dog—dogs bred to follow scent are a different breed."

"But Rascal loves him!" Tears glittered in Zori's eyes, and Stella heard the barely voiced "Just like me" as the girl burst into tears. "We have to try," she sobbed. "We can't just let him disappear—what if they put him in a ship, take him away—"

"It is a dog, sera," the Security officer said. "Isn't it true that dogs can track individuals through cities, even?"

"Some dogs," Stella said. It was at least an idea, better than some. She patted Zori's shoulder, feeling at least sixty. "Zori, you really should go home—"

"I—I can't," Zori said. "I think my father—I told them—"

"Sera Louarri has made accusations against her father," the officer said. "Until those allegations are resolved, it would be better for her to have no contact with her parents." He gave Stella a meaningful look; it took her a long pause to catch on.

"Oh, no. You want *me* to take her in? In the middle of all this?"

"It would be a great kindness," the officer said. "And in accordance with our customs." That sounded more like a forced exchange of hostages than a kindness. "It might be helpful in our investigation of your cousin's disappearance," he continued. "Sera Louarri seems to be linked to more than one problem. Otherwise, I'm afraid she'll have to stay in protective custody in jail, and we have no facilities for that, really."

"I do not think I can take the responsibility for another juvenile," Stella said. "Not when I've already lost one."

"You will have our assistance," he said. "Please, sera . . ."

Zori looked at her, tears obvious. Stella could not ignore that, any more than she could have ignored Toby. "But is it legal?" she asked.

"You will become her warden under our regulations governing protective custody."

"The problem I see is that my ward was abducted and his escorts attacked—one of them killed. I'm not sure I can keep Zori safe, if someone comes after her—and her family certainly may."

"We will notify her family that she is in protective custody. They will understand what that means under our laws and customs. We will provide additional security for you—quite reasonable, as your cousin was abducted—and this should deter potential attackers. You are free to use your own security service, as well, and make such additional arrangements as seem best. We would recommend that she not attend school tomorrow."

"Very well." Stella thought a moment. "I would like an

official vehicle, with shielding, for our return to my apartment; whoever went after Toby may have intended to go
after Zori as well. And she needs a chance to clean up
and get some rest."

"I don't need rest—!" Zori burst out.

"Are you sure the dog can't help us find him?" the
officer said.

"Not absolutely certain," Stella said. An idea glimmered
in the back of her mind; she needed time alone to figure
it out. "And it is an idea to be tried, perhaps."

FOUR

Back in the apartment, Stella prepared for whatever might come next, opening the first drawer of a locked cabinet to look at the array of knives there.

"I didn't know you had weapons," Zori said, eyes wide. "You're a businesswoman."

Stella smiled. "That's true, but even businesswomen may have weapons."

"Toby said you weren't just a . . ." Zori's voice trailed away as Stella considered the row of weapons in the next drawer and chose two.

"Just a pretty face?" Stella said. In the same drawer was a complicated web harness; Stella eeled into it, attached holsters, and slid the weapons home, then removed them and laid them out on the desk. "That's been useful, Zori, a few times in my life. People see the pretty face, the yellow hair, and they think that's all I am."

"I didn't mean to insult you," Zori said, flushing.

"I'm not insulted," Stella said. She locked that drawer and opened the next, each compartment stocked with a different ammunition. "I'm flattered that a girl your age would think me pretty. You're beautiful yourself, and you know it. Often that creates a rivalry."

"I'm not—" Zori started to say, then stopped. "You think I'm beautiful?"

"Don't be silly." Stella loaded the propellant canister in one weapon, then the flechettes, their tips translucent; in the other, a roll of thin wire. "Do you know what these are?" She tapped the containers of wire rolls.

"No," Zori said. She sounded more interested than frightened.

"The flechettes are high-velocity chemstun rounds. The highest concentration allowed to non-law-enforcement personnel. The rolls are tangle-tie. Expand on impact, stick to anything until they harden, which takes five seconds. None of this is lethal, thus none of it is illegal. Never be illegal if you don't have to, that's what my Aunt Grace always said."

"Your Aunt Grace . . . Toby said she's now the Rector of Defense of Slotter Key?"

"The same Aunt Grace."

"And the . . . er . . . blades?" Zori looked at Stella's sleeve, which showed no bulge beneath it.

"Insurance," Stella said.

"What am I supposed to have?" Zori eyed the drawers with more eagerness than Stella had expected.

"A good night's sleep, Zori. You will be quite safe here, with all the security around the place."

"You can't expect me to stay here while Toby's in danger—!"

"I expect you to do exactly that," Stella said. "I'm not risking your life, too, and I don't need to worry about you in a tight situation."

"But—but I'm the one who thought of using Rascal!"

"And I'm grateful for the idea. But Zori, you have no training—"

"I can handle a weapon—I have my own pistol at home!"

"Zori." Stella took the girl by both shoulders—stiff, resistant shoulders. "I don't doubt your courage, your intelligence, or your willingness to help. But I have done this sort of thing before—I got Toby away alive from people who wanted to kill him at Allray—and I will have trained, experienced personnel with me. I need to know you're safe. Toby needs to know you're safe. Yes, this is the boring part—but the boring part is useful, too." Zori's stubborn expression didn't change. Stella thought of something. "There is something you can do, something very important."

"What's that?"

"I have the transcript of a message sent by pirates—intercepted by my cousin Ky during a battle. Toby recognized some of the words as those you'd taught him, but he can't read the whole thing. Would you give it a try?"

"It's really important?"

"So far, only the pirates understand pirate jargon. If we had a translation . . ."

Zori's face relaxed a little. "Yes . . . I can see that might help, and it's something to do while . . . while you find Toby. I know I couldn't sleep."

"And Zori . . . whatever you do . . . do not contact anyone outside. Not your family, not friends, no one."

"But if I want to tell you something—"

"I can't risk it breaking my concentration. Believe me, I want Toby back safe as much as you do. Do the translation, if you can, Zori."

Stella finished her preparations, put a lead on Rascal's collar, and picked him up. He squirmed a bit, then settled into the crook of her arm. In the next room, she briefed the two men she had chosen from her private security to come along.

The corridor outside was quiet; the single apparent

guard was, Stella knew, only one of many in the area. She made her way to O'Keefe's, where she was allowed in after a brief check with police headquarters.

"According to his escort, he was sitting here, sera," a policeman said, leading her to the booth. She put Rascal down next to it; he scampered over to a puddle of melted ice cream on the floor and started lapping at it.

"Rascal, no—*find Toby*—"

Rascal glanced up, rolling his eyes and flattening his ears, took a last swipe at the puddle, and lunged for a lump on the floor that might have been part of a sandwich, dragging at the leash.

"Rascal!"

He had the lump, whatever it was, and gulped it down, then dashed in another direction winding the leash around Stella's legs, scrabbling at the floor, and giving short yaps.

Stella followed him, unwinding the leash, with the sense of time passing . . . she knew, she'd been told, where Toby was sitting—over there, on the left—and that Toby was taken out the back of the place, through the service area and kitchen. Rascal showed no interest in either the booth or the most likely path to the service area. This wasn't going to work. She herself had no experience with dogs that followed scent trails, but the ones she'd read about kept their noses to the ground and the trail made sense. Rascal looked eager and excited, head up, pulling hard toward the far side of the room at first, but then veering aside to grab another lump off the floor. This time Stella could see the bit of meat in it.

"It's not working," she said to her escort. "He's just fooling around. I warned them he might not be able to do this."

"The girl said it was a sanitation van . . . but there are hundreds on the station . . ."

"Sera Vatta!" Stella turned to see a policeman waving at her from near the entrance. Her heart clenched.

When she came nearer, she saw that he had a datapad with a visual display up. "Sera, we have a little information, not much. This is combined from the station gravity report and two surveillance vids . . . a vehicle massing approximately the same as a sanitation hauler and four adults, but not on the normal route of a sanitation vehicle in this branch, moved on this route—" It was highlighted in yellow, Stella saw: inward to the trunk and up two branches, out almost to the tip, spinward. "—and it passed these eight vids on that route, but only two were functioning. We are attempting to ascertain the cause of the malfunction."

Enemy action, of course, but they were being correct and polite. Stella said, "Thank you for sharing this information. If you'll excuse me . . ."

"Sera, you should go home and wait—we'll keep you informed."

Stella smiled, nodded, and left the mess behind. "Get us backup," she said to her escort once they had cleared the line outside.

"Sera? You aren't going—"

"I want medical, some heavy—"

"Sera!"

"I am not going to go home and wait. That child will not die or be taken off this station because I did nothing."

The escort opened his mouth, then shut it, and instead punched at his datapad. Stella led the way through the still-crowded corridors toward the trunk. The quickest way upstation was the airlifts, which she normally avoided because the pressure changes made her sinuses ache, but this time . . .

"Sera, for your safety—"

"Ganz, I'm wearing armor. And I'm armed. And I'm going."

The airlift tube made conversation impossible except by skullphone. It spat them out on the correct branch, and Stella quickly reoriented to the branch layout. Ahead, she saw a meaningful bustle—vehicles, pedestrians, some in uniform. Had they found him?

Toby felt he was making progress. With the medpad lying to his captors, and the paralyzing drug leaving his system, he'd soon be able to do—whatever he was going to do. But how could he get up—when he could get up— without revealing to the room's audiovisual surveillance that he was mobile? If his abductors were close enough, they could rush in and dose him again before he could get away.

He accessed the implant's security cluster—Stella had insisted on it over his protests. He hadn't believed he needed that stuff. He had bodyguards.

Now he extended the sonic and infrared probes. The next room to his right had neither sound nor heat signals. Nor did the room to his left. Beyond that, he could not be sure.

His eyes still stared straight up; he could not see the door or its lock. He had to know if he could get out that way.

Wait . . . if he could access the hardwired connections of the medpad, could he then infiltrate all the wiring, via the monitors the medpad reported to? Was there any way—? What had Rafe taught him about the simple way some ansibles had been disabled?

Simple in concept, difficult in execution. His implant could trace and identify circuits. Sure enough, a standard magnetic lock. His implant could not create, on its own, the kind of electromagnetic pulse that would disable the lock. But medical monitors had devices to multiply the signal, and these devices were software-controlled.

With the local circuitry in his implant, Toby knew exactly what to tweak and how, using the medpad's access via the medical monitors. Could he now call for help past the shields? Not without detection. Would there be back-splash into his implant? Not if he disengaged in time. The really tricky thing would be getting his door's magnetic lock open after he'd fried the circuits.

He set up the commands, put them on a timer, checked his biological status—drug almost completely metabo-lized, only a light dose still helping him lie still as if par-alyzed. It would clear in seconds . . . and then he would blink.

He felt the growing excitement, a mix of nausea—quickly suppressed by his implant—and glee. Then he blinked, and the lights went out. He blinked again. Still dark. Utterly dark. Not even a gleam of light . . . he sat up, blinking. He had imagined everything except how dark it would be.

His implant threw up a ghostly visual of the room. Toby stood, amazed at the quick response of his body, the steadi-ness of his stance. But this was not the time to stand still. He took the two quick strides to the door. Locked, of course. Without his usual tool kit, he had no way to open it easily, not with the whole system down.

Ky wouldn't stand here like an idiot. She would do something . . . and he'd heard about crawl spaces and ventilation spaces all his life. Toby stood on the bed and reached up. He could touch the ceiling . . . and the ceiling panels shifted as he pushed. It was harder than he'd expected to move one aside . . . and then he had to jump, with only the virtual light of the implant's view of the room. His fingers scrabbled on the frame that held the panels. What if it wasn't strong enough? What if it gave way and he fell back and broke something?

Voices in the corridor outside . . . angry voices. "I don't care—we have to be sure—blow the damned door!"

He had to try. He leapt up, flailing for the framework, caught hold, and hung a moment, legs kicking wildly, before he levered himself up into the cold, machine-smelling space above. He felt around in the dark, and pushed the panel he'd dislodged back into place. It probably wouldn't confuse them, but it might slow them down . . . though that was the only logical way he could've gotten out.

Even as he thought this, he was crawling along the framework, careful to put weight only on the frame itself. The implant gave him a peculiar fuzzy view a short distance ahead; it was detecting different materials with one scan method and distances with another, and he had to keep looking down so it could define the framework well enough for him to stay on it. How far did he have to go? How far had he come?

Behind him, he heard a crash, and a brief spurt of light revealed ahead of him a line of gleaming material that looked like a solid barrier. The light went out; he smelled acrid burning . . . if they did that to the framework, he'd fall through.

"He's got to be up here," a voice said. It sounded faint, though, not like someone in the same space. "I can't tell which way . . ."

Toby flattened himself as much as he could, holding his breath.

"We'll need a light," said another voice. "But he can't get far. The firewall's only twenty meters inboard."

Firewall. Of course. Toby's heart sank. He had moved

in the right direction, inboard, but now he was stuck. Firewalls had no openings at all between decks . . . but there were maintenance access ports on either side, running up and down between decks. The men could start their search at either end and trap him against the tip of that section or the firewall. And if he dropped out into a room or corridor . . . they might be there. They must be part of a larger plot; there must be other enemies to fear and evade.

Even as he thought this, he put more distance between himself and the room where he'd been held. The men were going for lights, or at least IF detectors . . . he had a little time to get away from them.

He angled across the framework now, heading for the far corner of the space his implant told him—when he lifted his head and let the implant scan it—was out at the tip of one of Cascadia Station's branches. Inboard was definitely the way he wanted to go. If he could move fast enough, get to one of the corridors where the firewall had an opening . . . they'd be waiting, if they were waiting, where the access passage came down through the decks . . . so he needed a room nearby.

He was almost to the far side of the space when his implant picked up the noise and light of pursuit. What would Ky do? Toby set his implant to scan the space below . . . unoccupied, and open to another space or corridor. He scrabbled at a ceiling panel, but this one was solidly fixed . . . he felt wires and connections . . . a light fixture. The next, though, came loose. He peered down; his implant showed him a ghostly image that could have been an office—a room with furniture anyway. He rolled over the edge, holding the frame for a moment to slow his drop, and landed on the floor. He thought of pushing one of the furniture pieces over and trying to replace the panel to hide where he'd gone down . . . but he was afraid that might be seen. Instead, he moved quickly to the opening the implant showed him. Outside was a corridor, as he'd hoped, and now he had no doubt which way was inboard.

He ran his hand along the wall as he went, deliberately leaving traces. If things went badly, someone should know he'd been here. Ahead he saw a small bright blue glow . . . one of the Cascadia Station emergency comunits. They had their own power source . . . his stomach lurched. He could call for help. If it worked; if it wasn't blocked in some way.

He picked it up, punched in the codes for everything he could remember: fire, pressure leak, personal injury, crime-in-progress. He heard voices down the passage outboard, pushed TRANSMIT, and put the comunit back in its holder before moving on as quietly and quickly as he could. A faint glow showed ahead of him . . . he could be seen against it . . . he moved to the darker side of the corridor as the light grew brighter. The corridor curved sharply, as always near a firewall opening; now the light came in brightly from a section where he hadn't blown the power. People were standing around waving their hands, talking loudly . . . nobody coming in. Someone in a Station Security uniform stood in front of the gap, facing the crowd, where two people were already pointing past him at Toby.

Toby straightened up and walked forward, as casually as he could, with what he hoped was a friendly and innocent smile.

"Excuse me," he said. "I need help—"

Then the uniformed man turned to him, and he recognized a face with no smile at all.

*   *   *

Stella, doing her best to see past the people ahead of her, spoke to the Security headquarters. "What's going on?"

"Someone entered a multi-emergency call right where we were going. We've got units of fire, medical, and pressure on the way out there . . ."

"You see this crowd . . . why aren't they moving?"

"There's someone from Security at—oh. He's not Secur—"

"Toby!" Stella yelled as loud as she could. He might be where he could hear her . . . she felt Rascal squirm in her arms.

"Aunt Stella!" At Toby's voice, Rascal scratched and squirmed free of Stella's arms, yanked the leash out of her hand, then disappeared into the back of the crowd, where excited exclamations of *Dog—there's the dog!* marked his progress. Stella elbowed her way forward, ignoring Cascadia's standards of courtesy.

An amplified voice from ahead spoke then. "Don't anyone move—I've got him and if you move he's dead."

Stella could just see, between the people still in front of her, Toby held with an arm around his neck, a weapon pointed at his ear. It would be a tricky shot—her hand slid into her clothes . . . but a black-and-white flash dashed across the scant open space. Toby said "Rascal" in a strangled voice just as Rascal jumped up in his usual way . . . but the man struck at Rascal with the weapon. Toby twisted out of the choke hold, kicked him in the knee, and Rascal latched onto the man's wrist, snarling.

Stella said, "Excuse me," in her politest voice. The front row parted and gave her a perfect shot. Chemstun and tangle-tie both, and without a touch on either Toby or Rascal.

"There's more of them," Toby said. Stella looked at him.

Not much of the gangly schoolboy at that moment; he looked as dangerous as she felt.

"Then we'd best get away and let Station Security—the real ones—take care of them," she said. "I've got our team, somewhat augmented." He might not know that one of his detail had been killed; this was not the time to land that on him. "We've got a safe conveyance."

"I knew you'd be coming," Toby said, once they were inside it, Rascal now in his arms. He ignored the others, talking only to Stella. "But I didn't know how long it would take and I thought I should do something, in case—"

"You were brilliant," Stella said. "I'm so relieved—the last I heard you were being carried out as if paralyzed."

"I was," Toby said. "It was the implant that saved me— if I'd had the student-level I'd have been sunk. Did . . . did Zori ever show up?" All too obvious in that was his fear that Zori had been part of the plot.

"Not only showed up, but was crucial to our finding you," Stella said. "She's quite a young woman, Toby. I knew that before, but I didn't know . . . well. We'll talk more about this when we get home. I know Station Security will want to talk with you, but they've agreed that you need to have medical evaluation and some rest before-hand."

"Is Zori safe? If her family finds out . . ."

"She's as safe as we can make her. She thinks her father was implicated in your abduction, and possibly more . . ."

"She's right," Toby said. "That trade tongue is the pirates' language, and her father gave the orders for my abduction. I overheard things . . ."

"Medical first, then home," Stella said. "Then we'll talk." Toby was entirely too bright-eyed; something besides natural excitement was working in his system. "I'll call and let Zori know you're alive and well," she said.

"Can I talk to—"

"Not now. You'll see her later."

They were in the medical center—the staff had drawn blood to analyze for any dangerous residuals from his implant's deconstruction of the paralytic drug, and they were awaiting the results of the tests in a guarded room— when Stella got a call from someone who introduced himself as the Moscoe Confederation Assistant Minister of Defense.

"Excuse me?" Stella checked the origination codes; the call had originated onplanet, near if not in Cascadia's capital city of Holme.

"I know it is after business hours, but I felt this matter could not wait," he said. "It's about the accusations that some in the Nexus government have made—"

"Unless we're under imminent attack," Stella said, risking an accusation of rudeness, "I'm afraid it will have to wait until morning. I'm at the medical center here on Cascadia Station with my ward Toby, after his rescue from an abduction attempt; I have another child at home; I need sleep to think clearly."

"Oh." A long pause. "Oh. I'm sorry. I didn't know—"

"So I will contact you in the morning, shall I?" Stella said. "I have your contact numbers."

"Well . . . yes. That will be soon enough . . ." The voice trailed off; Stella shook her head. When Toby's tests came back indicating it was safe for him to leave, she ordered a secure conveyance and took him back to the apartment.

Zori met them at the door and flung her arms around Toby, burying her face in his shoulder for an instant, then pushing away. "Forgive me—that was very rude."

"I didn't mind," Toby said, red to the tips of his ears.

He reached up to pat her back but she had already backed out of reach.

"I am sorry," Zori said, looking at Stella. "It is very bad—not just hugging Toby without permission, but what I have translated."

"I thought it might be," Stella said.

"My father taught me some words . . . he said it was our secret trade tongue. I told you that, but now I know it was not true. Not our secret family trade tongue, but the secret language of . . . of pirates. I didn't know—"

"Do you think he knew?" Stella asked, in as neutral a tone as she could manage.

"Yes." Zori's voice wavered. "He . . . his company . . . is mentioned. And his private com code."

"Are you sure?" Toby asked.

"Entirely." Zori looked away. "I'm sorry, Toby. I have become an embarrassment . . ."

"You're not—!"

"Yes. My father is . . . must be . . . involved in a criminal enterprise. He will be adjudged a criminal. We do not have attainder here, legally—at least, I'm underage—but it is a disgrace and I will no longer be a suitable acquaintance for you—"

"I don't care," Toby said. Patches of color stood out on his cheeks, and his hands trembled.

"You're under my protection," Stella put in before Toby lost it completely. "Toby, you may need to ask your implant to normalize your chemistry—you're still hyper from your ordeal. I suggest a hot drink and a snack. Zori, you and I do need to talk. Your room?"

Zori nodded; Stella gave Toby a quelling look and he glared before turning abruptly toward the kitchen. Stella ushered Zori into the spare room, which she realized would be Zori's until . . . whatever happened, happened. When

Stella shut the door and engaged the privacy shield, Zori pulled a data cube from her pocket and held it out to Stella.

"Here. This is as complete as I could make it. I don't understand everything; there were words I didn't know. I . . . I sent a copy to Station Security. I hope that doesn't offend you."

"Zori, why would it offend me?" Stella could wish Zori had waited, so Stella could have sent it to the person she'd contacted before, but it did show Zori's essential innocence.

"I don't know, I just . . ." Tears welled in her eyes. "I am so ashamed. I wanted to do the right thing—"

Stella sighed. Adolescent guilt . . . just as difficult to handle as adolescent lust. And if Zori was anything like her own adolescent self, she could never believe that Stella really knew what she was feeling. She had thrown herself on the floor of her closet, wishing to die, when . . . for a moment she could not even remember his name . . . had made off with the contents of the house safe, and she had realized how stupid she'd been.

"It's not your fault, Zori," Stella said. Should she offer a hug? But local customs required asking permission, and that seemed ridiculous at such a time. "You didn't pick your parents." She did not fully understand the belief system Zori's family followed. There were belief systems in which a child was presumed to have chosen its parents . . . she was damn sure she hadn't chosen hers.

"No, but—" Zori looked away. "I know you probably think I've always been too rebellious, the way I schemed to spend time with Toby even though you knew my mother didn't approve, but really . . . I was brought up to be a good girl, and I've never been in any real trouble before. Now—the station police know that I refused to do what my parents told me—"

"And the police agreed you shouldn't go home to them," Stella said, trying to interrupt what looked like a dive off the guilt cliff.

"But they'll still think I'm a rude, disobedient child," Zori said. "I didn't ask them permission first."

"Zori, you may have saved millions of people—billions—from death and brutality. I think your not asking permission doesn't loom very large against that."

"My grandmama won't think so," Zori said. "Or my uncles . . ." Her voice trailed off.

Families. There was always someone ready to dump on the young one who made a mistake.

"You don't suppose," Zori said, "that they're all in it?"

"All?" Stella said.

"My uncles. His brothers. His mother. I can't believe my *mother's* family . . . they never really liked him . . ." For a moment in those dark eyes, Stella saw knowledge of family pain no young person should have.

"I think you'll have to leave that up to the authorities," Stella said. "The important thing for you is to know that you're safe here, and you have people who care about you."

"They shouldn't care about me," Zori said. "My father is a monster—a traitor."

"Your father is not you," Stella said.

"My mother . . . they say she's an accessory . . . but I don't think she is . . . I don't think she knew."

"You can't know what she knew," Stella said. She had both liked and pitied Zori's mother, and hoped for the best, but she could not promise anything. Cascadian authorities would do whatever they would.

"I can't . . . Toby . . . it would be bad for him. I should go somewhere. Somewhere far away." She burst into tears again.

Stella sighed. In a fit of frustration she now recognized as justified, her own mother had once told her that if she ever had children of her own, she would deserve whatever trouble they brought her. Apparently that bit of universal balance was going to land on her even though the child wasn't actually hers.

"Zori, you know Toby loves you."

An agitated jerk of a shoulder; Zori was curled into a ball now, face buried in a pillow. "He shouldn't," she said, her voice muffled by tears and the pillow both. "I loved him—"

Stella parsed this as referring to Ser Louarri, not Toby. "You were a child; children love their parents unless the parents are brutal."

At that Zori shivered. "I thought he loved me. He said—"

"He probably did . . . which is more than my father did."

"You—I thought you had a good family! Toby said—" Zori's tear-stained face came out of the pillow.

"I meant my birth-father, Zori. Didn't you hear about that, shortly after I first arrived? My connection to the pirates is even closer than yours. My birth-father was one."

"Really?" That had her attention. "Toby didn't tell me that."

"Yes. The people I thought were my parents adopted me. And they were good parents . . ." Even if she was still angry with them for not telling her the truth. "Now," she said, pushing that memory away. "You need to wash your face and go have a hot mug of something so you can sleep." Could she slip something into Zori's mug? Probably not. "You and Toby both need rest."

"I can't possibly sleep," Zori said, then yawned widely.

"I think perhaps you will," Stella said. "Let me get you

something to sleep in . . ." Zori had come with only the clothes on her back. Stella went to fetch one of her own night shifts, and when she came back, Zori was already asleep. *One down,* she thought, and pulled the cover up over the girl, who barely stirred.

Toby, in the living room, wasn't tired at all. "Is she all right? Can I help?"

"She's finally gone to sleep, Toby. The most help you can be is to be quiet." Stella yawned. "I don't suppose you feel like going to bed."

"No . . . when I metabolized the drug—"

"Can you explain how you did that?" Stella had heard Toby's first version, given to the medics who'd examined him, but it didn't make sense to her.

"Not . . . really. I mean, I can recite the chemistry for you, but you said you didn't know much chemistry. But what it amounted to was I found a way to convert the drug to increased alertness and strength."

"I had no idea that implant had so much functionality," Stella said.

"It kind of surprised me," Toby said. His face shifted into the concentrated, thoughtful look Stella had come to recognize. "You know . . . there ought to be a way to miniaturize ansible function enough to link it to the skullphone . . . the problem would be the power draw, but if you could hook it into a power source . . ."

Stella opened her mouth and shut it again. It had to be a healthy sign that he was having ideas, but she was not ready to deal with yet another technological outburst. "That's nice," she said finally. "You can work on that after you deal with your schoolwork."

"Schoolwork? I'm just missing tomorrow . . ."

"No. You and Zori both, by order of Station Security, are not returning to class until they're certain you'll be safe. I'll contact the school, have them send over your assignments."

"At least we'll be together," Toby said, brightening.

"Toby, I need to talk to you about her—"

His jaw hardened. "I'm not going to stay away—"

"Don't be silly," Stella said. "No one's asking you to stay away from your own home. If she's staying here, of course you'll see her all the time. No, this is to help her." Stella outlined the problem as she saw it, ending with, "She's a Cascadian; she can't blow up about it. She can't yell or use bad language without violating her sense of morality. And that very sense of being a good person is under attack because of her father."

"So . . . what should I do?"

"You said she was more relaxed around you—that she dared to use a few bad words—"

"Yes . . ."

"Just be the young man she loves and trusts—keep letting her know you respect her. And if she blows up, try not to be too shocked at what comes out."

"Oh. All right, I can do that."

"I know, Toby. You put up with me when I was so upset after finding out about Osman—so I know you will be what she needs right now."

"You're tired," Toby said, looking at her.

"Yes, I am."

"I should go to bed. I should at least go in my room and be quiet." That courtesy, after what he had been through, almost brought tears to her eyes. He was so damned decent, and she had almost lost him.

"If you can," Stella said, fighting for calmness. "But if you want to stay up—you're right, I must go, because there's a government agency that wants my brain awake in the morning."

"C'mon, Rascal," Toby said; the dog butted its head into his chest. "See you in the morning, Stella."

He hadn't called her cousin, or aunt . . . well, it wasn't the right time to call him on manners. "Sleep well," she said.

The call came halfway through breakfast the next morning; Toby had wakened early and hungry, and Stella had set him to cooking eggs. Anyone, she'd told him, could cook eggs. Stella answered, one hand full of plates.

"I'm so sorry," the same man said. "I didn't know, last night—I've been given all the details now—"

"I quite understand," Stella said. To Toby she said, "They're done when the whites go opaque, Toby."

"You're cooking breakfast?"

"My ward is cooking breakfast. I'm setting the table. Don't let it bother you."

"Er . . . right. The Minister wanted me to set up a call today, if possible at 1400, and give you a briefing data-burst first. Can you answer now on that, or should I call later, at your office?"

"No, this is fine." Stella felt a certain wicked glee at his discomfort. She let the forks clatter to the table while querying her implant for today's schedule. "Shall I initiate the call at 1400, or will the Minister?"

"The Minister will. Thank you."

"And can you give me a clue?"

"Is this a secure line?"

"I certainly hope so," Stella said. "But for absolute security, I should use the office equipment. I'll call you in one—no, I'm sorry, two hours, will that be convenient?"

"Er . . . yes, Sera Vatta, that will be quite sufficient, and I will have transmitted the supporting data. You might wish to look at it . . ."

Stella called the school while Toby devoured four eggs

and a stack of toast, and explained what she needed, then put in a call to Station Security. As she'd expected, Zori's parents were both in custody, and the house was under guard, Security personnel plowing through it looking for evidence.

"I need some clothes for the girl," Stella said when she was transferred to the officer in charge. "I'll be sending someone over to pick them up—"

"I can't let anyone come in," the woman said.

"Well, pack her a bag then. It ought to be obvious which is her room. At least a week's worth of underwear and outerwear."

"I can't do that. That room's not cleared yet. It's against protocol—"

"The girl slept in her clothes last night. I don't have anything her size, and if you check with your superior, you'll find she's not supposed to leave my apartment. She needs clothes. She needs things for school, too."

"Why didn't she pick them up last night?"

Stella rolled her eyes. "Perhaps you don't know the whole story. She did not intend to come here when she left home. She was going to meet a friend for ice cream, and then go home. Then things happened, and your people— Security—asked me to take her in temporarily. And before you ask, I had no opportunity to send for her things."

"She'll just have to buy something, then. This family is rich enough."

"I expect the accounts are frozen," Stella said. "But thank you so much for your cooperation." She ended the call, shaking her head. "Idiots." With another call, she learned that her suspicion had been correct: all Louarri accounts were frozen, and it would take a court order to give Zori access to her own possessions. "Toby, go see if Zori's awake; I need to talk to both of you."

Zori looked as if she'd been crying again, and her clothes were rumpled, but she had herself under control when she came into the kitchen.

"I can fix you eggs," Toby said, clearly eager to show off his new skill. Zori shuddered and refused, but accepted toast.

"Your school assignments will be delivered here by mid-morning," Stella said. "But Zori, your computers and your clothes are all captive to a very zealous security officer. All your family accounts are frozen, so your current credit cube is useless for the time being. I'm sure the court will make one account available in a day or so, but in the meantime you need things. Where do you usually shop?"

"Gibalta's," Zori said. "But—you mean there are people in our house?"

Was she really that naïve? "Yes," Stella said, as gently as she could. "You know your parents are in custody—"

"Yes . . ."

"Well, the authorities are looking for evidence. You weren't involved in whatever your father was doing, but they can't be sure."

"They won't look in my journal, will they?" Zori's glance slid over to Toby, and she blushed, then looked down.

Young love, again. Stella felt like laughing and banging her head on the wall both, and neither would help. Her own mother had found her journal, all those years ago, with all the damning things she'd written about that boy. "I'm afraid they will," she said, as gently as possible. "But Zori, they are looking for evidence . . . not . . . whatever you put in your journal."

"They'll read it, though, won't they?" Red to the ear-tips, Zori stared fixedly at toast on the plate.

"Probably. But—" How to say tactfully that law enforce-ment had no doubt seen the same, and worse, and wouldn't think worse of a teenage girl in love. Nothing would have salved her own adolescent pride; nothing, at this moment, would help Zori, except perhaps getting her mind on something else. "But the immediate problem is getting you some clean clothes, and for that we'll use my credit cube—"

"I couldn't possibly," Zori said. "You're doing too much—" Tears trickled down her face.

"You need clean clothes," Stella said. And she herself needed to get to the office, and the greater universe had worse problems to deal with than this girl . . . she pushed her irritation down. "Here's what I'm going to do. I have to get to work, but I'll send my assistant, Gillian Astin, and she'll help you order in what you need. There's our security and Station Security outside; you are not to leave, either of you, for any reason. Contact me if anyone claiming to be official tries to get you to leave." Toby opened his mouth. "No, Toby, don't even ask. You are not coming to the lab today. Not until the authorities have some answers they don't have yet." They nodded, finally, and she left, all too aware that she was leaving two lovesick youngsters alone . . . but not for long.

FIVE

Once at the office, Stella opened the databurst from the Ministry of Defense and started reading. Slotter Key's government, in sending the privateers to Cascadia, had made a powerful argument that systems needed to cooperate to protect themselves—no one system had sufficient resources. Stella had not been privy to any of those negotiations, or the treaty that resulted. Now she read the dense paragraphs at skimming pace, wondering why she needed any of this information.

Everything had gone smoothly, the briefing went on, until the Moscoe Confederation government had consulted with its old ally Nexus, inviting them to join this new alliance against a common enemy. Then InterStellar Communications raised a strong objection against Ky Vatta. Not that she was too young, or too inexperienced—something that would have been reasonable, Stella thought— but because she was a Vatta.

Stella stared at that paragraph, read it twice. Her first impulse was to place an immediate ansible call to Rafe, and damn any concerns about the time of day where he was. Why would Rafe object to Ky Vatta commanding ships? But she had promised to call the Assistant Minister.

Nexus II

Rafe Dunbarger stared down the boardroom table, meeting each pair of eyes. Mostly hostile eyes, now, faces scowling back at him. He had only four solid allies on the Board, and even those were not entirely happy with him. They understood the reasons for his insistence that Nexus' alliance with the Moscoe Confederation should be expanded to include Slotter Key—or said they did—but they had a fixed aversion to anyone named Vatta that he had not been able to budge.

"You have to see," Perris Vantha said, "that since the government agrees with us, the evidence is all on our side."

"It isn't evidence," Rafe said, trying to keep his tone even. "It's coincidence. *Post hoc* is not *propter hoc,* not in logic nor in law."

"Everything that's gone wrong started with a Vatta," Vantha said, as if she had not heard. She was a replacement for Termanian, a woman whose prior experience had been on the board of a large nonprofit. So many people had been eliminated because of possible connections to Lew Parmina, and at least she hadn't had that. But she also didn't have, he had discovered, the keen intelligence he would have expected. She was connected socially to his family. That turned out to be almost as big a problem as Parmina.

"That's not entirely true," Vaclav Box said. But his quick glance at Rafe was worried.

"It is," she said. "And it's not recent—it started years ago, with Parmina linking up with Vatta executives on Slotter Key. The same branch of the family who sent their daughter off to a military academy—" Scorn edged her voice. Vantha's own daughters were active in charity work, when they weren't parading around in fashionable clothes posing for the media.

"And how does that figure into this?" Rafe asked.

"Clearly they were planning a military takeover," she said. That got some puzzled looks even from those on her side. She sighed dramatically. "Look—they already have a pirate captain, Osman Vatta. Now they train up a military leader, supposedly legitimate. They fake an attack on the family, an excuse for this person to act out her training, and the next thing anyone hears she's commanding an armed ship and gathering allies. And—worst of all—she's got some rogue technician with her who's repairing ansibles without authorization."

"She didn't have a rogue technician," Rafe said. "She had me. I repaired them."

Perris' mouth opened and closed before finally snapping shut, but the argument wasn't over. Anton Bolton took it up.

"Osman Vatta somehow stole the prototype for the shipboard ansible," he said. "That's established, right?"

"Right," Rafe said. He had conceded that before. Osman was a thief; he stole things. Every family probably had one.

"And he manufactured more or had them made, and supplied them to Turek."

"Yes, but—"

"Lew Parmina was in league with Turek, which means he was in league with Osman Vatta, really—" Bolton had spread out one pudgy hand to tick off his points on his fingers. Rafe suppressed the desire to break the fingers.

"Only if you think the leak of technology from here went from Parmina to Vatta to Turek, rather than directly," Rafe said. They had not been able to determine, from the data in Parmina's implant, exactly what Parmina had done with the units, whether he had already been in contact with Turek or Osman Vatta then, or only later.

Bolton ignored that and plunged on. "And then this daughter of Lew Parmina's friend, Stella Vatta, steals our technology and starts manufacturing and selling these things on the open market—"

"She didn't *steal* it," Rafe said. "We never *patented* it. Parmina stole the actual machines and abducted some technicians, after the decision was made—" By the Board of Directors, some involved in that decision still sitting here glaring at him.

"Probably because Parmina, on Vatta's advice, told your father it wasn't necessary. That's what a merchant spacer would want, isn't it? Shipboard ansibles? To be free of ansible charges?"

"And besides," Perris added. "For all we know, this Gammis Turek is really a Vatta and hiding it to protect the family. We don't have any proof he's not."

They had mush for brains. They were so determined to damn the entire Vatta family . . . "Every ship in space would like that," Rafe said. "The decision not to patent or market them came, as you know, from the Board of Directors, on advice from my father—"

"Who was being pressured by Lew Parmina, who had Vatta friends," Bolton said, ignoring Rafe's facts in favor of his own prejudice. He threw himself back in his chair as if he'd proved something.

"And now," Rafe said, "you're going to point out that it was a Vatta on Slotter Key who turned that ansible back on, right? And that Ky Vatta was present when our ships were chewed up at Boxtop?"

"Your father says—" Bolton stopped, glanced sideways. Rafe said nothing. It was no more than he'd expected; many of these people had known his father for years, and they would pay attention to his opinions even now. They'd said they didn't want him back as CEO; they'd said they wanted Rafe instead, but old habits died hard. "Your father says it has to be Vattas. They're trouble, that's all they are. Hiding it for years, appearing respectable, just like Parmina, but actually plotting to destroy our monopoly, ruin us . . ."

"We've already lost billions in income," Vantha said. "Billions. Our fleet's useless, you say. Well, it is now, after that Vatta woman ruined it at Boxtop—"

"She didn't ruin it. She didn't fire a shot at it. Did you even look at our own commander's post-battle analysis?"

"It wouldn't have been there if she hadn't made an unauthorized ansible repair," Elise Dameron said. "You have to admit that."

He had to get new Board members, people with more brains and fewer social connections. He had no idea how to do that.

"It comes down to this," Bolton said. "You don't have the votes, if you push us to it. You haven't done that badly as CEO; you've rooted out a lot of the bad here, in our own ranks. I understand, if the others don't, that the origins of this are not your fault. But now you have to choose: follow that Vatta girl like a besotted adolescent and lose your position, or stay and understand that there can be no alliance with a rogue family, not in a crisis like this."

Rafe opened his mouth to tell them what they could do with their antiquated, outmoded, obsolete, creaking-at-all-joints corporation . . . the very thought of getting back out into what he now thought of as the real world, the place he belonged, was like a gust of clean mountain air in a stale, overheated room. But. But there were his parents. What would they do, without him to run interference? And Penny. She was better, but not yet ready for total independence. And he knew, just as they knew, that he was better at his job than any of them, or anyone they could find.

He had duties. Responsibilities. Things he could accomplish that no one else could, because no one else would understand how important they were and have the determination to carry them through. Nexus had to stay in the alliance or—if the pirates came—the whole planet could be taken over and the pirates could end up in control of everything—all the systems, all the worlds, all the people ISC had once served.

Aboard Vanguard, in FTL Flight

"One minute to transition." Ky could feel the tension on *Vanguard*'s bridge as they neared their second jump-point transition. As the chronometer ticked down, she watched the screens. Weapons hot. Shields full on. Insystem drive on and synched to the microjump controller, already programmed for the first jump.

Scan flickered then came alive, roiled with downjump turbulence; before it cleared, they had microjumped a half second. Scan blanked, came alive again, steadied.

"Hostiles—" That was Teddy Ransome, first out, reporting; he gave the coordinates.

She had changed the pattern of the post-downjump dispersion jump . . . and now saw that indeed the hostiles were positioned to attack the initial emergence pattern or the dispersal she'd used at the first jump point. Her skin felt tight. If they hadn't spotted that pursuer—if she hadn't changed the pattern—they'd be caught in the maelstrom that now filled space where they weren't. Twenty enemy ships were insystem, at least.

"Jump now!" she said. No time to strip the local ansible

of any further news. So they might come out at Cascadia a bit ragged; better that than not at all.

"That was interesting," Major Douglas commented when they were safely back in FTL. "They certainly knew where we were going and what route. I think my organization will be very interested in the speed and accuracy with which Turek learned all that."

"I hope they haven't hit Cascadia by the time we get there," Ky said. "And using twenty of his ships just to block a jump point—"

"He's getting frantic," Hugh said.

"Do you think he's heard about the Slotter Key privateers coming to Cascadia?" Douglas said.

"He'd have to," Martin said. "Your Aunt Grace may have sent the orders as secretly as she could, but there's no way the crews of thirty-odd privateers would all keep their mouths shut about sudden orders from home. It's not like they're regular military."

"He knows more about us than we know about him," Ky said. "Our allies are leaking information like sieves." She sighed. "At least this is the short end of the trip."

Vanguard, Moscoe Confederation Space

"That's different," Hugh Pritang said as scan cleared from a slow insertion into Moscoe Confederation space. "They've ramped up their defenses." He had already signaled their communications board to reply to the system's automated arrival challenge.

"As they should," Ky said. Her stomach knotted; now that she was here, face-to-face with the moment she both wanted and feared, it was hard to stay calm. "There they are—!" Slotter Key ship IDs, close to Cascadia Station . . .

they must have arrived days ago, for scan to show them on downjump.

"Those your command, Admiral?" Major Douglas had come up beside her.

"Some of them, anyway," Ky said, counting them up. Thirty-five. And she had seven already, if she counted *Dryas* the supply ship. Forty-two . . . that certainly sounded fleet-like. She took a deep breath. Time to go to work in earnest.

"Incoming calls via internal ansible from Stella Vatta and external from Traffic Control with an overlay from Moscoe Confederation Defense Department," the communications tech said.

"Hugh, you handle the external; I'll take Stella's."

Stella, on screen, looked tired. "Ky, we've got translations of pirate transmissions for you—"

"That's wonderful!"

"Yes, except it turns out Toby's girlfriend's father was one of Turek's men. Toby's fine now, but he was abducted briefly; the girl's parents were taken into custody, and I have Zori at the apartment with me."

"You?"

"It was a shock to me, too," Stella said. "You recall the speed of legal action here? Well, Zori's father's been executed already, and her mother is still in custody. Protective, this time. There've been assassination attempts against her."

"And you?"

Stella laughed, with an edge to it. "I'm hard to kill," she said. "So, it turns out, is Toby. Now: you need to know that Vatta products are in high demand—you *did* bring all of them with you, didn't you?"

"All but one," Ky said. "I left one with Mackensee, so we can have direct contact with them."

"And I'm sure you know the Slotter Key privateers are

here, being outfitted with theirs, and eager to meet you. They brought along some personal messages from Aunt Grace for both of us—"

"No fruitcakes?" Ky asked, grinning.

"Not fruitcakes," Stella said. She wasn't smiling. "But you will need to pick them up in person."

"I won't have much time," she said, hoping Stella would understand.

"Of course," Stella said. "You have important meetings—and so do I. There's a sort of summit going on here—Nexus, ISC, Moscoe Confederation, Slotter Key. Vatta Enterprises is in it because of our product. And because of you. There's a problem—"

"Excuse me," Hugh said. "Captain, Traffic Control has given us a priority route in and we have our docking assignment. And the Defense Minister needs to speak with you urgently."

"Stella, the Defense Minister's calling me on standard ansible—I should go."

"Call me later," Stella said. "I'll send you the transcript of those pirate transmissions in the meantime."

Ky moved over to take the call from the Defense Minister, a thin dark man who didn't seem to fit what she thought of as the Cascadian type. He wore an immaculately tailored dark suit with a broad green ribbon across his chest. "Polmar Gorikan, Minister of Defense," he said. "As soon as you've got a docking schedule, Admiral, we'd like to set up a meeting to discuss our strategy; we have representatives here from the governments of Nexus and Slotter Key as well as our own, and Mackensee Military Assistance Corporation tells me that you have aboard a liaison officer from them—he will represent them at this meeting—"

"We have a docking assignment, but no ETA yet," Ky

said. A representative from Slotter Key? Surely Stella would've mentioned if Aunt Grace herself had come.

"As soon as possible after your arrival," Gorikan said. His gaze moved across her. "And . . . er . . . perhaps a dress uniform?"

More braid, that must mean. Something that looked admiralish. She had nothing like that; she had a Vatta captain's uniform with some additional patches sewn on. "Of course," she said.

"If it's not too flamboyant," Gorikan went on, as if doubtful of her fashion sense. Ky felt a momentary urge to do a Teddy Ransome on him, ruffles, silk cape, and all, but she knew better.

"I'll let you know our ETA when we have it firmed up," she said. He nodded, tight-lipped, and closed the connection.

" 'Not too flamboyant'?" Hugh said, eyebrow raised. "What kind of idiot wears a shiny green ribbon across his chest and accuses someone else of intent to be flamboyant?"

"I don't have a dress uniform," Ky said. "And I don't think I'd better borrow one from Ransome."

"If I may make a suggestion," Douglas said. Ky nodded, and he went on. "Military outfitters are good at putting things together fast, for just such emergencies. Your cousin is there; she could arrange it."

"Stella would love to get me properly dressed," Ky said with a touch of bitterness, and then realized how silly that was. It had been her mother and her aunt, not Stella herself, who had extolled Stella's fashion sense and urged Ky to copy her. "But you're right," she said. "I'll call her."

Stella readily agreed to find an outfitter and take care of ordering a dress uniform; she was more interested in explaining to Ky the unexpected complications arising from the resistance to Vatta influence from the Nexus government and ISC.

"It's not Rafe himself," she said. "He says he thinks it started with Parmina—"

"I still have trouble believing Parmina was the villain," Ky said. "I met him; he was nice."

"I met him, too," Stella said. "But clearly he was bent, and for whatever reason he poisoned a lot of minds about Vattas, in different levels of ISC and, through Rafe's father, in the Nexus government. Everything we've done to recover our position, they see as sinister plotting."

"I can't change now," Ky said.

"Nor I," Stella said. "Just letting you know—this conference isn't likely to be smooth sailing. A sharp new uniform is a very good idea."

When *Vanguard* docked at Cascadia Station, the first delivery was not the manual on manners that had marked their first visit, but Ky's new uniforms, complete with a team of three from the outfitter's to check and adjust the fit if needed. Not just one uniform—a set of them, for shipboard and stationside use, a range from everyday working to full formal. Stella had even researched insignia from all four sources—three governments and Mackensee—and from that the outfitter had designed and cast rank insignia for the entire officer corps of the Space Defense Force, as well as buttons with the SDF logo.

Maybe she should have paid more attention to Stella's fashion sense, Ky thought as she fastened the last button and glanced at the mirror the outfitter's staff had set up in her office. It fit, and more than that, it was comfortable. Nothing pinched; nothing felt awkward. And yet, in the mirror, it looked—it made her look—totally professional and competent. Older, more formidable.

"This is the semi-formal," the outfitter's senior representative said. "Full formal, evening formal, has a white tunic. But we consider this one ideal for the kind of conference you're attending today." She pulled open a carrier bag. "And here—I believe these boots should fit you."

Ky had completely forgotten about shoes or boots—hers were, when she looked at them, decidedly worn, though clean and polished as always. The new ones, styled with a subtle difference, slipped onto her feet as easily as the uniform had slipped onto her body, and felt as comfortable. And looked as good.

"Your cousin didn't know your preference in head coverings, if any; we prepared a variety." The other outfitter's rep opened another carrier bag. "The Moscoe Confederation uses a soft cap, like this. Slotter Key, we understand, uses a cap with a hard, polished bill. Mackensee tells us they use both that kind of cap and one that folds flat, like a child's paper party hat."

Ky had no opinion at all except that head coverings you had to yank off to stick your head in a pressure helmet were silly. "What do you think looks best with this uniform?" she asked. It would be her policy, she decided in that instant, that crews on ships would go bareheaded except for protective gear.

"The soft cap, don't you think?" asked the older one.

"Oh, yes," the young one said. "The soft cap with this uniform."

"Fine, then," Ky said, putting it on her head. "And thank you." And she would have to thank Stella. In person.

Major Douglas and Master Sergeant Pitt waited near the hatch, in their own impeccable Mackensee semi-dress uniforms. None of the other Slotter Key captains had been invited, but Captain Pettygrew, as a representative of Bissonet's military, was on the list. Captain Ransome had declined to attend; he'd told Ky he wasn't representing his government and didn't think a long boring conference would suit him. She hoped he wouldn't get in trouble with local customs.

At dockside, they met a Station Security escort and, after an exchange of identification, headed to a part of Cascadia Station she had never seen.

Instead of the annoying little map tagger she'd used last time, she found herself in a closed vehicle that slid up one wall of the passage, locked into a track on the overhead, and slid smoothly past a few pedestrians before rotating on its axis, passing through a double air lock, and then—still on a track of some kind—rising on an arc to aim for the far end of the tree-shaped station.

"I didn't see this last time," Ky said.

"Reserved for official business," one of the escort said. "We didn't want any delays getting from the root to the tip." He handed her a data cube and indicated the cube reader in the seat armrest. "A briefing, mostly names and faces." Ky settled in to watch, shunting data to her implant faster than she could really absorb it herself.

The tip, when they arrived, was a series of meeting rooms and offices, all with spectacular views of space. In the room set up for the first of the day's meetings, Ky found the usual long table flanked by heavy chairs—and to one side a large viewscreen, with the blinking lights of ready-ansible signals. Waiting for her was a group of men and women in Cascadian business dress, including—to her complete surprise—Stella.

"Captain—or should I say Admiral?—Vatta," said a tall man, stepping forward with outstretched hand.

"Council Chair Petros Moscoe-Silva," murmured one of her escort. She knew already, her implant cueing her with the few facts she had about him.

"Captain will do," Ky said, shaking hands. "Chairman Moscoe-Silva—"

"Silva, please. Or just Chairman. It's true I'm descended from the colony founder, but the tree needs all its leaves. We welcome you, Captain, despite the grave news you bring, news which—I must say—we find more truth in every day. Let's sit down, shall we?"

He ushered her to a chair at one end of the long table, and took the other end himself. Along the sides, others sat. On the table in front of her, Ky saw an agenda; beside it was a neat stack of data cubes.

When all were seated, Silva nodded. "Let's be at it. I will outline what I know—some of which, since she has been traveling in FTL, Captain Vatta may not yet have learned." His summary began with the familiar: the increasing interruptions in ansible communications several years before and increased piracy that damaged trade and travel. "The attacks on the Vatta family and their home world—and on some other home worlds we have learned about only recently—signaled a more dangerous turn of events. What we did not know at the time was that the same conspiracy putting ansibles out of service and attacking planets had connections inside InterStellar Communications. A mole high up in that company . . . we still don't know how or why that connection was made, but we do know it existed."

Someone stirred along the inboard side of the table. Silva paused and glanced at the woman, who wore a sash of office over her suit. Subregent of Enforcement Katerina Fois, Ky's implant informed her. "With permission, Chairman, may I ask if the recent arrests here of a prominent trader had anything to do with the conspiracy at ISC?"

"That will be part of the briefing, Katerina. If I may—"

"My pardon, Chairman; no disrespect or insult intended."

"And none assumed. I am aware of your special interest."

That sounded . . . ominous. Ky smiled when Silva looked at her again. "Excuse, please," he said. "It is only the pressure of the moment."

"Of course," Ky said.

"Well, then. Recently—it was after you had left the Mackensee home world—a threat was broadcast by ansible from someone calling himself Gammis Turek. You would not have heard—"

"Excuse me," Ky said. "We did pick up such a broadcast from a jump-point ansible on the way."

"Ah. Then you're aware of the nature of the threat. We have had queries from other governments, including that of Nexus. You should know that the Moscoe Confederation and Nexus System government have been allies a long time, cooperating on regional defense, regional control of piracy, and sharing many of the same standards in commercial dealings. We have long had good relations with ISC as well. Vatta Transport—" He now glanced at Stella, who nodded. "—has had a trading route here for a long time as well. We knew we were only on the fringes of your company's routes, but we had no reason to surmise that you were other than honorable."

Ky felt her stomach clench. That did not sound good, and from the expression on Stella's face, quickly masked to a neutral mild curiosity, Stella felt the same.

"Stella Vatta's business dealings here have all been lawful and correct; we have no complaints. Her new venture, into the manufacture of small ship-mounted ansibles, has already shown enormous potential for profit and has been formally validated by ISC."

Another pause; Silva looked like someone trying to find a polite way to say that there was a rotten egg on the platter. "The problem is," he said finally, "that although the CEO of ISC has nothing against you—or Stella Vatta— or the Vatta family—others do. He feels—Ser Dunbarger, whom I believe you know—" Another pause; Ky nodded, and Silva went on. "He has found resistance," Silva said finally. "His father, who was CEO before him, and who recently suffered a grave injury, is convinced that the Vatta family is to blame for the mole in ISC. He is totally opposed to any dealings with Vattas, and the current CEO feels that he has pushed his Board as far as he can. The government of Nexus, as well, is concerned at the predominance of Vatta influence here, as they see it." He glanced down the table at a man who also wore a sash of office. Abram Veniers, Ky's implant told her, a high-ranking officer in the Diplomatic Corps.

"We don't want a break with Nexus," Veniers said. "We don't want to offend their government. Their government has begun distancing itself from the views of the current ISC head. His father had friends, you see, old friends. His father, though apparently still impaired by the injuries he received, still communicates with them. His father thinks the boy—he calls his son the boy—is besotted with you."

"What!" That got out before Ky could stop it. "I'm sorry," she said at once. "I did not mean to interrupt."

"No offense taken," Veniers said. "The father thinks the young man's judgment is clouded by an infatuation, and this has blinded him to the evils committed by your family. We—our government, that is—do not see it the same way, and yet we would not force a breach. The current CEO himself denies the charge publicly, claims to have respect for you but nothing more. But before we go further in any kind of . . . understanding . . . with you, we do feel it important to clarify the relationship you have with Rafael Dunbarger."

Ky managed to hold her temper in check, partly because it was so ridiculous. They were threatened with annihilation or invasion; they needed to be focused on that very real threat and ways to prevent it. Yet they were fixated on the notion that young people must always be in a ferment of lust or something? But she couldn't put it that way. "You all know that Rafe was on a ship with me for some time, from Lastway to here. So yes, I know him. But the fact that we were on the same ship does not mean we had a relationship." Just a shared cranial ansible, but that was still a secret.

"So you have no emotional attachment?"

"If you mean, am I in a romantic entanglement with him, the answer is no," Ky said. "As Ser Dunbarger told you. As he told a Mackensee officer in my presence." She felt her face warming at that memory. "We were in a crisis situation together, more than once. That creates a very different kind of . . ." She stumbled over the word. "Relationship."

"Ah." A glance passed from person to person, notably skipping past Stella, who stared at the table. "But it is not uncommon . . . I do not mean to be discourteous, sera— Captain—but in this case your private feelings, should you have any, have political implications."

"I don't have any," Ky said quickly. Firmly. Ignoring the treacherous little voice inside that told her she certainly did, that she had spent more time imagining what it would be like to see Rafe again than someone with no feelings would.

"If I might," Major Douglas said.

"You are the Mackensee liaison, are you not? Go ahead, please."

"Brilliant young officers, such as Captain Vatta, are often expected to have corresponding emotional weaknesses. For what it's worth, *our* professional assessment—made prior to an attempt to recruit her to MMAC—is that this is not the case with Captain Vatta."

"Thank you," Ky said, with an edge to her voice that she could not suppress.

"You're welcome," he said blandly. "It seemed relevant."

"It is," the Chairman said. "An independent, professional assessment like that is completely relevant." He sighed. "To be honest, if somewhat less than flattering, I was almost hoping you did have such an infatuation, Captain Vatta. It would then have been easy to insist that however valid your thinking about the military situation, you personally must be distanced from any response we make. We have been close allies to Nexus for . . . well, almost since the first Moscoe and other shareholders set up a colony that later became this . . ." He waved to indicate the entire system. "They will be angry with us, I fear."

No one spoke for a long moment. The Chairman shook his head sharply. "Facts are facts, whatever we might wish. The material you shared with us, on the weakness of ISC's fleet, is . . . shocking. I won't insult you by asking if you're sure, and anyway, Mackensee corroborates your account of the battle. I have spoken personally to the current CEO of ISC, Ser Dunbarger, and he tells me that we cannot expect much aid from Nexus, as ISC has always served as their external force, and ISC's resources are no longer sufficient. That being so, we must consider our own welfare, and choose the stronger ally. We must consider how you and we can work together, seeking for some way that will allow Nexus to accept the situation."

"I understand that you have tried to hire some of our resources," Major Douglas said.

"Yes, we have, and so has Nexus. Ordinarily, we would coordinate those requests, giving you, the professionals, the choice of assigning assets as a unified command saw fit. Unfortunately, if Nexus remains obdurate about the Vatta connection, we will have no access to whatever force they hire, and I imagine we will retain ours nearby."

SIX

Grace Vatta, now Rector of Defense for Slotter Key but always a Vatta at heart, looked at the background report on Vatta's new senior staff. All of the most promising successors to Stavros and Gerard had been killed in the initial attack on Vatta, and two in the next tier had been assassinated while she herself had been busy protecting Helen and the children, setting up the demise of those who had been in on the attack, and managing the day-to-day affairs of Vatta. But she had spotted the few likely candidates early on. With the change in government, with no new assassination attempts in the past half year, they were now running Vatta's much-reduced business: the tik orchards and the onplanet transport services—surface, sea, and air—that moved the tik harvest to market.

For some reason—Grace could not be sure because the ones who knew or might have known were now dead—the attackers had missed Vatta's newer installations at the air- and spaceports, as well as the two Vatta Transport ships docked at the planet's commercial orbital station when the attack occurred. One of those had been lost later, on its arrival in another port. Only one Vatta Transport ship remained in contact with Slotter Key, traveling a restricted circuit.

Now a new problem had arisen. Vatta Transport had one corporate headquarters here, on Slotter Key, where its registered legal presence had been for the past several hundred years. And it had another corporate headquarters on the Moscoe Confederation, on Cascadia Station, where Stella had set up her offices. With the system ansibles out, that had made sense—had been, in fact, the only way to keep going. But now, with ansible service restored—at least temporarily—it meant that two head offices were a confusion instead of a godsend.

Maxim Vatta-Termanian, running the local office, seemed to be honest, hardworking, and just barely capable of handling his new job. He was Vatta by marriage, had taken the Vatta name only after the disaster in which his wife—an accountant at corporate headquarters—was killed. Maxim, a botanist, had been halfway through a ninety-day internship at a remote research lab on the far side of the planet that day, working on a project to make tik trees more resistant to follicle rust. When first appointed, he'd expressed doubt that he could do the job, citing his lack of training and his love of research. So Grace would have expected Maxim to be happy for a chance to get back to a lab somewhere, and turn over leadership of the company to Stella . . . but that wasn't proving the case.

"I'm not doing that badly and I'm learning every day," Maxim said. "I'm a quick learner." He was thin, intense, leaning forward into the video pickup, his fingers drumming on the arms of the chair.

Grace looked at the pulse in his throat. Was he on something?

"Just because Stella's his daughter doesn't mean she should inherit his job," Maxim went on. "I mean, look at her past. And Stavros made mistakes . . . if he hadn't, none of this would've happened."

And Maxim would have been just another married-in scientist. "Do you really blame Stavros for what happened?" Grace asked. "What mistake do you think he made?"

"He didn't see the threat coming. He didn't know about the charges—"

"That wasn't his job, Maxim."

"Well, putting someone in charge of company security was his job, and he didn't do a very good job of picking whoever it was—"

"That would be me," Grace said.

Maxim paled. "You!"

"Yes. And before you try to get your foot out of your mouth by saying something else, let me give you a few reality checks. I was not tasked to infiltrate the Slotter Key government and find out if elements in it were cooperating with offplanet criminals determined to attack Vatta headquarters and personnel. If you want to blame me for not knowing that the President, senior officers in Spaceforce, and others in the administration were involved . . . fine. Blame me. But that—the collusion of Slotter Key's government—is what made the attack possible and continued to make attacks on our people possible until I brought down the government."

"You . . . brought down the government?" Now he was even paler, sitting back away from the pickup as if to put as much distance between himself and Grace as possible.

"With some help from others, of course. But yes, the reason you are still alive today is that I acted in Vatta's best interest." Maxim said nothing; Grace waited a long moment, then went on. "The job of a corporate security chief is complex enough without considering that a government that has always been friendly and cooperative may be yielding to blackmail or other pressure, and becoming hostile. I dealt with internal matters specific to Vatta and with long-standing threats from without, such as piracy. The day of the attack, I had a new report to show Stavros . . . but never had the chance to deliver it."

"Well . . . all right . . . but that still doesn't mean Stella should be CEO. She's not even here—"

"No, she's established a successful branch of Vatta where she is—where she started alone, with minimal resources, and now has sixteen tradeships up and running and a very successful manufacturing program for a unique and highly desirable product. Her profit ratio's climbing fast; yours isn't."

"But she's—she's—"

Grace broke in on whatever unforgivable thing he was about to say. "Maxim, you don't have the votes. You can either fight and lose what you have, or leave gracefully."

"I have more votes than you think. Lots of people don't think Stella would be that good. They remember what an idiot she was." He still sat back, but with the kind of mulish expression Grace knew meant a mind made up in spite of evidence. It was a shame. He wasn't a bad man, but he would have to learn that in some things, Grace had far more power than showed on the surface.

Within a few hours she had arranged for Stella to vote her shares via Helen, for Helen to be fully briefed on what to do, and had checked up on her other family allies and enemies. On a whim, she looked up Maxim's genetic profile, and stared at a sequence now too familiar.

Maxim, like Stella, was another of Osman's bastards. He'd been placed with a non-Vatta family, so he hadn't made it onto her private list. And how had he come to marry a Vatta? She checked further. He had gone to the same university, having grown up in a respectable family—

Grace could find nothing wrong with the Termanians on Slotter Key. Why hadn't someone noticed his gene scan before they married? Everyone had gene scans before marriage, to find out if they carried a genetic disease and thus their DNA would need some cleanup surgery. But of course, that was the only purpose of such screening, to find genetic problems. Habit alone made her dig deeper. Where had the Termanians come from?

Termanian had first shown up in Slotter Key census records eighty or ninety years before, listing Nexus, of all places, as their system-of-origin. Medary Termanian, specialist in industrial colorants and dyes; he'd been recruited by Cosax Chemicals right out of university. A brother, Esarn, had followed four years later, to work for the same company. The next generation, born on Slotter Key, were all involved in science or technology—men and women both. Nothing that looked like an attempt to move into power positions— they had been both lab bench and field scientists, plant managers, that sort of thing. Grace did notice that there was a pattern of adoption, including adoption from relatives back on Nexus, and even then families were small. In that family, Maxim had seemed to fit—botany for an agribusiness job.

So . . . had he been adopted from Nexus, like others? And how had Nexus come by one of Osman Vatta's by-blows?

Now that the Slotter Key ansible was back up, she could query Nexus' own database for information on the Termanians. There, they were a prominent, wealthy family with strong influence in government and ISC both. A Termanian had been on the Board of ISC until very recently . . . until, in fact, he'd been shot dead by Rafe Dunbarger for being allied with Lewis Parmina.

It was beyond belief that an Osman bastard, adopted into the same family that had produced a traitor in ISC, married a

Vatta girl and ended up safe during the catastrophe, rising to become—even temporarily—CEO of Vatta, by accident.

The only question now was whether Maxim Vatta-Termanian knew he was a mole. He could have had his implant programmed to hide that from him, when he was a child. Still, the important thing was to get him out of his present position, and under surveillance. And to comb the databases for any more of Osman's surprises.

"Mac." She called MacRobert on their very private and very secure com.

"Problem?"

"Yes." Grace explained all the connections. "I'm thinking total surveillance until I can get a quorum together and get him voted out."

"You're sure you have the votes and he's sure he has the votes?"

"Stella's and Ky's shares tip it easily."

"But they aren't here."

"But Helen is Stella's proxy, and Ky gave permission for Stella to vote hers when she left Stella at Cascadia. Just took care of that."

"We put a guard on Helen," MacRobert said. "I'll do that first. What about your other votes?"

Grace sent a datafeed of the list. "You don't think I'm being paranoid?"

"Only as much as you should be. Make sure they all have protection. And I want you to take precautions, too."

"More than I am?"

"Yes. I'll be at the office before you leave."

Days earlier, she had invited Helen to bring the twins over for a visit. Now she could have used more time for research.

"Don't fret," MacRobert said. He walked on her left, and the rest of her security team, before and behind, knew which way to jump if she needed to use her own weapon. "The visit won't take that long. You'll figure it out."

"You're becoming a mind reader," Grace said.

"Practice," MacRobert said. "And innate talent."

She chuckled. "I may need to talk to Helen privately. Can you handle the twins?"

"I would like to think that having herded all those cadets, I can handle two young children. On the other hand, they are Vattas. I promise nothing."

Helen tried not to look at Grace's arm; the twins stared. Jo's children, now centimeters taller than they had been the summer before. They would have inherited her intellectual curiosity, Grace thought.

"It's grown quite a bit," she said. "Come on over and take a look."

"Gramma said we shouldn't stare," said Shar, who had been.

"It's not staring if I say you can look," Grace said. They both came over, wide-eyed; Helen grimaced behind them. "They saw the worst," Grace said to her. "They might as well see the healing."

"What's the green stuff?" Justin asked. "Shouldn't it be pink, like our insides?"

"Or clear?" Shar asked. "So you can see better?"

"Children—" Helen began. Grace waved her hand: *Hush*.

"It was almost clear pinkish until two tendays ago," Grace said. "It's grown enough that they switched to the green—I don't completely understand it myself, but it has something to do with enhancing skin formation. Because the bones and muscles are growing faster than normal, the skin must grow faster, too, and it can dry out and split more easily at this stage."

"Oh." Justin frowned. "Is the skin going to look like a

young woman's skin, when it comes out? Or wrinkly like the rest of yours?" Grace didn't have to look to know that Helen was rolling her eyes at this breach of manners.

"It will look smooth," Grace said. "And yes, it won't match. I don't care."

"I thought it would be baby-sized," Shar said. "And it's as big as our arms now. Can you wiggle the fingers?"

Grace wiggled her fingers; both children drew in a breath. "I have to wiggle my fingers; I have to bend the elbow and everything, or it would come out too weak to be useful," she said. "It'll be in the sheath only another four tendays, and then I'll start serious work with it." She didn't mention the painful therapy she was already getting three times a week. Some things children didn't need to know.

"It has *fingernails*," Shar said.

Grace almost laughed. The twins looked so interested, and so like Jo at that age, and Helen looked just as horrified as she had when she'd found Grace showing Jo how to field-strip a pistol. "How would you like some cake?" she said instead. Two little noses wrinkled.

"Fruitcake?" Justin asked warily. He had been offered fruitcake last holidays and after one large bite refused more.

"No. Pound cake with ice cream on top."

"Yes, please!" they said.

"Go on into the kitchen," Grace said. "Through there." The twins darted off. To Helen, she said, "It's all right, Helen. They're looking good—happy, curious, normal children."

"It's a lot harder without Stavros," Helen said. "I thought I did most of the parenting before, but I realize now what a balance he gave."

Grace led the way to the kitchen. "None of the others have stepped in?"

"We're all overloaded, trying to keep things going, deal

with the legal tangles. I have help, of course, but it's not the same."

In the kitchen, MacRobert was scooping out ice cream, and the twins were up on stools, leaning over the counter, watching him.

"You'd think I never fed them," Helen said. "Once their appetite came back—"

"It's the age," MacRobert said. "In a growth spurt, aren't they?"

"Do you have children?" Helen asked him.

MacRobert pushed the filled bowls over to the children and handed them spoons. "Not of the body, no, sera." His tone left no room for questions about that, but Grace could feel the pressure of Helen's curiosity. She had not expected to find a man in Grace's kitchen . . . though she should have. They hadn't hidden anything. MacRobert had been around ever since the shooting.

"Have you heard from Stella?" Helen asked now.

"She's in Cascadia—"

"I know that," Helen said. Her mouth tightened.

"And she's doing a fine job of running Vatta Enterprises there."

"I know that, too. But she hasn't contacted me yet, not once."

MacRobert raised one eyebrow and went out the kitchen door to the back of the house where his office was.

"Is this the time to get into it?" Grace asked, glancing at the twins.

"I just want to know. Is she all right? Is something wrong? Is she upset about . . . something?"

The two little pitchers at the counter paused, spoons partway to their mouths; their eyes slid sideways to watch the grown-ups. Grace could practically see their ears stretching out sideways.

"She's upset about finding out at the trial," Grace said, trying for something the twins wouldn't understand. "She blames both of us." Helen most, of course.

"She thinks I should have told her . . . but you know why I didn't—"

"I know," Grace said. She knew the reasons; she had argued, years before, against those reasons and had lost. "And she'll get over it."

"You think?"

"She will," Grace said. "Because she's your daughter. And because . . ." She realized she could not explain the whole reason: that Stella was now *in loco parentis* for Toby and Zori, and discovering for herself the difficulties of parenting.

"I just . . . I love her," Helen said. She didn't say *And she's all I have left,* which they both understood. "If she doesn't—"

Grace sighed. Except for that one brief period, she had never considered becoming a parent, and Joel, bless him, had understood that when they married. "She will," she said, and made a mental note to tell Stella to call her mother. Fight with her, yell at her if necessary, but at least call her.

"What about Ky?" Helen asked next. "Do you think she'll get over this military thing and come back to the family and help Stella run the business?"

"Probably not," Grace said, as mildly as she could manage. Helen was a nice woman, and a fine mind in her own field, but really . . . how could anyone not see what Ky was, what Ky had always been?

"We need her. She should marry and settle down," Helen said. "It would be good for Ky, give her a base . . ."

MacRobert came back into the kitchen, as if Grace's wish for an interruption had summoned him. "Ky marry?" he said. "I doubt that. Now she's not besotted over that good-looking boy—"

"She has a boyfriend?"

"Had. Not anymore." MacRobert looked grim for a moment, then smiled. "I don't think she's the marrying kind, Ky."

"Well, something has to bring her back. She can't spend her whole life running around the galaxy having adventures. She's Gerard's daughter; she's his heir; we need her here."

MacRobert cleared his throat; when Grace glanced at him, he flicked a finger signal that meant *Calm down*. She realized then the back of her neck was hot. "If she lives through this," he said, politely enough, "she may come back—but I suspect they'll tap her for work in the new combined fleet. Perhaps the family can buy out her interest."

"But she's Vatta," Helen said. Then she noticed the twins, smeary faces intently watching the grown-ups. "Justin, Shar, go wash those faces." The twins slid off their stools and headed slowly for the kitchen sink. "In the bathroom," Helen said. "Down the hall on the right. And your hands. With soap." When they'd gone she shook her head. "They have so much energy."

"It's not going to be the same, Helen," Grace said. "Ky and Stella won't be like Stavros and Gerard."

"I know that," Helen said. "But—"

"Stella will run Vatta . . . she's doing it, she's good at it, and Ky will give her the votes. You'll get Stella back, Helen. But Ky is not just a Vatta anymore."

"There's no *just* about Vatta," Helen said.

"I didn't mean it that way," Grace said. "Mac, if the children want to play outside, would you take them into the yard?" Water had stopped running in the hall bathroom, and one of the floorboards had creaked. Not only little pitchers, those two, but sneaky little pitchers.

"I'm sure they'll want to," he said with a grin and

headed back toward the hall. "Hey, you two," he said. "Come on outside; your Aunt Grace has put in a whole playspace for you . . ." It was her own exercise space, but they didn't have to know that.

When the back-door chime binged, Helen looked at Grace. "Is he yours? Who is he?"

"Master Sergeant MacRobert, retired from Spaceforce. He was at the Academy when Ky was there; he's been working with me at Defense."

"That's not exactly what I meant," Helen said. "Are you going to marry again? It's been so long . . ." Joel had died over twenty years before.

"No," Grace said. "But I am sometimes going to have friends you don't know about, Helen, just as I always did." She took a sip of her coffee. "And it's really none of your business."

Helen flushed. "I asked because I care, Grace."

"Well, then, if you care—Mac and I are very good friends, these days. We don't intend to marry, and I doubt we'll move in together. We like our independence. But I don't necessarily kick him out of the house before bedtime. And yes, we've shared a bed."

Helen's flush deepened. "You didn't have to—"

"Tell you everything? I haven't. But remember, Helen, what I told you last summer. I won't ever tell you everything, and usually I won't tell you what I don't think you need to know. That's the rule I lived by for decades, working for Vatta, reporting to your—to Stavros. He understood; I hope you will."

"Is that the reason Stella isn't calling me? She doesn't think I need to know something?"

"It may be," Grace said. "But she was angry with both of us. She has to communicate with me—pure business, relating to deals between the Slotter Key Defense

Department and Vatta Enterprises. We don't chat; some-times it's her people talking to my people. She doesn't have to communicate with you . . . so any reason not to may seem sufficient to her."

"I wish I had told her," Helen said. "You were right, I was wrong—but you know, Grace, people can get very tired of one person always being right. You demand that people trust you; you keep secrets; you taught Stella to be sneaky—"

"Now, that I didn't do," Grace said. "I taught her to be skillfully sneaky, but the girl was sneaky before, or she wouldn't have gotten past you, with those relationships—"

"And there you are, being right again." Helen's face twisted. "Dammit, Grace, would you please be wrong once in a while? Just to give me a little comfort?"

Grace shivered; she couldn't help it. "Helen . . . I have been wrong more times than I can count. Maxim pointed out that I missed the conspiracy against Vatta . . . I told him it wasn't in my brief, and it wasn't, but it was the biggest mistake I ever made. You can blame me for that, as he does, if you want—your husband dead, all your chil-dren but Stella. Don't think I don't blame myself—I do. And last summer, this—" She lifted the developing arm. "This is another mistake."

"You saved the children!"

"Yes. But I didn't prevent the attack. And that was my job, and I knew it. I stayed up too late; I overslept; I should have been up to notice the perimeter alarms—"

"Or you should have told me how to read them," Helen said. "You can't do everything yourself, Grace."

"For years I had to." She had learned, was learning, in this past year, how to delegate, how to depend on others more, but it was not easy.

"Well . . . if you admit you aren't always right, I guess

I can learn to stand it when you are," Helen said. She shook her head. "Two poor old ladies, you and I . . ."

"You're not old!" Helen was still beautiful, now that her grief was slowly healing.

"I feel old sometimes. Especially when the twins are at their most energetic." Helen shook her head again. "Well, we've got that settled, I guess. What's all this about needing extra security coverage and Maxim? He seemed harmless enough, if not very talented . . ."

Grace explained in more detail than she had in the earlier contact. "So," she said, "that's why Mac wanted more security on you and the children until this is over with. Maybe Maxim's just putting the same determination into staying on here as he put into his research—maybe the connection with Termanians on Nexus is just coincidence—but there are a few too many coincidences in the situation for me to be complacent. Better safe, and so on."

"His performance, compared with Stella's, certainly justifies removing him from consideration as a permanent CEO. But we do need someone in charge of operations here, and Stella can't do it from there."

"I don't suppose, since you're feeling better, you'd consider hiring more help and doing it yourself?"

"Or Stella could come home," Helen said.

"Not at present," Grace said. "There are . . . things . . . going on there, and she needs to be where she is."

"I don't think I'm suited," Helen said. "I really don't know that much about the business, though yes, I do understand the agricultural end. And I don't want to turn the twins over to staff only at this point."

"Well, we have to find someone, and I'd hate to go outside the family. Think about it."

SEVEN

Cascadia

Immediately after the close of that first meeting, Ky was ushered into another, with the Moscoe Confederation's Assistant Minister for Military Deployment, Omar Edgerton, and several high-ranking members of their military establishment. Edgerton introduced her to Admiral Fossey, in charge of System Defense, Admiral Handlin, in charge of defense forces near Cascadia, and Admiral Trey, in charge of strategic planning. All were a head taller than Ky, and decades older; she registered the moment of disbelief and then the courteous recovery. She also met Commander Dowitch, head of the military construction and repair yard in orbit around Cascadia, Commander Beliss of Oak Squadron, Commander Corleone of Pine Squadron—Ky wondered how the spacefaring culture that had settled Moscoe System had ever become so fixated on trees. Not that there was anything wrong with trees.

"Admiral Vatta, delighted to meet you!" Commander Dowitch didn't wait for the meeting to convene. "You've been in touch with us about the availability of modular combat command centers—"

"Yes, we have. And received the details shortly before

docking here. I have a few questions, but this may not be the time." Ky glanced up the table at Fossey and Edgerton, who looked a little annoyed.

"Now that the government's decided to commit to alliance with Slotter Key, and you're designated to command the Slotter Key ships," Edgerton began—a subtle hint that she might command nothing more; that decision hadn't been made—"we must figure out how to work with you."

"Though our agenda's fairly fluid and dependent on you," Fossey added, with a quick glance at Edgerton.

Ky wondered if it would be discourteous to ask if this meant the government was committing actual ships to the cause, and decided it probably would be. After a long moment of silence, she realized they were waiting for her to make a start.

"As you know, I just arrived today," Ky said. "And just got out of a meeting with your government. So I'd like to hear what ideas and questions you have for me, before we start on mine for you."

"Do you have any idea where Turek will strike next, or what kinds of targets he's after?" Commander Beliss asked.

"Our group thinks he'll go after shipyards manufacturing large warships," Ky said. "The Bissonet yards, which he captured along with much of their fleet, are tooled for smaller ships—they can build only a few large ones at a time. In several encounters, we've seen nothing larger than a Bissonet cruiser—in fact, they were Bissonet cruisers. We're also concerned that Turek may now have accumulated enough capital to simply order ships built for his force."

"Surely no one would build ships for a pirate!"

For money, Ky knew, some people would braid a noose for their own necks, but before she could think of a polite way to say that, Commander Dowitch spoke up. "Molly, you should see the things I get in from contractors. Some people have never grasped that if you cheat your protection, you don't have protection. I'm sure that somewhere in the universe, some profit-mad shipbuilder is quite willing to supply the means of his own destruction."

"Turek could be ordering ships through governments sympathetic to him in some way," Ky said.

"Why would anyone be sympathetic to him?"

"Mackensee—the mercenary company—pointed out that there's been a resurgence of anti-humod sentiment and violence in a number of systems. It's a minority, but a fervent and sometimes militant minority. The intel you shared with me in the briefings you sent before we landed showed that the man you believe was Turek's local agent held memberships in several anti-humod organizations. Gretna—where we're sure Turek had dealings—is a vehemently anti-humod society, to the point that they refused basic assistance to a ship full of refugees—all humods—from one of Turek's attacks. And though we think he attacked Polson because of its six-vector jump point, he was particularly brutal to the population, killing everyone who could not cram into one of the few ships to escape; Polson's entire population were high-mod."

"What does he have against humods?" Admiral Trey asked.

"I have no idea," Ky said. "I'm not even sure that he personally does—but anti-humods are a minority group that he might have targeted as potential allies. We expect he's also made contact with, or taken over, some traditional criminal organizations." She waited for comments; none came. "We started compiling a list of construction yards that build large warships—I'm sure you know there aren't very many—and the next step, now that we're here, is to contact those whose ansibles are still working and find out if they've had orders for new ships, or have ships in storage."

Admiral Handlin looked at Commander Dowitch. "Ben, what's your take on this?"

"Moray's the nearest big yard to us," Dowitch said. "Their ansible's still up, and I have a contact there. What specifically do you want to know?"

"Have they had orders for large warships in the past— oh, say three—years, or orders from governments of systems they know are anti-humod—religious or secular, doesn't matter."

"Religious would be like the Miznarii, right? Think even implants are modifications some deity wouldn't like?"

"That's one," Ky said. "My understanding is there's a range of strictness about it, and different groups have different names. They're all concerned with the purity of the human race, though. Whatever they mean by that."

"I'll call them as soon as we're done here," Dowitch said.

"One thing we would like from you is your analysis of the tactical and strategic implications of these new ansibles," said Admiral Trey. "My staff have worked on that, but we have no experience, and yours would be most helpful."

Ky handed around the data cubes she'd brought. "We have experience only with the older type, the ones the pirates are using. Those communicate only from unit to unit. The ones my cousin Toby invented also communicate with system ansibles. Here are some post-battle analyses of our two most recent actions."

"Is there any communication while in FTL flight?"

"No," Ky said. "But you can communicate immediately after downjump—there's no waiting, as there is with scan, for the signal to clear." She paused, but they were waiting for her to say more. "As you've probably realized, instantaneous communication ship-to-ship greatly improves command and control before and during combat. Your ships can be more dispersed, and yet fully aware of one another's position and movement—"

"Is the discrepancy between communication and scan distracting?" Admiral Handlin asked.

"It was until we figured out how to display the scan data from one ship on another." Ky saw confusion on all their faces. "We don't have the right setup," she said. "But it works like this: a ship two light-hours there—" She pointed down the table. "—can load its current scan data for transmission by onboard ansible to a ship here." She pointed to herself. "So—if I have a spare screen hooked up—I can see that ship's scan data, in real time, on my ship."

Astonishment replaced confusion. "So—in effect—you can make scan instantaneous as well?"

"Only if you have a source with minimal lightlag near what you want to scan," Ky said. "I imagine with a sufficiently large AI and the right software, with enough data sources, you could form a near-real-time integrated model of a battle area."

"I still see the potential for a lot of confusion," Admiral Handlin said.

"Turek is using stealthed observer ships," Ky said. "We captured one with most of its electronics intact. Apparently he's using something like this, but with only a few data sources—the observer ship itself and one or two of his warships. I'm not sure if the AI is capable of really complex modeling, but it can receive and send scan data from multiple sources, and make at least a crude model. You'll see the effect of that in the Boxtop battle on those cubes."

"We had not thought of that approach," Admiral Fossey said. "I'll need to speak to R and D right away." He glanced at Edgerton, who hadn't said much yet. "I think we could break for an hour—give me a chance to ping R and D, and Ben to send a message to Moray."

"Fine," Edgerton said. "And we might also let Admiral Vatta arrange what she needs with Commander Dowitch."

Ky sensed that some resistance had given way, though she could not tell what had done it.

"I've looked at the design data you sent me," Commander Dowitch said. He lit a display, and *Vanguard*'s schematics came up. "The only place we can put the CCC module— our smallest—is here." His finger pointed to the aft starboard cargo bay in the original plan, now occupied by the starboard weapons bay and munitions storage and the firing range.

"All that?" Ky said. "It must have room for twenty people—"

"No, Admiral, only a half dozen, and it's cramped inside. Some of the gear you need in there is bulky, and it's built with hull-grade bulkheads. It's completely self-contained, with its own limited life support, so if the ship's damaged, you'll still have functionality. Originally, these were designed as command centers for automated insystem supply convoys . . . one ship would run up to three others, so it was essential that if the ship it was on took damage, the AI could still control the others."

"But that takes out my aft battery on that side . . . I was hoping you could fit it into my office and stateroom area—"

"Not a hope, I'm sorry. Even for the forty or so ships you'll have on your first cruise, you'll need a lot of gear. You'll have not only a mirror of the sensor suite on

Vanguard, but ansible-boosted mirrors of others—direct to you, no waiting. Well, direct to your scan crew: three of them. The command unit—your command seat—is again self-contained. Should something breach the CCC, you'll have at least twenty-four hours of life support. Full displays mirrored there as HUDs, tunable with your implant once we install the software."

"I see," Ky said.

"We can make larger ones, but ideally a CCC for a large fleet would be built in from the beginning, designed in. That may be what Turek would find most useful in a purpose-built warship."

"How soon can you start, and how long does it take?" Ky asked.

"As soon as you clear whatever you need and find quarters here, we can move her over and get to work. Maybe twenty days, if we're lucky. Thirty otherwise."

"Turek's not going to sit still and do nothing for thirty days," Ky said. Dowitch started to speak, but stopped himself. "I know," she said. "It's not your fault—that is fast. We just have to hope that he doesn't hit here. I'll tell my people to pack up—do you need them all off?"

"No, only anyone who bunks in that area and anyone you want here. The yard has basic support, and we can use the extra help as well."

"Thanks, Commander. I'll send for my things right away, and I'll have Hugh Pritang contact you when the ship's clear."

Finally Ky was free to meet with the other Slotter Key captains; she had talked to several of them before arriving, but this would be the first time face-to-face. She had their dossiers—though privateers, they had all trained primarily as merchanters, and represented a dozen of Slotter

Key's minor shippers. She'd asked Argelos to meet with them first, along with Hugh Pritang, who would be her flag captain on *Vanguard,* in case she was late—and she was, because she was buttonholed in the corridor by the Slotter Key ambassador, who needed fifteen minutes of her time right that moment.

For this meeting, she had chosen a site closer to the branches where most were docked. The room wasn't as luxurious as the offices upstation, but the Cascadians had moved in the necessary table and chairs, and installed a good display system.

All were older, and most looked other than delighted to be where they were. Their military advisers had much the same expressions, ranging from politely noncommittal to frankly negative.

From the dossiers Slotter Key Defense had forwarded, Ky had identified five who might cause serious trouble; one had not shown up at all—perhaps delayed in transit, perhaps simply refusing to come.

The military advisers had all stood up quickly, acknowledging her rank, but most of the captains stayed seated. That was not a promising start, Ky thought, but she said nothing, walking instead to the head of the long table where a place had been left for her. Argelos moved to the empty seat on her right, and Yamini, after a quick smile and nod to his fellow military advisers, sat at her left.

Ky sat down; the military advisers also sat. "I'm Admiral Vatta," she said. "I'm presuming you all received information on me from Slotter Key Defense—is that correct?"

A mumble—some yes, some no. One captain— Cannelos, her implant informed her, one of those she thought might be a problem—said, "Grace Vatta's your relative, right? How's that qualify you for admiral, at your age?"

Ky grinned. "Grace is a relative, yes. That's not why I'm an admiral. I'm an admiral because I'm the only person who's commanded a force against our enemy, and the only person besides Turek who has fought space battles, plural, under the conditions now operating—with instantaneous communication between ships during the battle."

"Oh, right—I'm sure you have *so* much combat experience," said a lean gray-haired woman next to Cannelos. Captain Gillian Merced; someone had noted on her dossier that her ship *Termagant* was aptly named. Complaints had been lodged against her for attacking tradeships, but she had five confirmed pirate captures to her credit, second only to Captain Coufal.

Ky looked at her; the woman shifted in her chair, but did not look away. "Since that little affair at Sabine II, which I believe was covered in the news awhile back—" The woman gave a tight nod. "—during which my ship was captured by mercs, assigned to hold officers of other captured ships, and we had a mutiny which I personally ended by shooting the ringleaders—" There was a stir along the table, a subtle withdrawal. "—Since then I have fought multiple engagements, including capturing a larger, armed pirate vessel with my unarmed trader. Some of you might remember an old, small Vatta ship called *Glynnis Jones.*"

"You captured something with old *Glynnis*?" someone asked. Tardin, not expected to be a problem. "How'd you do that, play possum?"

"Something like that, yes," Ky said. "And they didn't know I had EMP mines aboard." Silence; they were all attentive now. Just as well; she didn't want to answer the question of where she'd gotten the mines and why. "You're aware of the attacks on Vatta, I'm sure," she said. "I was on Belinta, delivering cargo, when that started; after that,

I was the target of multiple assassination attempts as well as ship attacks. Later, realizing the need for a multisystem force, I started trying to organize one. That's when Captain Argelos, another Slotter Key privateer, joined me." She nodded at Argelos. "Tell them about that, if you would."

Argelos pulled out a control for the room's display functions. "We had seven ships, to start with. The admiral wasn't commanding; she'd chosen to let an older, supposedly more experienced officer from Bissonet command—three Bissonet ships were with us, plus the two of us, a ship from Ciudad, and someone who turned out to be a plant, one of Turek's people. No way to know that at the time." He put up a graphic of the system where they'd gone to train.

"Thing is, that commander hadn't had experience with the onboard ansibles, the way the admiral had, and she couldn't adjust her battle plans. The Ciudad ship left the group—" He glanced at Ky, but she didn't yield; she had insisted that they not complicate the explanation with a personality and cultural conflict. "—and then returned to warn us that the other captain had been a traitor and that enemy ships were in the system, about to attack. He tried to intervene, delay them, and his ship was blown. The admiral and I had been arguing for a more open formation, but the Bissonet commander just didn't trust the ansibles. So we were in tight when the enemy attacked, and only three ships made it out—one of the Bissonet ships chose to follow the admiral's orders."

"We were lucky," Ky said. "Got off with minor damage. We had a full load-out of munitions, but that wasn't the deciding factor. They expected us to do what their spy had watched us train for, only—I changed things." She skipped over the fight at Gretna—not really a space battle—and the interval at Adelaide. "We picked up some more allies, Ransome's Rangers—"

"Is that those fancy boys in all that gold and glitter?" Merced interrupted.

"Very competent ship handlers," Ky said, ignoring the rudeness. "Invaluable in what came next. We came into a situation at an empty system, where a merc company— you've all heard of Mackensee, I assume—was holding a training exercise, and had been attacked by Turek's force, which outnumbered them. We were able to break up their attack and then assist in the recovery of wounded. But a second battle occurred some days later, when an ISC fleet had arrived to deal with us for repairing the relay ansible in that system."

"You fought an ISC fleet?" That with a tone of disbelief from Coufal's military adviser, Major Steen.

"No," Ky said. "Turek had come back with what he thought was enough ships to take our small force and the rest of the mercs. What he didn't know was that the ISC force was due to arrive—"

"How'd you know that?"

"Later," Ky said. "Suffice that I did. I also knew that a merc convoy was on its way to trade out training cadres. There was considerable confusion—the ISC commanders thought I was the enemy; the merc convoy knew better; Turek returned in force, using ships they'd gotten from Bissonet when they overran that system and they claimed to be something called Blueridge Defense. Luckily I'd been able to establish good communications with the mercs by placing one of my smaller ships—one of the Ransome's Rangers—close to the merc ship and another as an observer and relay." She had their full attention now, even troublemakers. "It was . . . interesting there for a bit."

"We've been briefed on this onboard ansible thing,"

Bocanegro's adviser, Griffith, said. "I don't understand how Turek ended up with some and we have some—and they aren't what Vatta Enterprises is now selling, are they?"

"We still don't know how Turek found out such things existed, though I believe there are people in ISC looking into that," Ky said. "How we got them—found out about them at all—is that first ship I captured. There were a lot of them on it, along with other illicit cargo. I didn't know what they were at first, and I certainly didn't grasp their military significance until later. I didn't know Turek had them—I didn't even know who Turek was, or have any idea of the scope of the attacks he had made and was making."

Griffith nodded. "I see that—so you think this ship was transporting them to Turek?"

"There's evidence that Turek and this ship were working together, yes," Ky said. She did not want to get into the tangled family mess that Osman Vatta represented. "Whether it was transporting them to Turek's fleet from some manufacturing facility, or to Turek's agents in various systems, we don't know. I expect others were also involved. But the existence of onboard ansibles explains how Turek and the other pirate groups were able to co-ordinate their attacks and overcome planetary defense forces. We've always depended on lightspeed communications—and tactics in space required consideration of lightlag."

"Does this mean we're going to see instantaneous scan, real-time data, anytime soon?"

"I'm the wrong person to ask," Ky said. "My concern is how to use the technology to advantage in combat."

"Which brings up the point—just how different is it to fight with ansible communications among ships? That ought to improve control—" Major Steen again.

"It does," Ky said. "I've been working on new tactical

formations and moves, as has Turek's force. What we've discovered is that he usually sends in more than one stealthed observer—small ships packed with scan and communications gear—positioned in different parts of the system he plans to attack. We have no post-battle analyses of his successful attacks, other than from Bissonet. There, he used his surveillance of System Defense training to determine when they would be lowest on munitions and fuel, least able to fight. He probably did the same in other systems, but we have no proof. Captain Ransome captured one of his observers in the Boxtop battle; it's now part of this fleet."

"What about security?"

"We've modified the ansibles we first captured. As it is now, we can listen in on Turek's force—though we don't know the language, or code, or whatever it is—and so far they've shown no indication they can listen in on our transmissions. But as with any ansible, these have both general and directed capability. When they're talking with directed ship-to-ship, we can't hear them. All we get are the general announcements, and possibly not all of those."

Only three faces were still closed, showing resistance. Ky picked up the display controller and switched it on.

"Here's a simulation of Boxtop, phase one," she said. "This is taken from a combination of scan data from our ships, with some additional data Mackensee gave us, rendered in Poro-space, with Time Zero as our downjump. The blue icons are the Mackensee ships; red are Turek's; green are ours. Notice these two in particular—" She made their icons blink. "These are the stealthed observers. Now, this is what we saw on scan at downjump—" On another display, she put that up. "If I hadn't seen their attack formation before, I would not have expected it, because without real-time communication, those ships would shoot each other, not just the enemy."

"So what did you do?" Captain Coufal asked.

"This." Ky changed displays on the second area. "Because we had onboard ansibles, we could spread out, come in on different vectors." She ran through the rest of the sequence, using the simulation to indicate weapons vectors, integrating scan data from all the ships. "Now, this is what we all need to be able to do. I know that some of your ships have only limited microjump capability and that all of them may have problems resulting from conversion to armed traders."

"What kind of problems?" Captain Popelka asked.

"Structural. Those of you with beam weapons may have fatigue in the support members resulting from excess heat dissipation and inadequate coolant capacity. I'll need a complete combat history for each ship—how many engagements, what load of weapons. For missile attacks, the ratio of firing between missile batteries. For beam weapons, total time of fire."

"I never heard of that before—" Captain Merced said, scowling.

"I hadn't, either. But Mackensee Military Assistance Corporation, which started its existence with conversions similar to ours, discovered the problem with its first ships, and warned me about mine. Tradeships just aren't built to handle the additional stresses of sustained or repeated combat. When they did the engineering analysis, sure enough there were signs of stress in the mounts for the beam. Cascadia doesn't have the capacity to check all your ships at once, and we dare not have so many out of commission, so you'll need to help with a complete review of maintenance and repair, plus those details I just asked for, on your ship's combat exposure. If you did live-fire exercises, include those as combat. Also any damage taken, with details on repair history. From that we'll prioritize use of the facilities here for evaluation and—if time allows—repair."

"Can structural strain be repaired?" Coufal asked.

"It's possible to make temporary repairs," Ky said. "But bringing these ships up to full equivalency with purpose-built military vessels would require complete rebuilding and would take a minimum of a year."

"And we can't wait that long," Coufal said. "That's obvious. So you want us to go into battle with ships that might fall apart, against military-grade ships? Isn't that—" He paused.

Merced jumped in. "Stupid," she said. "That's what it is, stupid. Why didn't the Rector send real warships, if that's what's needed?"

"The two of you," Ky said, "with your rate of pirate capture, have probably got the most hours of weapons-use on your ships. I will certainly understand if you feel it's too risky to take part in this venture." Merced smiled and sat back, armed folded. Coufal looked watchful. "However, if you choose not to join, then your letters of marque will be rescinded, and your ships and yourselves will be held here until I deem it safe to let you travel again."

Merced came upright, fists clenched. "You can't do that! You've no right!"

"On the contrary, I have authorization from the Slotter Key Defense Department, from which your letters of marque were issued. The Moscoe Confederation government is unwilling to allow armed but unaligned vessels to operate in its space in a time of war."

"Those—" Merced began.

Ky made a sharp gesture. "Silence!" Merced stopped, mouth open.

"This is Cascadia," Ky said, glancing around the table. "Some of you, as new visitors here, may wonder if the Cascadians really enforce their strict laws of courtesy. I can assure you they do. A former Vatta Transport captain was executed here for culpable rudeness to an official. While I have no intention of enforcing the laws to their fullest when we are not in public, you should know that Cascadia has superb surveillance, and this compartment was supplied by the Cascadian government. Open contempt for the government will not be tolerated. It might get you killed, but—worse than that—it will imperil our mission."

"But you're saying we have to join you or be stuck here, with no ship and no income," Cannelos said.

"That is unfortunately the situation," Ky said. "It's not a situation I manufactured. I didn't ask the Rector to re-assign you; we weren't in contact when she did it. Like you, I think Slotter Key Spaceforce would have been the more appropriate choice." The military advisers looked thoughtful; none of them spoke. The captains, their expressions ranging from barely suppressed fury to apparent resignation, also said nothing. Ky went on. "In order to brief you at all, I had to reveal the existence of not only onboard ansibles, but also the modification that made our communications secure. So far as we know, the pirates still don't know about that—and thus those of you who do, and are not bound by the oath the rest of you will be asked to take, must not be free to chatter about it."

"I don't chatter!" Merced said.

"Captain, tell me why I should believe you. Or trust you."

Merced glowered a moment, glanced from side to side at her fellow privateers, and—getting no encouragement—finally shook her head. "I suppose . . . I suppose you have no reason to, other than my . . . my record."

"Your record," Ky said, "emphasized that I would find you troublesome. I won't quote it—"

To her surprise, Merced laughed. "Oh, go ahead. I wager everyone who knows me could come close without even looking at it. Stubborn?" Ky nodded. "Thought so. Defiant, resists advice, reckless, combative?"

Ky could not resist her own chuckle. "Pretty much. 'Quarrelsome, disrespectful, hypersensitive, argumentative, reckless.' "

"You know I was kicked out of Spaceforce Academy in my second year thirty-one years ago," Merced said. "Unable to maintain military courtesy under pressure, they said. I decked a senior cadet."

"And you surely know I was kicked out," Ky said.

"But you were in the Honor Squad. You were the goody-two-shoes kind; I heard about you. Vatta's daughter, straight arrow—"

Ky leaned forward. "You can always spend the rest of this war in custody here, which will be no fun at all—"

Merced did not flinch. "I can't be a straight arrow. I can't be a butt-kisser. I can fight like blazes—anyone, anywhere, anytime—but I can't just sit back and be given stupid orders by a—" She stopped again.

Ky pulled out her Rossi-Smith and laid it on the table in front of her. Utter stillness in the room; eyes shifted from her to Merced and back. She pushed up one sleeve, showing the sheath of one of her knives. "If you feel it necessary, Captain Merced," she said, "we can adjourn for an hour to the gym assigned to our crews, and you can find out just how straight-arrow I am these days. This—" She touched the Rossi-Smith with her index finger. "—is my personal firearm. I won't notch a bloodbeast-tusk grip, but I assure you it's been blooded more than once. And this—" She touched the sheath. "—is just one of my personal knives. I gutted a man twice my weight with the big one, fighting hand-to-hand in zero gravity, to save my ship. So if my being too innocent worries you, get over it. One on one—" Ky looked Merced up and down. "—you wouldn't stand a chance." She had no doubt of that. The older woman was fit, and no doubt had won her share of brawls, but Ky had seen enough to know Merced lacked the training she herself had.

Ky—and she was sure everyone else—saw the realization come slowly to Merced's expression that Ky was as formidable as she claimed. "It might be . . . fun . . . to find out," Merced said. "But you said we had a war to fight."

"We do," Ky said. "Do you want in on the fight?"

"I suppose—" And then, as Ky continued to stare her down, Merced nodded. "All right, yes. I do. And I'll try to be good—"

"No," Ky said, correcting her. "I need your best performance, and your record says that comes not from being good in the traditional sense, but from being the wild card."

Merced's face lit up again. "I don't have to stay in pokey formations?"

"Sometimes, but not always. When we get to specific battle plans, I'll tell you about it. But now—" Ky looked around the table again, collecting everyone's attention. This time it wasn't hard. "—I need to know, from all of you, whether you can commit fully to this. It's not like privateering. We intend to fight, and we must fight as a coordinated force."

"I'm in," Merced said before anyone else could. The others all nodded, with varying degrees of enthusiasm and not a few glances at the pistol as Ky picked it up, spun it for emphasis, and reholstered it.

After that long day, Ky headed back to *Vanguard* to see how Hugh was coming along in preparing the ship to go to refitting and acquire its modular CCC. She knew she would have to move to quarters on Cascadia Station—and Stella's guest room was already full—but not tonight. She was tired but excited at the same time. At last there would be a joint force, and—she grinned to herself at the thought—she had handled the Slotter Key privateers, even Merced.

"Isn't that Rafe Dunbarger?" Hera Gannett, Ky's escort, spoke suddenly.

EIGHT

Rafe in a perfectly tailored business suit still looked like Rafe, but without the familiar edge. Was it just his clothes? He also looked older, and tired, and in some subtle way defeated. His smile, though, when he met her eyes, was much the same. Her heart raced.

Ky nodded to him, trying to damp the excitement she felt. "Rafe," she said. She choked back the *At last* that would have been natural, along with the very unmilitary desire to grin like a fool. After all, she'd told a roomful of dignitaries that she had no feelings for him. She must not be seen by anyone, even her bodyguard and his, making the opposite obvious.

"Ky. I'm glad to see you," he said. No mockery in the tone at all; he might have spoken to a casual acquaintance as calmly. She felt her heart lurch in her chest. Did he feel nothing? Was she being a silly schoolgirl?

"You are—?" Changed? No longer interested? Someone else entirely wearing Rafe's face?

"Well," he said. "Quite well. And you?" Still that tentative, gentle tone, as if she might shatter.

"I'm fine," Ky said, slightly annoyed. He should know her better than that. What kind of game was he playing? "And your family?"

His eyes sagged shut briefly; his smile now seemed forced. "They're much better. My father's recovery is still progressing, albeit slowly. Penny—my sister—is working for the company now."

They might have been distant acquaintances, politely reintroducing themselves. Ky felt a surge of impatience. Couldn't they get beyond that? "So . . . you're here for the conference?"

"Yes. ISC and the Nexus government are, as I'm sure you've been told, closely related. Nexus has depended on our—the ISC's—fleet for a long time, and they are not pleased to find out it's not very good. And as Stella may have told you, one of our subsidiaries here holds a license to manufacture the new ansibles on Cascadia. So my presence was considered necessary." He said nothing more. The awkward moment lengthened; the obvious bodyguard at his side stared at Ky and then murmured something to Rafe, who startled. "Oh—sorry—Ky, I want you to meet Gary. He was instrumental in rescuing my family."

Gary looked like a very hard case indeed. Ky could feel Hera Gannett's alertness like a radiant heater. The man smiled suddenly, a remarkably open smile for someone so obviously dangerous. "Gary Marrin," he said. "Rafe knew me a long time back. I have—had—a private security company; now I'm working mostly for him, something I would never have expected."

"Rafe can be quite unexpected," Ky said. She felt Hera's slight relaxation.

"That he can," Gary said. He glanced at Rafe, a look somewhere between fatherly and mischievous. "But I understand you, too, can be unexpected."

"It's considered appropriate in commanders," Ky said, rocking back on her heels for a moment. "Surprise being one of the principles of successful warfare."

Rafe snorted; this time his grin looked natural. Gary shook his head. "You told me, Rafe, but I didn't believe it. And this is the woman—"

"Enough," Rafe said. "Or I'll be late for the meeting. Ky, you'll excuse me. If the alliance holds, we may meet again to discuss the status of the ISC fleet." He nodded, turned away; Gary shrugged and followed.

"*The woman*—?" Hera said. "Is he talking about you, Admiral?"

"Rafe has probably told him that I'm an innocent child-warrior with a ramrod up her rear," Ky said, more annoyed than she wanted to admit. "And he's surprised to find that I'm not sixteen or something."

"I'm not sure I like this place," Hera said, leaving that topic firmly behind. "It's so polite, I keep thinking something else is going on."

"Trade and profit," Ky said. "I know that much."

"Where there's money, there's trouble," Hera said. "Spies, thieves, crooks of all kinds . . . if Turek doesn't have agents here, I'll be very surprised."

"He certainly did," Ky said. "Toby fell in love with the daughter of one, and there's no knowing if the locals ferreted out all of them. But I don't think they'll do anything on the station, do you? Not after they caught Zori's father."

"If they can. Get rid of you, they've gotten rid of someone they already know is a dangerously efficient commander." Hera paused. "Ma'am, if you don't mind . . . what do you really think of that man?"

"Rafe's bodyguard?"

"No . . . Ser Dunbarger. He's . . . he's different than I remember him. What do you think?"

"I think he's gotten stuffy and boring," Ky said. She was appalled at her own honesty, but she went on. "He was a rogue, that much was obvious before, but at least he was entertaining, and he'd quit treating me like an imbecile. And he gave me good advice. But now—I guess he's distancing himself from all that—from everything in his life as it used to be, and I'm—I was—part of that life. I don't think it's just the present diplomatic problem." She felt sad, even hollow. It wasn't as bad as what Hal had done, but it hurt in the same places.

Hera started to say something, then very obviously stopped herself. Ky didn't want to think more about Rafe, about the bond she had been sure they had, but she could not quite push him out of mind.

"Quite a woman," Gary said, when they were out of earshot. "So that's the infamous Ky Vatta . . ."

"You don't know the half of it," Rafe said. Seeing Stella again had been difficult enough, but for both of them their official positions as heads of their respective enterprises had enforced a business attitude. No doubt at all that Stella was well over him, that he could not shake her sense of self—not that he wanted to, these days—and he had never been that connected to her. But seeing Ky—realizing that he had not forgotten the least detail of her face, her expressions, even her smell—that shook him. It was impossible.

"She's not what I expected," Gary said.

"And what did you expect?" Rafe asked.

"From your family and the gossips at ISC, some hard-faced, overmuscled criminal type. From her cousin, a juvenile military martinet."

"How did you read her, then?"

"I'm not sure. The military part shows, and clearly she's young—in years anyway—but there's something else. I'd say she's a natural killer—"

"She is," Rafe said.

"And you would know. Yes, well, she's not as one-dimensional as your family and her cousin seem to see her . . . she expected more from you, you know."

"I know." Rafe walked on. "I expected . . . I don't know . . . that it would be different."

"What? You, her, the meeting?"

"All of those." Once, he had imagined a meeting that ended with a life together, a life that suited both of them.

Gary gave a sharp nod. "You want her."

"I . . . did."

"Do. Come on, Rafe, I've known you for years. Even the years you weren't there, I'll bet I could name the scams you pulled, the messes you got into . . ."

"You always did have good intel," Rafe said. He could feel the back of his neck heating up.

"Did you ever try with her?"

"Once. She dumped me on my back."

"You are doomed," Gary said. Rafe glanced at him; he was grinning, without losing any of his concentration on their surroundings. "Man like you, woman who can meet him head-on . . . you are doomed. She might be the making of you, though."

"I can't," Rafe said.

"Why? You're not that much older; it wouldn't be cradle-robbing."

"She has her life; she needs to concentrate on it . . . and politically, right now—you know how the Vattas are regarded on Nexus."

"And maybe she wouldn't want you? Or maybe at some level you wonder if your family's right about the Vattas?"

"Not that. Never that. Not about the Vattas as a whole, and absolutely not Ky. But I can't subject her to that kind of situation, where others are suspicious of her." He took a breath. "And anyway, she's busy."

"And you're busy, and the beauteous Stella is busy, and everyone's busy . . . right, there's a war on, I'm not forgetting that." Gary's opinion of that excuse stung.

"I thought at first . . . she was too young, too strait-laced . . . I really didn't have any interest in her beyond teasing her, trying to get her off balance—"

"I tell you again, Rafe, you're doomed."

"It's not me. I haven't been . . . that way . . ."

"In love?"

Rafe felt the heat in his neck rise to his face. "Whatever you want to call it. Interested in that way, anyway. For a long time, if ever. I never thought about marriage—what did I have to offer, renegade of the family, living on the edge? And why would I, anyway? I was having too much fun."

"I understand," Gary said. "When I finally settled down, it came as a surprise to me, too. And now I have children—"

"You?"

"Yes. Carefully kept away from the business. But I see them whenever I'm not on a job. Their mother—well, she's not exactly like your Ky—"

"She's not *my* Ky."

"Yet. Thing is, men like us have to find women who understand men like us, and will stick with us anyway."

"She's not—"

"Rafe . . ." Gary shook his head, then went on. "You may not be the snake I thought you were—at least, not to people you care about—but you still don't get it. That's a remarkable woman. She was looking at you that way—"

"I didn't see it—"

"Your body did."

Rafe struggled with the combined desire to scream out loud or clobber Gary, neither of which was a good idea on Cascadia. He tried to pull the Ratanvi identity out of its drawer and put it on, but it didn't fit now. He was here as himself, as his father's heir, the head of ISC. What worked with Stella, the CEO persona, wouldn't work now.

"Tell me," he said, hating the timbre of desperation in his voice, "that she didn't see that."

"Oh, I don't mean that way," Gary said. "You can relax about that part."

"Thank you."

"But I'm trained to read people and I read them very well. The little signs . . . they were all there. You knew, or your body knew, that she knew that she wanted you, and you chose to ignore it. She's not going to be happy about that."

She wouldn't be. She would think he'd snubbed her. She would try to explain it to herself as her fault—she'd mistaken the earlier interest, it was all on her side. She would, being Ky, take herself in hand, lock down her shields, blaming herself . . .

"I should talk to Stella," Rafe said.

"You should put your head in a meat grinder, you mean," Gary said. "Talk to the family? Now I know for sure you're doomed. The old Rafe would know better than that without thinking about it. It's not even lust—it's love."

"It's a mess," Rafe said. "And I don't want to talk about it."

"You let her alone," Stella said. They had scheduled a meeting to discuss the manufacture of the new ansibles; the Nexus government wanted them badly enough to pay a premium for the right to have them made on Nexus. That business done, Rafe had mentioned that he'd met Ky briefly. Stella stiffened at once and pounced.

"I'm not doing anything," Rafe said.

"No? You're certainly exuding interest in that direction. And she doesn't need to be hurt again."

Rafe felt a surge of irrational anger. "Who hurt her? You mentioned that once before—"

"It's none of your business. It happened while she was in the Academy—or rather, after she was kicked out."

Rafe sat very still, refraining from saying that though it was none of his business, Stella seemed ready to share the gossip.

"I don't know much about the man," Stella went on, lacing her fingers. "A fellow cadet, I know that much. I heard her father telling my father about it . . . he approved, I think. Family not as wealthy as ours, but respectable. Ranked very high, like Ky. Hal, I think his name was; I don't remember the rest of it. My father said he might be after Ky for her money, but her father said not." She looked at Rafe. "Am I boring you?"

"No. But you said it wasn't my business."

"It's not. It's just . . . I saw the letter. She forgot, left it behind in the ship after she transferred to Osman's. As a breakup letter it was about as nasty as you can imagine. Clearly distancing himself from whatever trouble she was in. Insulting—even sent back her class ring all mutilated." Stella quoted a few of the juicier phrases. "I kept it, in case she ever remembers she left it there and wants it."

"Stupid young twit," Rafe said, in as light a voice as he could manage, while rage blurred his vision. He could imagine the depth of pain that would cause a woman like Ky; his knuckles ached to meet the fellow's face.

"Yes. Scared, too, I think. Ky stirred up a political storm, you see, just trying to do a good deed. But my point is, Rafe, that she's been hurt, and she doesn't need your kind of man upsetting her."

"I would never . . ." Rafe began. Stella held up her hand.

"Rafe, even granting that you may have changed enough to take over at ISC and act the part of a respectable corporate executive, I know you too well . . . you might not intend to hurt her, but you would."

"Because . . . ?"

"Because you are not serious about her." Stella held up her hand again, though he had said nothing. "You have never been serious about anyone, though I admit you now seem to be serious about ISC. And your own family, perhaps. But you are not serious about Ky; I do not see you giving up what you have now—ISC, your family—to court and marry her and be with her for the rest of your life and hers. Can you tell me that's what you're thinking?"

He was not thinking . . . he was feeling, and what he felt was outside his experience and his expectation. "I love her," he found himself saying.

"You *think* you love her," Stella said. "But if you do, it's as a little sister—"

"No," Rafe said, ignoring the upraised hand. "I have a little sister, a little sister I care for and protect. What I feel for Ky is not that." He took a deep breath, looking past Stella at the Vatta Transport logo on the wall behind her, then met her eyes again. "It's up to me and to Ky herself, Stella, what we do. Not you."

She grimaced. "I was afraid you'd start sounding like Toby and his girlfriend. Rafe, you're too old for that nonsense. You have responsibilities, as have I. Ky has responsibilities—and if she's distracted by you, or anyone else, we may all be lost. You cannot—you must not—distract her."

"I thought of that—I *did*," he said, when she looked dubious. "It's why I didn't tell her anything. But the war will be over, one way or the other . . ."

"You're not right for her, Rafe. She needs someone with the same interests, the same expertise. She's not ever going to be a corporate wife."

"That's her decision." Stella just looked at him. Rafe shrugged. "I know. She's not—but I don't want her to be . . . to be like my mother or anything. I do care, I do . . . love . . . her."

"Then let her alone," Stella said crisply. "I know you, Rafe, remember? Not just that time we had, but the background I did on you for Aunt Grace."

"I am capable of change—"

"Maybe. And you aren't the same as you were the last time I saw you, I'll give you that. But you still aren't what she needs, not after that Hal fellow."

"I won't hurt her that way."

"She doesn't need to be hurt *any* way."

"I'm not going to," Rafe said.

"Well, see that you don't. Because I'll be watching."

She was watching. The Nexus government was watching. His father and his father's old friends in ISC were watching. All, like vultures perched on a cliff, eyeing a lame wild sheep limping slowly along below. Waiting for it to fall. Hoping it would fall. Like Parmina, in that way, in wanting him to prove how base, how faithless, how incapable he was.

Rafe slid into his CEO persona as easily as into a well-tailored jacket and met Stella's gaze with bland equanimity. "I'm sure you're right," he said. Stella gave him another suspicious look, which he met with all armor on. She could not hurt him. She could not stop him. Nobody could, except Ky. And if, for reasons even he had to admit were—for the time being—operable, he could not have Ky . . . nothing could stop him from the pursuit of the man who had hurt Ky. *Hal.* He knew better than to ask

Stella for the rest of the man's name, but someone he knew would know someone who knew or could find out. Presumably he had graduated from the Academy; presumably he was, or had been, an officer in Slotter Key's Spaceforce.

"I'm serious," Stella said, a fine line now between her brows. Rafe forced himself to smile, the neutral and acceptable smile of one CEO to another.

"I'm sure you are," he said. "But now, I must go, because I have to meet with the Deputy Minister of Defense, who will I'm sure want to know what we are doing to ensure the reliability of the system ansibles here."

"If she weren't my cousin and an orphan," Stella said, "I could be more sympathetic."

Rafe waved a hand, dismissing the entire topic. "Let me assure you that damaging your family is far from my mind—and that also means I'm fighting the Board on behalf of Vatta Enterprises."

"I know," Stella said. "I was told that by our people here." She glanced at the clock. "Don't be late for your meeting. I'll see you at the dinner tonight." *And I'll be watching,* that meant.

Ky had not realized how many uniforms an admiral might need—how many public appearances must be made, at what levels of formality. She fastened the last button on her new evening dress tunic, mentally reviewing the various sensitive areas she must avoid this evening. She would meet, for the first time, the Nexus diplomats, and Rafe would be there. Well, she could handle that part. No more romantic fantasies. Everyone should be well satisfied that she was a cool, adult professional with no adolescent yearnings for the unattainable CEO of ISC. The Slotter Key ambassador should not be a problem, nor his military attaché. Dan Pettygrew had been invited, again, as Bissonet's representative, and Teddy Ransome as head of Ransome's Rangers. Teddy, uninterested in meetings, had accepted the dinner invitation, and Ky decided to let the watchers assume that's where her affections, if any, lay.

Teddy, it turned out, had chosen the most flamboyant of his uniforms—white with gold, at his side a sword that Ky suspected was not merely ornamental. Gold buttons, gold braid, gold stripe on the white trousers . . . at least his shoes were black and had no tassels. With her white dress tunic and dark slacks they made, she was aware, a striking pair. Especially as Teddy, enacting his Romantic mind-set, paid her every gallant attention. Never mind. It would divert attention from the unacceptable.

She smiled, greeted the honorable this and the distinguished that, the names going straight into her implant, while her mind drifted . . . where was Rafe? Would he even speak to her? Teddy had gone off to the drinks buffet, promising to return with one for her.

Stella appeared in front of her. "You look superb," she said, very softly.

"These uniforms," Ky said. "You're a genius."

To her surprise, Stella flushed slightly. "I'm glad you like them. I was worried—all those times your mother told you to copy me."

Ky shook her head. "Let's bury the mother–cousin thing, shall we? I needed help; you gave it; I'm grateful. I couldn't have managed this on my own, not on top of everything else. And the other officers like the insignia design for the SDF, so again—thanks."

"I did just want to say—are you having any problems with Rafe?"

Ky's heart stuttered. "Problems?"

Stella gave her a hard look. "You know what the problems

are—is he doing anything to make it seem like . . . like . . ."

"Like we're more than acquaintances?" Ky said. "No. On the contrary." Her voice was a little more clipped than usual; she could hear it, and she saw Stella react to it.

"I'm glad you're not . . . involved," Stella said. "I didn't think you were, but besides the political problems it would cause now, he's just not the right sort for you."

Ky bit back *As if you knew,* and said instead, "You've not met Captain Ransome yet, have you?"

"No—" Stella looked around. "Which one is he?"

"Captain Ransome!" Ky spoke a little louder, and Teddy whirled, his cape swirling out. "Come meet my cousin Stella."

"Good . . . heavens," Stella said. She had no chance to say more, because Teddy had already produced an elaborate bow that caught everyone's attention. Nor did he spill either of the glasses he carried.

"Stella, this is Captain Theodore Albert Driscoll Ransome, commander of Ransome's Rangers, who has gallantly attached himself to our force. You may recall I told you about him, when I was at Adelaide. Captain Ransome, my cousin Stella Vatta, currently CEO of Vatta Enterprises."

He was looking at Stella in the way men often did—and women, too, Ky had to admit—but the shock of her beauty did not impair his speech. "My utmost admiration, Sera Vatta," he said. "May I offer you this?" He held out one glass.

"Thank you," Stella said, taking it, whereupon he immediately seized her hand and kissed it. Ky felt a bubble of laughter for the first time that day; Stella looked dumbfounded.

"And you, Admiral, here is your favorite." Ky took the glass he offered, and watched with mounting amusement

as Stella reacted to Teddy Ransome's effusive praise . . .
she had never seen that particular expression on Stella's
face.

"Excuse me, Admiral Vatta—" That was one of the
diplomats from Nexus; her implant gave her his name and
title.

"Of course, Ser Tallal."

"You do not, pardon me, look much like your cousin . . ."

Ky smiled. She was familiar with this one. "You're right,
Ser Tallal. My family were all darker; she takes after her
mother's family, the Stamarkos family, who are mostly
blond. And of course, she is beautiful."

"Ah. I meant no insult—"

"And no insult was taken, I assure you." If they thought
Vattas were villains, she could at least be a courteous,
smooth villain.

"I was . . . I know you must have heard that on my
planet there is concern about your influence on the young
Ser Dunbarger."

"I have no influence," Ky said. "We are acquaintances,
merely; I'm sure he has told you the same."

"Yes, but . . . his family history . . . he did not have a
good reputation as a young man. I would not bring up any
details now, considering his present position, but . . . it is
thought that perhaps he might . . . shade the truth."

If only that were the case. If only she could believe
that. Ky shook her head. "By happenstance, we traveled
on the same ship for a while, and in his capacity as an
agent of ISC he repaired some system ansibles. When
we arrived here, he chose to leave the ship and return
home."

Tallal looked at her long and hard, then glanced aside
at Teddy Ransome, still chatting with Stella. "Is that young
man . . . a friend?"

"Captain Ransome," Ky said carefully, "commands Ransome's Rangers, and joined our force in Adelaide. His unit is quite effective for certain special assignments."

"He is actually a ship captain? He seems so . . ."

"*Colorful* may be the word you're looking for," Ky said.

"Yes . . . and you find him . . . attractive, perhaps?"

Ky looked at him. "Ser Tallal, one cannot help noticing that he is decorative, but I am a military officer, and he is in my chain of command."

He scowled, but dropped that topic. "It struck many of us that quite a few Vattas survived and seem to be involved in our affairs—" His glance slid past her and fastened on Stella. "You, your cousin, your aunt on Slotter Key—and these . . . privateers . . ."

"It bothers you that they're privateers?" Ky said. She hadn't heard that before.

"Well, they're really just pirates, aren't they? Given license to attack any ship they suspect of being an enemy?"

Ky wondered if any answer would change his mind, but she had to try. "Letters of marque and reprisal specify what types of ships a privateer can lawfully engage," she said. "They are legal under the code that your government and many others signed."

"Lawfully . . . but who is to say they stay lawful. Osman Vatta didn't."

"Osman was never a privateer," Ky said. "He was an outlaw from early on; the family threw him out—"

"They gave him a ship, a ship with weapons—"

"No, he stole the ship. And armed it himself—it was an ordinary tradeship before."

"You say that now—" He stopped short as two Cascadian government officials within earshot turned to watch, their expressions disapproving.

Ky softened hers intentionally. "I'm sure you didn't mean to imply that I am less than truthful, Ser Tallal."

"Er . . . no, not that, but you're young; you might not know—"

"The Slotter Key ambassador can, I'm sure, furnish you with the data you require," Ky said. "Vatta filed a report with law enforcement and with the insurance company when the ship was stolen."

He looked unconvinced, but the Cascadian officials had come closer. One was the minister Ky had met in that morning's first meeting.

"Admiral Vatta," he said. "I wanted to ask you about that very decorative young man chatting with your cousin."

"Captain Ransome," Ky said. "Of Ransome's Rangers."

"A privateer company?"

"No. I'm not sure what you'd call them. Gentleman adventurers, perhaps. They come from a society with a very unusual—to me anyway—approach to identity. Right now, Captain Ransome is exercising his Romantic intelligence, he will tell you."

"Romantic, as in chatting up pretty women?" Ser Tallal said. His tone would have peeled paint.

"Romantic as in heroic," Ky said. "He believes in honor, gallantry, heroism, and style. Whatever you think of his present costume, he has shown himself courageous and able in combat, which is after all the measure of a warrior."

Tallal looked at her as if she'd sprouted horns. Clearly, nothing was going to change his negative opinion.

"It is said that some of our founders had a Romantic streak," the Deputy Minister said. "We always considered it something the young grew out of, with experience."

"The same on Slotter Key," Ky said. "But on Ransome's home world, people apparently cycle through extremes of personality, or attitude—I'm not sure which. His parents, he says, are 'being Irrationalists'; he's being a Romantic, as is his friend Captain Baskerville. It led them to seek adventure, first against pirates in their own system, and then to venture afar. We met them on Adelaide, where they asked to join us."

"How very interesting," said the Deputy Minister as a chime sounded. "But I believe they're now signaling it is time to go in, and if I recall correctly, the ambassador from your home world—yes, here he is."

"Admiral Vatta," Estro Rajani said. "May I take you in?"

"Thank you," Ky said, with considerable relief. She left the Deputy Minister to sort out the Nexus representative. From her seat far up the table, she saw Rafe being perfectly polite beside Tallal, hardly looking at anyone else, and certainly not at her. He looked, in fact, like the embodiment of a stuffy, somewhat glum senior executive. Probably for the best, she told herself. She herself chatted with Ambassador Rajani about conditions back on Slotter Key and with the Moscoe Confederation Defense Minister on her other side about the education of young officers in both systems.

"They will be sorry not to claim you as a graduate," the Defense Minister said toward the end of dessert.

"If I'd graduated," Ky said, "I'd be a very junior officer on a ship somewhere."

"And we would be lacking your experience," he said, nodding. "So their loss is our gain."

NINE

Over the next few days, Ky gathered data on the privateers' combat history and repairs, and began to organize maintenance and training schedules for them. Every ship needed an ansible installed, and crews needed training in their use. Some also required repairs; others, resupply. Minor repairs and supply ate up the first ten days of *Vanguard*'s refit, but in addition to shepherding the Slotter Key fleet, Ky now had Cascadian ships. Commander Dowitch's contact at Moray's Tobados Yards reported that Moray had indeed taken on a contract to build sixty to ninety of their largest design, a contract made two years before.

"It got them out of a depression," Dowitch reported. "They're delighted; there was an upfront payment, another a year ago when they were on schedule with the job, and they expect to deliver the first ships in about forty days."

"How far away is Moray?" Ky asked. "And did you warn them?"

"I let the Minister do that," Dowitch said. "Government-to-government. But it's going to be tight, if that is indeed the target. We're pushing flat-out on your ship, Admiral, but you won't have time for practice runs. Moray's a solid twenty-day run."

"I'll need to talk to their defense people," Ky said. "I can warn them what they're up against, and suggest a few tactical things to make up for what Turek can throw at them."

"I expect Admiral Trey will help you with that," Dowitch said. "But what if it's somewhere else?"

Ky shrugged. "We don't know of any other large-ship yard that's gotten an order in the right time frame. Piccolo's only got one on order and it's eight months from completion. Defornis doesn't have anything but light cruisers, and only four of those. I'm betting on Moray, especially as they said the government was Stepparn, and we know they're anti-humod."

Time blurred over the next days as she consulted with Moray Defense, Moscoe Defense, the privateer captains, Cascadian captains. She managed only one hurried meal with Stella, in the apartment with Toby and Zori. "Rafe's gone back to Nexus," Stella said, halfway through the meal. "Nexus has pulled out, the idiots."

"I was afraid they would." Ky ate hungrily; she hadn't had a regular meal in days, just grabbing a bite whenever she could. "That Nexus ambassador or whatever, Tallal, seemed to think I was a monster."

"It's Rafe's father," Stella said. "That and our fathers being friends with Lew Parmina. They didn't know—but the Nexus idiots don't know they didn't know."

Ky put that aside—nothing she could do about another system's government—and turned to Toby. "I hear you had quite an adventure," she said.

He glanced sideways at Zori. "It was, kind of."

"And you, Zori," Ky said. "You translated all those things I sent—you must be really good at languages."

She looked at Toby, then down at her plate. "Only because my father is—was—a criminal."

"That doesn't matter," Ky said. "You aren't."

"How can you be sure?" she asked, flashing a glance at Stella then looking straight at Ky. "I thought I knew what my parents were, but I didn't. He was horrible all along, and I didn't see it."

Ky had only the bare-bones story from Stella, nothing to suggest the level of distress Zori was showing. Stella gave Ky a look that meant something, but she didn't know what. Deal with this? Fix this? Then she got up and started clearing the table. When Zori offered to help, Stella told her it wasn't her turn. Nobody could have missed the obvious signals that left Ky and Zori alone. It was ridiculous. Why would Stella think Ky could help Zori? But she had to try something.

"Tell me," Ky said. Maybe directness would work. Zori looked at her, eyes already shiny with tears.

"I love Toby," she started. "But I loved my father once, and now I hate him, and I didn't understand about my mother."

Ky tried not to sigh obviously. "Go on," she said, trying for a voice somewhere between commander and friend.

"I can't tell Stella. She's been so good to me. She wants to help me. She thinks she understands because of her—because of Osman—but she doesn't. It's not the same. She never loved Osman."

Stella had misplaced trust, too, Ky thought, but perhaps there was a reason having fallen for the gardener's son wouldn't work. She nodded, saying nothing.

"It started—I mean, I realized it started—when I was in the kitchen at O'Keefe's, the night Toby was taken, and I had fallen on the floor, and there was this little girl . . ." Tears were flowing now, but Zori's voice shook only a little. This was a story she'd rehearsed to herself.

Ky knew—everyone knew—that some marriages were

unhappy, that some were even violent, but the story Zori told still shocked her. It linked in her mind with the violence done to her class ring; she wondered if Hal would have been that kind of spouse.

"And I ran right to him," Zori said. "My mother was hurt and I didn't even see it; I just let him hold me and pet me and feed me cookies . . . I *liked* being his favorite. And all the time he was hurting her, I believed what he said . . . believed it was her fault, that I was better—" Her head drooped. "I feel so guilty—I am so guilty—she should never forgive me—"

"Have you talked to her since?" Ky asked. "Do you know she's angry with you?"

"No. Stella has. I—I can't. It's all my fault."

"It's not," Ky said. "You were a child . . ."

"That's what Stella says, but I'm not a child now and I still didn't see it."

"Are you more afraid she'll hate you, or more afraid she won't?" Ky asked. She had finally realized that her own fear of telling her parents about her reaction to killing had both components.

Zori looked up, surprised. "I—I don't know."

"Stella has her own issues with her mother," Ky said. "Did she tell you?"

"No . . ."

"You might ask her sometime. But here's what I see. You were a child; your father used you against your mother, and you could not possibly have understood that—"

"I'm supposed to be smart," Zori said, glowering.

"So part of what you're upset about is that you weren't as smart as you thought you were?" Ky said. *That* she understood. She herself had been so smug about not making the mistakes "that idiot Stella" made—then she'd missed the cues that her Miznarii protégé was using her and that Hal's affection was really ambition. She'd hated feeling stupid more than anything.

"I . . . guess so," Zori said. "I didn't think of that."

"I've been fooled," Ky said. "And that was the worst of it for me. Stella and I grew up together, you know, and I always thought I was smarter than she was, even though I was younger. Then I went and fell for a sob story and got myself kicked out of the Academy."

"Really?"

"Really," Ky said. "Look—I'm not a therapist, and maybe a therapist would help you more. But I do know it's not your fault your father fooled you. By what you said, he may have used drugs as well—and possibly programming in your implant—to shape your perceptions. You made the right deduction at the right time, to save Toby, and you've now realized what the truth is. See your mother. Talk to her. If she's hostile, then you have to deal with that. If she's not . . . you'll have a chance to rebuild your relationship. At least she's not dead." *Like mine,* she thought but did not say. This was about Zori, not herself.

"The cookie," Zori said. "I did get sleepy."

"Yeah. You said that. I'll bet he used treats more than once. Not a nice man, your father."

Zori straightened up. "I know she wants to see me. She's asked Stella. Stella won't make me . . . but now . . . all right."

Ky reminded herself that adolescents could change moods in moments—she had, Stella had, Toby'd been the same. Then her comunit chimed. "Drat." She pulled it out. "Zori, I'm sorry. I have to leave."

"That's all right—I mean, you've helped." Zori seemed to sparkle with renewed energy.

"Stella—I have to go," Ky called. Stella and Toby came out of the kitchen.

"Already?"

"Unfortunately, yes. I'll try to call you later." Ky noticed that Zori was murmuring something to Toby. Stella glanced that way and gave Ky a finger-flick: *Good.*

Ky caught the shuttle over to the yard where the newly installed CCC was ready for calibration runs. *Vanguard* was shrouded in the vast bulk of a repair dock capable of handling a ship twice her size. Riggers were now rebuilding the hull around the inserted CCC; the interior of the ship was mostly aired up, and Ky could enter from the normal hatch.

The ship looked different even on the route from the personnel hatch to the CCC. Ky had known that her former spacious cabin and office would be cut into quarters for more crew, but it felt strange to see hatches where none had been before. Where she had fought Gretna's intruders along the aft weapons-deck passage, she now faced a bulkhead with a single hatch that looked much thicker than usual.

"Remember I told you the CCC has hull-thick construction," Dowitch said. "Go on in."

"Where are the connections to the ship's systems?" Ky asked.

"Already covered," Dowitch said. "The breakfrees are on the ship side—I can show you later, if you want."

Inside, the CCC was every bit as cramped as they'd said and smelled of freshly molded plastics and resins, machine oil, and an acrid bite from soldering just finished. Protective film still covered some of the screens and control boards. It looked too fresh, too clean, but that would not last the first tenday's use, Ky knew. Soon there would be smudges, stains, the paths humans left behind them wherever they worked and lived.

Ky wove between the lumpy shapes of the armored stations for Scan and Communications and the intrusive bulk of the onboard ansible to the command seat. It looked much like the one on *Vanguard*'s bridge, except the shield that would close her in was opaque, a peculiar blue-gray.

"I thought it would be translucent," she said.

"It will be," Dowitch said. "When you turn it on and choose that option. But it will respond to certain kinds of shock by going opaque. Doesn't matter; you'll still get the data. What you're seeing there are the laminae for the displays." He nodded toward the chair. "Go on—sit in it. I want to calibrate it for your size and weight."

"Shouldn't I have my suit on?"

"Yup. Your suit locker's by the hatch."

Ky suited up, wondering who had moved her personal suit from her former quarters, then eased into the command seat.

"Let your arms lie naturally on the armrests," Dowitch said. He touched the controls of a remote; the chair seemed to squirm under Ky, gently lifting, falling, nudging . . . "How's that?"

"Very comfortable," Ky said.

"Setting one," he said. The seat quit moving. "That's your default. Now look to the right. Good—and to the left. Now pretend you see something right in front that you want to point out—yes, just that much movement. Now I'm going to unlock it again. Lean back—you're tired; there's a break in the battle, and you need to relax, shift, unkink your muscles, but you're not sleeping—yes."

Ky leaned back, stretching her legs out a little; the seat moved, supporting her, easing her back.

"I'm going to start the massage function," he said. "You tell me how much is too much—"

In another five minutes, he had the seat's support functions set for her.

"Now the displays. I know you'll practice, but I want to take you through them first. Left hand, thumb knob: that's your translucency. Right hand, thumb knob, lift and lower the canopy when it's not automatic. If it won't open, there's a reason: don't fight it." He waited until she nodded, then went on. "Now: lower the canopy."

Ky lowered it; in front of her, a dark field, like space itself. She thumbed the left-hand control, and it faded until it was wholly translucent; she could see Dowitch watching her.

"How's the sound?" he asked. It sounded as if he were inside the shield; she said so. "Good. Your scans can be chosen as the primary data from any of the stations, or as an integrated view of all of them. I've put a simulation in the CCC scan units, so we don't panic Station Security by setting off live scan this close. Scan controls are left hand, communications are right hand. You have armrest controls, but you can also choose point, touch, or gaze direction."

In front of her, hanging in the air, miniature scan screens came up. Ky switched from one mode to another. She could enlarge any screen; she could combine screens. In the simulation, the familiar acceleration cones—orange for approaching, blue for receding—showed ships in motion. She hunted through control hierarchies and found how to mark ship icons as enemy, unknown, friend.

"How much of this can be controlled by my implant?" she asked.

"Probably all of it," he said. "We just need to get your implant and this set of subroutines melded. Now—if you find the visual background confusing, try reducing the translucency."

Ky thumbed the control again, and the canopy slowly

darkened; the displays seemed brighter now, and she could still see Dowitch—she continued until the displays seemed to hang in space as vast as that between stars.

"Sound still good?" he asked.

"Fine," Ky said. "I've never seen anything this elaborate—"

"The command chair's based on what they use at Moray," he said. "You've got direct feeds for communication—we're still figuring out how to connect the onboard ansible, though. It's easy in the other ships, but here we want to tie it in to the one on the bridge but have independent use optional."

"Have you asked Toby?"

"Your cousin's ward? No . . . I thought he was still supposed to be restricted."

"I can spring him—and he knows everything about ansible hookups."

"Fine . . . but for now let's go over the safety features." Dowitch explained the conditions under which the CCC would close automatically from the rest of the ship, and when the command seat would seal. Temperature, pressure, acceleration, atmosphere: some of those, Ky realized, would not be met unless *Vanguard* blew. She was not going to think about that.

Back out of the command seat's enclosure, Ky called Stella and told her they needed someone—Toby, for preference—right away, to link the onboard ansible.

"And while I have you—what about ansibles for spares, and to take to Moray?"

"You'd have to clear that with Moscoe Defense," Stella said. "We're putting them in as fast as we can." She started explaining more than Ky wanted to hear about the difficulties involved in tooling up for a completely new product and maintaining quality control as production scaled up through set points that required unit expansion. Ky tried to listen patiently, but finally interrupted.

"Bottom line, how many units can we have?"

"I just told you," Stella said. "It depends on Moscoe Defense."

At least there Ky dealt with someone who didn't want to explain everything, who had answers.

"Ansible units for Moray?" he said. "Sure—that's been dealt with at the policy level. Moray asked for a demo model but will purchase enough for their new-built ships, and pay in ships. It's lucky your Slotter Key contingent are privateers; they have more cargo capacity. For safety, we'd prefer to ship no more than five per vessel."

"You're sending that many?" Ky asked. "What about technicians to install them?"

"Oh, there's a manual now, standard format training materials. Anyone who can install a standard comunit can do it. We're providing technical assistance as each is installed, and after that each ship's communications specialist will be able to help install others at Moray. All you have to do is give the orders."

After the struggle to keep her few ships supplied, this seemed unreal . . . surely it wouldn't continue. The rest of supply—food, munitions, water, cultures for environmental chambers—went almost as smoothly, but only because, Ky suspected, her newly commissioned Supply Division used the same tactics as they had in their privateer days. Gordon Martin, on *Vanguard*, had counterparts on all the other privateer ships and on the Cascadian ships committed to their fleet. Martin had not wanted to command Supply; a Cascadian officer, Commander Michel Moscoe-Corian, held that post, and supplies poured onto the docks in what Ky considered astonishing profusion.

"How are we paying for all this?" she asked him one day.

"Paying?" he said. One of his bushy eyebrows rose, and a sly grin crooked the corner of his mouth. "Did you think you were supposed to pay for something?"

Ky grinned back. "Are you trying to give us a bad rep, Commander?"

"No, ma'am. Never that. But when Moscoe Defense tells me to be sure the ships are fully supplied—well, I'm just following orders, see? They didn't give me a budget, exactly."

"A free hand, then?" Ky asked.

"Not exactly," he said. "More like—prove it's necessary. Anything doubtful, get approval for. Now—just between you and me—I might not have the same definition of *doubtful* they do. And they know you're not trained by them—and over half your ships aren't ours, so we don't necessarily know what they need."

"Did you ever consider privateering?" Ky asked.

"Me? My family would have had a fit," he said. "And this way there's no question about the legality of what I'm doing."

Ky laughed. "It would be rude to suggest anything else, wouldn't it?"

"Yes, Admiral, it would. I'm glad you recognize that, because I would hate to see such a fine officer err in matters of professional courtesy."

"I'll keep that in mind," Ky said. "I'm supposed to meet a Major Anson in about an hour, something about personnel transfers—"

"Bobby Anson? You'll like him. You need more crew, don't you?"

"Yes." She had been short of crew even before reaching Cascadia, where several more of the civilians on *Sharra's*

Gift and *Vanguard* had asked to leave. With need for a fleet staff and crew in the CCC, she'd had to ask Moscoe Defense to help.

"He'll do you right. People are clamoring for a chance to be on your ship."

"I want to talk to my mother," Zori said to Stella during breakfast, the day after Ky's visit. She had wakened with that thought foremost. Whatever her mother said to her, she herself had to try to make up for years of neglect.

"Are you sure?" Stella asked.

"Yes. What Ky said—it's not all about me. I'm hurting her more by not seeing her." Zori took a swallow of juice. "I didn't think of that. Is she at our—the house?"

"No, she's staying at Sprucewood; it's in the directory." Stella looked as if she wanted to say more but hesitated. Then she went on. "She's been talking to her relatives, Zori, and she's had some disappointments. She wanted to move back downplanet—"

"Where the family estate is," Zori said, nodding. She looked at Toby. "I don't want to—I don't want to leave Toby."

"I don't think you need to worry about it," Stella said. "She'll tell you, I'm sure, but her family's being difficult. Something about your father and the estates." She glanced at the clock. "I've got to get to the office; feel free to invite her over here."

Zori stared at the contact number a long time before calling.

"Zori, I don't blame you." Her mother wore a simple blue dress and no jewelry.

"I blame myself. I should have seen . . . I should have known . . ."

"And then he would have hurt you. Zori, you were a tiny child . . . it was better as it was."

"I can't believe that. You were hurt—"

"You don't want to believe that. Zori, listen to me. This was not the worst life, and you can have a better one. Maybe with Toby, maybe with someone else. You deserve it."

"And what about you? I should take care of you—"

"No." Her mother shook her head. "I am an adult. It's my job to take care of myself. I'll be fine—"

"You won't . . . what will you do?"

Her mother laughed, a genuine laugh. "For one thing, I won't let you run my life . . . Zori, relax. Please. It's true that my family are angry with me right now, and they don't want me back home—back onplanet. But I still have some resources. I'll get by, and you'll finish school—"

"You should move in here," Zori said. "Stella would let you—"

"No, you should move in with me," her mother said. "Not because I want to keep you away from Toby—he is indeed a very nice boy, quite suitable—but because you and I are a family, all we have left of what we had. Yet we don't know each other that well, and we need to."

Zori thought about it. "Would we go back to the house?"

"No. Never. That life is over. I've had all your things moved into storage; we can rent an apartment—"

She didn't want to move. She wanted to stay near Toby forever. She liked Stella. But it was hard, too, living in the same apartment and yet not ever doing any of the things they weren't supposed to do. And Stella probably wanted her to move out . . .

"I won't force you, Zori, but I think it would help you. And me."

"I think so, too," Zori said. She reached out, and her

mother was there, holding her, both of them crying a little, but more in relief than pain.

Stella, at the office, stared at her comunit and bit her lip. Zori was talking to her mother. She, Stella, was not talking to her own mother. She had to. She knew she had to. The white-hot rage she'd felt when she'd first learned of her true parentage had long since died down to a sullen glow.

But that still left the dilemma. How honest could she be with a woman who had not been honest with her? She no longer wanted to hurt Helen, but healing the breach between them would require honesty from both of them. Could Helen stand that?

She checked the time zone for Vatta headquarters on Slotter Key. Early evening now. Helen might be out to dinner, or shopping or . . . home.

She could not let Zori outdo her in courage. She opened a circuit to the system ansible and placed the call.

As the work on *Vanguard* neared completion, Ky's days grew ever busier. She needed to be in at least three places at once; she wanted to get the ships that were spaceworthy into training, she had to be available for conferences with Moray and Moscoe government officials, and she was sure that the admiral's presence would speed work on *Vanguard*. Argelos and Pettygrew, because they had been in combat using the shipboard ansibles, took over much of the training. Ky had daily reports, and logged in by ansible whenever she could, but she knew she needed experience in commanding from the CCC. Yet she could not spare the time to be ferried to and from the dockyard to sit in the command seat while the others worked on their assignments.

Finally, *Vanguard* came back to Cascadia. Ky moved her

gear back aboard. Her formerly spacious quarters were now the size of the captain's cabin on *Gary Tobai,* but she didn't care about that. She wanted to run an exercise from the CCC as soon as possible. Though Turek had not sent another broadcast, she knew his next attack could not be far away.

"Those ships at Moray will be within days of completion by the time we can get there," Ky said to her assembled captains, some on Cascadia Station and some attending by ansible. "We can't afford more than two days of exercises; they'll be intense. We can sleep in FTL." A few groans, but no real resistance. In the presence of Cascadian ships and officers, the privateers had become competitive ship handlers, determined to show that privateers weren't sloppy merchanters. She passed out the updated information she had on Moray's own defense system, the basic tactics used, the contact codes they'd been given. Moray Defense used clusters: two maniples per cluster, a cluster per sector, scattered around the system and dependent on the system ansible for rapid communication. "Moscoe's given us the entire Sector Twelve to play in; we'll rendezvous there at 1800."

"Today?" Coufal asked.

"Today," Ky said. It was 1400. "Dismissed."

She was as exhausted as the others when she finally gave the order to form up for jump to Moray System. But in those two days she had come to feel that the forty-six ships under her command were functioning as a fighting unit, even the transports. Moray's last report before they entered FTL was that construction proceeded normally and no threat showed.

"A lot can happen in twenty days," Hugh Pritang said.

"We're as ready as we can be," Ky said.

TEN

Lozar Phittanji, Assembler Third on the second shift of number thirty dock, headed home at the end of the shift with nothing more on his mind than whether Jari, his wife, had brought home a fish for the betrothal feast. Though he would never rise above Assembler Third—as a devout Miznarii, he refused to consider a cranial implant, and more senior grades required implants—he had a comfortable life, especially now that ship orders were up.

Besides, he had that small but very welcome stipend from the Faithful, making the betrothal feast possible. And for nothing, really—for nothing but attaching a few tiny datadots to each ship he worked on.

"It is nothing harmful," the Amadh of their local congregation had told him. "It will only tell Miznarii who have a little reader that the ship was partly built by Miznarii, that's all. You can see for yourself."

Lozar had taken the reader he was offered and passed it over the dot, and the message came up—the quotation from the Book that ordered the people to use their own brains and not partake of machinery, and the words "This vessel contains work made by the mind and hand of True Humans, the Faithful."

So Lozar had attached many such dots to the ships he'd worked on without anyone noticing: one near the main hatch, one near the bridge. Yes, it was against the rules to attach any extraneous materials to the ship, but what harm could it do? Even if the infidels had readers and found the dots, even if they determined who had placed them, his conscience was clear.

"Hey, Lozar, wait up!" Lozar glanced back. Gerry and David, both on his shift but non-Miznarii, were almost jogging toward him. Though they were senior, thanks to their disgusting implants, he had come to consider them friends.

"Didn't I hear you say your daughter's betrothal dinner was tonight?" Gerry asked.

"Man, you can't face something like that right after work. C'mon. We'll stand you a round at the Rigger's Friend. Least we can do." David patted Lozar's shoulder.

"But Jari told me to come straight home—"

"Wives always do," David said. "Bet you she doesn't really expect it, though. Mine never did. You're facing the in-laws, right? You need a little fortification. Jari doesn't really want you around when she's putting the final touches to the dinner. What time is it for, anyway?"

"Twenty hundred . . . later than usual because it's formal . . ."

"Then you have plenty of time." David hung an arm across Lozar's shoulders. "And I promise, we'll see you get home in time to change and all that."

Despite David's assurance, Lozar left the Rigger's Friend so late that he had to take the shorter back way through a service corridor—not strictly legal—and Jari glared when he came in.

She was not nearly as annoyed as the substitute candy salesman at the cart parked in D-ring, Corridor 34—on the direct route between Lozar's work site and his apartment, the route he took almost every night.

Paddy Kendelmann looked at the daily statistics with half a mind on his son's school performance. He'd paid for the enhanced student module for the boy's implant, but Paul still struggled with math, and the teacher talked about special testing and learning disabilities. Lisa had been furious, blaming the teacher and Paddy alternately. If only he'd been put in the other class; if only Paddy had bought that enhanced module the year before . . .

Now, that was odd. He pushed aside the problem of Paul's math performance and squinted at the readout, where Dispatch had flagged certain entries. On a station this size, twenty deaths in a standard day, plus or minus three, was about right. Most were natural or accidental, the causes obvious: the very old, the sick, the accidents that will happen anytime serious construction work is going on, the occasional drunken brawl or domestic dispute ending in death-by-intent, though not nearly the level it used to be.

But the past twenty-four hours had produced twenty-nine deaths, a notable bump. And here were three unexplained deaths in previously healthy men of early middle age. Not accidents, not assaults, no real reason . . . all sudden deaths, dead before the medics could arrive and do anything. Heart failure. Heart failure, in men so young, men whose last medical checkup had been clean? Modern diagnostics didn't miss things like that. No wonder Dispatch had flagged them for investigation.

And all worked in the yards. Coincidence? It had to be coincidence, didn't it?

But five lines down he saw another. A woman's sudden collapse in a public place, death too quick for medical intervention. How common was that? Forty-year-old women—she was, or had been, an accountant, Paddy noted, in the same firm one of the men had worked for—didn't have sudden death from undiscovered heart disease. Not in this era. Not with mandatory health tests . . .

Lisa always said he had a streak of paranoia, and right now that streak was buzzing up and down his spinal cord, raising the hair on his neck. He initialed the autopsy requests, marked them URGENT, and sent them on. The dead Miznarii's family would no doubt try to prevent the autopsy, but the law was on his side.

Could this be related to the alert they'd had three ten-days before? He glanced at the master schedule. They'd been briefed that an attack might come when a frame of ships neared completion, and Frame Six was within days of completion . . . they were expecting the customer to arrive to take delivery.

He looked at the list again. The dead Miznarii had worked on Frame Six and Frame Five both, as assemblers. Another had worked only on Frame Five. But the other dead man had been a specialist in control systems, and he had worked on Frame Six.

Paddy pulled up the man's record. Banamir Attanda, unmarried, no close relatives in Tobados Yards station. No obvious legal problems . . . but his financial records were peculiar. Everyone had had problems in the dearth of ship orders a few years past, but his balance had sunk faster than most . . . faster than some married men with children to support. It couldn't be drugs, not with his performance reviews. Women? Or gambling? It had to be one of those, Paddy thought.

Surveillance videos in the local gambling halls showed

Banamir's face at table after table. The uneasy feeling intensified. Gamblers—serious gamblers—were easy to manipulate. They always thought they had a system, but gambling led to debts—often large ones—and too often debts led to embezzling.

Paddy shook his head as the files opened to show a familiar pattern. Embezzling . . . then blackmail.

The question was, what had Banamir Attanda used to pay his gambling debts?

Vanguard dropped out of FTL flight at Moray System on schedule and in the approach vector Moray's defense command had requested, a low-relative-velocity insertion at a high angle to the ecliptic, far out on the fringes of the system, four light-hours from the primary. Ky, in the new combat command center, stared at the duplicate scan displays. She felt isolated, her familiar bridge crew replaced by specialists, some borrowed from Cascadia, on duplicate scan stations. The only familiar face was Master Sergeant Pitt, who'd asked permission to observe here. Major Douglas had elected to observe from the bridge, at Hugh Pritang's invitation.

As scans cleared from downjump turbulence, ship icons appeared, most—with wide uncertainty bars—clustered near the fourth planet and its shipyards. Until they had more information, all the icons were neutral yellow. Behind *Vanguard,* more and more of Ky's fleet dropped out, their two stealthed observation ships tucked neatly between larger vessels. Each ship reported in, and a broad vee of green icons built behind her. They had kept excellent formation; Ky transmitted congratulations to all of them by shipboard ansible, then turned to the communications officer.

"Report our arrival to Cascadia."

He shook his head. "We're not getting an ansible signal, Admiral."

Ky looked at him. "No system ansible at all?"

"Nothing. I've pinged it . . . we wouldn't get a reply to that within a couple of hours if the booster tech is down, but I'm thinking it's something else. I can use the ship-board—"

"First IDs coming up," one of the scan techs reported. "Uh-oh. Blueridge is a red-tag, right?"

"They beat us to it," Ky said. "Use our onboard ansible; report that to Cascadia." That leisurely visit with the Mackensee commanders, that trip back to Cascadia, the time necessary to transfer ansibles from *Vanguard* to the other privateers, to install the CCC in *Vanguard,* all had given the enemy time to strike its logical target. They'd warned Moray, but a few tendays wasn't time enough to develop a plan against a massive invasion, especially when the enemy had onboard ansibles.

"If they have the ships—" someone muttered.

"All right . . . steady on. We need to know more before we charge in." Across the screen, icons flared to red. Some remained yellow. Those could be neutrals, or natives, or enemy not yet identified. The new military-grade battle analysis computer, a gift from Cascadia, should give them better real-time data on the flow of battle . . . including the location and identification of outlying ships, presented in a 3-D holographic display. Ky wasn't sure she trusted it; the unit had been purpose-built to work with onboard ansible data as well as conventional scan data, and they'd had so little time to test it—

"Anomaly here," the scan tech pointed. "Mass consistent with small ship. Could be stealthed observer."

"Probably is," Ky said. "What're we picking up on communications channels?"

"We've got just one ansible tuned to the pirates' channel set. A lot of chatter, can't understand it. Lightspeed com will be old—"

Lightspeed would be, most likely, Moray's own defense services. "Capture all we can, put someone on it for history." History might tell her how this had happened. She'd warned Moray Defense, before her fleet left Cascadia, to be alert for attacks; they'd said they were prepared, but they had refused to release most of their plans until she arrived. Prudent, but now another complication. She could not coordinate with them without knowing specifics.

She glanced at Yamini and Douglas, tiny icons on her command chair display. "Recommendations?" They had insisted on preparing two battle plans for a similar situation: arriving to find the pirates either already in possession of the yards, or just arrived in the system.

"More data," Yamini said.

"I'd say plan C-one, in ten minutes, to collect a little more data," Douglas said.

"Two hours," Yamini said. "We'll have a better picture—"

"In two hours, it could be over," Douglas said. "I interpret the present ship positions as indicating combat ongoing for at least four hours. Already, microjumping into position puts us at risk of weapons tracks. As well, if they have stealthed observers, as we think, the pirates now know where we are; if we sit here—"

Ky nodded. Space congested rapidly as a battle progressed, filling with the lethal detritus that included ordnance, fragments of blown ships and other structures . . .

"C-one, but twenty minutes," she said. "Preceded by a two-light-minute dispersal jump . . ." If any of the pirate ships weren't fully engaged in the battle, if Turek had a reserve, she needed to get her force into unpredictable

motion quickly. It would make recombination more difficult, but not beyond her captains' abilities. The real
problem—the one no one mentioned as the ships jumped
on her order—was the possibility of jumping into the path
of weapons fired hours before. "And we need to let Moray
know who we are, even if they don't get the word for hours."

"The enemy can pick up that transmission."

"With any luck, the enemy is busy at the moment. Use
tight-beam, the 'Snowflower' set."

The dispersal microjump ended; all ships reported in.
Partrade, on *Angelhair*, had moved closest to Tobados
Yards. "All the ships in the yard appear to be there still,"
he said. "I should be within two hours of them." A pause.
"I . . . er . . . overjumped."

Fatal, if he overjumped into one of their own ships.
But no time now to regret the lack of training time, the
lack of calibration she'd insisted on with her first little
group.

"Forward your scan data," Ky said. "Then all captains—
use your new scan data to refine your microjump calibration. Last chance."

The data poured in; the new battle analysis computer
combined data from *Angelhair*, their own stealthed observer
left back near the downjump exit, and all the other ships
to produce a best guess with narrower uncertainty bars
and the first movement cones. A debris field now blurred
scan where the first contact had come. One Moray
cluster—ten ships—was simply gone. Others were frag-
mented; without the system ansible, they could not communicate well enough to coordinate their actions.
Maniples tried to hold together, within easy lightspeed
communication, but this made them fatter targets for the
enemy.

"He's thrown a lot at them," Douglas said. "We've got

. . . forty-eight enemy icons, at least. If half those yellows turn red, we're in for it."

"We'll be in for it worse if they get those warships," Ky said. "Except for the Bissonet ships, he's got the same kind of ships our privateers have, and he's fought enough that they should also be showing structural problems by now."

"Unless he picked up more military ships somewhere," Douglas said. "But yeah, he needs more."

"Coming up on twenty, Admiral," someone said.

"Execute," Ky said. "Then recalibrate." It wouldn't be as good as if they'd calibrated before the battle, but it should help reduce some of the inaccuracies.

Vanguard skipped and then returned to normal space; new data popped up on the screens. Now some thirty of the enemy ships hung less than a light-minute from the yard, their acceleration clearly marked on the trace, while eight were poised on the far side of the debris field.

"Got voice recordings, Admiral," one of the communications techs said. "Moray Defense challenged an apparent official mission from the government that ordered the warships. Moray told them to halt and be inspected at an outer station. They must have thought they might be challenged, because that's when Turek's force attacked the nearest cluster. Other Moray Defense clusters responded to that area, but they came in singly—Moray's lost half its on-duty clusters at this point."

"Defeat in detail," Yamini murmured. "And there's nothing left to defend the yard; it'll be over before the other half of their defense force realizes it's started."

"We have the local codes," Ky said. "And they have our beacon IDs. Send our ships to their cluster stations, use lightspeed com to tell them what's going on . . ."

"And tell them to do what?" Yamini asked. "Their doctrine would have them support the cluster under attack; that's how the closest ones got hammered."

"Tell them to stick with our ships—follow their orders—because otherwise they're dead or useless."

"Moray's yelling for help—they've picked up our closest ships' beacons . . ."

"Tell them we're here, and we'll engage shortly. Wait—what are those ships leaving the station?" Seventeen blips, none with working beacons, had lifted from the station an hour ago, in no particular formation. "Are they Moray-crewed, or what?"

"There's a problem . . . a lot of radio chatter I don't understand it all. Sabotage, they think, but also . . . some hotheads took some ships out to fight off the invaders, only the ships aren't really commissioned."

"Which is which?" Ky asked. Scan recognized the ships as large, some of them as armed, weapons hot. If those were the enemy . . . half her own ships were now dispersed to offer support and communications to surviving Moray clusters. Some of those were beginning to move together, following Ky's battle plan.

"Eight have crew, they think. Not trained crew, though. Dockyard workers, riggers and the like. The others are under some kind of remote control."

"Can they blow them from the station? How long ago did they undock?" Ky touched her own scan controls, enlarging and shrinking until she found the views she wanted, estimates of the ships' velocity, acceleration, course.

"They don't want to destroy them, they're saying—those are brand-new warships, worth a fortune—"

"Idiots!" They could lose not just ships, but the station, the entire system, if the enemy got away with those ships. But her force was now engaged . . . some of it.

Those ships weren't her problem yet . . . even without proper beacon IDs, they were pinned on scan. Without working weapons systems, they could be blown anytime. More important to get Turek and his ships.

Tobados Yards

Lozar woke to the blare of emergency sirens, with Jari pulling at his arm. His head felt the size of a humri drum, and pounded like one, too.

"Waas goin' on?" he muttered.

"What's going on is that you and that bunch of unbeliever ruffians you drink with came in staggering drunk last night . . . you went out again after the betrothal dinner . . . and now there's an emergency—"

"My head hurts—"

"I hope it bursts," Jari said.

He peered up at her. She looked really angry, not mild and forgiving as a wife should.

"You disgraced the family. You brought those men home; you insisted they stay to dinner; if Pasandir breaks the betrothal it would not surprise me—"

"They were happy for me; they are my friends—"

"And you smelled of liquor even before the dinner began. How could you?" She looked ready to cry now. Jari crying had always melted his heart. "And they aren't even believers! How can you call them friends?"

Lozar rolled over and pushed himself up to sit on the edge of the bed. Pain lanced through his eyeballs. What had he drunk, after they headed out to celebrate? Something they called "shiny bock"? Why hadn't he stuck to the same green Stellar Special he was used to?

"Hurry up," Jari urged. "Whatever it is, it's important."

"I'm coming . . ." He tried to stand, staggered onto her; a hard elbow in the ribs finally got him upright. "I need a shower."

"No time. The red lights are flashing."

A serious emergency, then. He stumbled into the 'fresher, his stomach churning, and threw up a foul-smelling mess. He ran the water as hard as it would go, just to rinse off the smell, and put on the clothes Jari held out while still damp.

"Here," she said, still grim-faced, holding out a bulb of black liquid. No need to ask if she'd sweetened it or put in the stomach-protecting powder: he'd have to drink it black and bitter as the regrets of a fool, which is what he felt like.

It ran down his throat in a fiery, acidic wave, shocking him more awake. He looked again at his wife, his wife whom he loved. "I'm sorry," he said.

"You're a good man, Lozar," she said. "But you're too easily led." She sniffed. "Friends, indeed."

They *were* friends, but he wasn't going to argue. Not all the humods were bad people, the part of them that was people. It was only the nonhuman part that was bad.

He hurried out of the apartment and down the passage toward his emergency station, his head still pounding. What was going on? Around him, others hurried as well, just like in drills, but traffic thinned even as he neared dockside. His emergency station, across the construction arm from his workplace, served ships within days of launch.

"You look like you was run over by a cargo lift," Gerry said. Gerry looked disgustingly fit, to Lozar's gaze, only a little red around the eyes.

"How much did we drink?" Lozar asked.

"You," David said, coming up on his other side. "The

right question is how much did *you* drink, and the answer is, you tried to match us. You know you can't do that, not without an implant to detox for you."

"You need a tab," Gerry said. "Here—" With a quick look around for any proctors, he unpeeled a tab and pushed it into Lozar's hand.

"It's not allowed," Lozar began. Its little cloud of short-lived nannites was just another form of humodification, according to their cleric.

"It's an emergency. What kind of god is it that won't forgive you when it's an emergency? C'mon, Lozar, we need you alert, and you ain't within a kilometer of alert."

Lozar palmed the tab into his mouth. He imagined he could feel the illicit little demons—they were, in the Law, the same as demons—crawling through his taste buds into his bloodstream. He shuddered. In moments, the sour taste in his mouth vanished; his stomach no longer burned; his vision sharpened.

"Did that have other—"

"Oh, just a little stimulant. No, I promise you, the nannies are short-timers. Gone in five minutes."

"I have to pee," Lozar said a minute or so later.

"And that'll be all of it," David promised.

The sirens stopped while he was in the crank; he came out to the mutter of low voices, the rustle of clothing and shuffle of feet on the decks.

"Phittanji! Over here!" His shift boss waved. "We need all you fellows without implants . . ."

Some scut work no doubt, something low-level for the supposedly handicapped pure humans. Lozar looked around for Gerry and David, but they were in another group now.

"This is an attack, not a drill," his shift boss said. "Remember that broadcast? They want our ships—we think they're trying to control them remotely, and we have to stop them. The first people we sent in collapsed—apparently there's some kind of electronic attack aimed at cranial implants. You Miznarii don't have to worry about that. We need you to get aboard and disable the controls."

Lozar's stomach clenched. He looked sideways. Simsan Attara, a member of his congregation, looked back, face shining with pride. Real humans were going to do what humods couldn't . . . Miznarii were about to be the heroes, about to be recognized . . .

"If you can figure out what's causing the attack on implants," their shift boss went on, "turn it off. Destroy it. Doesn't matter how much damage you do; we can't let these guys get the ships." He glanced down at a datapad in his hand. "Gottlin and Pelinnha, take Dock One. Serranja and Metablos, Dock Two . . ." As he called the name, Miznarii at the front of the group moved up, picked up some kind of toolcase, and headed down the row to the designated docking spaces.

Lozar, at the back of the group, went to Dock Thirty with Veenaji Pestanza, trying to remember the shift boss' hasty instructions. Turn on the E-scanner on entry, report any anomalies, moving directly from the entry to the control nexi in the ship's axis. Behind them trailed an insulated cable like a slick black tail: a hardened communications line supposedly proof against EC interference.

Veenaji, nursing his damaged arm in a sling, held the hardened communications device; Lozar carried the toolcase and its probe. The probe bleeped; Veenaji turned to look. "What's that?"

Lozar grinned at Veenaji, and gestured for him to kill the microphone.

"It's proof a Miznarii worked on the ship," he said.

"How did you know that?" Veenaji asked.

"I put it there," Lozar said, feeling once more that little surge of pride. "I put them on every ship, like a seal that says, *A Miznarii worked here.* That it doesn't take humods to build spaceships."

"Let me see," Veenaji said. Lozar put the probe directly on the datadot and turned the screen so Veenaji could read it.

"It doesn't say we worked on it," Veenaji said.

"Of course it does," Lozar said. "I've read them; our Amadh showed me."

"Look."

On the screen, instead of the pious message Lozar had seen before, lines scrolled past: . . . STATUS SECTION 14.3 COMPLETE, STATUS SECTION 14.4 COMPLETE, STATUS SECTION 14.5 . . . CONTROL INITIATION CODE 112, CODE 297, CODE 410 . . .

"What is that?" Lozar asked. His belly clenched; he felt cold all over.

"Nothing good," Veenaji said. "Lozar . . . what did you *do*?"

"I didn't," Lozar said, but his clammy hands told him he had. "Elder Marjee told me I should talk to our Amadh, and he said for this service to the Faithful, I would be paid a little for my trouble and the risk I was taking—"

"But you . . . but this . . . Lozar, these things you put— how many?—they're harming the ships!"

"I don't understand," Lozar said.

"How many?" Veenaji demanded.

"Uh . . . one by the entry hatch, so the Faithful coming aboard—" The expression on Veenaji's face stopped him. "Uh . . . altogether . . . seven. One here, one blessing . . . er . . . one on the casing for each control nexus, one on the bridge . . ."

"Burn it out," Veenaji said, his voice harsh. "Burn them all out, quickly! I can't believe you—and they'll think we all—Lozar, you are so . . . so stupid!" He yanked on the trailing cable. "I have to think how to say it so they don't blame us all."

Ears burning, Lozar pushed the nozzle of the probe onto the datadot and pushed the button he'd been told to. Something cracked, and a trickle of smoke rose. He moved on into the ship, to the next site, half scared and half angry. Had the Amadh lied to him? Surely not: holy men did not lie. Had someone lied to the Amadh? That must be it. Miznarii did not lie; Miznarii did not break the law; Miznarii did not break even rules . . . the memory of the tab he had taken, the demonic nannites he'd put in his mouth, rose to mock that assertion.

The probe bleeped again, this time at a cross-corridor. He had placed no datadots here. He ran the probe up the walls and found something that showed up on the screen as EMP EMITTER: STRENGTH 9.2. He wanted to ask Veenaji what to do but Veenaji had not come with him. He decided to burn it out, whatever it was. The probe found another on the other side of the passage, and then another—four in all. He burned them all. Now the screen said NO FUR-THER EMP RISK. Surely that was something he should report. Maybe workers with implants could come aboard now.

Maybe now his handcom would work. Lozar pulled it out, flicked it on, and the little light came up, bright and blue. But they hadn't given him a code number to call; they'd just said the handcoms wouldn't work if implants didn't.

ELEVEN

He was still wondering whether to call when he heard footsteps coming. Lots of footsteps. Veenaji at last . . . but when he looked, it was not Veenaji. Gerry and David and two younger men he'd seen in the Rigger's Friend but didn't know—all carrying toolcases like his. "David," he said. "Gerry—I do not think it will hurt you now; I burned out the . . . the EMP emitter."

Gerry sighed; David shook his head. "You poor stupid Mizzie bastard," Gerry said. "You don't even know what you've done."

"And now we're in trouble because you're our drinkin' buddy," David said. "Other guys got assigned to weapons, backup to Station Defense; they might even get to shoot at somethin' with real actual missiles. We get stuck comin' in here after you. By the time we get back, there won't be any weapons positions left . . ."

"Buford, take his toolcase," Gerry said. Buford slouched forward.

Lozar clutched the toolcase to his chest. "I didn't mean anything bad! The Amadh said—"

Buford spat. "Amadh! That slimeball! Bastard sold out the station—"

Gerry put up his hand. "Buford, don't talk trash about

religion. It may not be our religion, and it may be a stupid religion to us, but Lozar takes it seriously."

Lozar saw sympathy in Gerry's face; it moved him to explain. "He said it was just to show that Miznarii could build ships—at least in part—without modification. He showed me the dot readouts; they said we had worked on the ships, and that was all—"

"But that's not what they say now, is it? How do you think that happened?"

"I don't know," Lozar said. He felt hollow inside. "I didn't do it; that's all I know . . ."

"Are you sure the dots you placed all read the same as the one he showed you? Did you read them all?"

Lozar stared. "I—of course not. I do not have a dot-reader at home, and I could not take the time at work. Surely you do not think the Amadh—"

"What does it matter?" Buford said, shifting his feet. "I don't care which Mizzie did it. Fact is, the ships're all infected—"

"Take it easy, Buford," David said. "Let the man talk."

"Did you get the rest of 'em on this ship?" Gerry asked.

"Not yet," Lozar said. "My detector bleeped, and I found four EMP emitters here, at this crossway."

"We oughta beat the stuffin' outta this Mizzie bastard," Buford said. The other man, who hadn't said anything yet, nodded, fists bunched.

"Just hold on there, boys," David said. "Other things're more important right now."

"Come on, Lozar," Gerry said. "Show us where those other dots are; we'll help you burn 'em out. We'll worry about who did what later."

Lozar set off toward the core control nexi, very aware of the four big determined men behind him. He could hear Gerry and David both muttering into handcoms. He felt worse and worse. He could imagine what Jari would say; he could imagine the betrothal dissolving, his poor daughter remaining unmarried for life because of her father's disgrace. Worse, he could imagine the anger of the non-Miznarii, so obvious in Buford . . . his family abused, even killed, because of what he'd done.

When they arrived at the central core of the ship, he saw that bulkhead panels now covered the nexus pod covers where he'd put the datadots; they had to pop each panel off and then locate the dots with the probes.

"We ought to strip these messages," David said. "Have a record of what it said."

"Why?" Buford asked. "Faster we scorch 'em, sooner we can get back—"

"Maybe it'll help on the other ships," Gerry said. "Just a few seconds can't hurt." He plugged a dot-reader onto the dot, and his handcom into the dot-reader. "I've got it going straight to Security. Lozar, show Buford the next one."

Grumbling, Buford did the same as Gerry. "Go on," he said. "Take Bub here to the next."

They were halfway through burning the nexus dots when a mechanical voice announced: "Seals closing in five . . . four . . . three . . ."

"What?" David whirled to look at Lozar. "What'd you do?"

"I didn't do anything . . . I'm just standing here—"

"Seals closed . . . secured . . ."

Down the passage, Gerry and the other two came running. "What'd you do—what happened?"

"Nothing," David said. "Ship sealed itself, I reckon. Or someone at dockside did it."

"Worst case, whatever was going on finished and now the bad guys have control—"

"The bridge," David said. "We've got to get to the bridge." He looked at Buford and Bubba. "You two—you know where to look for the nexus datadots now. Keep going. We're takin' Lozar to the bridge."

The ship shuddered. David and Gerry looked at each other. "Now," Gerry said. "C'mon, Lozar."

They ran upship, taking the direct route along the core, past the CCC, past the environmental tanks, past the mounts for the forward weapons. David smacked the controls for the personnel uptube, but Gerry shook his head. "I don't trust any of that now," he said. "Whoever's doing this has to know we've burned some dots; they know someone's inside. They could trap us . . ."

"And we don't have our full kits, right." They turned away from the uptube and went up a ladder. Suddenly the ship seemed to lurch, and Lozar's feet lifted off the rungs. Above him, Gerry seemed to be lying on air.

"Oh, bugger," David said from behind him. "They're playing with the artificial gravity. Lucky if they don't hit us with hypergrav in a few seconds . . . hold on with something . . ."

They'd made it to the deck below the bridge when gravity returned as suddenly as it had disappeared. Lozar slipped and landed hard on the deck. David and Gerry merely staggered. "Here," Gerry said, offering Lozar a hand up. "Implant compensators . . . too bad you don't have one."

"The other ships?" he asked.

"Don't know," David said. "When the ship sealed, we lost contact. If it's launched itself—"

Lozar made the connection himself. A sealed ship ran on its own internal power, or had none. The lights were on; air moved out of the ventilation grilles they passed. So at least the insystem drive was up, and that meant . . .

that could mean . . . they were out in space, undocked, going . . . who knew where?

"We told 'em what we found here," Gerry said. "Veenaji had already reported on the datadots and how many, and some of the other teams had found dots on the other ships—I heard that dockside—so maybe they were disabled elsewhere faster, and those ships are safe . . ."

"We aren't safe," Lozar whispered.

"No, but we also aren't bored," David said. "Whatever you say about today, it's not the same old same old." He grinned at Gerry. "Remember that old story I told you about in Rigger's last week?"

Gerry scowled. "If you mean that grandstander talking about a good day to die—"

David spread his hands. "What else? And if it has to be—"

"Death in the protection of true humanity is a great boon," Lozar offered.

"I wouldn't exactly call it a *boon*," David said, starting up the last ladder; they should come out in the bridge vestibule. "But if you hafta die, you might as well find a reason in it."

"My wife is not going to be happy about this," Gerry said. "Shari's told me time and again not to get mixed up in any daredevil stuff."

"You didn't exactly ask for it," David said. Lozar knew that David's wife had died seven years before; he himself had never met the woman, but from everything he'd heard she'd been as good a wife as an unbeliever could be. "She'll forgive you."

Gerry shook his head. Lozar thought of his own wife again with a pang of guilt. Would Jari forgive him? Would his daughters and his in-laws? Would the Almighty?

Then they were on to the bridge deck, in the little

vestibule, and the bridge hatch itself was still open.

"Where's the dot up here, Lozar?"

Lozar looked around. A lot more had been fitted into this space than bulkheads . . . communications equipment, seats for future crew covered with protective wrap, connectors for equipment that hadn't been installed yet. The entire vestibule had been open then.

"I—I'm not sure."

"Probe should find it," David said, waving his around. "There . . ."

Gerry had moved past David and now entered the silent bridge, about half its displays lit. In the center, a holo model of the station seemed to float in midair, little bright shapes around it.

"Lookit that," David said. He had burned the last dot, and now hung over the waist-high railing with Gerry. "That's the station . . . and where are we? Oh."

One tiny shape wore a gold halo. David pointed at it.

"Bugger," Gerry said. "We're undocked."

Lozar looked around. He had never been on the bridge of a completed ship before. So many displays, so many instruments, so many chairs. On storycubes, bridge crews mostly consisted of a captain seated in a big fancy chair. Like that one . . . Lozar went closer. Under the protective wrap, he could see a thin wand in its sleeve. He knew at once what it was: the command wand, famous in so many storycubes for breaking, failing, or falling into the wrong hands. For an instant, he had a fantasy of picking it up, sitting in that chair, and . . . and what? Saving the ship? Saving the station? What would the Almighty want him to do? Only those with implants could work ship controls, he'd always been told.

"Gerry? David?" He hated the way his voice wavered. They turned. "I found the captain's chair," Lozar said.

"Won't do us much good," Gerry said. "None of us knows squat about running a ship."

"We can try," David said. He ripped off the protective cover. "Look, here's the thingie—"

"David, you aren't serious—"

"Gerry, we're on a warship out in space with no trained crew, and the bad guys are running the ship. Sounds like a time for initiative to me."

"You read too many of those old books," Gerry said.

David was already in the seat; with his weight on the cushion, status lights in the armrest came on, and a screen rose out of the deck to position itself in front of him. "This is even better than the holosim," he said. "Watch this—" He slid the command wand out of its sheath. "There's gotta be a slot around here someplace."

"David, I don't think you should—"

"Aha!" David pushed the wand into a slot in the console.

AUTHENTICATION REQUIRED appeared on the screen. INPUT LICENSE NUMBER WITHOUT PUNCTUATION.

"Damn," David said. "I don't have a captain's license."

"Told you," Gerry said.

"But I do have a trade license . . . let's see." David stuck out his tongue, concentrating, and entered a long numeric string.

"It won't work," Gerry said. Lozar agreed silently. A Rigger One license wasn't a captain's license . . .

The screen flickered briefly, then WELCOME ABOARD CAPTAIN DAVID R. WATSON. CAPTAIN ON DECK. CAPTAIN'S ORDERS TAKE PRECEDENCE.

"Told you back," David said. "It doesn't know one license from another; it just needs numbers."

"David, you aren't a captain . . . you don't know—"

"I am now," David said, grinning. "Would you look at

that!" The display in front of him had a menu of choices, including ARM WEAPONS and RAISE SHIELDS. He touched RAISE SHIELDS, and other screens around the bridge came alive. "Gerry, get over there—" He pointed. "That chair. You're going to be my weapons officer—"

"David, you're crazy. I don't know anything about—"

"The ship doesn't know that. Lozar, I don't want you near any weapons, but I need someone on drives. That's . . . lemme see . . . over there."

Lozar went to the seat David had indicated. His mind whirled uselessly, like a child's holiday top. David wasn't a ship captain. Gerry wasn't a weapons expert, and anyway the ship's weapons hadn't been mounted yet.

"Hey, Gerry!" came a hail from the passage. "You'll never guess what we found—" Buford strode onto the bridge. "Oh, wow! Lookit this! It's like a storycube only better!"

"I am the captain, I am the captain!" David half sang, laughing. "The shipbrain accepted my trade license, can you believe? Boys, we got us a real spaceship!"

"What we've got is a real mess," Gerry said from the other side of the bridge. "David, you have gone plumb off your rocker. We're stuck on a ship none of us knows how to use, and it's controlled by whoever's invaded us . . ."

"It's not," David said. "You saw that message. Captain's aboard, captain's orders take precedence."

"Never mind that," Buford said. "We found the weapons."

"What weapons?"

"Well, they look like weapons. The ones in the story-cubes. There's one of those big long things with power warning stickers all over it. The mounts at this end of the ship are empty, but at the back—"

"Where's Bubba?"

"I'm here, Uncle Gerry. I went lookin' for more weapons and found racks of these long tube things, and some holes to put them in—I'll bet they're missiles."

"Don't touch those," Gerry said. Lozar saw the look that passed from Buford to Bubba.

"Er . . . Uncle Gerry . . . we kind of already did, sort of."

"What did you do?"

"Well . . . we thought if they were missiles, then they ought to be in the missile tubes where we could fire 'em. And Buford sort of thought he'd see if the missile control station was active—"

"And?"

"It wanted some kind of ID," Buford said. "So I input my station ID, and that did it."

"Boys, you don't even know how to aim the things—"

"It's easy, Uncle Gerry," Bubba said. "There's this screen with little ship icons and crosshairs and everything, just like a game."

Lozar's mind clicked on again. "These men—you are their uncle?"

Gerry grunted. "My sister's boy, Buford Claiborne. My brother's boy, Bubba . . . well, his real name's Beauregard Eustis, but we call him Bubba."

"And his real name's Gee-yorgy-ih Ham-eel-car D—"

"Shut your mouth, Buford," Gerry said. "You can't even pronounce it right yourself."

"All of you shut up," David said. "I gotta figure out where we're goin' and where we want to go. And if we can talk to anybody . . ."

"This is the communications board, isn't it?" Bubba asked. "I'll bet I can make it work . . ." He leaned over the seat and poked at the controls. "Dang, it wants another number."

"Just make one up," Buford said. "It won't know the difference."

Bubba tapped at the board. "Yup. Here it comes . . . Uncle Gerry, should I put it on speaker?"

"Might as well," Gerry said.

"—hear this? Can you hear this? Ship that was in Dock Thirty, can you hear—?"

Bubba leaned closer, both hands splayed out on the console for balance. "I can hear . . . who's this?"

A burst of static, then: "Take your fat finger off the TRANSMIT, you idiot!"

"There's no need to be rude," Bubba said, and took one hand off the console. To the others, he said, "How'm I supposed to know which is the TRANSMIT button?"

"Who am I talking to? Who's in charge?" demanded the voice.

Before Bubba could reply, David fumbled on the arm-rest of the captain's chair. A microphone rose from the back of the chair and curved around to his mouth. "This is Dave Watson, Rigger One on Frame Six. We got all the dots burned out."

"Where's the Miznarii spy? Isn't he on your ship?"

Lozar froze as four pairs of eyes stared at him. "I'm not—" he started to say, but his voice faltered.

David said, "Lozar's not a spy. He's just an idiot. He didn't know what he was doing."

The voice still sounded angry. "You just say that because—"

"I say that because I know him; he's our friend. Come on, we got him drunker'n spit last night, and had to listen to the whole story of how his second daughter landed the son of somebody important in their congregation, and how this meant his wife wouldn't have to suck up to someone else's wife, and all the way back to the girl he didn't marry because her father thought he wasn't good enough. And he was hungover this morning . . . you can't fake that, not that green look around the mouth and the red eyes. And since we've been on the ship he's been just . . . an idiot. He thought the datadots were harmless messages to other Miznarii."

"Messages to someone, and not harmless," the voice said. "We want you to put him in confinement and come back here so we can take him in for interrogation."

Lozar hunched in his chair. He could imagine all too well what that would be like.

David looked at him, and then at Gerry, and then over at Buford and Bubba. "You'd be usin' what kind of interrogation?"

"Whatever it took. Hell, the Mizzie deserves a mind-wipe and a scutter implant, for what he did . . ."

Again glances passed back and forth. David cleared his throat. "Well, you know, there's a problem."

"What problem? I can tell you how to link the ship to the station traffic control computer; it'll bring it in. Just don't let that Mizzie touch any controls."

"See, the thing is," David said slowly, "the ship thinks I'm the captain."

"You?" the voice said. "You aren't a captain!"

"I am now," David said. "Seems the ship just wanted a license number to hand the controls over to me, and my Rigger One license did the trick. And Buford and Bubba here, they've activated the weapons controls and communications, and Gerry's got shields, and old Lozar's on drives, so the thing is . . . I don't think this ship's gonna just roll over for any traffic control computer."

"But you have to make it—you can't bring it in by yourself; you don't know how."

"I don't want to bring it in," David said.

"You're one of *them*?" The voice rose to a shriek.

"Don't be stupid," David said. "I'm not one of those damned pirates or whatever, and I sure ain't a Miznarii. But we have invaders in the system, and I have a warship and a crew and some weapons—"

"You have *weapons*?"

"And if the bad guys think this ship is empty, maybe they'll come close enough we can blow their heads off."

"You . . . that's insane."

Gerry nodded vigorously from his seat, but with a grin on his face. David's grin was even wider.

"Hey, Thirty!" That was a new voice. "This is Seventeen—you gonna go fight?"

"Is that you, Allen?" Buford asked.

"Yeah, it's me. We got sealed in—you too? Beth and me, Ruta and Ferris, and Simram—he's a Mizzie but he's people, whatever they say on the station. Would you believe the ship took my license and made me captain! We got a forward beam, too: what've you got?"

"Stern beam, at least one, and some missiles."

"I've got a whole slew of mines," another voice chimed in. "Hemry here, in Eleven. But I'm not the captain. Lee got here first."

A gravelly voice broke in. "John, let your captain do the talking; I need you down there figuring out how to launch those damn things. Hey, David, how's it goin'? George is here and we've got Durgin, Burrell, and Fletcher with us. It's like a Swords meeting."

"*Be quiet!*" That was the station again. "None of you are going anywhere; none of you know how to—"

"We're wastin' time," yet another voice said. Precise, a different accent than the others. "Jody here, on Ten. Bill's here with me; we've got Kristine, the Schwartzes, and the Bonds. *Swords of the Spaceways!*"

"James on Nine; Rachel's here of course, and the Kerchevals and Godwin. Swords forever!"

"Underwood on Twenty-two. I never thought I'd get to be a spaceship captain for real! May and Nazarian are with me. Have we got the whole club? *En garde, mes amis!*"

"Twenty-eight, Hise here. I'm not sure how to run this thing but it took my number."

"Of course you can, Tom. Let me take over communications . . . Gorlison seems to be our pet Mizzie, and we've got Smith, Susan, Esther, and Clough from the club and a few others." Lozar recognized Jan's voice.

"Will you all shut up and *listen!*" The station again. Lozar watched David and Gerry just laugh. It was the Stationmaster himself now; they shouldn't be laughing.

"Latner here with Twenty-six. We have Richerson and the Zrubeks from the club. No, wait, Julia's here too. And Madeleine. Swords forever!"

"Mostly the Swords of the Spaceways club," David said. "I guess that figures. All the ships undocked?"

"No, Seventeen," Lee said. "But only eight have our people on 'em. The rest are still docked, but three more have sealed up, and there's no communication with them yet. Must not've reached the bridge. Say . . . is it true the Mizzie on your ship is the one who put the dots in?"

"He says so," David said. "But he didn't know what they were."

"Station wants him bad," Lee said.

Lozar hunched lower in his seat, watching David.

"They can't have him," David said. "He's not the brightest egg in the carton, but I'm not turning any friend of mine over to be mindwiped and forcibly implanted, no matter how stupid he is. It wasn't his fault; he was duped."

"Can we get video with this thing?" Allen asked. "I want to see this bozo."

"Come on, Lozar, nobody's going to hurt you," David said. On shaky legs, Lozar made his way around the central display tank to the communications console.

"I've seen you before," Allen said, when Lozar came into vid pickup range. Lozar barely remembered the balding redhead. Behind him, a thin woman with curly blond hair leaned for a look.

"Oh—I know you," she said. "Isn't your wife, Jari, on the Corridor Four children's activities committee? And isn't Mir your younger daughter? Our Meg is a friend of hers."

"That settles it," Allen said with a laugh. "We can't let anyone do anything to Lozar. Meg would have a fit."

Lozar remembered the blond woman and her redheaded daughter. "Please," he said. "Take care of my wife, my daughters—"

"Can't do that," Allen said. "We're in the same situation you are . . . all aboard the one-way express."

"Oh, Allen, don't be that way." The blond woman nudged him, then smiled into the vid pickup. "Lozar, don't worry. Even if we don't make it back, Meg won't let anything happen to your daughter."

"But if people hate Miznarii . . . because of me . . ."

"Don't worry about it. They won't take it out on her. Meg won't let them. And most people aren't like that anyway."

"She may not ever marry—"

"Is she pretty?" Buford put in. "*I'd* marry her if I get back alive—"

"Buford!" Gerry said. He sounded shocked.

Lozar *was* shocked. His daughter marry an unbeliever? He hardly listened to the banter that passed back and forth among captains Watson, Hartman, Martindale, Fawcett, Underwood, Sikes, Latner, and Hise, except to note that they kept making references to the long-running serial *Swords of the Spaceways*.

"We really ought to have some kind of plan," Gerry said suddenly. "Those things are a lot closer."

"Ram 'em," David said. "That always works in the vid cubes. Lozar! Give us full speed ahead or whatever that is . . . straight at 'em."

Lozar looked at the controls, none of which said anything like "full speed ahead." He prodded one sliding bar tentatively. On the screen in front of him, colored bars climbed up a set of lines, both with scales he couldn't read. He nudged the bar farther. It stopped. On one side was a red button with OVERRIDE engraved in the top and a warning notice beside it: OVERRIDING AUTOMATED ACCELERATION LIMITS IS NOT RECOMMENDED. REQUIRES CAPTAIN'S AUTHORIZATION.

"It won't let me make it faster unless you say it's all right," Lozar said.

David touched a control. "Try it now."

Lozar pushed the red button, which lit up from inside; a metallic voice said, "Warning. Max acceleration approved. Warning. Take hold."

"What are they thinking?" Major Douglas said. He knew from experience that if he'd been in the CCC he would not have had as good a view of scan—everything was angled for the admiral's convenience—and besides, he could comment to Hugh Pritang without distracting Admiral Vatta. The scan data on two of the rigger-crewed ships showed them accelerating rapidly straight toward two of the pirate ships. "That's a stupid course; they're dead meat—"

"They're not trained, Moray Command says," Hugh said. "I don't know why they didn't go back and let someone with expertise take over . . ."

"Look, there goes another one—" This time on a different course, apparently trying for another one of the attacker groups. "And those—" That for a group moving together, away from the combat zone toward the jump point.

"Uncrewed. Command thinks they're controlled by the pirates, due to some kind of sabotage—" Hugh paused to acknowledge Ky's order to microjump into attack position on the raiders.

"Too bad the riggers didn't just blow *them* up."

"They seem to have a suicide wish. Like something out of an entertainment vid."

"Maybe they're Romantics, like Teddy," Lee put in. Douglas looked at the pilot sharply, but Hugh shook his head. Nothing would convert Lee to full military courtesy.

"Riggers? I wouldn't think so," Hugh said. "I've met a lot of that sort and they're usually solid, sensible—well, except when drinking. But they do watch a lot of commercial entertainment, and if that's all they know about tactics—"

Vanguard, in concert with six other privateers and one Cascadian ship, now had a good angle on ten of the enemy. Hugh nodded to *Vanguard*'s weapons officer, and the ship quivered as the forward batteries launched. The enemy's counterlaunch came a full second after their own, and they were no longer there to receive it. Four of the enemy ships took damage; none of their own had more than a sparkle on the shields.

"Seems odd not to have Ky—the admiral—on the bridge," Hugh said. "She's better than I am—"

Douglas shook his head. "That looked good to me; we're still in one piece. Her ship dispositions seem odd— dispersed like this—but they work. I'm still not used to having instantaneous communication." He looked back at scan, relayed now from Baskerville's ship, close in to Tobados Yards. "Damn." The first of the rigger-crewed ships came under fire, its shields sparkling as pirate missiles struck them. "Well, at least they have their shields up, and they got some off—" Launch signatures, multiple. "Wonder what fusing options they'd used . . . if they've even heard of fusing options."

"There's another—" Now four of the eight rigger-crewed ships were engaged, though their methods made Hugh wince. "They have no idea how to range their shots, do they?"

"Why don't they engage their targeting computers?" Douglas said. "That's a good strong beam; they might even burn out a shield with it—"

"They probably don't know they *have* targeting computers—" Hugh said. "I can't understand why the ships let someone with no qualifications take control. Unless the sabotage damaged their AI somehow."

"See if Moray Command will relay some of their chatter—I have a morbid desire to know if they realize they're all going to die," Douglas said. "Or maybe we can give them some direction."

Moments later, Moray Command fed some of the previous minutes' transmissions from and among the rigger-crewed ships. Major Douglas shook his head as he listened. "I've never seen or heard anything like that. It's ridiculous; they're untrained civilians, not even ship crews, but—damn, they're brave."

"If only they knew what they were doing," Hugh said. "Wonder if they'd listen to us—there goes one—" The first of the rigger-crewed ships blew, though it was impossible to tell why, just from scan. "Listed as Nine, captain was Hartman."

Now all eight were engaged, tossing out missiles with

more enthusiasm than skill, stabbing away with their beams. Turek's ships microjumped out of the way after firing their own salvos, and ship after ship ran into a deadly fusillade and blew. The stolen warships, under enemy control on safer courses, were now accelerating toward the distant jump point.

Ky, in the CCC, at first missed the easy banter she'd had on *Vanguard*'s bridge when she was captain, but with every minute in the combat zone she appreciated more and more the wealth of data pouring into the CCC, the lack of distractions. She lost track of time, concentrating on the movement of the enemy ships, her ships, the Moray ships. For the first time she felt she had full understanding of what was happening in real time. Her orders could be more precise, more tuned to the situation. She had seen the rigger-crewed ships' erratic and ineffective maneuvers, but she also noticed that in evading them the pirates had put themselves in position for her ships to attack. She concentrated on that, moving ships with the best microjumping accuracy into position for attack and back out.

At first the enemy ships didn't realize what was happening, but after the first three blew, the others ignored the easy prey and returned more effective fire. Ky had positioned *Vanguard* between Tobados Yards and the jump point she expected the invaders to use for their escape, well outside the expanding danger zone, but most of her other ships were in the thick of it, shields flaring as debris or weapons intercepted their course. Moray's defenders, unused to her style of fighting and unsure of her commands, were slower to respond; two more of them died as she watched.

This time Turek's force did not stick to the familiar X-attack pattern they had used before. Ky struggled to analyze the difference. Douglas and Yamini had located a copy of Baines' *Practical Tactics for Regional Conflicts* and Ky had loaded it in her implant, but had not come up with a good way to classify the variations. If Turek was using only that one book—and yes, there it was, finally. Baines didn't list the ideal countering moves, but logically—she moved five of her ships, and sure enough they were able to blow another of Turek's with only minor damage to one of hers.

Still, the attackers stayed in formation and continued to fire on Ky's forces, though they were retreating slowly away from Tobados Yards and Moray's main planet—and a third of them formed a protective shield around the eight uncrewed ships they were controlling.

"Keep after them," Ky said. "If you can get something through to take out those warships—" But so far the new ships' shields had held and their guardians kept her ships far enough away that no close straight shot was possible.

TWELVE

Three enemy icons moved against the flow . . . as in the battle at the Boxtop ansible, Ky noticed the aberrant movement even before the computer analysis pointed it out.

"Twenty-seven," she said on her all-ships channel. "That's their commander and his escort."

"They read like Bissonet ships, but their IDs aren't the same as at Boxtop," Douglas said. "They've changed ship-chips again."

"That's not the point," Ky said. "That's Turek heading for safety. He made it at Boxtop; I'm not going to let it happen again—"

"Everyone's engaged—"

Ky could see that. Only the little group of three turned from the area of battle to move directly toward the jump point.

"They think they won't be noticed," she said.

"Or they really need those ships and are hoping to distract us."

"They're covering Turek's escape," Ky said. "And we're the only ones with a vector on him."

"You can't go after him alone!" Yamini said. "Remember your structural damage—"

"We're the only ones with a chance. And we still need to knock out those other warships if we can." The displays made that clear. She called the bridge. "Captain Pritang, we have a chance to stop Turek before he makes it to jump. We need to be in range for a max-power beam—if we can paint him for ten seconds, that should do it. Looks like we have a clear place to microjump."

"Yes, ma'am," Hugh said. He sounded eager.

Quickly, Ky told the unit commanders that *Vanguard* would be in pursuit of Turek, but to continue with their engagements.

"We can come help," Teddy Ransome said.

The last thing she needed was Teddy's lightly armed little ship getting in the way.

"Stay where you are," she said. "Everyone needs your observations."

"My stuff's too lightlagged to be of use now," Teddy said. On the scan, his ship had already begun moving on an intersecting course. "I can help you—"

The idiot. The loose cannon. Other labels raced through Ky's mind but she ignored them. If he got between her and her target, that would be his problem. "Stay out of range, and out of my line of fire," she said.

"Yes, ma'am!" he said, as if he hadn't already disobeyed one order.

Hugh chose an initial microjump to bring *Vanguard* a half hour closer to Turek's ship, then boosted with insystem drive. Minute by minute, *Vanguard* closed in. Ky watched the range diminish.

"Target in range," he said finally. "Forward batteries—"

The missiles were away, but would that be enough? They were close enough now for the beam. Hugh would have to drop the forward shields for a sustained burn, but Turek was fleeing; he'd offered no attack. There'd been nothing on scan from his escorts, either, no sign of live munitions being dropped.

"Beam?" Hugh asked.

"Go ahead," Ky said. "But watch the temperature on those mounts. Let's not tear our own ship apart."

"Yes, ma'am," Hugh said.

Ky watched on her readouts as the beam stabbed out, pinned Turek's ship—sparkling and then steadying on its shields. She began counting seconds . . . one, two, three, five . . . surely Turek's shields would have to fail soon. Was that a flare—? But the beam readout surged upward suddenly. Had Hugh missed it? She started to speak—

The canopy blanked, locking Ky into the command chair; her head snapped back, smacking into the back of the chair hard enough to stun her. Her body tugged against the restraints as the CCC's gravity compensators took over from Vanguard's. She felt the shove of acceleration again, and then again, before the gravity compensators caught up. Then something else hit her head and she felt nothing for a time.

She woke from a dream of loud music in a strobe-lit nightclub. As she blinked, dazed and unsure what had happened, her HUD showed miniatures of the screens in the rest of the CCC—half of them blank after a flare of white. Red warning lights flashed on and off. She heard nothing but a ringing in her ears.

"Helm!"

No answer.

"Lee? Hugh?"

No answer. She toggled to ansible with a moment's satisfaction at having insisted that she have one, checked that she was on their most secure channel.

"Vanguard, Vatta here. Report!"

"Admiral Vatta! You're alive—!" She didn't recognize the

voice but her implant parsed it as *Treebear*'s Captain Moscoe. "How many others are with you?"

"I don't know," Ky said. If they thought whatever had happened might have killed her, the ship must have been holed. "I get no answer from the bridge—"

"*Vanguard* blew." That was Pettygrew's voice, and *Bassoon*'s icon, familiar. "You were using the beam—" She remembered that. "—and we think they'd left a mine-burst the beam triggered."

She remembered now, seeing the readout for the beam climbing into the danger zone—she'd been about to tell Hugh to shut it off, but Turek's ship had been so close . . .

"We'll send someone, now that we know which chunk of debris you are," Pettygrew said. "How's your life support?"

"I'm fine," Ky said. Chunk of debris? So . . . had anyone else survived? A wave of black misery swept over her— had she killed all her friends? "My chair canopy's blanked, but I should have up to twenty hours. What about others?"

"We've got some suit beacons," Pettygrew said. "No contacts so far, though."

Ky touched the control that should have opened her chair canopy if life support in the CCC had held. The canopy did not move. Neither, she found, did the chair rotate on its base, as it should. She could feel the faint vibration of the servomotors, but no movement occurred. Could she even clear the canopy? She found that control . . . the canopy cleared more slowly than usual and showed her the wreckage beyond, lit by the chair's own emergency lights. Something had come through the armored bulkhead—the supposedly impregnable armored bulkhead— and severed one of the other chairs at what had been its occupant's waist. Whatever it was—a jagged piece of something she could not identify—protruded from the bulkhead beyond. Another chair, its canopy closed and opaqued, tilted crazily to one side. Only one was upright, sealed. A suit of space armor, off to the left, moved slightly, like a weird insect found under a log.

"Situation?" But even as she asked, several of the displays came back on. "Wait—I'm getting data. I'm seeing enemy icons about two light-hours outbound—is that right? And all our other ships are undamaged?"

"Right, Commander. *Vanguard*'s the only one with significant damage."

"What do our scouts report?"

"Clean sweep. No enemy chatter for the past hour—" Hour? How long had she been out of contact? Had she blacked out and not known it? "No gravitational anomalies that might be stealthed observers."

"Then we need to pick up survivors but be alert for a sudden return. If they realize they've blown *Vanguard* they might jump back in . . ."

"Moray Defense is working on that, ma'am. They've sent crews to their remote installations, though it'll be days yet. We need to get you to one of the stations first."

"No, I'm fine. Pick up any suit beacon first." Ky stared at the monitors, forcing herself to think only of the situation outside. "Did they get any of the new ships?"

"Yes. Nine of them. What we're hearing from Moray is that agents had sabotaged the ships, allowing the enemy to gain control. All those crewed by riggers were lost—that happened before you were hit."

"Nine . . . that's not so many, except that they're new. Weapons mounted?"

"Weapons aboard, not all mounted. Not fully loaded out, though."

Ky thought again, then made her dispositions. Cascadian contingent here, to do this, in case of trouble.

Slotter Key contingent there, ditto. Ransome to transport someone to do ansible repair, if Moray didn't have the resources.

"Ransome's gone, ma'am."

"Gone? Killed?"

"No, ma'am . . . right after *Vanguard* blew, he torched up and went in pursuit of the enemy ships. Didn't answer hails or anything. Went into FTL about the same time they did . . . er . . . zero point oh one seconds after they did. Moray Defense was asking if I thought he'd been a conspirator . . ."

"No, he's being a Romantic," Ky said. If she could have laughed at anything, she'd have laughed at this idiocy: one little ship, chasing after Turek's entire fleet. "What about Baskerville?"

"He followed Ransome . . . two loose cannons . . ." Pettygrew had never liked Ransome. Pitt was looking at her now, and tapping her helmet cover.

"Excuse me," Ky said. "People are waking up; I'll give you a report later."

"Admiral's aboard," Pettygrew reported. "*Bassoon*'s headed in."

Ky looked around. The Bissonet ship, much smaller than *Vanguard,* nonetheless had a pure military feel that *Vanguard* had never quite achieved. It had its own tiny CCC off the bridge—hardly more than a closet, but packed with electronic gear. The crew saluted her and Pettygrew smartly. Nothing looked at all merchant-like.

She felt shaky, which annoyed her; she had a blinding headache and ached in every muscle. The medics in *Bassoon*'s tiny sick bay insisted on putting her down for a few hours while they checked her over.

"No bones broken, no internal bleeding, but Admiral,

we strongly advise you take it easy, and you definitely need to be checked out in a real medical center when we get back to a station."

"I'll be fine," Ky said. She was not about to lie in bed while other people's bodies—her crew's bodies, her friends' bodies—were scattered in a debris field and could not even be gathered for decent disposal and memorial. She struggled off the exam table and started dressing. "I need to speak to the captain."

"I know the system ansible's still down," she said to Pettygrew a few minutes later. "But it occurred to me that if Turek saw my ship blow, he might think I was dead. And that might be good for us. So please inform the other ships that no one is to mention my being alive on any transmission outside this system. I'll tell the Moray government as well—"

In the three standard days it took to reach Tobados Yards station, Ky learned more about Pettygrew and his crew than she had in the long months before. He was married and had three children—if they were still alive back on Bissonet. Over half his crew were from the same district, Valrhona Hills, and most were also married.

"We try not to think about it," he said, when Ky asked how he was dealing with the possibility that his crew's families, as well as his own, were dead or under control of the enemy. "We know you lost your whole family and you're staying focused on the task at hand. If you—pardon the implication that you might be expected to be less able, but you are younger—if you can get past that, we can. We must. Our families' only hope is our victory—our return to free them, if they are alive."

"If we knew his total force, we could guess if he'll have to pull people off Bissonet to take Nexus."

"If he takes every ship there, destroys the shuttles and

the ansible, the downside population won't be able to do anything. All the shipyards are up in space. He could pull his occupying force, if he left one, and it wouldn't help."

When they arrived at the Tobados Yards station, Moray's senior military commander had already set up meetings with shipyard and military personnel, and Tobados itself had already decided (perhaps with help from the Moray government) that the best use of its remaining heavy cruisers would be under Ky's command.

"I have too much on my plate to spend time lounging around a clinic," Ky said. She had accepted an initial evaluation to satisfy Pettygrew, but she was not going to check in. "Yes, I have a headache. Yes, I'm sore. I'll get over it. We have a war to fight; we've got to stop Turek." This was her first conference with her captains since the battle. "Much more critical than my very minor injuries is recognizing your very important actions—you saved not just some warships from Turek's control, but these people from certain death. And you proved that a multisource force can fight together and be effective."

"With the right commander," Argelos muttered. Others nodded, even Merced.

"Most of you had never fought with me before—or with each other—or with onboard ansibles—and yet in a short time you were able to learn how to do it and remember it in the stress of combat. Every one of you—" She made eye contact with each one in person for those at Tobados or on screen for those on patrol, and named them, one by one. "Each of you played an essential part in this victory, and I commend you all."

"But he ran," Merced said. "He took his ships away; it wasn't a complete victory."

The collective sigh from the others made it clear that Merced had been saying the same thing before. Vassli,

Merced's military adviser on *Termagant*, looked particularly pained. Ky chuckled. "Captain Merced, driving the enemy to retreat is usually considered victory. But you're right, one rout does not make a victory. It will be victory when we have destroyed Turek's fleet, and killed Turek— and that will come. You will have plenty of fighting in your future, Captain Merced."

"As long as you don't stop now and think the job's done," Merced said.

"Turek killed my entire family," Ky said. "I'm not likely to stop now."

Merced subsided, and Ky led the discussion where she intended, to the next steps to be taken.

Teddy Ransome suspected that Admiral Vatta would not have approved of what he was doing. But that gallant officer had surely died with her ship, and he was not going to let her death go unavenged.

It was risky in the extreme to tuck little *Glorious* into the tail of the formation Turek led. Everyone knew it was impossible to tail ships in FTL space. Undetermined location and all that. But . . . *but,* he told himself, no one had ever tried it the way he was trying it. He knew the science was vague, even vaguer in that science had never been his favorite subject. But he could do nothing more for Admiral Vatta in Moray System, and if he could avenge her—it was worth any risk. Moreover, the discovery that his comtech could tune their shipboard ansible with that of a pirate vessel suggested to him that the space-folding of ansible physics and the indeterminate space of FTL might have something in common. Was it enough? He would find out.

His ship had gone into jump on the heels of Turek's fleet, and they had been in FTL space for six days now.

Not a long jump, as jumps go, but he might be jumping in the wrong direction, for all he knew.

His mind replayed the death of *Vanguard* over and over. It was one thing for his friends to die, as Dennis had done. He knew this was the death they had wanted to die. But Ky Vatta was—had been—different. He suspected she did not believe everything he said, thinking him the soppier sort of Romantic, but she had been the one true thing, the one ideal woman—beautiful and exotic and brilliant and brave—and he had seen himself protecting her, fighting alongside her, finally winning her regard and—in the rosiest of his visions—joining him in partnership forever.

And now she was dead. Blown apart, not even fragments to rejoin and mourn in a funeral service, to be laid in a proper mausoleum where he could come with wreaths and mourning scrolls, and water the stone with his tears.

Just dead. Worse, he had not protected her. He had not been between her and danger; she had outstripped his honor and taken danger on herself, and if this made her even more a hero, even more his soul mate, it was too late.

He would make up for it as much as he could. Turek would die by his hand.

After the meeting with her captains—only the first of many, she assured them—Ky met with local officials of Tobados Yards and the station government.

"Right before the alarm," Kendelmann, the station's security chief, said, "we had some anomalous deaths way outside the statistical norms. All were healthy professionals working for subcontractors at the shipyard. No prior health flags on their records, completely unexpected. But when we looked, they'd all had opportunities to do something, get in at least second-degree contact with the ships in production. We dug deeper, turned up some interesting details: gambling debts, embezzlement, scandals of one kind or another. Aside from that idiot Lozar, whose friends are sure he was duped by his religious leader, they were all blackmailable, every one of them. If they were killed to prevent their talking later—"

"Then someone higher up in Turek's organization is still here."

"Yes. We halted all civilian traffic as well as blocking ansible access. But we don't know who—we haven't found anything else. It's difficult here. Moray's older than you younger worlds, closer to the Central Alliance. We get people from all over, and always have. With travel and trade down, our economy tanked, but I don't know why anyone would think pirates were the right answer."

"Hungry people will listen to any promise of food," Ky said. "They were promised business, profit. You had new contracts for ships enough to restart your economy . . . that would make a lot of people happy."

"We need to find their agent," he said, scowling. "Or agents."

"If they're using Turek's private language," Ky said, "I can help with that. We have a lot of transmissions, a lot of text, and at least partial translation. I think you should monitor the ansible traffic out of here, as well as look for one of the small portable ansibles we use on our ships. Turek has them, too, as we told your government before we left Cascadia. Someone here might have one."

"So . . . someone here might have told him that you're alive?"

"If they had such an ansible, yes. Even if not, they'll probably pass a coded message through the system ansible. Thing is, if they use one of the pirates' ansibles, they can communicate only with Turek's people—so any rumors of my death will have come through his network, his agents."

"We haven't opened ansible service for private communication yet," he said. "We've said we're still working on damage repair."

"I'd keep it that way," Ky said. "In the meantime, if you want, I'll bring you a file of code phrases to watch for. I won't ping it to you—I don't know how secure your communications are."

For an instant, he looked offended, then he shook his head. "Too long a peace, too little suspicion," he said. "I was acting like a police chief, dealing with ordinary crime, when I should—"

Ky shook her head. "Don't start that. Guilt's a luxury sometimes. You know more about the station and its people than anyone else—we need you."

He stared, then laughed. "I can see how someone your age got to be a fleet commander. Sorry. Yes, of course. Please let me see just as much of that as you think I need to keep an eye out. Meanwhile, since there very well may be one of Turek's people here, I assume you're taking precautions yourself?"

"Indeed yes," Ky said. "But I would prefer not to tell even you what all of them are." Though Master Sergeant Pitt could not look like anything but what she was, a combat veteran, she passed well enough as a civilian security escort, and between her and the others on the team, Ky felt as secure as any logical target of assassination could.

Nonetheless, walking down the concourse later that day, on the way to a conference with Moray's senior military command, she was on full alert. The concourse looked normal—as normal as any business area shortly after an enemy attack, at least. Stores were open; pushcarts to either side sold flowers, trinkets, small electronics.

People moved in and out, no longer looking grim and frightened as they had the day she arrived. Some turned to look at her; some smiled.

Ahead, at a cross-corridor, someone looked, then shifted back. Ky stopped abruptly; her rear escort bumped into her; the one to the right stumbled. Ky dropped, rolling left, as she said "Scatter!" She heard a click as something struck the tiles near her, and slapped a mask on her face before she stopped rolling or took a breath. Yells came from up the corridor, sudden noises of things crashing, breaking—and Pitt's voice over all.

"Got one!"

"'M all right," her escort on the right mumbled. "Vest stopped it . . ." He, too, had put on a temporary mask, slapping it on so hard that it had pulled one side of his mouth awry.

Ky looked at the object on the tiles . . . a glassy blob that disappeared as she watched, sublimating and leaving behind a colorless residue. Her escort reached out a gloved finger.

"No!" Ky said sharply. "That's for forensics, and they'll need a hazardous materials team. My guess is it will go through ordinary fabrics."

"My armor—?"

"We'll get you to a secure medical facility, just in case." Ky queried Pitt as Station Security arrived.

"There were two," Pitt reported. "One's dead; I got a telltag on the other and I'm following but with caution. I don't know what they're using."

"The round I saw was clear; it disappeared and left a liquid residue," Ky said.

"Typical assassin's round, then. Anyone hit had better go to med, and have it cleaned off very carefully before disrobing. If they're alive."

"He's alive," Ky said. "How long will ordinary armor hold up?"

"Maybe an hour. If Station Security's there, can you send me backup? Tsongo and Eklund for preference."

"Right away." Ky told Tsongo to link with Pitt, and pointed out the residue location to Station Security. They'd brought a medic, who immediately called in transport for Evans and a hazmat team to clear up the residue. She checked in with Argelos.

"You should come back aboard—we can keep you safe—"

"I still need to make that meeting with the Moray military," Ky said. "Station Security's got an escort for me."

"Are they as good as Pitt?" he asked. "Or my people?"

Ky smiled at the worried-looking senior security officer in Moray green. "I'm on their turf; I'm sure they'll take care of me."

"We can't afford to lose you," Argelos said. "Seriously."

"I understand," Ky said. "Though I don't necessarily agree. I'll report in when I'm in the meeting." She closed the connection and turned to the officer. "What's bothering you, besides having an assassin running around your station?"

"Your people chasing the assassin," he answered. "How are we supposed to know which is which?"

"Your database has all our people. Master Sergeant Pitt says she has a tagger on one assassin, and Tsongo and Eklund are with her or close behind."

"Ah. I'll tell the boss—he'll send out those IDs. We don't want to get your people by mistake. And now, Admiral, we need to get you to that meeting. A vehicle?"

"Not unless you think it's necessary," Ky said. "A vehicle's a bigger target."

On the way, two more of her own people showed up

to augment the escort, and Pitt called in to report that the assassin had gone through a hatch she couldn't open without breaking regulations as well as the locks.

"This station's as secure as church cheese," she said. "The bad guys apparently have at least some of the security codes. Best tell your meeting that, and hope nobody drops anything in the ventilation . . ."

"I have a mask," Ky said. "The important thing is to keep whoever it is from using an ansible and letting Turek know I'm still alive."

"If you get killed, then it doesn't matter," Pitt said. "You know, you're a stubborn woman, and I couldn't say that to just any officer."

Ky snorted. "Certainly not one in your chain of command."

She could almost see Pitt shaking her head, from the tone. "Ma'am, I begin to be glad I *couldn't* recruit you."

Ky's staff and Argelos were already there when she arrived at the meeting. Moray's senior military command stood when Ky came in. "We heard what happened." Admiral-major Hetherson, stocky and gray-haired, shook his head. "What is it coming to, with assassins roaming our concourses?"

"Nasty kind of war," Argelos said. "If they'd gotten you—"

"I'd be dead," Ky said. "Pitt says she got one; pursuit continues . . . I hope whoever it is doesn't get to their ansible."

"You think they have their own?"

Ky nodded. "It would have been reasonable for Turek to give each of his main contacts in different systems one of the small ansibles, even though most of their communication may well have been through the commercial ones. No one suspected they existed; there was little risk until

I captured Osman's ship. And if they're using the same model I found, anything as big as an ordinary desk might conceal one."

"Security's on it." Pitt entered, her uniform marked with a single suggestive spot on the upper right arm. "Admiral, I'd like permission to contact Mackensee HQ about this."

Major Douglas, still in a sealed medical unit, should have been the one. The medical center had done its best but made it clear they did not expect him to live. Only three other intact suits had been found; all the people in them were dead.

"I'd prefer not to let anyone out of this system know I'm alive," Ky said. "Too many chances of leakage."

Pitt's expression said she didn't think Mackensee communications channels would leak, but she merely said, "Yes, ma'am. I understand."

Ky stared into the darkness. She had not slept well since the battle, and worse after the assassination attempt. Though she'd instructed her implant to put her to sleep, once more she'd wakened early, exhausted, her bed soaked with sweat. Once more the faces of her dead had loomed over her as she slept, once more their sad or accusing expressions had melded with remembered sounds, smells, sights.

A soft noise from the far side of the room brought her upright, heart pounding. She flicked on the bedside light. The top sheet of a stack of plasfilms, its edge waving in the air current from the air vent, flicked not-quite-rhythmically against the handle of a mug.

She lay back against the pillow, trying to slow her heartbeat, but her thoughts raced down one mental corridor after another, banging into walls and closed doors, whirling

and racing another way. Her father—she hadn't told him—
she hadn't confided—what would he think? Her mother—
her father's view of her dead mother's face in the
swimming pool, his reaction to it, all still lay embedded
in the implant's synthetic memory. She had considered
deleting those cells, but how could she destroy the last
memory, the last sight?

And now the others crowded in . . . Gary Tobai, who
had died to save her. The enemy spy murdered by his mas-
ters right in front of her . . . and now all those on *Vanguard.*
She had a list of the names; she had made a list of the
names, and now her implant fed them to her, one by one.
Those who had been with her from the beginning, like
Lee and Mehar. Those who had joined later . . . and later
still . . . she named them all. Even Teddy Ransome, that
Romantic fool . . .

Why was she still alive? Who was she to still be alive,
when so many good people were dead, because of her? It
felt as if a whole universe of virtuous dead were crushing
her into their scorn, their anger. They had been brave; they
had been steadfast; they had been loyal. She . . . she had
led them to their deaths, and yet . . . she lived.

Once, she might have taken refuge in her faith, her
family's legacy of belief in the harmony of the universe,
the sweet cycle of color and sound that she had been
taught from childhood would sustain her in any trouble,
calm her. But she had lost that faith some time back, when
she could not visualize the cycle of colors that had always
worked before. Was it because she had killed? Because she
had enjoyed killing? Because she had enjoyed killing a
Vatta, Stella's birth-father?

Do not judge, her mother had told her. *We are Saphiric
Cyclans; we do not judge; we do not create disharmony.* Which
was silly . . . her mother judged all the time—she judged

people by their clothes, their education, their professional qualifications. But that was different. She'd been told it was different.

We are not exactly pacifists; we agree that self-defense may be necessary, her mother's remembered voice went on. *But we take no pleasure in violence.* One of many lectures she and her brothers had received, after someone came home with cuts or bruises from mock battles in the tik plantation. Ky and San had privately agreed that grown-ups must be very different indeed . . . neither of them could imagine not enjoying a clod fight.

But now she, Ky, had taken such pleasure in violence, as an adult. She had killed, up close. She had blown up ships—ships like the one she had lost. She didn't even know how many people had died because of her . . . and that some of them were bad people, who had spent their lives hurting others, didn't make much difference this dark night. She shivered.

Rafe might understand. But was understanding what she wanted? If it was wrong—and everything in her background told her it was wrong, that her parents, if alive, would be appalled and ashamed—then she should not be coddled, comforted by agreement that it had all been necessary.

The alarm chimed, breaking her concentration. She rose, showered, dressed without looking in the mirror— she was the last person she wanted to see—and went directly to the staff room set up for her. She had no desire for food.

Pitt was there, laying out folders with the steady concentrated expression characteristic of her. Ky felt her shoulders tighten. Pitt's senior officer was another death to be piled on the stack of Ky's guilt. He had been a good officer, as steady as Pitt; he had been the sort she'd gladly follow.

And he'd chosen to observe the battle from *Vanguard*'s bridge, while she had taken refuge in the CCC. He had been recovered, barely alive . . . he had died two days after arrival at Tobados Yards.

Pitt glanced up, having placed the last folder. "You're early, ma'am."

Ky muttered, "Morning, Master Sergeant."

Pitt took a step toward her; Ky struggled not to flinch. "You look like hell," Pitt said after a moment. "What did you have for breakfast?"

"Wasn't hungry," Ky said. She opened the folder at her place. Why did every meeting have to start with the same boring, useless trivia?

"Supper?" Pitt said.

Ky shrugged. "I don't remember. Something." List of attendees and their positions. Report of the previous meeting by someone—a Moray officer, she forced herself to notice. Agenda.

Pitt came closer; startled, Ky whipped around, hand reaching for her weapon. Pitt stopped short; her eyes widened for an instant, then narrowed. "Admiral," she said, in a voice softer than her usual. "You need something for breakfast. I'll order—"

"No!" Ky was shocked at the tone of her own voice. She sounded angry and frantic both. "I don't need—"

"You need food and sleep," Pitt said. "With all due respect, ma'am, I do know what's eating you and what you need—"

"You don't—" Ky said. Her eyes burned—not tears, she was not about to cry, she was just so tired, not sleeping.

"It's over an hour to the meeting. You have time for food—and you're not doing anyone good the way you are—"

"You think I don't know that?" Ky glared at Pitt, but Pitt didn't budge. "I have to be—"

"Fed," Pitt said. "Sit down, now."

As if someone had hit her behind the knees, Ky half fell into the chair.

"I'm going to bring you food. No one will come in; I'll secure the room."

It was entirely too much like Master Sergeant MacRobert and the day she'd been kicked out of Spaceforce. Ky fought back a giggle she knew was half hysterical. Her head hurt; her eyes hurt; every muscle and bone . . . she leaned forward, holding her head in her hands, pushing into them until she couldn't feel them tremble. She squeezed her eyes closed.

"Start with this," Pitt said. Under Ky's nose she put a tray full of food: eggs, potatoes. For one moment it smelled delicious—then suddenly nauseating.

"I can't eat all that," Ky said.

"Give your stomach a chance," Pitt said. "You've skipped too many meals. And don't hurry."

Ky took a cautious bite. From inside her mouth, the taste and smell went straight to her brain, it seemed. She didn't realize she'd eaten it all until it was gone.

"A start," Pitt said. "Drink your juice." Ky hadn't noticed the juice; when she tasted it, it was tart and refreshing.

"What time—?" Ky began; Pitt held up her hand.

"Don't worry about that. I put the meeting back an hour. Said you had something you had to do."

"But—"

"And you do. Now, this is not the way I usually operate, you understand. But you and I, we have an odd situation here. You outrank me, but I'm not in your chain of command. And yet you're the only commander I have on scene. And yet, again, I'm older than you are and I've seen a few more wars than you have. Not nastier, but more."

Ky pulled her scattered wits together. "So?"

"So, with all due respect, and that's a lot, because like I told my people way back when, you are a remarkable young officer . . . with all due respect, you have dug yourself into a hole and we need to get you out so you can go on doing what you do best." She cocked her head; when Ky didn't answer she gave it a quick shake. "What you do best, ma'am, is command in combat. You are a natural, and you have enough training to add skill to natural instinct."

"I thought I just got my friends killed," Ky said.

"Ah. And that, you see, is the hole you've dug yourself into." As Ky shifted uneasily, Pitt held up her hand again. "Everyone does it. All the decent people, anyway. Nobody gets out of combat without scars. You, me, all my friends, everybody you know. Nobody. Most of us—well, lots of us, anyway—were brought up to be good, decent citizens of wherever we grew up. Religious, some of us. We had all sorts of social rules for how to behave, among them not killing other people, and not letting friends get hurt if we could help it. You had that kind of raisin', didn't you?"

"I guess so . . ."

"And now you kill people for a living."

Said that way, as stark as that, it hit like a blow to the belly. Ky sucked in a breath, stiffened. Pitt went on.

"But the thing is, if you didn't, the people who do nothin' *but* kill for a living would win. If you hadn't come in to Boxtop and shot up some enemy ships, I'd be dead, for one. So would a lot of my friends."

"I . . . can't . . ."

"Can't think of it that way? That's the hole you dug. You can undig it, but you need some help."

"You're a therapist?" Ky said, her voice rough.

"Not me, ma'am. But you need one, right enough."

"I don't have *time*," Ky said. Her fists had clenched without her noticing.

"We—and I'm talking everyone here and everyone waitin' back at Nexus for you to show up—don't have time for you to go crazy on your own and do something stupid and maybe not live over it."

Ky's head came up; she glared at Pitt. "What do you think—"

"I know. I know what someone like you—an honorable person who's been through eight kinds of hell since you left home—is likely to think and, worse, do if you don't get the help you need."

"And you think Turek will wait while I take a rest cure?" Ky said.

"No. An' I'm not suggestin' a rest cure. You don't need that; you need five days of appropriate military-based mental health intervention, followed by a period of appropriate medication—no, I don't mean drugging you into not caring. I mean what clears your head enough to think straight, which right now, ma'am, you are not doing. The way you tore into that poor guy in yesterday's meeting . . ."

Ky could barely remember that. She had been angry, that's all . . . but the food had cleared her head just enough.

"I'm not sleeping well," she said. It was not an excuse, she knew that, but it was in part the reason.

"I figured," Pitt said.

"I tried the implant setting—it used to work—"

"Your stress hormones are up about five notches," Pitt said. "It's set for normal brains." She paused, then leaned forward a little. "Have you ever cleaned out the stuff your father left when he died?"

"How'd you know about that?"

"Martin told me. And I'll tell you what they told me: archive it all in external storage, as many copies as you want, but get it the hell out of your head."

"It's my *mother* . . ."

"It's not. It's someone else's memory of a horror involving your mother, I'm assuming your father's memory. And then he died. I don't care what your religion says, carrying around that kind of memory is like sleeping with a rotting corpse—"

Anger flared; Ky fought it down. "What *they* told you?"

"Personal, ma'am, the details. But I had something in my implant as toxic as what you have in yours. Thing about implants, they told me, is it's worse than traumatic memories in the brain itself . . . the implant can't forget and can't remodel the memories to something tolerable. You can treat the trauma in the brain, but if you don't get it out of the implant . . . it always comes back."

"I don't know . . ." Ky said. Her stomach rumbled.

"External storage preserves it, if you need it, but you shouldn't access it for half a standard year, minimum. I kept mine five years, then dumped it. Knew I didn't need it, wouldn't want it. The wetware memory was enough to deal with, and I had dealt with it. I'll be back . . ." Pitt left the room again.

Ky felt shaky, as if the room itself were trembling. She put out her hand . . . no visible tremor at least. It was ridiculous. She didn't have time for this. She didn't have energy for this . . .

"Second course," Pitt said. "Get this into you, but slower."

Ky was halfway through that plateful when she realized she had not taken any of the precautions against possible toxins that she had been advised to take until they caught the assassins. She stopped with the fork halfway to her mouth.

"It's all right," Pitt said. "I checked it. But you see what I mean. You're not fit, right now."

"I have to be fit," Ky said grimly.

"Yes. Which means you're going to have to do something about it. No one can make you. Nobody in your force outranks you; you don't have a proper medical assessment board set up yet; the Moray people are halfway between worship and stark panic. You're the only one who can get yourself fit."

Ky thought about it, realizing even as she did that it was far too hard to think. If she tried developing a battle plan and commanding in battle as cloudy as she felt . . .

"So . . . what do I do? What facilities do we—they—have?"

Pitt just looked at her for a moment. "Here's what I think would work to maintain your command's confidence in you, and return you to full capacity as fast as possible. It's based on what Mackensee uses, with available local resources . . ."

"Which you've already researched."

"Yes," Pitt said, with an expression that dared Ky to object. "Yes, I did, ma'am, and for a good reason. Staff should always be prepared with what the commander needs to know."

"Right," Ky said. She took another bite of the food.

"You tell your command—your captains, the senior Moray officers—that you've realized you're having more sequelae from *Vanguard*'s blowup than you knew, and you want to get it worked on while they're fitting out the new ships. You've got people qualified to supervise that, and until you hear from Cascadia if that girl's been able to figure out where Turek's headed, you can't do much planning." She paused. "Though you do need to build a new staff, same organization basically, and just a suggestion—include some Moray officers."

Ky's head ached again, but less. Through the fog she could now perceive, all this made sense. "They'll think I'm . . ."

"Very wise," Pitt said, before Ky could finish. "Look, ma'am, I know I'm way out of line, but I'm the only one who can talk to you this straight. What you do is go back to your quarters, shower again, put on a clean uniform—"

Ky looked down at herself . . . she had just grabbed one without checking, she realized, and that was completely unprofessional.

"—and come back here and tell them," Pitt said. "Make your own dispositions, of course, but I'd recommend you include a Slotter Key officer and Captain Pettygrew in the team to ramrod the ship preparation alongside the Moray people. Cascadia, Moray, and Captain Argelos to organize a staff for you . . ."

"How long?" Ky said.

"You have forty-five minutes," Pitt said. "And a clear path—your security's waiting outside this entrance." She gestured. "I'll just clear up here and have everything ready for you."

Ky made it back to her quarters, showered, checked hair and teeth and all carefully, and made sure the uniform she put on was freshly cleaned. She felt better—almost better enough to think she could make it without taking a few days off for medical nonsense, but . . . but that had gotten her into such a state she didn't even know she'd put on a soiled uniform. No. Hard as it was, she'd do it, whatever it took.

THIRTEEN

The men and women facing her in the conference room looked anxious as she came in. She recited what Pitt had suggested, almost word for word; their faces relaxed slightly.

"I've been irritable," Ky said, at the end. "My apologies to anyone I've bitten. A more thorough medical evaluation should take care of everything—you know they told me when I first came in that I shouldn't check out so fast—"

"Don't worry," Argelos said. "We'll take care of everything, and if we need to hold departure awhile—"

"I doubt that will be necessary," Ky said, "as long as I do what I'm told." She managed a grin. "I may be as stubborn as all the other Vattas, but I can follow orders . . . sometimes." There was a chuckle in response that sounded almost natural. "Feel free to not tell me anything you're doing—I'm sure you'll be fine without me. For a while, anyway."

It was hard to turn away from the table, hard to make herself leave the room, but inside she felt a shift, a change of something indefinable that told her she was making the right decision.

Moray's medical staff had assembled a team, men and women in their version of hospital uniform; it was almost like walking into the conference she'd just left, except that no one looked scared of her.

"I've been assigned to manage your treatment." The speaker wore a green-and-cream-striped tunic; the cream stripes were narrower. "I'm Psych-Phyz Fumaro Adjan; these are Neuro-Phyz Milian Cortsin, Neuro-Psych Kember Tasani, Implant Tech Vasti Bak, and Incare Specialists Maran, Zlaznin, Vitsi . . ." Ky nodded, knowing her implant was picking up faces and names and could retrieve them when wanted.

"We understand the urgency," Adjan said. "And the need for you to reach your usual level of performance . . . but we understand you have no baseline data . . ."

"Baseline data? I'm not sure what you need. It's possible that something could be obtained from Slotter Key. Medical records, is that what you mean?"

"A baseline brainscan with and without implant would be helpful. Information about your implant—how long you've had it, any upgrades—"

"I can tell you that," Ky said. "Though ship time isn't always accurate with a lot of jumps, as we've had in combat."

"You can explain that later," Adjan said. "Right now, if you can get us some baseline medical information, that would be very helpful. I assume your home world was advanced enough to do regular childhood exams including biochemistry?"

"I had to go to the clinic every year, but I don't know all they did," Ky said. Now that she thought about it, where were her medical records? Had they been at the house—and lost in the explosion—or had they been at the clinic?

"We'll need to do our own examinations for present data, of course. But briefly, can you tell us your own understanding of your situation?"

"I thought you'd know," Ky said. Irritation edged her voice; she heard that and fought it down.

"It's always helpful to know what you think the problem is," Adjan said, almost primly. "Your degree of insight is an indicator." She did not say of what.

"Well . . . I'm not sleeping well. I have bad dreams. I'm irritable and I'm not thinking as well as I should."

"Anything else?"

"I . . . can't stop thinking about them. The ones who died." The ones she'd killed, with her incompetence. The ones she'd killed, on purpose.

Adjan nodded. "Well, then, we'd best get to work. Maran will take you to get changed, and then to the lab for the necessary medical implants."

"Medical implants?"

"Yes, of course. We'll want continuous monitoring of too many variables to use external monitors or periodic sampling of tissue and blood."

"You won't feel a thing," Maran said. He was a chunky, cheerful fellow who reminded Ky all too much of Lee, who had died with *Vanguard*.

An hour later, Adjan reappeared, along with Cortsin, Tasani, and Bak. "We have a group working on your biochemistry results," Adjan said. "Slotter Key Spaceforce Academy is sending us your medical data from your time there; luckily that includes a scan without implant. Now for the interview and history."

Ky answered questions about her childhood health to the best of her memory. More data might be buried in the family section of the implant, but she still did not want to go there. What difference could it make, anyway?

"Do you consider yourself a humod?" Adjan asked next.

"A humod? No," Ky said. "Why would I? I mean, there are anti-humods who may think I am, but I'm not." She wiggled her hands. "Two hands, ten fingers, no sensory enhancements—"

"Um. Technically, brain implants—even as far back as the first cochlear implants for those with hearing loss—made permanent intentional modifications to the human brain that are medically considered to be modifications in a different way than external hearing aids or corrective lenses or mechanical prostheses."

"That . . . seems extreme," Ky said.

"Your implant can put you to sleep, can it not?"

"Yes, but—"

"And wake you at a specified time? And it augments your memories, and expands your effective retrieval space?"

"Yes—"

"And allows you to interface directly with other electronic and neuronic equipment, such as your ship's controls, right?"

"Yes . . . but . . . I didn't realize that was what a humod was. I thought it meant direct modification of the body—like a tentacle in place of a hand, a chemical sensory module or something. Something changed in the genes."

"Implants are so common that most people don't think of them as an actual modification. But in fact, you were modded in infancy, and it's likely your parents chose a genetic enhancement to make implant use easier, if they did not carry those mods themselves."

"I never knew that . . ."

"That's why I need to know about your implant history. You started with a childhood model, I'm sure."

Ky nodded. She'd had several implant changes before leaving for the Academy without one.

"You had no problems with adjustments?" Adjan asked.

"Not until the last time—it was so rushed, you see, and it was my father's—"

"Wait—you're telling me that after traumatic brain injury and emergency brain surgery, your next implant was someone else's? Uncalibrated?"

"It was a long time after," Ky said. "And the implant was my father's . . ."

"Why?"

Ky explained, though she did not mention that her Aunt Grace had baked the implant into a fruitcake to smuggle it off Slotter Key. "I wouldn't have put it in right then," Ky said, "but I needed direct access to the ship's sensors and the Vatta command set for the other ship—"

He looked at her with a curious expression. "You put in the implant your father had when he died—presumably your aunt had . . . um . . . cleared some things out."

"Not that I know of," Ky said. "Why should she?"

"It's a wonder you lasted as long as you did," he said. "What happened when you put it in?"

"The usual—I was dizzy, staggered around a bit more than usual. I didn't have time to sleep overnight with it, so the adjustment was a bit difficult, but then things were happening . . ."

She went on with the story. She hadn't ever had time to put the whole thing in order before, from her disgrace at the Academy through the capture of her ship, the mutiny, the loss of her family, the attacks at Lastway, loss of credit, Stella and Toby, Rafe, Osman's death and her decision to take over *Vanguard* . . . and on and on.

"It's all been a bit crowded," she said finally, coming to the recent battle and the loss of her ship. She felt drained.

"Ummm. Any one of those things would be enough to

give most people a significant problem. We have a lot to deal with. Let's start with the implant. You'll need to delete all the files pertaining to your parents' death. You can download to external media, if you wish, but I don't want you accessing them for a minimum of a standard year. They're well into your own neurology by now—"

Ky had expected that, but not the next.

"Now—as this was your father's implant, it will have information stored on you—things he valued for some reason. Could be school records, images made of you at different ages, anything. Have you been accessing those files?"

"No." She had deliberately not done that.

"Good. I want you to delete all the family-connected things—anything not needed for your work. I assume you'll want to keep Vatta business-specific information, but everything else needs to come out. Again, to external storage, but not for immediate access. I'll want to review it—"

"But it's personal—"

"Yes, and he's dead." Adjan sighed. "Look—it's not ideal to do a rush job on this kind of problem. It's possible that he stored things like educational assessments, test scores, even biodata, in that family file structure. If you try to find it for us, you'll get tangled in it—you'll be wondering why he saved that image of you and not another, or what he meant by keeping some scrawl you wrote at the age of three, or you'll start looking at images of your siblings who died—and as you pointed out, there's some urgency. We need all the information we can get on your pre-morbid condition, but we don't need you complicating matters. So I need access, once you have the files external."

Though she knew it was not true, she felt that the implant was emptier, lighter, when she had deleted those files. She'd been tempted to go below directory level and sample the files she'd never explored . . . even to revisit, painful though it was, the last day of her father's life. She forced herself to go on, unload the files in huge chunks . . . and now someone else had those memories, those images and words and feelings.

"Now we're going to normalize your hormones," the next doctor said. He started an IV and also plugged something into her implant's external jack. "They've sent me your genetic profile; we don't have reference data for Slotter Key, but some of your ancestors probably came from Seahallow, which supplied a lot of colonists to Slotter Key a few centuries ago. Let's see . . ." Ky fell asleep, waking a few minutes later as he murmured on. ". . . an interesting response. Let's see now . . ." She felt as if she were floating in the warm sea, the sea near her home. Then something tingled in her veins and she was awake and alert, but calm. "How's that, then?"

"Uh . . . that feels wonderful," Ky said.

"A tick less, I think" he said. The alertness receded; the calmness remained. "Your stress hormones were way off norm. Not unexpected, but you'd adapted. You're going to sleep long and heavy for several days, and when you wake up you may feel thickheaded. Don't worry about it. We've got to reverse the adaptation. Ordinarily we'd do that over several weeks, but in the interest of getting you back to service . . ." He murmured on, but Ky slid back into sleep.

She woke with a mild headache and the feeling that she had slept too long. When she turned her head something tugged slightly; a voice spoke out of dimness. "If you'll hold still a moment, I'll get that off your head . . ." Ky held still; hands touched her hair and whatever it was lifted off, leaving a sweaty patch behind. "And now a little light . . ." Light revealed a hospital room and the pleasant broad face of a woman in a green smock. "I'm Annie; let me help you up. You need to walk around a bit."

Dizzy at first, Ky soon steadied enough to make it into the hospital bathroom for a shower and hair-wash and so on. By then she was hungry, and after a meal came sessions with one specialist after another, a nap, another meal . . . and finally bed, where again she slept at once and heavily. That set the pattern for the next several days.

At the next medical conference, Ky felt much better. Well enough, in fact, to leave. Her team had a different opinion.

"We've stabilized your biochemistry," the chief neurologist said. "But we're concerned about residual damage from that brain injury you suffered at Sabine. The surgeons did an excellent repair, considering the conditions, but our scans show several areas that could be improved. Besides, we haven't yet dealt with the retraining you need. The two together will take another five days, but your fleet tells us the ships won't be ready to depart for at least seven."

"You're sure I really need this?"

"The retraining, definitely. We could excise the memories that led to the trauma, but that might impair your judgment the other way. Retraining will help you modulate those memories, control their intensity."

Ky agreed, and underwent a treatment that involved having short-lived nannites inserted into her brain, where they removed excess scar tissue from the surgery at Sabine and from a childhood concussion, then several days of adjustment trials to her implant controls and biofeedback work that was supposed to optimize both physiological and bionic response to stressors. Every day she felt a bit more clearheaded, until finally the team dismissed her.

"Here are the copies of material sequestered from your implant," Adjan said. "They belong to you; they are from your implant. But I caution you that under no circumstances should you review this material for at least one standard year. Ordinarily we would ask you to deposit it with a trusted relative who would then lock it away—the temptation to snoop has caused more than one patient distress and required re-treatment. This is not possible for you, as you have no relatives here."

"I could get a lockbox at Crown & Spears and leave it there," Ky said. "With instructions to destroy it if I'm killed. Would that do?"

"That would be very wise," Adjan said.

"I'll arrange it, then, and let you messenger the cubes over. Then you won't have to worry that my insatiable curiosity will undo your work . . ." She grinned at them all.

She dressed once more in her uniform, called to let her security detail know she was ready to leave, called to arrange a lockbox at the local Crown & Spears. Then she called Pitt.

"What's my agenda? They're kicking me out."

"Well, if you're able, there's a string of memorial services where your attendance would be welcome. They've been holding off on the *Vanguard* one, hoping you'd be out in time."

"Of course," Ky said.

"With so few of us surviving—" And so few remains, Ky knew. "—it'll be brief."

Someone had thought to send along a mourning band with her security detail, so Ky was able to go directly from the hospital to a small chapel. She recited the ancient

words commanders had used in Slotter Key for genera-
tions; others gave their memories of those killed. Argelos
and Pettygrew attended but did not say much. The names,
recited together, were too long a string to remember; Ky
remembered faces, expressions, the sound of a laugh or a
curse.

While she'd been gone, someone—she assumed Pitt—
had gone through her quarters on the station and moved
everything to her new flagship. Ky had been asked about
that name, and agreed with the others that it should be
called *Vanguard II.* The new *Vanguard* looked and felt very
different from the old one. It smelled different; it sounded
different; it was much bigger.

She felt different, too . . . not the kind of fresh-paint
quality that gave the ship its distinctive smell but something else. She had the memories she needed, the memories that had given her the experience to do what she
must now do. But she felt stable again, steady . . . she
had not realized—had not had time to realize—how long
she'd been struggling to stay upright, as if one mental leg
had been lopped shorter than the other. The implant's
software addition, tweaking her biochemistry, kept it in
an allowable range, the doctors had explained. She could
still get angry, be scared, feel grief and triumph . . . but
extremes would not create feedback situations that maintained an abnormal level.

Pitt had visited, the last two days in the clinic, and so
had Argelos and Pettygrew. She'd been fully awake by then,
still on an IV to boost neural retraining but able to have
visitors for an hour. Both captains had offered her data
cubes, but—obedient to the doctors' orders—she'd refused
them. Now she'd have to tackle them. She felt well able.
Moray had an extensive library of military science, tucked
into the larger database of technical material. Though their

own space force had been, like Slotter Key's, intended for System Defense only, their archives held the records of many previous conflicts, going all the way back through human history to the origins of war.

Ky downloaded the sections she found most relevant: strategy for large, diverse units, information on how best to organize units from different original governments into a unified force, and how to organize the staff for such a large force. While space warfare had always suffered from lightlag in communications, even after system ansibles become common, pre-space warfare with its much shorter distances had dealt with instantaneous communication—its value and its problems—for centuries. Strategy for surface warfare had to be translated into multidimensional terms, but she found ideas that no one else had used for a long, long time.

She pulled her attention out of this fascinating topic to attend another memorial service, this time for those who had tried to use the sabotaged ships against Turek's force.

Unlike the small private service for the *Vanguard* dead, the memorial service for the civilians killed in their attempt to fight off the invasion packed the largest hall Moray Station could find. Despite the urgent need for ships, construction work halted long enough for the ceremony, because riggers closed ranks around their Miznarii co-workers and their families.

Ky and her escort had a space near the front; they edged through the already crowded room. At the far end, on an improvised stage, someone had mounted images of those who had died. Along the sides of the room, as outside, a line of station police kept watch. Ky had to shake innumerable hands, nod and smile innumerable times. Everyone, it seemed, wanted to speak to her, touch her. She was glad this was the last such service—for now—she would have to attend. That for the crew of

Vanguard, delayed until she was out of treatment, was only a day past.

On the professional side, what the riggers had done was foolhardy and even stupid: once they'd undone the controls the enemy had placed on the ships, they should have let the station take over control and bring them back to dock. But that would have meant turning their Miznarii friends over to Station Security as saboteurs, exposing those families to legal scrutiny and public scorn, or worse. Instead, they had chosen to make heroes out of potential suspects. Moray's senior security officer, Kendelmann, had shared with her the initial record of the conversation between riggers and the station on the ship they called Thirty.

It would've been remarkable if even one of the crews had done this, but they all had.

"They're a tight-knit bunch, the riggers," Kendelmann had said. "And this particular group all live in the same neighborhood. The Miznarii keep to themselves somewhat, but the neighborhood leaders are all unusually gregarious."

"So do you think this Lozar knew what he was doing?"

"No. I think it's like his friends said. He was just barely bright enough to be a rigger, and he was always a go-along kind of fellow. That new cleric of theirs, though, he knew what those datadots were for, and he knew Lozar was gullible enough to believe what he was told."

Now, surrounded by friends and relatives of those who'd died, Ky was ushered to a seat in the second row, next to a stocky dark-haired middle-aged woman and a girl who was obviously her daughter . . . neither with implant bulges. On the far side of them sat a young redheaded woman, her implant bulge showing through hair pulled back to a bun. She had her arm around the shoulders of the daughter.

"Phittanji's widow and daughter," someone murmured from behind her. "It was poor Lozar—"

They could not know that she, Ky, had a reason—distant and minor, comparatively—to be less than sympathetic to Miznarii. The woman turned to Ky. She looked miserable and exhausted, but she summoned up a weak smile. "Thank you for saving us from those pirates," she said.

"I wish I had been able to save all your families," Ky said.

"It was not—it was not possible to save Lozar, once— once he—" Her shoulders trembled; tears overflowed her eyes. "He only did what he was told—"

Ky was not sure what was culturally acceptable; the Miznarii woman would consider her—anyone—with an implant a humod, and so might consider contact a contamination. But the woman's obvious distress required something—she put out her hand, and Sera Phittanji clung to it.

"I don't know what to do," she said. "We have no savings; my daughter was to be married and we had spent everything on her—" In a low, rapid voice, she poured out her troubles as if Ky should be able to do something. Lozar's disgrace, the rent due, the death of her daughter's suitor on another of the ships, the confusion of the congregation when their cleric turned out to be one of Turek's agents, everything. All Ky knew to do was listen, let her hand be squeezed out of shape, and hope that the ceremony started sometime soon.

When it did start, Sera Phittanji let go of Ky's hand at last. Each rigger's family had a chance to speak, usually telling some anecdote about the family member. They were taken in order of the ship numbers. When number seventeen was called, the red-haired girl three seats down got up and made her way forward.

"Both her parents," Sera Phittanji said, tears running down her face. "Both of them dead, and her mother was the sweetest woman. We worked together on some committees. I don't know what Meg will do . . ."

Ky froze; she had been where Meg was, only this girl was younger. She could not speak; she wanted to be somewhere, anywhere else rather than here. At least no one had asked *her* to give a speech after losing her parents in a violent attack. Unlike the other speakers, Meg did not talk about her parents specifically; instead she talked about their decision—all the riggers' decision—to try to attack the invaders and in the process save their Miznarii friends.

Silence held the room as she spoke, her earnest young voice catching now and then, but clear. "It was the right thing to do," she said at the end. "And they did it. And we need to do it, too." Ky felt tears stinging her own eyes.

When the time came for the families of those who died in Thirty, Meg stood up with Lozar's daughter and helped her to the front. The daughter read from a sheet of paper, now much-crumpled: her father had been loving and honest. He had not known—her voice broke there. He had been a good friend to his friends, and his friends had been loyal to him . . . her voice broke again and she ducked her head. Meg patted her shoulder and helped her back to her seat.

Ship Thirty was the last of the "hero ships," as the local press called them, and when a co-worker of D. Watson, who had no family at the memorial, had talked about the man's fascination with the same entertainment series many of the group enjoyed, *Swords of the Spaceways,* a government official handed out medals from the stage.

Then family members lined up to walk past the row of pictures while others stood around in clumps, talking and waiting their turn. By the time she left, Ky had a dozen invitations to lunch, dinner, a couple of birthday parties, and various private wakes.

"Good bunch of people," Pitt said.

"Yes . . . I can't get over that girl—Meg. When my parents were killed, I don't think I'd have been so forgiving of someone who'd made it possible."

"She was already friends with the families," Pitt said. "She and that Phittanji girl had been in classes together. It's different when you know the people."

Ky tried to imagine how she'd have felt if she'd known that someone in the office at Corleigh, some gardener or the mechanic at the airfield, had been involved. She'd played with their children, years before . . . and no, she couldn't see blaming Ekar or Adadi if one of their parents had been involved.

"It's a good thing they were all so close, then. Kendelmann told me he thought there'd be riots when people found out, but the riggers wouldn't let nonriggers into their neighborhoods for days."

"Did she break any bones?" Pitt asked, glancing at Ky's hand.

"This? No, but I was afraid she would. Poor woman. She's got more problems than most, at this point."

"If I could make a suggestion—"

"Of course," Ky said.

"Have the fleet—your fleet—set up a fund for those families. Let everyone toss in a few credits; it'll add up. Kind of back up that solidarity they have."

"Good idea," Ky said.

"I borrowed it," Pitt said. "It's something Mackensee does, spread a little butter around on something other than bars and brothels and weapons suppliers. Seems to create goodwill, anyway."

Back at the ship, Ky took the time to download and

install the new command data set for this ship, then review
the news that had stacked up even in those few hours.

Moray Security had located one of the small ansibles
in a shop stockroom; the owner claimed no knowledge of
it, but was in custody, and one of the employees, under
interrogation, had suddenly died. Despite an intensive
search, they'd found no more of the ansibles, and felt that
they'd blocked local agents—if there were more agents—
from communicating with Turek. Moray had technicians
capable of restoring service to the system ansible, which
they had done, but only for government use.

"What's the latest on Turek's force?" Ky asked.

"One of the transmissions picked up—translated by
that expert at Cascadia—said they were going to finish
getting the ships ready and supply them at their base. The
translator doesn't know if the coordinates were in clear or
a code. There is a system where the coordinates are, but
of course that could be a feint. Mackensee has been
working with us on that; if that is the system, the closest
place to do a supply would be Gretna—"

"I don't think they'll be lucky there," Ky said. "We left
a bit of a mess . . ." Argelos chuckled.

"I doubt that would stop Turek," the Moray officer said.
"And there's Rosvirein. Both systems with dubious repu-
tations, but both with plenty of arms on hand at last
report. Mackensee has an agent at Rosvirein, but not at
Gretna. They think they can pinpoint where Turek is, if
his people come to Ros for supplies."

"What do we know about the system they might be
in?"

"Unmanned ansible platform—just a relay, basically.
There was an unsuccessful colony there, something went
wrong . . . I'm not sure. Mackensee may know."

Ansible communications—especially via one of Toby's

special units—should be completely secure, but how secure was Stella herself? She would be furious if she were left out of the loop completely, if she thought Ky was dead. But if anyone found out that she wasn't . . . if Stella, after a communication from Moray, walked around looking happy . . . that could compromise their only chance to make a surprise attack on Turek's force.

Ky wished she could talk to Grace, but suspected that her communications lines were even less secure than Stella's. Too many ansible relays between Moray and Slotter Key, and the codes Grace had given her might have been compromised.

No. She would have to let Stella worry. She had just decided that when a Moray officer came in with a cube of messages received on Argelos' shipboard ansible.

Grace, of course. Hers was terse, voice-only. Ky ran it through the code filter. "Heard about big battle. Expect confirmation you're alive as this is prerequisite for sending Spaceforce ships finally released by idiot government." How had Grace heard about the battle? More worrisome, how had she heard enough to wonder if Ky was alive? The system ansible had been down . . . was Turek spreading the word, and if so, why?

Stella, next, video and voice, uncoded. "The Moray ansible is still down, but I'm sending anyway. I've got an invoice from Crown & Spears on Gretna, and I remember your telling me something about this, when you were at Adelaide, but you never sent me any paperwork. Should I pay this out of Vatta accounts, or apply to the Cascadians for it as a military expense? You weren't actually authorized to draw funds from Cascadia then, but it will mess up my books if I pay it out of Vatta, since I don't have any corresponding value received. Also, you forgot to give me the details of your transactions with Ransome—the sale of those ansibles—and that should be cleared up so the Vatta accounts are clear. Please do that immediately. The auditors will be checking our books in a few tendays . . ."

Ky shook her head. Surely Stella should have realized by now that Vatta Transport or the expanded Vatta Enterprises and its accounting were the least of her concerns. She felt like calling Stella just to give her a good talking-to. And she had no idea what documentation Stella really needed, and anything there might have been had blown up on *Vanguard*. She could have put it in her implant—it had been in her implant, as a record of conversations, but she'd offloaded it as a nuisance and now it was locked in a Crown & Spears box.

Some merchanter's daughter she was! Wrong instincts every time. But the pang of guilt eased as fast as it had come, and the implanted therapy module dropped a few pearls of cognitive realism into her awareness. Stella had a legitimate problem: auditors. She herself had a legitimate problem: the war. Who else might have the data Stella needed? Well . . . Argelos might have stored it. Ransome would certainly have the records of his purchase. And she had staff.

"Evelyn . . ." The trim Moray officer appeared in the hatch. "I need to send my cousin on Cascadia some information, via shipboard ansible, that does not appear to come directly from me. Here's what she needs, and here's where it might be. Contact these officers, find out if they have it, and if so have them transmit it by shipboard ansible."

"Right away, ma'am." Evelyn saluted, took the list, and disappeared. Ky grinned. Staff was good. Now for Aunt Grace. That was still a problem, and she needed to consult the experts, such experts as she had.

"The only way I can imagine that word got out from here is via a shipboard ansible," Ky said. "It could be Turek trying to spread the word that he's won, trying to intimidate more governments. That makes sense, in a way. Or one of his agents here got something out before we caught them . . . they had hours to do that. But Aunt Grace addressed me, and said she wanted confirmation I was alive; she didn't seem to be asking if I was alive. That suggests to me that she got word, somehow, that there'd been a battle, that there was some rumor of my death—that would logically be Turek, I think—and that I was in fact alive. Anyone else have ideas?"

"No, but I can't think who'd have done it," Pettygrew said. "I know I didn't. I would have no reason to contact Slotter Key. Well, if I'd known you were dead, maybe . . . but even then I'd have contacted Vatta on Cascadia first. I've met Stella; she's the logical contact."

"I didn't, either," Argelos said. "When the ship blew, before we knew you were alive, I was thinking how to tell Grace Vatta, in her role as Rector of Defense—but like Dan, I'd have gone through your cousin, most likely. I suppose one of my crew might, without my knowledge—" His face was grim.

"Excuse me," Pitt said. Ky turned to her. Pitt's expression, for the first time in Ky's experience, showed embarrassment.

"Yes?" Ky said, fascinated in spite of herself.

"My orders, orginally, were to support Major Douglas in his role as Mackensee liaison to this fleet." Pitt paused; her mouth twitched. "I know that . . . the admiral is aware that this usually involves some . . ." She seemed to be struggling for the right words.

"Spying?" Ky suggested.

"Gathering data useful to Mackensee, yes, ma'am. If

the admiral recalls, upon leaving our headquarters—" Ky noted that even now Pitt did not specify the location— odd, since they all knew it. "—the admiral told us about Grace Lane Vatta's new position and the fact that Slotter Key privateers would be joining us at Cascadia. The admiral may recall that Major Douglas asked permission to contact Rector Vatta and present credentials."

Ky had forgotten that, but she remembered it now.

"The major was aware—but I don't believe the admiral was aware—that in the earlier events at Sabine, when Mackensee was forced to put up a bond by ISC, and the admiral's—then captain's—performance had impressed some of our senior officers there—a certain amount of preliminary background checking began. And was continued after the events at Lastway, but terminated when the admiral chose to pursue a privateer career."

"I wasn't aware of all that, no," Ky said. It was unlike Pitt to be so roundabout, but she must have a good reason.

"In checking up on the admiral's time in Spaceforce Academy, I happened to make contact with one Master Sergeant MacRobert. He thought a lot of the admiral as a cadet." Now the faintest of blushes colored Pitt's cheek. "We . . . um . . . corresponded now and then."

"About me?" Ky asked.

"Sometimes. He was interested in how Mackensee saw the wider issues—piracy and the like—and after the attack on Vatta on Slotter Key—which to him looked more like an attack on Slotter Key itself, at first—he contacted me to see if I had any word on the admiral. Which, right then, I did not." Pitt took a breath. "The long and short is, ma'am, that Master Sergeant MacRobert has been my source, as it were, for Slotter Key. And he's now working closely with Grace Vatta, and apparently was before the old government fell and he may have had something to do with that."

Fragments of memory coalesced in Ky's mind, forming a pattern that almost made her laugh hysterically. Those fruitcakes. That spaceship kit with strange parts. MacRobert and Aunt Grace? Together?

"It didn't seem something you needed to know, and he and I were both fully cognizant of the need for security—"

"Are you a double agent?" Argelos asked suddenly. "Have you been all along?"

"No, sir. My primary loyalty's to Mackensee, same as always. But Mackensee saw, after Sabine, that Slotter Key and the Vattas were going to be important to know about. MacRobert knows that. He never passed on anything I could use to hurt Slotter Key, even if I wanted to. But there was a connection, and I was part of that connection, working of course under Major Douglas' orders, as Master Sergeant MacRobert knew. The feeling was that two senior NCOs chatting was less . . . obvious . . . than Major Douglas calling the Rector of Defense. The thing is, after the—after Major Douglas died, all the responsibility fell to me. And I did think, after we knew the admiral was alive, that this was something to be passed along, with care."

Ky shook her head, fighting off the urge to burst out laughing and scream simultaneously. The others were less restrained.

"What the hell—!" began Argelos, just as Pettygrew said, "That's treasonous!" and the other officers muttered things Ky didn't catch.

"Master Sergeant Pitt," she said. The others subsided. "I am to understand that you have been in contact with MacRobert ever since Sabine?"

"Off and on," Pitt said.

"I hope you won't take this the wrong way," Ky said. "You saved my life, after all. But what you're describing would put you in the position to cause some of the trouble you've always seemed to deplore."

"I was almost killed at Boxtop," Pitt said.

"Allies have been killed to cover tracks," Ky said. "What strikes me is that you may be telling the absolute truth—and I know you have been truthful with me in the past—but if you were clever enough, you could be backstabbing Mackensee, and us, and Slotter Key. Major Douglas is dead; we have no independent confirmation of your past history; we have no way—without breaking the communications ban I feel is necessary—to see what Mackensee thinks about all this. Assuming that Mackensee is as it has presented itself."

"I understand, ma'am," Pitt said. "It is logical . . ."

"I've trusted you, and I like you, but you've put me in a position where I can't continue to trust you. You know I wanted my survival to remain secret—"

"Begging your pardon, Admiral, but you had not given that order at the time I contacted MacRobert. Even believing it was important for your people to know, I would not have done it against your orders."

"You can say that now, but . . ." Ky shook her head. "I want to believe you. I will check on the timing of your transmission, which I presume is logged on whatever ansible you used—"

"Yes, ma'am. On Captain Pettygrew's ship—" Pettygrew seemed to swell in his seat.

"If, as you say, your transmission preceded my orders, then that's a point in your favor. But until we are in a situation where I can again contact Mackensee command myself, I cannot allow you to access communications equipment, and you must consider yourself confined to quarters."

"Yes, ma'am. I understand, and I apologize for causing you this difficulty."

"Corporal Decker will escort you to your quarters."

Pitt did not object, as Ky half expected; she saluted and left, with Corporal Decker behind her. The moment the hatch closed, Pettygrew exploded.

"That—that arrogant, meddlesome—"

Ky raised her hand. "Dan, I know she shouldn't have done it, and I know you didn't mean to let anything like this happen. Please do check your logs, and check the time stamp on that transmission. My concern now is damage control. Grace Vatta knows, and Master Sergeant MacRobert knows. Would Grace have understood how important it is that no one else knows?"

"Turek must've spread the rumor of your death," Argelos said. "Your aunt knows you're alive—her message makes that clear, and Pitt told her—told this MacRobert, anyway."

Ky was still thinking about MacRobert and Aunt Grace as a team. No wonder the bad government had fallen. How many had died in that, she wondered. And what was the status of the Commandant of Cadets? She pulled her attention back to the present. "We need the Slotter Key Spaceforce ships; if Grace needs confirmation . . . I wonder what will satisfy her?"

"There's always fruitcakes," Argelos said with a grin. He had found the original fruitcake story hilarious.

"Not a bad idea," Ky said. "In fact . . . I think I can devise a message not even Turek's best can figure out. Too bad we don't have instantaneous matter transmission—I could just send her a fruitcake . . ."

"That would make a military nightmare," Moray's senior commander said. "I don't want to contemplate matter transmission, thanks."

Ky nodded. "I'll take care of Aunt Grace. Now let's consider how to deal with Turek . . . with what we've got left.

It's a mercy that putting the CCC into *Vanguard* meant we had to put the extra ansibles we brought you folks into *Sharra's Gift* and *Helvetia,* or they'd be debris like the rest of her."

Argelos looked at her with a curious expression. "Could've been a worse loss than ansibles."

"It was," Ky said, thinking of Hugh, Martin, Douglas, the Gannett family. "But the ansibles are the key to our ultimate victory."

FOURTEEN

Rafe Dunbarger, acting CEO of InterStellar Communications, stared out the window at what had been an avenue of blooming cherries until the freezing rain withered the flowers. The view expressed his mood precisely. Every time he thought he had his life rearranged into something livable, a disaster moved in.

"Rafe?" His sister Penelope, with her own problems.

Rafe suppressed a sigh and turned to her with a smile. "Penny! You look lovely." And she did, having regained the weight she'd lost in the aftermath of losing her husband and her baby. Physically, she was fully recovered. Emotionally, Rafe considered her still fragile.

"I feel . . . better." But even as she said it, tears glittered in her eyes. She shook her head. "I'm sorry. I—I can't help thinking . . . a year ago . . ."

A year ago she had been recently married, pregnant, the wealthy and indulged youngest child of a wealthy family, married into what had seemed a secure relationship.

"No apologies, Pennyluck," Rafe said. He held her for a few moments, until she pulled back a little, then released her. "Dinner still all right?"

"Yes." She pulled out a tissue and blew her nose. "Yes. I need something to celebrate."

He didn't have much to celebrate, except that he had saved her life, and his parents' . . . and in the process lost the most fascinating woman he'd ever known.

"Tell me about Ky Vatta," Penny said, tucking her arm into his. "She was in the news again—well, her cousin Stella was, but talking about Ky. What did you think of her?"

Ky Vatta was the last person Rafe wanted to talk about. "Stella's interesting, too," he said. "Gorgeous creature, like a fine sculpture—"

"I saw the pictures," Penny said tartly. "I am not in the mood for gorgeous creatures . . . Ky doesn't look so . . . so impossibly perfect. Did you hate her so much?"

"Hate Ky? No." He guided Penny gently out of the apartment, pinging their security with his skullphone to be sure the driver would be ready. Arral, the evening number one, fell in behind them; Madoc, the evening number two, was already at the elevator.

"You don't talk about her; I wondered if—"

"She's hard to describe," Rafe said. "Not physically, of course: you've seen the pictures. But that mix of commercial and military background gives her . . . unexpected qualities. She's . . . feistier than Stella. Not that Stella's bland."

Penny looked sideways at him. "You're hiding something."

"I'm not. I'm trying to answer your question."

"You are. I can tell. I thought you were in love with the other one, the gorgeous Stella."

"Not in love with," Rafe said. "We had a brief fling. And I'm not proud of those years, Penny. She was a little younger than I, less experienced in what she was trying to do. I enjoyed escorting her, of course. But—" But any love had been on Stella's side, and she'd clearly gotten over it.

"So you're in love with the dangerous one," Penny said.

"I'm not a character in a play," Rafe said. "I don't have to be in love with either of them."

"Right," Penny said. Her voice was lighter now, teasing, as they rode down to the dock where his driver would be waiting. "You only rescue people, pretend to be a rake-hell—"

"I am—I *was* a rakehell."

"Inside, I mean. I don't believe you ever were, inside. And you've fallen for her. The rumors were right. Don't bother to deny it."

"I never argue with beautiful women," Rafe said. He handed her into the car, checked with his security team that all was well there and aboveground, and then entered himself.

Rafe had invited his personal assistant, Emil, to join them; a birthday dinner needed guests, and Penny had agreed that Emil would suit her. Winterplain suited her, as well: a restaurant whose dedication to privacy and comfort almost equaled its pricing.

"Let's talk about something else," Rafe said, fastening the safety web. "Like how you're doing—I hope you won't find it insulting that I've been surprised and delighted by your work so far."

"Really?"

"You have a nose for fraud, Penny—you've found one bent account after another."

"So you thought you'd bury me in paper and keep me busy and out of trouble—" He could not tell from her tone if she was angry or not.

"Guilty as charged. I knew you needed work to do,

some way to feel productive. And I was sure you weren't a crook yourself. I had no idea I was turning a ferret loose in a rabbit warren. You're talented at this, and you're valuable to the company—or anyone else you want to work for."

"It's easy," Penny said. "Anyone could—"

"No, they couldn't," Rafe said. "I can read people when I'm with them and spot the crooks that way, but I'm not nearly as good as you are at following cold trails through the books. You've found problems I never suspected."

"Were they all Parmina?" Penny asked.

"I don't think so," Rafe said. "Too many diverging vectors of motivation . . . I think he created a climate in which fraud and embezzlement and simple incompetence could thrive on the margins of his own intent. Lying, cheating, and stealing became the norm; people who weren't on his team shrugged and went after their own interests."

"And you're changing that," Penny said, patting his knee.

"I'm trying—but an organization like ISC has a lot of inertia. Convincing people to quit doing what profits them is tough. I can't fire everyone and start over."

"Why didn't Father notice any of this?"

"I don't know, Penny. Parmina was working him, for one thing, and for all I know could've been feeding him poisons literally . . . something to dull his perceptions just that little bit. Unless Father was in on it—"

"No!" Penny shook her head violently. "No. He was as surprised as I was when we were taken, and I'm sure he didn't know about the rest of it. Though it does seem incredible that he wouldn't . . ." Her voice trailed away; her expression, in the dim light of the vehicle, showed doubt and fear. Not emotions Rafe wanted her to feel on her birthday.

"Let's talk about something else," he said for the second time, racking his brain to think of something. With war looming, with the company foundering, with their father still mostly incoherent and their mother still in denial about his condition, with the woman he loved facing death in combat . . . what other topics could they talk about?

"I had lunch with Lucy Parmina last week," Penny said. "I don't think I told you, I gave her the name of my therapist after—you know."

"How's she doing?"

"Much better, I think. She's not actually using my therapist, but another in the same practice. She's started painting again, and she showed me some images—I can stand to look at them."

"Mmm?"

"Well, when we were in school, she painted, but they were such horrible things—bleeding bones and faces that scared me—green stuff coming out of the eyes, barbed teeth—that I couldn't look at them. Now she's painting landscapes, and kind of stiff-looking people. But people, not horrors."

"I was an art dealer once, you know," Rafe said. "Well, art and antiquities, anyway."

"You?"

"Oh, yes. If she wants an agent sometime—if she wants to pursue a career in art—tell her to ask me. I know people."

Penny gave him an odd look. "I would never have thought of you as knowing anything about art. She does hope, she said, but I don't think she believes she'll make it."

"Her father's faults can't be allowed to ruin her life," Rafe said. "How's her mother doing?"

"Not as well," Penny said. "Lucy says she won't leave the house, won't consider going into therapy."

The car slid into the secure parking area below Winterplain. Rafe handed Penny out and redirected the conversation again, this time to artists he'd known and things he'd learned about the business. They chatted about art all the way up to their private dining nook, where Emil had just arrived. Rafe let Emil take over the conversation— he was eager to tell Penny about a musical show he had seen, and soon the mood lightened. Music—why hadn't he thought of music? Thanks to their mother, Penny had had lessons and played two instruments at near-professional level; they'd had musicians staying with them on tour. Emil's family had always had season tickets to the opera and the symphony; he, too, had had lessons.

"But I didn't have talent," he said, grinning. "My parents took me to teacher after teacher, and they all gave up. I love to hear good music; I can't make it. Do you still practice, Penny?"

"I haven't in a while," Penny said. "I should get back to it, I suppose . . . but I'm not really the soloist type."

"Some of my friends have an amateur group—you might consider them. I could introduce you."

Penny glanced at Rafe, then said, "I'd like that, Emil. I'm rusty, but if I had a goal, I know I'd practice—I'd have to move instruments from my parents' house—"

She was looking happier; she was relaxed. If health for Parmina's daughter meant going back to painting, then maybe health for Penny meant going back to music. Rafe ate the rest of his entrée with genuine pleasure.

A tap on the door of their room startled him. No one should be able to find them, let along interrupt—but the door opened, one of the restaurant staff and a man in business attire.

"So sorry to interrupt, Ser Dunbarger."

Rafe's implant ran a rapid check. Alois Malendy,

Assistant Secretary of Defense. He felt his pulse race, controlled it. "Not at all, Ser Malendy. I hope it is not too urgent; this is my sister's birthday dinner."

"Sera, my pardon—ser—" The man paused, glancing at the others. "Ser Dunbarger, I am truly sorry, but this is a matter of considerable urgency. If I could just speak to you privately."

"Very well." Rafe rose. "Emil, will you take over as host, in case this takes longer than a moment? Penny, my apologies."

"It's all right." In company, she had acquired a glow and looked happy and relaxed. Rafe rose; his other security guard moved with him as he and Malendy moved to an alcove just outside the room.

"Ser . . . we have received word that a large force—the conspirators or pirates or whatever they are—have attacked Moray System. This information is relayed from the Space Defense Force."

Ky's force. A battle. He felt suddenly cold.

Malendy went on. "You may not be aware that Moray has military shipyards—very high quality—and apparently the pirates had ordered ships to be built, under pretense of being a legitimate government, and then arrived to steal them."

"That's . . . how far away is that?" Rafe used his implant to query the ISC database. Sure enough, Moray's system ansibles had gone down some hours before.

"The system's two tendays' FTL travel, plus—"

"Plus the usual insystem time. Yes. What else did Commander Vatta say?"

"It . . . er . . . was not Commander Vatta herself. In her name, from the Space Defence Force. Commander Vatta's ship was destroyed—"

"What?"

"They said to notify you that although they interdicted some of the thefts, the pirates got away with six fully armed warships. They also have information received indicating that the same group has many more warships than previously known, and they believe an attack on either Nexus or Cascadia will follow. I know you told the Secretary that ISC could not provide useful defense, but we've always depended—"

"But what about Commander Vatta?" He could feel his body tightening around that question, his heart racing.

"Well, you know we have always had our doubts about the Vatta connection . . . in light of Vatta's theft of ISC technology, and the rumor that Vatta was involved in your parents' abduction—"

"It *wasn't* our technology and they were *not* involved in the abduction! How many times—!" Rafe lowered his voice; people in the larger room were looking around. "What about Commander Vatta?"

He had spoken quietly and distinctly; why was Malendy backing away, a sheen of perspiration on his forehead? "I—I believe—she was lost with her ship. They said the ship exploded—"

Everything stopped for an eternity Rafe could not measure. Sound, movement, all stopped. Nothing existed but Malendy's face, a pale blur, and the darkness around him. Ky. Dead. His heart beat again, a single beat like a drum. *No.*

Something twittered in the distance. Rafe tried to focus on it. Malendy, still talking. "—thing is, if they attack here, I must know how many ships—"

"Go. Away." He did not know if he said it aloud. He wanted only to hear no more from Malendy . . . no more horrible, life-destroying news, no more impossible demands, nothing.

"But Ser Dunbarger! It's important—the Secretary demands an answer—"

Inside, he felt a cold black explosion, the opposite of a nova, darkness spreading at the speed of light, faster even.

"I have no answer." His voice startled him: colder than ice, colder than anything he had ever heard. He struggled with himself, and managed more. "Look: I did not know about the battle; I did not know about Commander Vatta's death. It was my sister's birthday; I had arranged a special dinner—" He looked at Malendy.

"But—"

"I will have an answer for you shortly . . . are you still in ansible contact with Moray?"

"Er . . . only by relay through the Space Defense Force. Moray's ansible hasn't been repaired yet. They're working on it."

"Good," Rafe said. He was hovering over the brink of an endless drop . . . no, he was engulfed in horror . . . no, he was Rafe Dunbarger, acting CEO of InterStellar Communications. If Ky was dead . . . if the report was true . . . she would expect him to do what he needed to do, whatever that was. He had always known she was likely to be killed; he had told himself that over and over. Why then this shock? Had he not really believed?

"I'll talk to Moray myself," Rafe said. "I will need the code for the relay through SDF." Malendy handed him a data strip; Rafe did not look at it, but tucked into his jacket pocket. Maybe the report was wrong. Maybe it was another ship; maybe she had somehow survived. Maybe she would not be there to stop him from killing whoever had done this in the most vicious way he could think of.

"But ships—"

"I'll have that information for you later," Rafe said. "Tomorrow morning."

"We can't wait—"

"You must," Rafe said. "At worst, no one can reach us from there for twenty days at least. You said that yourself. I will be gathering data. It will take me that long to be sure it is accurate. You want it accurate, I take it."

"Er . . . of course."

"Then tell the Secretary I will have the data for him by 0930. And now, if you'll excuse me, I must get started."

"But—"

"Good-bye," Rafe said. One of his security—Arral—stepped forward. Malendy backed away. Rafe turned his back on the man, reminded himself to breathe, and spoke to Arral.

"They have an ansible booth downstairs," Rafe said. "Stay with Penny, Arral; Madoc can come with me. I'm going downstairs to make an ansible call."

"Right, ser."

"Tell Emil to check the status board; we have another system ansible down; he's to arrange a repair."

The Winterplain ansible booth was large enough for two, but Rafe left Madoc outside. In moments, his priority code gave him access to the closest satellite, with punch-through to the ansible platform itself. He downloaded the original message to the Defense Department, even as he placed the call. Status lights changed; the screen blinked twice then gave him a steady image of a uniformed woman he did not know.

"This is Rafe Dunbarger of ISC. I need to speak to Admiral Vatta." Maybe it would work; maybe his need to talk to her would conjure her out of the ether.

The woman's face changed to a careful expression. "The . . . you haven't heard? Her ship . . . her ship was lost."

Lost could have many meanings . . . he told himself that, to keep his voice steady. "And Commander Vatta?"

"Was . . . she's gone, Ser Dunbarger."

Ships could be lost, misplaced, and yet whole and sound, along with those inside them. People could be gone, not here, and yet alive.

"Who's in charge?" Rafe asked.

"Of Space Defense Force? Acting commander is Commander-Senior Murphy, of Moray."

"Then I need to speak with Commander-Senior Murphy," Rafe said. "I was contacted in response to a call from Space Defense Force to the Nexus Ministry of Defense."

"Yes, ser."

Commander-Senior Murphy looked nothing like a senior military commander to Rafe. His tall frame had generous bulges: jowls and chins and wrinkles where his stomach had grown over the years. But his eyes were shrewd; he nodded at Rafe. "I know who you are. Admiral Vatta briefed us before her ship blew; she believed Nexus was likely the next target for this fellow Turek. Nexus or Cascadia, and she was leaning toward Nexus."

"How did it . . . happen?" Rafe asked.

"We aren't entirely sure. Turek's force laid a minefield as it fled, but we don't think that was it—or wasn't all of it. The ship was firing its beam—"

Rafe remembered what Stella had told him about Ky's ship. It needed a major refit; Ky had not taken the time— or changed ships—

"—and we think perhaps the beam set off a number of mines at one time, too many for the shields. But our investigative teams haven't completed their analysis."

Stella had said something about a CCC, some kind of module that was supposed to give the ship . . . something. He couldn't remember what. He didn't ask about that. Instead, "Can you give me any information on the state of the Space Defense Force? Is it still operational? Will it be pursuing the enemy, or—"

"I cannot give you any operational information, you understand. I can say the force remains a useful organization. If the government of Nexus requests our assistance—"

"I'm sure it will," Rafe said. "I have been asked to assess the readiness of ISC's forces and respond to the Secretary by morning—it's late night here. Did Comm—Admiral Vatta tell you anything about the ISC forces?"

"That they weren't worth the trouble to blow away, yes, she did. I'm surprised you people have the reputation you've had—"

"Yes, well . . . it came as a surprise to me, too, when I took over this job. Apparently it was part of the same sabotage that resulted in my family's abduction."

"Do you have anything that's combat-ready?" Murphy asked bluntly.

"Yes. Less than I could wish. I can't tell you anything operational, either . . . I'm in a public ansible booth at a restaurant, and though I've engaged encryption it's not as good as our own. But as soon as I found out our fleet had serious . . . deficiencies . . . I set about remedying them, putting all our resources into our best units."

"Contact me again from a more secure location, will you? It's midmorning here, but feel free to contact me anytime."

"Thank you," Rafe said. "It's nighttime here—not late; we were at dinner. I'll be briefing our Secretary of Defense in about . . . um . . . twelve of our hours. So I should be getting back to you within four."

He closed the connection, and leaned his head on the

console a moment. He had promised himself that when the crisis was over, when Turek had been defeated, and ISC was on firm ground, and his father recovered . . . he would go and find Ky Vatta, explain why he'd acted the way he had on Cascadia, see if she could forgive him. Now it was too late. That could never happen. His future lay before him, one bleak stretch of unpleasant duty, to the end of his days.

He sat up, shook his head sharply, and composed himself as well as he could. He had acted so many parts in his life; he could do it now. When he went back upstairs, Penny and Emil were finishing dessert, still chatting about music and musicians.

"I'm sorry it took so long," Rafe said, forcing a smile. "ISC fleet problems, Emil. I'm afraid I must ask you to meet me at the office; I'll take Penny home first."

"Of course," Emil said.

Once more in the car, Rafe turned his face away from Penny's; he wasn't sure he could control it.

"It was a lovely dinner, Rafe," Penelope said. "I'm glad you organized it."

"Glad you enjoyed it," Rafe said. Outside the car, the world was dark and wet and cold, but inside . . . inside was too small, stuffy. He wanted to throw open the door, jump out, take his chances out there, with risks he understood, on his own again. "So did you and Emil have a nice chat while I was gone?"

"Do you want me to marry him?" Penelope asked.

He turned to stare at her, her profile outlined against the faint glow of late-night street lighting. "Marry him? Whatever made you think I did?"

"Only that you've had him hovering over me since the first day you brought me into the company. Only that you keep telling me how responsible he is, how reliable, how honest, how unlike Parmina."

"I only wanted you to feel safe, Penny," Rafe said. Safe with someone other than him. And she had sensed that, sensed that withdrawal he had hoped never to reveal to her.

"I'm not upset," Penny said. "Don't worry . . . I just want you to understand that although Emil is a nice fellow, I'm not nearly ready to think about marrying anyone."

"That's good," Rafe said. "Since I told him not to make any moves in that direction."

She gave a little chuckle, the most relaxed laugh he had heard from her since the rescue. "I wondered . . . there he was, always ready to be an escort, to take over for you, but . . . I was beginning to wonder if he thought I was ugly or something. You scared him."

"I . . ." He had meant to scare Emil; in the mood he'd been in, back then, he'd been willing to scare anyone.

"Rafe . . . we need to talk."

His heart sank. What now? What little-sisterly problem or plan needed his attention now? With an invasion on the way, with Ky lost, with his enemies on the Board and in the government constantly looking for reasons and ways to bring him down. He forced a smile to his lips, and gentleness into his voice.

"What's the problem? What do you need?"

"You," she said. "You are the problem."

"Me? What have I done?" He tried for lightness, but he couldn't help thinking *After all I've done* . . .

"Rafe, you're on the edge. I don't know if others can tell yet, but I can. You're working so hard to be so good, so professional-business-steady-upright . . . and you're a good actor, I'll say that for you. You can't be this good all the time without going crazy," Penelope said.

It took his breath away; how had Penelope, of all people, caught on to that? "I'm doing the best I can," he said after a moment.

"I know. And you're doing wonderfully. But for—how many years—you did what you pleased, good or bad. I don't mean you were bad the way Parmina said—I don't believe that for a moment. But you were free; you could go anywhere; you could be anybody. And ever since you've come back, you've been tied down here, to family and business—"

Just what he was thinking; just what he must not think. Not now, in this crisis. Not now, when the escape hatch he'd promised himself was gone forever.

"You're very good at it, but you can't keep it up forever."

"When Father's better," Rafe said. Even to himself, his voice sounded unconvincing.

"He'll never be better," Penny said. "You know that; we read the reports and you explained them. And even if he were, the Board won't trust him, not now."

"They don't entirely trust me," Rafe said. Even Vaclav Box, who did trust him—or seemed to—was chafing at the changes Rafe had made. "You know what they told me about the alliance with the Moscoe Confederation, on account of the Vattas."

"No, but you're strong enough to handle them. He won't be. He never had to fight a contrary Board the way you have. Only . . . I can't see you doing it forever. Or really, for much longer."

"I have to," Rafe said. "There's no one else . . ." He felt squeezed; he could scarcely breathe.

"If you had her," Penelope said.

"Who?" The pressure increased, the sense of time passing, time lost, things that would never be.

"Don't be stupid!" She punched him lightly in the arm. "You know perfectly well who . . . Ky Vatta. She sounds like another adventurer, like you . . ." Now her voice was a little wistful. She had come so far, recovered so much, but even as a child she had not been the most daring of his siblings, and he could not see her as an adventurer.

"She's busy," Rafe said, the first thing he could think of. He did not want to tell Penny that Ky was dead, not now. He needed time to grieve by himself. Time he wasn't going to have, he could see. "So am I. We may never meet again . . . if . . ."

"If she gets killed. True. So you ought to tell her."

"Penny—!"

"Rafe, I'm not saying this just as your little sister, but as a woman—a woman who has been married. It's stupid to waste more time. You love her, don't you?"

"I don't . . . know."

"Oh, please! You do, and it's obvious enough that all the anti-Vatta people guessed it, are still gossiping about it, worrying . . . you might just as well admit it, jump into the fire, and come out with the horseshoe."

That reference to the old children's story made him laugh even in his anguish. "You think I can talk my way past the fire demons?"

"I think you have to do something—you have to tell her, you have to tell the others to go . . . jump in the ice pit or something."

"I can't just . . . she's not like the . . . others." And she was dead, dead, *dead*. Whatever wise advice Penny came up with, it was too late now.

"Of course not. So do it properly. Not like the others . . ."

"You don't know how I—"

Penny put up her hand. "I heard, Rafe. I'm not that much younger than you. Your conquests had siblings, some of them my age."

Rafe was glad for the darkness in the car; he could feel

himself blushing. It was one thing for his conquests to know, or his contemporaries, but his little sister . . .

"And don't waste time being embarrassed," Penny said. "I'm a grown woman; it's not like I haven't heard plenty about other people's sex lives. You weren't any worse than some others I heard about."

"I just never thought about you finding out," Rafe said.

"My point is," Penny said, "it's clear to me—experienced widow that I am—that you really care for this woman. Yes, she might die in the war. Yes, you might be assassinated by an infuriated Board member or one of Parmina's co-conspirators. So? Use what time you have. I'm also the expert on how little time you might have with someone you love."

"I can't just call her up and tell her—she's really busy right now—"

"When is she going to be less busy? When are you?"

"I . . . I'll think about it."

He made sure Penny was safe in her apartment, then went on to ISC headquarters. Work kept his mind off Ky for as much as an hour at a time. He sent Emil home after midnight but stayed on, gathering the material he would need to present to the Secretary of Defense in the morning.

FIFTEEN

"I can't believe you let us get into this state!" Alois Malendy smacked the arm of his chair, as if that would accomplish anything. "You're going to tell me you weren't here—that it's not you personally, but—but Nexus has depended on ISC—it's part of the bargain—"

The bargain no one wanted to talk about openly, the bargain where no sums were ever mentioned, no concessions ever openly discussed. ISC got what it wanted, and in return money that supposedly went for Nexus Defense could be spent . . . elsewhere.

"You're wasting time," Rafe said. He had heard this and similar diatribes all morning, and he supposed he would hear another from the last few men at the pinnacle of government. "It's not news to either of us, the shape the ISC fleet is in. I told you about it myself, weeks ago. What you need to do now is prepare the defenses you do have—"

"That we *don't* have, because of your company's irresponsible behavior. Your father's dereliction—and here you are, beneficiary of his power, when you've done not one thing—"

"Scolding me isn't going to change anything," Rafe said. "What you need to do—"

"Scolding you won't, but getting you out of that plush office might," Malendy said. "You coldhearted bastard—I heard all about you—"

"Really." Rafe sat back, folded his hands. "And from whom, I wonder? Lew Parmina?"

"At least while Lew was over there we had someone who listened to us—this mess didn't happen on his watch."

"Actually it did," Rafe said. "Actually it happened *because* of him . . . so what did he tell you?"

"It was in the news reports years ago—playboy, sex-crazed cradle-robber—" That would have been Ilsa, Rafe thought. He did regret Ilsa, but really—she had climbed into his lap that night, pressed herself on him, and he'd been only eighteen . . . "—all you care about, all you've ever cared about, is protecting your sugar-tit . . ." Malendy's voice trailed away. Rafe realized that he'd let his hand slide down, approaching the part of a gentleman's suit that—if the gentleman carried—would hold what it did in fact hold.

"Let's calm down," Rafe suggested. "Let's look at the timetable, if you want facts and not the insinuations of a known traitor. Funds were misused—yes. They were misused for years—at least six years—while I was not on Nexus or anywhere near it, and while Lew Parmina was your friendly voice at ISC. You trusted him, and this is what came of it. Some of the documentation disappeared, but some we've managed to reconstruct: Lew Parmina, using my father's name, authorized expenditures of two types: funding those now our enemies, and funding those whose votes he wanted to control. Not just within ISC but also in Nexus governmental circles."

"You can't make wild accusations—"

"And you can? Come now, Malendy. If you're wondering

if your name was on the list, you must have been a very minor beneficiary of Lew's generosity . . . it's not on the lists we've found so far." Rafe watched Malendy's face run through a sequence of expressions, ending in sullen resignation. "So . . . whatever you think of me, whatever you think of ISC, we're going to have to work together if Nexus is to survive."

"Someone else should head ISC," Malendy muttered.

"In the long run, yes," Rafe said. "But for now, you have me. I'm not quitting, and you can't force me out—I have too much on your government and the means to make it public if you force my hand."

"That's . . . that's blackmail."

"No. That's the result of stupidity and greed on all sides. ISC is culpable but so is the government of Nexus. And we have more important things to worry about than who's most to blame for this mess. Now, quit acting like a primary teacher with a naughty boy and get me the SecDef."

"He'll have some serious questions for you!" Malendy said.

Rafe's patience snapped. "I have questions for him, too." Like why he had not yet met with Rafe, instead passing him from one flunky to another. Did he suspect the data that Rafe held, or was he looking for leverage?

Humphrey Isaacs did not rise when Malendy finally ushered Rafe into his office. He overflowed his chair, pudgy hands clasped on the edge of his desk, and glared at Rafe. "We are not pleased with ISC's performance," he began. One of the secretaries from the outer office darted in with a folder of data cubes for Isaacs' desk, then withdrew.

"I wouldn't expect it," Rafe said. He pulled one of the heavy, leather-seated chairs to one side of the desk and sat down before Isaacs could stop him. "Let's get

past all the recriminations, shall we? ISC, in the control
of Lew Parmina, did not maintain its fleet to the standard it should have. This impacts not only ISC's ability
to defend its monopoly, but Nexus Defense's ability to
defend the system, because you depended on us. All
that's a given—"

Isaacs' cheeks puffed out. "It's a disgrace. You promised—"

"Correction." Rafe interrupted with a raised hand. "*I*
did not promise anything. I wasn't here, remember? ISC,
a long time ago before my father was even born—before
you were born—did a deal with the Nexus government to
provide protection in return for certain government accom-
modations. Like any protection racket—" Rafe noted with
pleasure that Isaacs did not like that wording, so he
repeated it. "As with any protection racket, it weakened
the protected. I will stipulate that ISC has had far too
much power in Nexus for far too long. But that is not the
immediate issue."

"I could have expected that you would attempt to evade
responsibility—"

"Do you confuse the entity with the individual?" Rafe
asked. "Or do you want me to consider you fully responsible for everything the Nexus government has done over
the centuries, as it crawled into bed with ISC?"

"That's preposterous!"

"Is it? I think not. I think history offers many exam-
ples of relationships between business interests and governments that ranged from benign marriages to outright
prostitution. Nexus was founded as a company planet.
You know that; you took Jesperson's history course at
Central, and he always laid emphasis on it. That's why
they fired him."

"Damned radical," Isaacs said. "Trying to stir up

trouble—" He picked up a letter opener, turned it around and put it down, then picked up a pen and twirled it in his fingers.

"Not really," Rafe said. "Trying to point out the stress points in our system where trouble might erupt. As it has here. Nexus was founded as a company colony; the government has always considered the interests of ISC above the interests of other citizens . . . and always tended to believe whatever the leaders at ISC said. When these leaders were honest—and many of them were—Nexus prospered and was no worse off than it would've been with a different system. Financially *better* off. But the goals of a corporation are always both broader and narrower than the goals of a government. Broader here and narrower there."

"You never went to business school," Isaacs said, gelid gray eyes narrowed.

"Oh, but I did," Rafe said. "I went to a very hard, very unforgiving business school."

"Where?" Isaacs said, his tone challenging. He put the pen down then picked it up again.

Rafe looked him over as he might have looked over a side of beef. "How long would you survive if you were exiled? And how?" Isaacs looked angry but said nothing; Rafe went on. "I had of course grown up among businessmen and women. But when I was thrown out, I had to care for myself—"

"You had a remittance—"

"I had a pittance," Rafe said. "And I didn't use much of it, because I became a businessman. Several times over, in different systems, with different laws and different economic possibilities. I learned more there than any business school can teach about what interstellar commerce is really all about. What it depends on, what sustains it, what damages it. I had a perspective that you—who have never traveled beyond the Moscoe Confederation, who have never started your own business—lack. If you want to assess my understanding of business in general, and corporate structure in particular—bring in someone who knows something about it. I could not have found what was wrong in ISC as fast as I did, if I'd been as ignorant as you seem to think."

Air huffed out of Isaacs, and he seemed to shrink a little. "It's still wrong—"

"Many things are wrong, but we cannot deal with all of them now. What we need, you and I, is a clear grasp of reality as it is right now, today: what the threat is, what our resources are for meeting that threat. The past is, for the moment, irrelevant." The past that included Ky Vatta alive and his feelings for her, his father undamaged, his belief that ISC was as powerful as it had always been.

"So what do you think reality is?" This time Isaacs opened the cube folder and began to roll several of the cubes in his hand.

"We—meaning the Nexus System and the people who live in it—are in imminent danger of attack by the same force that has attacked and overrun other systems, growing stronger with every resource captured. And—unless you have a nice modern fleet hidden away in a box somewhere—we're as defenseless as a baby in a snow-storm."

"And I suppose you have a solution?"

"No. I can help define the problem, but I do not have a solution."

"Well, I do." Isaacs tapped one of the cubes on the desk for emphasis. "You—ISC—are going to hire a fleet to protect us, and it's not going to cost us a penny. You got us into this mess; you will get us out, if—" Isaacs stopped abruptly. Rafe was paring his thumbnail with a knife. "Where—how—"

"Calm down," Rafe said. "If I wanted to cut you, you'd be bleeding. I had a hangnail. Now let's be serious. We can't hire mercs for you. You're the government; you have to do that or it's illegal—"

"You have to pay—"

"We don't have the money," Rafe said. Isaacs stared at him, jaw hanging. "For over a standard year, our income has been well below norm, thanks to ansibles being out of service. No calls, no income. Second, when I got into this job, I found that a lot of our reserves had vanished. Some of that's been traced to plain ordinary embezzlement, some to fraud, and some directly to the government. Third, as soon as I found out our fleet was in the shape it's in, I started spending what was left to upgrade and supply it."

"So it's not that bad?"

"No, it is that bad. Do you have any idea how much it costs to run a fleet the size we had? You should, in your business, but then you always depended on us—" Rafe let some of the bitterness he felt about that edge his voice. "Cheaper to privatize, let ISC do it. Put it this way: if I sold everything my family owns—the houses, their contents, the clothes off my back and my sister's and parents' backs, my mother's piano and harp—it would not supply one single warship for one single engagement. Our ships can't even use modern munitions, most of them. It's fortunate that rocks in space are lethal weapons because we're in the Stone Age when it comes to ships."

"How did it—who let this happen?"

Isaacs himself let it happen, among others. No use to say that. "That doesn't matter," Rafe said. "As near as I can tell, it started some thirty years ago, with budget cuts for the fleet because there wasn't any need. To that you can add chicanery, not only in ISC but in your department, where inspectors were supposed to ensure that our fleet was maintained to standards you thought appropriate. They didn't."

"We depended on you—"

"Yes. For a consideration."

"You can't tell me—"

"I can tell you that I have a list of individuals in this department—and others—who took substantial bribes in return for not doing their jobs. And as I told your assistant, if you're wondering whether your name is on the list, you know you're guilty."

Isaacs flushed. "I don't recall," he said. He dropped the cubes he had been handling and picked up another.

Rafe shrugged. "Fine. But be aware that the list exists, in more than one secure storage location, and that I have no more concern for the welfare of this government than you have for mine. As for hiring assistance, you will be lucky, at this date, to find anyone. I put you in touch with Mackensee months ago; you chose to delay and now they're working for the Moscoe Confederation—"

"We have an agreement that I can still have some—"

"Good. But understand this—we can't pay for them. I have already cut executive salaries, including my own of course, and all but essential expenses. We must keep the working ansibles going, and we must repair the ones that others can't. That's critical to military action. We don't have any spare money—"

"You can borrow it—"

"And so can the Nexus government, at lower interest. Now I'll need authorization to talk to your senior commanders, whoever you're going to put in charge—"

"What senior commanders?" Isaacs said. "We don't have anyone capable of running a real defense. You know that. We're just the local police force."

Rafe looked around the luxurious office, bigger than his own as CEO. "You . . . you fraud. So . . . what do you want to do now? Quit? You must have someone you think has some ability, unless you've done nothing for six years but sit here until you filled your chair side-to-side. Call 'em in, tell 'em to take over. Not Malendy, of course; he's an idiot."

"I can't believe it's that bad . . ." Isaacs was shaking his head. "Your father—Lew Parmina—they never said—"

"My father never knew—Lew Parmina knew, of course, but he was hiding it. Look—we need to get the Premier in here, contact Mackensee right away, get the commanders—"

"There's no time," Isaacs said. "They're on the way—they'll be here any hour—" He looked outside at the blue sky streaked with wisps of cloud. "They could be entering the system now—"

Rafe suppressed a strong desire to grab Isaacs by his jowls and shake him. "They could not," he said instead. "The early warning system's fine; if something jumped in, we'd be told."

"We?"

"I'm linked to ISC's Emergency Report Center, aren't you?"

"No . . . why should I be? That's for a specialist . . ."

"Well, then: there is no enemy spacecraft in our system at this time—"

"You're sure—how can you be sure?"

"The rubigilliam hypercontractivity generator," Rafe said with a straight face. "Put into service only four days ago."

"Oh. I didn't know about that."

The man was worse than Malendy. The man was insane. Could he possibly be dragged back to what must be done? And if the rest of the Defense Department was this brain-dead, which of his own staff and commanders might take over?

"The Premier," Rafe said. "And Mackensee . . ."

"Must inform the Premier at once," Isaacs said. "Shocking—impossible—must—" He looked grayer. "Something—something's wrong—"

Rafe threw open the office door. "Secretary Isaacs is ill—he may be having a heart attack—"

Malendy and several others rushed into the room while Rafe moved aside. Odd. Very odd. Humphrey Isaacs hadn't been that muddled when Rafe first called to tell him about the problem with ISC's fleet. Something had happened to him in the interim. Something had happened . . . before the conference on Cascadia Station? After? And why hadn't anyone in the government noticed?

He stepped into the outer office as a squad of medics arrived, and picked up the headset one of the secretaries had abandoned. The desktop had a direct link to the Premier's office, as he'd expected.

The Premier's secretary was sorry, but the Premier was fully engaged . . . if Ser Dunbarger cared to leave his number? Rafe explained that Secretary Isaacs was suddenly unwell, some kind of emergency, and that he had information of urgent import.

"Ser Dunbarger. What's going on?" The Premier's resonant, reassuring voice replaced that of his secretary.

"Secretary Isaacs had some kind of medical emergency while we were in a meeting; I called assistance and they're with him now. He was on the point of contacting you himself—"

"Why would he do that? We have a regularly sched-uled meeting tomorrow morning."

"You're aware of the situation on Moray?" Rafe said.

"An invasion beaten back by that force from Moscoe Confederation and Slotter Key? Yes, what of it?"

"When the Secretary reported that, did he tell you that Moray is reasonably sure the attacking force is now headed this way?"

"What? No! Where are they?"

Isaacs should certainly have told the Premier at the daily briefing—why hadn't he?

"I don't know, sir. I do know that Moray is a minimum twenty-day transit in FTL, plus time insystem."

"Thank heavens we have your fleet to protect us! Will you need any assistance from insystem patrol?"

Rafe felt a ball of ice falling down through his body. "Excuse me?"

"I mean, you do have enough of your fleet here, don't you? Or you can retrieve them from someplace. Humphrey—the Secretary—would have arranged that—"

"I'm afraid not," Rafe said. "I told him back when our fleet was defeated at Boxtop—"

"Defeated? What? Where?"

"Mr. Premier, I believe I should brief you immediately, but not over this unit. We have a situation."

A moment of silence, then the Premier said, "How soon can you be here?"

"Twenty minutes," Rafe said. He heard a muffled cry from the Secretary's office. "Just a moment—" He stepped to the door. Isaacs was stretched on the floor, medics working on him. "Excuse me," Rafe said to the nearest person, someone he vaguely recalled sitting at a desk outside. "The Premier's on the com. What should I tell him?"

"Give me that!" Malendy said, turning abruptly and striding toward Rafe. "I'll deal with him."

"I'm on my way," Rafe said to the Premier before handing the headset to Malendy.

"You're not going anywhere," Malendy said. "It's all your fault."

"No," Rafe said. "It's not, and I'm to go to the Premier's office as soon as possible."

"Why? So you can kill him, too?"

"I did not kill the Secretary," Rafe said. "I wasn't even—"

"You probably poisoned him or something," Malendy said. "He was perfectly healthy before you showed up. And you threatened me."

"Don't be ridiculous," Rafe said. "I had no reason to kill either of you. Even if it weren't illegal. Secretary Isaacs had a heart attack or a stroke or something. I had nothing to do with it."

"You're a dangerous rogue," Malendy said. "You always have been; you always will be."

Rafe just stopped himself from saying that Malendy was an idiot and always had been and always would be. So far, no security personnel were in the room to hear Malendy's accusations, but they were probably on their way.

"I'm going to meet with the Premier," he said, in his mildest voice. "Thank you for all your help."

Malendy's jaw dropped; in that moment of confusion, Rafe slipped out of the office and—instead of going to the elevator his own security was already holding for him, he signaled that he would take the utility stairs. He removed the official visitor's pass he wore as he walked down the hall, peeled off the telltag on its back, and— hardly breaking stride—opened the door to a men's toilet and slapped it onto the inside wall above the light switch. From his inner jacket pocket he took the small packet containing an apparent twin to the telltag, slipped it out, and pressed it onto his pass. Preprogrammed for just such occasions, the "tag" now deactivated door alarms and informed area controls that he was authorized anywhere in the building and also for unplanned entrances and exits.

Nobody stopped him on the way down to the ground floor; the stairs there opened into a side passage invisible from the main entrance, and one of his own team was there to meet him. "Elevator stopped on four—Security let Curran go when you weren't in it; he'll meet us outside."

"Idiots," Rafe said. "Did you retag?"

"Not yet."

"Do it now," Rafe said. Even Gary, always suspicious, had thought providing the entire security detail with fake telltags was unnecessary. Rafe had agreed, but insisted on having them anyway.

With his escort retagged, Rafe led the way toward one of the utility entrances. Guests were not normally allowed in this area, but the few employees who saw them were obviously more interested in the break room they passed than in strangers in the corridor.

No live guard at the entrance, even. There was a full suite of electronic surveillance, but the loop for storage was brief and the equipment was old, not working properly even before Rafe contributed a little more damage. They had come out into a small paved space; Rafe's other escort stepped out from behind a trash bin.

"Best this way," he said, and led them along a paved lane just wide enough for a trash truck, between windowless walls, to a larger parking area. A sidewalk led off to the left, around the corner of the building and probably, Rafe thought, to the front, but his escort nodded instead to the car park itself. Just beyond, his car waited.

"The parking attendant hadn't heard?" Rafe asked.

"Small alterations," his escort said. "And this car park has a separate exit."

Moments later he was in the car, reporting to Gary what had happened. "Malendy's going to claim I killed the Secretary," he said.

"I'll alert your legal team from here," Gary said. "You'd better get back here—they'll expect that, but—"

"They think I'm headed for the Premier's office," Rafe said. "I'm supposed to meet him—"

"Don't," Gary said. "They'll be ready for you."

"I know that," Rafe said. "But I still need to talk to him. Isaacs hadn't told him about Boxtop; the Premier still thought ISC's fleet would be able to protect this system."

"Isaacs was in on it—"

"Must have been." Rafe sighed. "I knew he was taking bribes, but I thought he was greedy, not a traitor. Just when I think it can't get worse, it does. Dammit, I can't save the world all by myself. Somebody else has to be honest and competent—"

Gary laughed. "Come on, boyo. You know this is more fun than sitting in your fancy office looking at spreadsheets."

"It was fun when it didn't mean a billion people could die if I screwed up," Rafe said.

Gary snorted. "I still can't get used to you being all sober and responsible. I've seen you at it for three seasons now, and I keep expecting you to break loose and do something crazy."

"I'm reverting to my boring corporate roots," Rafe said.

"From what I see of these guys, they're as crooked as you ever were. That's not boring . . ."

"No, right now it's terrifying. Our fleet's worth zilch, except for that one special unit; Nexus Defense has nothing that can stop Turek, and I have no doubt he's coming. We're the helpless virgin as the barbarian comes in the gates—"

"Don't go literary on me," Gary said. "What about Admiral Vatta? You could ask her."

"I could, if she weren't dead," Rafe said.

"What!"

"Last night. Heard it last night. Fleet action at Moray System—twenty-day FTL jump from us. She drove off the enemy attacking their naval yard, but in the process her ship blew up."

"Rafe—I'm sorry."

"I knew it was likely," Rafe said. "I told myself, *Just think that she's died, don't think about her* . . . we're not supposed to be . . . aren't . . . anything to each other."

"Are you sure she's dead?"

"As sure as the Moray officer who told me," Rafe said. "Her ship blew up; she was in it." He struggled to keep his voice steady. "Of course, our brilliant government refused to ally with Moscoe and Slotter Key, so even if she were alive, she might not come."

"You think the alliance wants Nexus to fall?"

"No, but I think they won't come without being asked by the government, and if the government is convinced I killed—or attempted to kill—the Secretary of Defense, then they are less likely to yell for help."

ISC's headquarters loomed ahead. Farther ahead, something with flashing lights sped toward them. Too close. "Use the tunnel," Rafe said to the driver. The car turned aside, drove a short distance between nondescript buildings, and went down a ramp to an underground loading dock, then made a sharp turn into what was actually an underground parking garage. At the bottom level of that, a blank wall slid aside, revealing a narrow tunnel. The car eased in; the wall slid closed behind them. The tunnel ran down, curving slightly to the right, then emerged into a cavernous dark space; the headlights picked out something shiny in the distance. "At one time," Rafe said to his escorts and driver, "I would have thought this high adventure. Now it's a nuisance."

Shiny was a grate, which slid up at their approach, letting them into a car-sized lift. To one side was a smaller lift for personnel and a hardwire comport. Rafe stepped out of the car and plugged into the comport.

"Gary?"

"Here. Front gate's crawling with cops. No sign any of them spotted your car. You did button up the tunnel—"

"Yes, Gary. Both ends. Can't do anything about the thermal into the garage, though. I'm in sublevel C. Best route?"

"I'll send a truck in to start foxing the thermal. Your best route—leave the car down. Take the lift up to sub A, turn right, take the second corridor to the left, second staircase, right again, there's a lift to the eighth floor. Go into Archives, and at the back left there's another lift. I'll meet you there."

Rafe followed this complicated path without incident, except for dodging someone in a Technical Services tunic pushing a wheeled cart with a big gray metal box on it down the corridor. The man quickly pulled the cart to one side and Rafe strode past, nodding thanks. The door dragon at Archives, where he'd been before, simply smiled and said, "Good day, Ser Dunbarger. Can I help you find anything?"

"No thanks, Sera Vozan. I'm just taking the shortcut today."

"It's all right for you, Ser Dunbarger, but I will not have those infants from Survey coming in here, pretending to look for charts, and then sneaking down the back lift to lunch an hour early . . ."

"And quite right," Rafe said. "I trust you make them look at charts until noon?"

"I certainly do," she said. "Or send them right back to their section."

The lift was waiting when he reached it, with Gary inside. As it moved Gary shook his head. "You kicked a very large anthill, boyo. The Secretary is indeed dead, and they're saying it looks like poison. They want your hide stretched on a hoop."

"I didn't poison him," Rafe said. "Is Emil all right? And Penny—where's Penny?"

"Both here, both doing their jobs. You know, your sister's really come a long way. Quite a young woman."

Rafe looked sharply at Gary, but the man seemed sincere, no edge to his voice.

"Emil did say to tell you the Premier's office called; he wants to talk to you at your earliest convenience."

"I'll bet he does," Rafe said. The lift stopped. Gary exited first, then waved Rafe out.

"That other one—Malendy?—says you pulled a weapon on him, and threatened him, and he's saying he should never have let you in to see the Secretary."

"I should have just killed that little bastard last night when he interrupted Penny's birthday dinner, and called it an affair of honor," Rafe said. "What I threatened him with was exposure of his incompetent little financial fiddles." He came in sight of his offices; Emil was out beside the receptionist's desk. He waved at both of them.

"Ser—"

"I know," Rafe said. "One of those interesting days I wished for when I was a bored little boy." He smiled at his receptionist. "I would love to give you the rest of the day off, but I'm afraid that would result in your spending some hours being grilled by officials. Instead, could I offer you the comfort of one of the guest suites?"

"The children—" she said.

"Right. They're nine and thirteen, aren't they? In school, then an after-school program? Here's what we'll do, if you agree. We'll avoid all the media and official attention and move them and you somewhere out of reach. It's near the end of term."

"I—well—yes, that would be nice."

"We'll need your authorization to have one of our people pick them up from school. We should do that before anyone makes the connection and tries to intercept them when school's over."

"I'll make the travel arrangements," Gary said. "Quiet house, suitable for children that age, a couple of security, just in case."

"Emil, come fill me in." Rafe led the way into his inner office.

The light blinking on his desk was the direct connection from the Palace to ISC—but he could not answer that until he knew how close to the cliff edge he stood.

SIXTEEN

Moray System

Ky Vatta's message to her Aunt Grace was as terse as Grace's had been, and even more cryptic. "Fruitcake contains one K, no filler. Only one fruitcake, positively no S in fruitcake. S does not belong in fruitcake." From the generations-back family code stored in her father's implant—surely Grace would know that one—she added "Tik harvest less than projected by fifteen percent, propagation of seedlings strongly discouraged." Translated: "Do not propagate this message." How could she tell Grace that Pitt was suspect. That maybe MacRobert was suspect? "Tik pitts—" A simple misspelling that she hoped would pass for a mistake to anyone else. "—may be infested with fungal disease from the source. Isolate any storage bins used by suspected lots. Source may be unreliable." Did she really think MacRobert was unreliable? He had sent her the letter of marque and set up the delivery of those mines disguised as cleaning materials. If he had been the traitor who opened Slotter Key to the enemy, would he have done that? Would he be Grace's—whatever he was to her? She could not believe it. She did not want to believe it, rather, any more than she wanted to believe Pitt was a traitor.

What she wanted to ask Grace was where Grace had heard of the battle and her supposed death. What she wanted to tell Grace was that Turek probably still had an agent or two on Slotter Key. But Grace would not thank her for that information. Grace would give her that Aunt Grace look, and would understand being kept out of the loop.

Pettygrew called in. "Pitt told the truth," he said. "She requested use of the ansible right after you came aboard. My comtech assumed that it was a message you had asked her to send, so he let her have the board. It was another hour before you ordered the shutdown. You asked me if anyone had communicated outsystem, and I asked my comtech, but she didn't tell me about Pitt, because she thought you already knew. A stupid mistake on my part; I'm sorry."

"Not your fault," Ky said. "I'm relieved that Pitt wasn't lying about that; it would cast doubt on Mackensee's agenda." Now what could she do about Pitt? The transmission might have been innocent in intent. The log showed that the only transmission had been to Slotter Key. But why hadn't Grace told Ky that MacRobert and Pitt were communicating—if she knew.

Argelos reported that Stella had accepted his and Ransome's financial data without asking for a direct contact with Ky. "She said she supposed you were busy, and she was sorry to bother you but the auditors were coming."

Auditors. Of course the survival of Vatta Transport was important, but why couldn't Stella understand that Ky had more important things on her mind?

Slotter Key

Grace Vatta looked at the printout she'd been given. Straight data, no voice, no visual. It had come from a shipboard ansible, one of two mounted on Ky's ship, but had it come from Ky? Could the enemy have figured out how to intercept such messages and then use the originating code on a different unit? And "fruitcake." Too many people knew about the fruitcakes now. As long as she'd been seen as the dotty old lady who handed out inedible fruitcakes, fruitcakes as code were safe, but now some people—some of Ky's crew, for instance—knew that the fruitcakes might have more than fruit and nuts in them.

Fruitcake contains one K. That might be Ky. Or something else. No S. Not Stella. But if the message was from Ky, why would she say Stella wasn't with her? Of course Stella wasn't with her. Ky knew that Grace knew Stella was on Cascadia. And the last part, the old outdated Vatta code for "deep secret, do not share."

"What's that?" MacRobert asked as he appeared with her afternoon tea.

"Either confirmation from Ky that she's alive, or a clever fake," Grace said. "It's almost—I can imagine her doing something like this, but—does she think communication through her onboard ansible is compromised? And what else is she trying to tell me?"

MacRobert looked at the printout. "Ah. Don't tell Stella. Definitely from Ky, and—oh, my."

Grace looked up at him. "What? You understand this nonsense about tik seeds?"

MacRobert looked amused. "Yes. At least, I think I do. Ky's found out that I've been in contact with the Mackensee liaison, Master Sergeant Pitt. And she's trying to warn you. She's wondering if I'm reliable."

"You!" Grace shook her head. "Of course you're reliable; what was she thinking?"

"Girl's learning," MacRobert said. The corner of his mouth twitched. "What would you think if I hadn't told you about Pitt?"

Grace shrugged. "All right. I see what you mean. But she knows you—"

"She knew me years ago, when she was younger and naïve," MacRobert said. "She's been through a lot. She's not the same Ky, Grace."

"I know that," Grace said. "That's why I wanted to talk to her on Cascadia."

"You're still miffed about that, aren't you?" MacRobert rubbed her shoulders. "You know, if you'd been Ky, you wouldn't have waited, either. She had to go; she heard trouble coming . . ."

"But—"

"She's a good—I can't call her a kid anymore—commander, I'd have to say now. Remarkable, in fact."

Grace glowered at him. "You're glowing."

"I'm not. Well . . . maybe. Look at it like this: I'm the closest thing she has now to a father."

"If my arm weren't the size of a child's I'd hit you with it."

"All right. I won't push it. But I am proud of her. It was obvious from the first term that she'd be right at the top—and she was, and not just academically. She had the right kind of mind. We get brilliant cadets who don't, and we try to shunt them into positions where their brilliance can be used without destroying them or their mates. I had high hopes for her as a commander . . . and she's fulfilled those hopes, though not in our Spaceforce."

"You kicked her out of your Spaceforce," Grace said.

"Not me. I had nothing to do with that decision and

you know it. And anyway, it's your Spaceforce now. You know the political pressures on it."

"Fewer," Grace said. "But yes."

"And if she hadn't resigned, if she'd been the most junior officer in a cruiser in our home fleet . . . which is where the good ones are assigned . . . she wouldn't have been available to do what she's done. Which may very well be to save us all."

"It doesn't hurt that she doesn't fully trust you now?"

"Hurt? No. It would bother me if *you* didn't."

"Very well then. I will inform the President that she is alive, and ready to take command of Slotter Key forces when they arrive."

"We still have to figure out where the rumor came from," MacRobert said.

"Tonight?"

"No . . . I suppose it can wait until morning."

"Good . . . because my therapists are annoyed with me about the arm . . . horizontal exercises, they prescribe. They insist I must do them."

"Horizontal exercises . . . I think we can manage that."

Moray System, Aboard Vanguard II

Ky called Pitt into her office. As always, Pitt looked perfectly professional as she came to attention in front of Ky's desk.

"Ma'am."

"The log bears out your story, Master Sergeant. But I can't say I'm happy about the fact that you were in contact with Slotter Key behind my back for . . . years, it must be."

"Yes, ma'am. I understand that. If the admiral will permit—"

"Go ahead," Ky said. She was well aware that Pitt was using formality to maneuver her.

"Until Major Douglas died, the admiral will understand that there was no conflict of interest: I was, as I am, a member of Mackensee Military Assistance Corporation, and my loyalty belonged to that organization." Pitt paused, head slightly tilted, and Ky nodded her understanding. "So," Pitt went on, "it would have been inappropriate for me to discuss with you any of my contacts, anywhere."

Ky thought that over. She had never been drawn to the shady side of military work; intel was something she wanted, but did not want to obtain herself. "I see," she said, her tone neutral.

"If the admiral thought the contact was inappropriate, it was a matter between the Slotter Key government and my high command."

"But I didn't know," Ky said.

"No, ma'am. I understand that, but . . ." Pitt sighed. "Ma'am, it's been a very odd situation between you and me from the start, like I've said before. We're not in the same chain of command. We're not enemies. We're allies of a sort, but normally you would interact only with officers of your own and related ranks. Yet—" The faintest color came to her cheeks. "You could, in age, be one of my children."

Ky just managed not to blurt out *You have children?* in a tone that would have been insulting.

"But you aren't, and you outrank me, anyway. I do not know exactly what Major Douglas' orders were, as Mac's liaison. Of course I never saw them, and my orders were to assist him as required. But from what he did say, I gathered that he was to assist you, without giving up any of Mac's secrets. Though we were not, then, officially in alliance with you—and I don't yet know the terms of our alliance, because they were in the files that were destroyed with *Vanguard*—I considered it my duty to be of assistance as well. Especially after he died. I did overstep my authority, ma'am, both by contacting Master Sergeant MacRobert and by urging you into treatment, but . . . I did so thinking it was in the best interests of my command."

"What you aren't saying," Ky said, "but I'm hearing, is that I can't really expect you to be loyal to me, and neither is, or was, MacRobert."

Pitt looked thoughtful, not worried. "It's not exactly that, ma'am. As I understand my duties, my loyalty to Mackensee—which is of course primary—requires that I assist you, and your endeavors here, in any way I can. That is what I have tried to do. As a matter of fact, not that it should make any difference, I happen to like and respect you personally. But if you were a sothead idiot, I would still have the same duty to assist you. And though I like and respect you personally, I cannot allow that to affect my duty."

"And your understanding of MacRobert?"

"He has his duty, to Slotter Key, as I have mine to Mackensee," Pitt said. "He will do what he thinks is best for Slotter Key, despite what he feels for you . . . though, like me, he respects your ability and character."

"Do you know if he has told Grace Vatta about his contact with you?"

"Oh, yes," Pitt said. "He told me that he told her, and that she had been amused. She is quite a woman, he says."

"She is indeed," Ky said. "And she also doesn't give much away. But my question now is, how much can I trust you?"

Pitt frowned. "Ma'am, I will not lie to you. I will not divulge anything I think might be harmful to Mackensee, now or in the future, without specific authorization from my own command structure. When we can, I would like you to contact them, in my presence, and I need clarification of my orders. However, I know from Major Douglas, and the articles of alliance you showed me, that my orders will, at the least, be to assist you—and that means being straight with you. If you ask my advice, it will be the best I can give—though I'm only a master sergeant."

Ky snorted, humor having overtaken indignation. "You are not 'only a master sergeant,' and if you're not going to lie to me, let's start there." Pitt gave a short nod but said nothing. "Well, then. I suppose my lesson learned is that all intelligence personnel are tricky at best. Including MacRobert and my very unsainted Aunt Grace. You have my permission to continue your contact with MacRobert— since I suspect you'd find a way to do it anyway—but please keep in mind the advantages to secrecy."

"Yes, ma'am."

"You're no longer confined to quarters; you've already been all over the ship, so there's no reason to cause us both inconvenience that way. I'll want you at the staff conference at 1330 hours. If we can arrange a secure link to Mackensee before that, I'll contact you so that you can speak to your command."

The Mackensee officer who appeared on the screen introduced herself as Colonel Watkins. Pitt saluted, assumed parade rest, and gave a succinct report of events since her last official report, without mentioning that Ky was alive.

"You were on the orbital station, then?" Colonel Watkins asked.

"No, ma'am. With respect, ma'am, is this a secure connection? Entirely with the Vatta-type ansibles?"

"Yes," Colonel Watkins said. "Why?"

"Ma'am, what I need to say is extremely sensitive and should be shared only with Section Four."

Watkins' brows lifted. "Would you prefer to speak to the senior Section Four officer aboard?" From the tone it was a request Pitt should not make.

"That might be best, ma'am. There are . . . strategic implications."

"I see. Can you hold the connection at your end?"

"Yes, ma'am."

A pause, a flicker at the edge of the screen that cleared, and another officer appeared, also a woman. Ky, watching from out of range of the video pickup, saw a flick of hand signal, which Pitt acknowledged with a twitch of her own.

"Master Sergeant Pitt, I'm Colonel Paraits. I understand you have sensitive data for us?"

"Yes, ma'am."

"But you're not alone." It was not a question. Ky wondered if the finger flick had conveyed that.

"No, ma'am, but the officer here already knows it, and has reason to mistrust me."

"Ah. Go on, then. I was monitoring your transmission before; I'm caught up."

"Yes, ma'am. I was in *Vanguard* when it blew—but in the CCC, which survived, though not without casualties. The most critical information to protect is that Admiral Vatta also survived. We know from local transmissions and remote reports that the enemy believe her dead, since her ship was destroyed."

"I see. And you are now . . . where?"

"Moray System, ma'am. And in the past days, after Major Douglas was killed, I've been operating on my own—but I could do with some orders, frankly."

"I'm sure, Master Sergeant." The colonel looked thoughtful. "The problem is . . . we don't have anyone to send out your way right now. I can have some orders cut, but as for sending an officer—" She paused again. "And— what was that about an officer there having reason to mistrust you?"

"If the colonel will refer to my report history, under the code name Foxbat-Victor," Pitt said, "the colonel will find that I have a contact on Slotter Key—"

A few moments later, the colonel nodded. "I see that, yes."

"Well, ma'am, the officer did not know I had a contact on Slotter Key and considered it a breach of security. As it happens the officer was acquainted with my contact and was concerned about his loyalty as well."

"Um. I can think of only one officer that might be," Paraits said. "The subject perhaps—?"

"Yes, ma'am. Who is also here with me, observing this transmission." Pitt radiated caution.

"I see. Actually I don't see, as it were, but I do understand. Let me assure this officer that, as Mackensee is now contracted to both Nexus and Cascadia, to augment their defense forces, any prior surveillance on . . . this officer . . . will certainly not be used in her detriment. And I am confident that, should I confirm Master Sergeant Pitt in her present role as temporary liaison between the . . . commander in your present location . . . and Mackensee, the master sergeant will obey all your orders and conform to your needs." Paraits paused, then went on. "It might be easier if I could talk to this officer directly, though I understand that this might present an unacceptable security risk."

"I'll talk to your people," Ky said, waving Pitt away, and moving into pickup range. "Colonel Paraits, I see that you recognize me."

"Yes."

Ky explained the circumstances that had led to Turek thinking she had died with her ship.

"So you think that if Turek thinks you're dead it will give your fleet a sufficient advantage?" Paraits asked.

"An advantage, certainly. Sufficient . . . we can't know that. He won't expect us to respond as quickly, and perhaps he will not expect the same level of tactical control," Ky said. "Not that there aren't other competent officers, but I'm the one he's seemed to worry about."

"With reason," Paraits said. "But won't he be suspicious of a continued communications blackout from Moray?"

"No—he'll think it's my death that's being concealed. And it is, in a way. We know that Turek had agents here, and at least one of his pirated ansibles . . . but those can communicate only with others like them. So if word of my death gets out, it's almost certainly through a network of his agents, and it might be possible to backtrack and locate them by those leaks."

"Ah," Paraits said. "Very ingenious and quite possibly workable. I doubt you'll smoke them all out, but you should get quite a few. Do you have your strategy for attacking Turek planned yet?"

"No. It depends on where his supply base is and how long he'll need to be there. Moray tells us that the ships he made off with will need at least another six to seven days in dock, with competent workers, to do the final weapons fitting, the stocking up, and so on. Longer without a skilled crew and the facilities they have here. If he wants to calibrate the weapons and fine-tune the navigation computers, to maximize his control in combat, he'll need still another seven to ten days. Moray has given us the ships he didn't take, and they're now very close to fully operational." Miracle, that was, considering the number of expert riggers who'd died, but the Moray government had gone all-out.

"If he thinks you're dead, if he thinks that will make a real delay, he could move either faster or slower. And have you considered the effect word of your death may have on your other allies?"

"It should stiffen their spines," Ky said. "If it doesn't—well, they wouldn't stick it out if they knew I was alive."

"I think you underestimate your effect, Admiral Vatta, but I won't argue."

"You're not going to believe this." The Moray senior scan tech handed over a data cube. "We have all the details of Ransome's departure untangled from the rest of the scan data that day. The ship identified as *Glorious* accelerated toward the enemy as the enemy fled, and appears to have gone into jumpspace at the same relative distance from the scan station, as if they thought they could pursue through FTL space. The other Ranger ship was behind by some minutes, but went into jump within ten thousand klicks of that location."

"Idiots!" Ky said. "And no transmissions at all?"

"Not to the fleet and not to Moray. They just took off. Do you think they were actually associated with the enemy all along?" Moray's suspicions were still active, Ky realized.

"No," Ky said. She glanced at Pitt.

"I agree with the admiral," Pitt said. "These young men were impulsive and extravagant, but they weren't traitors."

"Well, what did they think they were doing? Nobody can follow in FTL flight . . . they wouldn't have the coordinates or anything."

"And a blind jump can dump you out anywhere," Ky said. "But . . . could they have had the coordinates? Could they have been monitoring the enemy transmissions? We have a record of those, don't we?"

"Yes, and the translations—but he couldn't have had the translations that fast—"

"Do the translations give any numerical data?"

"Er . . . yes . . . I suppose those could be vector and duration—if you knew which was which . . ."

"So he could've swung over to get on the same course, which gives him vector . . . and duration . . . and he might come out at the same place."

"Might. Unless it was multiple jumps."

"But he might have thought he had enough data—"

"Then he's crazy."

"Right now, he's gone," Ky said. "And since we don't know where, or when—if ever—he'll be back with us, we might as well go on to the next item."

The next item, crewing the Moray-built ships, took much longer.

"You'll have to take one of them as your flagship," Argelos pointed out. "And none of us knows diddly about them; you should use Moray crew for Moray ships."

"Moray's own space navy doesn't use this model," Ky said. "You could learn. *Sharra's Gift* shouldn't go into another combat—you've seen the stress charts."

"Um. We could be second-tier . . ."

"You could also be dead. We need to replace the ships with the worst stress levels, and you know it. You're not the only one who's being shifted."

Argelos looked grim. "*Sharra's Gift* has been my ship since I got into the business. She's like my other arm—"

"I understand. But this is war, not privateering. If you're to be with me, you're going to have to move to a ship that's capable of sustained combat."

"Can I at least name it *Sharra's Gift II*?"

"I don't see why not," Ky said. "None of them have names yet . . . all their ship-chips are just numbers at this point."

"What about Dan? Are you going to make him change ships, too?"

"*Bassoon* isn't showing the same damage. We have worse in the fleet. *Tangeld,* for instance, and *Sapphire Radiance.* Captain Peters and Captain Tardin will both take over cruisers."

"What will happen to my—to the original *Sharra's Gift*?"

"You owned her outright, didn't you?"

"Yes . . ."

"Then you could sell her, or let Moray do the refit, either to military grade or back to a merchanter. For that matter, if Moray pulled her armament, she could run as a merchanter now."

"I won't have time to do that—to run her, I mean. I suppose I could sell . . . but I don't know . . . I feel I'm losing my connection . . ."

Ky noted his expression. "You're not happy with all this, are you?"

"Who would be?" Argelos asked. "I don't mean you— you've been a good commander—"

"Look . . . do you want to quit and go back to being a merchanter? A letter of marque doesn't force you to be a privateer—it's permission. If *Sharra's Gift* were unarmed . . . you've earned a rest."

"It's a commission," Argelos said. "I said I'd take on Slotter Key's enemies."

"Yes, but not in the same way it was when there were kings and things. Legally, I think you'd have no problem, if that's what you want. I'd back you."

"I don't want to get blown away by Turek's bunch—

and I would, unarmed and alone. I guess . . . I never really thought of myself as a Spaceforce captain. Being a privateer, I could be mostly a trader and only sometimes have to worry . . ." He scrubbed at his head. "And now I've been in . . . is it only three battles? Four, counting that mess at Gretna, if that qualified as a battle, and I guess it did. Should, with some of my people dead. I don't know, it's just . . . I think I'm not good enough."

"You're good enough," Ky said. "But you need some of the same treatment I got. I should've thought of that."

"No . . . if you think I can command a Moray-built warship, then I guess I can command a Moray-built warship. But I'm going to miss old *Sharra's Gift*."

"You'll get her back someday," Ky said, and then wondered if it was an empty promise.

"It won't be the same," Argelos said. "But it'll be nice to have this over with. So—where's the book for my new ship? I know the first rule: RTFM hasn't changed since before the Dispersion."

One by one, Ky found captains for her ships, some transferred from aging privateer vessels, and some from Moray's own space service. Since Moray didn't use heavy cruisers in its home defense fleet, none of the captains had prior experience with that model, but the Moray officers were familiar with much of the software. Ky set up classes. Crews for the new ships would come mostly from Moray—she did not have the people, in her other ships—to fill out the necessary positions, nor would she have even if *Vanguard* had not been lost.

SEVENTEEN

On the seventh day in FTL flight, Teddy Ransome experienced the kind of internal change known in his culture as "brain-bend." Some people planned their progress through their various intelligences: so many months in each. Others waited on whatever biochemical signal switched off one and turned on another . . . and something turned the switch.

It felt mentally just like falling out of bed felt physically—that moment of blissful weightlessness, followed by a hard thump when he hit the floor. He had been a Romantic; he had enjoyed being a Romantic; he had secretly planned to die as a Romantic, never completing the cycle of modalities that was supposed to prepare one for full maturity.

Only he wasn't a Romantic anymore. Safe in the cocoon of uncertainty that defined FTL flight, he stared at the banks of instruments visible from his command chair and wondered how he'd ever convinced himself this was a good idea.

Even his uniform disgusted him. Sky blue, gold braid, white facings? He looked around the bridge. More light blue, more braid . . . brightly polished metal in decorative shapes. Had he really thought that was practical? It looked theatrical, not at all workmanlike . . .

He reached mentally for the mantle—no, the flamboyant swirling cloak—of his Romantic period, but it was gone. He couldn't be Teddy Ransome, pirate hunter . . . Teddy Ransome, noble, gallant, daring . . . he shivered. Who was he now? Theodore, not Teddy? It sounded stuffy; it felt . . . much less stuffy than it would have even a few hours before. Which intelligence would come to the fore, and would it be one he could stand?

A cool, severe voice rose from his brainstem to point out that he had put himself in harm's way repeatedly—including now—in hopes of impressing a woman who was, when you came down to it, nothing but a merchant's daughter with a perfectly ordinary face. A merchant's daughter with considerable military skill, yes, but far from the glamorous figure he had created in his imagination.

And now here he was, with his ship, in FTL flight, not knowing where he was going, when the enemy would drop out into normal space . . . he had gone blindly, without thinking, assuming she was dead, and she probably *was* dead, but that was no reason to do what he'd done.

Seven days on an uncharted jump. They could be anywhere. They could downjump into a star, into a planet, into a stupid chunk of rock. He'd been an idiot; he wouldn't be an idiot one moment longer.

He called up what navigation charts he had and looked them over, something he hadn't bothered with before. It was impossible to tell where he was, yet in general the longer a ship was in FTL flight, the farther it went, and there were some accepted correlations. If Turek's entry vector had been this . . . and if Turek had not already made other jumps on other vectors . . . then they should be somewhere in this area, within three to four light-years. Unfortunately, not one of the safely blank areas, but still—

"Bajory, prepare for downjump transition," Teddy said.

He could hear the different timbre in his voice; the entire bridge crew glanced at him.

"Time, Captain?" Bajory asked.

"As soon as possible," Teddy said.

"Excuse me, but are you—are we—giving up the pursuit? Or do you have information—"

"We're dropping into normal space for navigational purposes," Teddy said. Again the curious looks. He'd better do something about that. "I . . . have had an episode." Now they looked worried. "Brain-bend," he said. They still looked worried.

"So . . . you're not a Romantic anymore?" Bajory said.

"Not at the moment, no," Teddy said. "And it's not settled yet, but I see no reason to run on blindly . . ."

"Captain Baskerville, sir?"

Damn. Brain-bend had affected his memory temporarily. Des Baskerville, commanding *Courageous*, was probably speeding on, still in his Romantic phase, unless he, too, had suffered an episode of brain-bend. And Des was one of his oldest friends. They'd sworn to stick together forever, back in school. But—with no way to contact Des while in FTL flight—he couldn't tell Des he was dropping out.

"We don't even know if he's still on our trail," Teddy said. "A lot can happen in seven days."

"So—"

"So we will drop out of FTL, try to get a location, see if anyone's had word of Captain Baskerville, and then— if it seems reasonable—continue the pursuit."

"Yes, Captain." Bajory nodded sharply and turned to his work, while Teddy leaned back in his command seat and tried to figure out what he'd become.

Sometimes brain-bend did simple reversals—from Romantic to Cynic, for example—but he didn't feel partic-

ularly cynical—not as he understood cynical. He felt almost
. . . analytical. The way he imagined Ky Vatta thought,
weighing options, considering plans of action . . . really,
even if she was a merchant's daughter from Slotter Key, she
was remarkable, if she could think like this.

Downjump, when it came a few minutes later, felt
normal, but emergence was at high relative vee and scan
showed nothing useful in real time. Teddy sweated out the
interval before they had slowed and scan began to show
reliable data. Their own downjump had left a noticeable
disturbance, the typical concentric-ring dimple, sharper for
being a high-vee insertion. Scan picked up no ships at first
run, which only meant nothing was nearby now. No accurate position yet, but the uncertainty box was within the
segment he'd expected. He felt happier now.

"When scan clears, see if there's any trace from
someone coming through in FTL." Unlikely, but any malfunction in the FTL drive might show a temporary effect
scan could pick up. "Contact *Courageous*," he added.
"Let's see if Des dropped out somewhere. Then give a
listen on the pirates' channel, just in case we pick up one
of their general broadcasts. And then we'll call back to
Moray."

Moray System, Aboard Vanguard II

"Admiral! It's Ransome!"

"Ransome?" Ky pulled her attention away from the
chapter of Gershaw & Xrilin discussing staff organization
in multinational forces; it took a moment to think who
Ransome was. "*Teddy* Ransome?"

"Yes. He's calling on his shipboard ansible. Says he has
important news. Do you want to talk to him yourself?"

"Yes," Ky said. "I want to see his face when he finds out I'm alive. Just in case he's playing both sides."

Teddy Ransome looked different, but Ky could not at first define the difference, in his slack-jawed astonishment. "You're alive," he said. "I thought you were dead . . . your ship blew up."

"Yes, it did," Ky said. "Care to explain what you thought you were doing?"

"You were dead and I wanted revenge," Ransome said. "So I followed Turek into FTL."

"Just like that," Ky said.

"Mostly." He bit his lip. "It was a lucky guess, I suppose you'd say. I was monitoring their transmissions, as you know, and heard the order to withdraw—well, I think that's what it was, but it contained navigation data, a blip to computers. I fed it into mine and—"

"And didn't come out in a star . . . where are you, anyway?"

"I've found them," he said. "They're in the same system."

"They didn't notice when you popped out of jump next to them?"

"Er . . . no. I didn't downjump here. That was days ago. What happened . . . I had . . . changed my intelligence. It happens sometimes. Anyway, I thought it too risky to just run blindly wherever they were going, and I still had the data in the computer. So we ran an analysis on that, and then followed very carefully . . ."

That didn't sound like Ransome. Charging headlong had always been more his style than following carefully. Ky pushed that thought aside. "You found them . . . where?"

"It's not really charted," Ransome said. "At least, not on my charts. I'll blip you everything we have, course and all."

"Good," Ky said. "What do you mean, *changed my intelligence*? Does it mean you're not a Romantic anymore?" His voice did sound more mature, less emotional. He hadn't gushed about anything yet.

"Exactly," Ransome said. "I'm not a Romantic. I certainly didn't plan to change. I have no idea what triggered it. But on the seventh day of FTL, it suddenly . . . changed." His expression was rueful. "It was more fun being Romantic, but I can't get back to it. So now I'm stuck in whatever I am."

An adult, finally, was Ky's thought. "You don't know?"

"No. It can take as long as sixty days, I've been told, for the new intelligence to declare itself, if it's singular. At home, I'd go to a specialist and be sorted out more quickly, but here—I don't know."

"How do you . . . er . . . feel?"

"Quite well, thank you. I ran through some evaluative tests, and apparently I'm thinking very well, and have no memory impairments or gaps in reasoning ability. I've instructed my second in command to inform me immediately if he sees any disordered thinking, but so far— nothing of the sort."

"So what—besides the data you just sent us—can you tell me about Turek's force? What are they doing?"

"There's significant time lag on their non-ansible transmissions. They don't use the ansible much when they're in their base, so what we've got is probably a day or so old. All we know is that they're provisioning their ships, taking on munitions. We did get a transmission from an incoming ship apparently loaded with munitions."

"Send us your recordings, too," Ky said. "And we'll send you the latest translation keys we have. But do you have any idea where they're headed next, or when?"

"No. They've never said, or we can't understand it."

"Can you stay where you are and keep monitoring?"

"Certainly. Are you going to come here and attack?"

"It's what . . . an eight-day transit?"

"More like ten, if you come in sneakily. And I know they've mined the entrance they used from Moray. But there are no jump points on the chart, and no big masses nearby. Anyone could come in other ways."

"If we're in FTL, we won't know if they leave. Or where they're going, even if you're able to tell us. Do you have any idea what the FTL time is from there to Nexus or Cascadia?"

"Not really. There are no mapped routes from here to anywhere on my charts; I don't know if they'd need intermediate jump points and, if so, where they might be. But they're definitely gearing up for a major attack, as you expected before Moray."

Ky found it easy now to believe that Ransome had changed in some fundamental way. No flamboyance, no flowery language, no compliments—not that she missed those—but the kind of sober, rational assessment any good officer might provide. His face even seemed older, less boyish. But if he wasn't the Romantic-hero-Ransome anymore, who was he? Was he, for instance, loyal to her, to their cause? If not, he could do them immense harm with that shipboard ansible.

"What about Captain Baskerville?" she asked. "He's with you, I presume."

"No, he's not." Ransome shook his head. "I have tried to contact him, without success. I had no way to tell him I was leaving FTL flight . . . I would have expected him to drop out by now, somewhere, but though we've tried a contact every four hours, there's been no word."

"I'm sorry," Ky said.

Ransome lifted his hand and let it fall. "We'll keep

trying," he said. "Now—what do you want me to do? If part of their force leaves, if they all leave—?"

"Contact us first, but also Cascadia Defense. If we're in FTL flight, they can pass the data on to Nexus Defense. If some of them stay, you stay put, so you can report on their movements; if they all depart, and you can't reach me, go directly to—" Where should she send him? Cascadia or Nexus? "Cascadia," she said.

"If I stayed here," he said, "I would be able to give you current information when you arrived . . ."

"That's true. Let me think about this for a few hours. I'll get back to you."

Ky called in her senior staff. Most attended on screen rather than take the time to shuttle to the flagship. She explained what she could about Ransome. "We need to figure out where he is on our charts, and then decide how to move next. If we could hit Turek in a base he thinks is secure—even a glancing blow could knock out some of his fleet. Ransome's is the only onsite intel we've got."

"The latest report from our people says there's been his lingo here—" Pitt pointed to a set of coordinates. "It's just a blip in the stream, for most traders—the only reason it was ever colonized was raw materials. It's only a two-day FTL hop from Gingervin; miners go over there and break off pieces. Finally someone installed a station, three or four space-based processors, and they have a kind of back-of-the-hills trade for anyone who drops in. Rough bunch. Anyway, one of our people knows someone who knows someone, and they reported some odd transmissions."

"Wouldn't they want a place with a relay ansible?" one of the Moray officers asked.

"No—they have their own," Ky said. "They don't need relay ansibles, and if they're in an empty system, or between systems far from an ansible, less chance of being noticed." She stared at the display. "Did they actually come to this miners' place, Master Sergeant?"

"Word was somebody made a beer run, Admiral. But it's thirdhand."

"I can't see Turek letting any of his people wander off just to find liquor—surely he'd have his own setup, if he allowed it."

"It's a way to find out what rumors are floating around," Major Steen said. "Hang out in a bar and listen, the same way the Mackensee informant did."

"Well, we can't sit here waiting forever," Ky said. "We're stuffed with supplies; we've done the run-in tests. We could always use more training, but I don't expect Turek to wait for us to move, and we dare not wait for him. At the least we need to be closer to his likely targets—and this is in the right direction."

From the sudden alertness in the room, Ky was sure that the others agreed. "Orders, Admiral?" asked the Moray senior commander.

"Make up formations," Ky said. "Just what we've talked about—we'll head for the jump point, use the same vector as Ransome, seven standard days in FTL, drop out and contact him. Maybe we'll get a better fix on location before we jump, but we have more extensive charts to use when we get there, even if not. Captain Yamini, I want you to be advance scout: precede formations to the jump point, extend your FTL to seven point two five standard days, and come in dead slow."

"Yes, ma'am." Yamini blanked his screen.

"Any questions?" Ky asked the others. No one had any. "Fine. I estimate we're twenty or more hours before the fleet's in formation on the right vector to the jump point; I'll have more detailed orders for downjump by two hours prior so you can pass them to your formations. Let's go."

Ky set to work drafting orders to cover the possibilities she recognized: Turek's force within firing distance, Turek's force light-hours, or -days, away, mines in the downjump destination, everything she could think of. The same basic five or six formation assignments covered them all, thanks to the work she and her staff had done in the past tenday. Shields up. Weapons hot. Passive scans only on downjump. She handed the draft orders to Pitt and Stanley, a Moray officer.

"Here. Nitpick. What did I forget?"

"What about microjumping the forward formations out two minutes? Your spacing's five, right? That'd give some margin of error."

"Good point," Ky said. With this many ships, and less training time than she'd have liked, best leave more room for the inevitable errors. "But into a pincer formation— gives us more options, whatever we find."

"Admiral Vatta, we have a location!" The navigation officer was grinning. "It's on a mapped route, but not a green one—it's yellow due to flux disturbances near a pulsar here—" He pointed. "In fact, there are mapped jump points all through this area—" With a touch he highlighted a region. "But no green routes. An open cluster here, a pulsar there . . . really more trouble to commercial vessels than ours, but it's a wonder Captain Ransome didn't run into something." Ky gave him a look, and he hurried on. "Turek's force is here. Mapped jump point PRTB-1512, in the current Pritchard-Robarts atlas."

Ky transmitted the navigation data and her orders to the rest of the fleet and watched as the ships edged into formation. Squadrons combining the new heavy cruisers from Moray, the Cascadian and Moray warships, the privateers, the support ships—supply, minesweepers, all moving to her plan.

It had better be the right plan. The wraiths of her dead rose around her for a moment, reminding her of mistakes made, deaths she had not prevented, and then her implant intervened. She would do her best; she had taken the best advice she could get; what happened would happen.

She left her office and began a walk through the ship after notifying her flag captain. Hugh would have known her routine, known she walked the ship daily, and they had their understanding of his limits and hers. This new *Vanguard* had become more familiar with every passing day, but it was not the old *Vanguard* and Captain MacKay was not Hugh. Its crew was a mix of Slotter Key, Moray, and Cascadia citizens . . . all new to her . . . she had them all in her implant now, knew the cooks in the galley—a space as large as the largest crew compartment had been in the old *Vanguard*—and the moles in Environmental, as well as the weapons crews and the engineers.

The ship smelled right, its original sharp odor from outgassing of new synthetics now mellowed by filters and hydroponics. Chemical sensors along the bulkheads checked constantly for toxic vapors, but Ky knew the human nose made a good early warning for some things. The ship sounded right, too . . . the barely heard vibrations were those of good adjustment . . . nothing was phasing in and out. The voices in compartments she passed had the right timbre, even if the accents were different. Crew were excited, eager, but not anxious.

The day before she had walked the portside first; today she started at the starboard bow. This *Vanguard* mounted multiple beams along the long axis; the massive supports and heat-radiating structures crowded the center of the ship on the weapons deck, narrowing both lateral passages. Ky reached out and ran a finger along the red stripe—the red Turek had ordered, and which she had not bothered to change. The deck gleamed under the overhead lightbars; the bulkhead itself, matte-finished except for the stripe, curved gently toward the bow.

At the starboard forward missile battery, Ky looked in. Chief McIntosh of Moray was drilling a team on fusing options; one of them spotted her and leapt to his feet. "Admiral on deck!"

"At ease," Ky said. Despite the obvious advantages to having uniforms that were uniform, only the officers had acquired Space Defense Force uniforms. Chief McIntosh, in a dark tan shirt and slacks tucked into brown ship boots, had a tartan armband with four black stripes angling across it; the team he was drilling included two in Moscoe Confederation green, and three in Slotter Key blue. "So, Chief, how's it going?"

"Fine, ma'am," he said. "Crews are meshing well. Never thought I'd get to serve on a ship like this, y'know."

"Nor I," Ky said. "I thought Slotter Key cruisers were big, back when I was in the Academy, but this thing's twice that size at least. I can spend more than a shift going from compartment to compartment and not see them all."

He grinned. "That's right, ma'am. We're one of the few places that can build 'em this size."

"Well, carry on, Chief. I'd better keep moving. Admirals are supposed to spread their interruptions around . . ." She moved aft, pausing in each of the weapons bays to speak to crews, all busy with something.

Cascadia Station

Stella Vatta pored over the financial data Ky had sent. She had in fact sold the ansibles to Teddy Ransome for the sum Stella had suggested. But she had given others away . . . there was the amount owed to Crown & Spears on Gretna, already taken care of. But the purchase of indentured servants was illegal here in the Moscoe Confederation. Traffic in humans was illegal most places . . . and she didn't think they'd understand that it had been the only way to save those people from a worse fate. Were any of them still with Ky? Could they testify if necessary? It would help if she could talk to Ky, not have to pass everything through her staff . . . silly, that. She was family. Family should always have access to family.

"Aunt Stella!" Zori tapped on the door. She had come to call Stella "Aunt" only in the past few days. Though she now lived with her mother, she showed up at Stella's at least once a day, trailed by her escort.

"Yes, Zori," Stella said. The girl might not be family yet, but she now believed it was likely to happen.

"I just heard something . . . it may be only a rumor, I don't know, but this boy at school said something about your cousin Ky, the admiral—"

"What?"

"That she . . . she died. Her ship blew up."

"What! No, of course she didn't." The icy wash that seemed to drown her for an instant passed. "I've had messages from her."

"Oh . . . ." Zori slumped against the desk. "That's a relief. I didn't really think Jed knew what he was talking about, but he said he heard it from a man who heard it dockside."

Except . . . Ky hadn't actually contacted her personally.

Of course that meant nothing; she was busy; she had a fleet to organize, enemies to watch out for. Still . . . she must be alive. Someone would have told Stella if she wasn't. Someone would have known, someone would have made contact, surely.

Still, it wouldn't hurt to check. Just to be sure. And if a rumor was going around that Ky had been killed, that might impact morale . . . she should let Grace know.

With that thought in mind, Stella placed an ansible call to Moray, and waited longer than usual for the icon to resolve into someone's face. Not Ky's face, but then she had staff . . . Stella tried to ignore the knot in her stomach. The uniform was unfamiliar as well.

"Admiral Vatta, please," she said. "From Stella Vatta."

"I'm sorry; the admiral is not available."

"Would you give her a message to contact me directly as soon as possible?"

"I . . . will transfer your call to a more senior officer. Just a moment."

Stella's anxiety grew.

Ky had just finished taking Teddy Ransome's latest hourly report when one of the Moray officers walked in. "It's your cousin," he said. "She wants to talk to you. She's on a secured line, but—"

Ky shook her head. "She can't know I'm alive. Stella wouldn't leak it but there's too much chance, with Toby and Zori there, and Zori's father having been one of them—"

"She'll be upset—"

"My concern is defeating Turek," Ky said. "We have only a slim chance of doing that anyway. I'm not going to give it away to comfort Stella. Tell her my ship blew up."

"Yes, Admiral."

"Sera Vatta." The senior officer in Moray uniform who had appeared on screen was an older man. "I realize this may come as a shock—I am sorry it is necessary to—"

"What?"

"When Admiral Vatta arrived here, we were under attack by the force we'd been warned of. In the battle that followed, her forces joined with our own defenses and drove the enemy away, albeit with losses. Admiral Vatta's ship blew up while in pursuit of the enemy."

"Her . . . ship?" Stella could not think for a moment. "But—but she was in a special unit. She should have survived—"

"I'm sorry," the man said.

"So . . . who's commanding Slotter Key forces now? And the coalition? Has the Moscoe Confederation government been informed?"

"All relevant governments have been informed," he said. "Clearly the alliance is still necessary. I believe Slotter Key is sending someone out to take command of their ships, and the overall coalition commander will be decided very soon. More than that I cannot say."

"Were there any . . . was anything . . . recovered?" Stella asked. She still felt numb, but knew that pain would follow.

"No. I'm sorry . . . the aftermath of a battle in space is . . . not . . ." His voice trailed away. "I wish I could offer some comfort—"

"Comfort!" White rage etched through the numbness; Stella fought it down. "I'm sorry; I have to go—no, wait. The government here hasn't made any announcement, so if they know—perhaps I shouldn't say anything—?" But how could she not?

"I believe the decision was made not to publicize Admiral Vatta's . . . passing . . . in order not to disturb the public. But you might want to speak to Garond

Seviera, in the Moscoe Confederation Department of Defense."

"Seviera," Stella muttered, entering it in her implant database. "What's he?"

"An undersecretary for propaganda, I believe. And sera, if anything is . . . recovered . . . you will certainly be informed."

"Thank you," Stella said.

After she'd disconnected, Stella sat motionless, waiting for the grief to strike. She could sense its approach, a giant block of misery . . . all the things she'd said she could not now take back or explain away, all the words unsaid that could not now be said. No. She could not wait for it. That first stab of anger at the Moray officer gave her energy. She looked up Seviera and placed a call to his office.

"Sera Vatta, how may I help you?"

"You can tell me if it's true that my cousin Ky is dead and you're hiding that fact."

"Sera . . . where did you hear that?"

"The young woman I'm taking care of, Zori Louarri, heard it from a schoolmate who heard it from someone who works dockside. She didn't believe it, and neither did I until I tried to contact Ky myself. And an officer of the Moray Defense Services told me her ship had blown up."

"I'm sorry you found out this way," he said.

"So it's true."

"According to the report we got, her ship was in hot pursuit of the enemy—possibly the enemy flagship—and suddenly exploded. I haven't heard anything more about the exact cause, if it can be determined. There have been other priorities. As I'm sure you're aware, the ship had some deficiencies that went uncorrected—"

"Yes, but she was supposed to be in that secure modular thing—"

"CCC, yes."

"That was installed here. I thought it was proof against anything—"

"Nothing's proof against everything. It's certainly a tragedy. And to answer your second question, it's true we've not publicized her death, and I hope to persuade you not to . . . the thing is, so many people were impressed by her, we're afraid her death would be a serious blow to morale. And if the enemy doesn't know she's dead, perhaps it will delay their next attack."

"I see . . . so you don't want me to tell even the family?"

"That's a difficult decision, sera. I do understand the desire to have family support at a time like this. But if word got out—and that reminds me . . . can you tell me more about how you found out?"

Stella recited it again—Zori, the classmate, the unknown spacer dockside.

"We need to plug that hole," Seviera said. "I don't want to bother the young lady; she's had enough problems. Do you think you could get the name of that classmate from her and let me know?"

"It was Jed-something," Stella said. "I could try, but I don't know if I—if I can keep the truth from her. I'm—"

"Upset, of course," he said. "You've suffered a terrible loss, on top of all the others your family has had to endure. I'll check the school registry first."

Stella closed that connection, and wondered what to do now. If Slotter Key's government knew, then surely Grace knew . . . and hadn't told her . . . but if they both knew, surely they could talk. She looked at the time where Grace was. Three in the morning. Grace might be up, but she wouldn't appreciate a call in the middle of the night. For just an instant she thought of calling Rafe—but that would not do, even if he also knew.

She tried to bury herself in the accounts, but she kept seeing Ky in everything Ky had touched. Images of the sturdy, stubborn little girl, the sulky teenager, the wary adult, all ran into one another and kept her mind from focusing on the figures. Another one of the family gone, every childhood playmate, gone.

She would not cry. She would not . . . but in spite of herself, tears rolled down her cheeks.

EIGHTEEN

Slotter Key

"So Ky isn't telling Stella she survived the explosion?" MacRobert said. "Tough on Stella. You told Helen." He handed Grace the padded grip of the exercise apparatus. She wrapped her small hand around it slowly, careful not to stretch the flexible sleeve that still protected it as it grew.

"Helen's not in the middle of a crowded space station, the sole licensee for a technology vital to the war, with two intelligent and no doubt naïvely nosy adolescents living with her," Grace said. She moved her arm back and forth in the range-of-motion exercises. "I can trust Helen not to leak it to anyone, and the children are too little . . . nobody's going to listen to them, even if they do insist their cousin Ky is alive."

"Stella's going to be furious when she finds out," MacRobert said. "With you, as well."

"Not when she's going to get the CEO-ship," Grace said. "If we can get Maxim out before he does something else stupid—"

"Do you still think he might be a Termanian plant in support of Parmina?"

"I'd like to think it, but no. Nobody else in the family has done anything suspicious, and he hasn't been offplanet. Yes, he's got the right genes to be an intended problem, but I think it's coincidence. We've looked—you and I both—and we've uncovered everything else." They had found Turek's agents in the local mafia, and located the portable ansible they'd used to keep in touch with Turek. Even deep interrogation hadn't produced any links to Maxim. "He's just young, in love, and full of innate stubbornness."

"Keep that shoulder level," MacRobert said. "You're compensating with a tilt."

Grace tightened her grip on the handle. "I wish this thing would grow faster!"

"It took you fifteen years to grow the first one—this one's growing pretty damned fast. Now remember—shoulders level, breathe with it—"

"How angry do you think Stella will be?" Grace asked, halfway through the next set.

"You know her better, but from what she told you about that trip with Ky . . . she really resented being kept literally in the dark. If I were you, I wouldn't let Stella get the idea you and Ky have a special bond—"

"We don't," Grace said, startled.

"You know Ky's alive. Helen knows Ky's alive. That's all the family. Stella—your protégée—is the only one who doesn't. And she's just made up with Helen, forgiving her for not telling about the adoption. Another secret she's locked out of? I think it's explosive."

"But Ky's reasons—"

"Make perfect sense from the military point of view. It's not one Stella's ever been really sympathetic to, is it? There's Vatta sense and military sense, and you're the only person who can make them overlap."

Grace unclasped her hand from the handle and flexed

the fingers. The arm ached now, instead of itching as it had earlier; it had skin and muscles and it moved, within its covering, almost without thought. Fine-motor was still a problem, but she was sure once she got rid of the protective covering it would come quickly.

"How could I do it without Toby finding out? And why would she accept it from me?"

"You're her mentor. You're senior in the family. You're the Rector of Defense. All those together. You can tell her it was essential for Ky herself to make no contact with anyone, anywhere. That you were the only one who could do it safely."

"That might work." Grace stretched the young arm forward, measuring it against her old one. "Ha. Look at that." The tips of her left fingers touched the base of her right palm. "Not long now." MacRobert took her hands, both of them, and lightly kissed them. "You're right, Anders, that should work. Ky wanted to tell her, but didn't dare get on herself—she wanted me to tell her—" She glanced at the clock. "I could call her—"

"Before she calls you, yes."

Cascadia

When the Slotter Key origination code came up, Stella wasn't surprised. Aunt Grace, of course. Probably Seviera had told her that Stella knew.

"Aunt Grace," Stella said when Grace's face appeared.

"How secure is your end?" Grace asked.

"Best I can make it," Stella said.

"And you're alone."

"Yes . . . look, I already know—" She felt tears stinging her eyes again.

"No, you don't," Grace said. "You have a privacy shield in your office, I'm sure."

"Yes, but—"

"Engage it."

Stella took the cylinder out of her desk and laid it where the video pickup would include it, then touched the nub on one side. "Engaged," she said.

"No one must know what I'm telling you," Grace said. "Not Toby, not Zori, not anyone, including that twit in the propaganda department."

"I know it's a secret," Stella said.

"But you don't know *what* secret," Grace said.

"Ky—"

"Ky is alive," Grace said.

"She—but they said—"

"Ky is alive. She could not tell you; she can't communicate outside the system she's in without risking the enemy finding out she's alive."

"But—but I thought it was her *death* that was supposed to be secret."

Grace shook her head. "It's a double cover, Stella. We seem to be hiding the fact that she's dead, but we're actually hiding the fact she's alive."

"But her ship—"

"Did blow up. She was nearly killed, injured but not too seriously; only being in the CCC saved her. And the enemy think she's dead, which we think—we hope—will give her a slight advantage in the coming battle."

"The coming battle?"

"Stella, I can't tell even you more than that. Most of the enemy got away; they fled shortly after she arrived. Here's the thing: because outbound communication from Moray via the system ansible is limited to official transmissions, we know that rumors of her death must be coming from the enemy—and we're using that to trace his agents—"

"Zori heard it from a schoolmate who heard it from someone who works on the docks—"

"Yes. Which means Turek has at least one agent on Cascadia they haven't found. Thing is, you and Toby are still in danger; you must play ignorant just as you did on your first assignments. Report rumors, of course, but if the Moscoe government chooses to announce Ky's death, just be the grieving cousin."

"I can do that," Stella said. "I was grieving—"

"Of course you were. Please understand—Ky could not risk talking to you herself, and it took awhile for the message to get to me—"

"I feel like I've been—yanked around," Stella said. "I understand why, but—"

"You have been," Grace said. "Anyone would feel that way. You've been under a lot of stress on other fronts, too. And you've done brilliantly with the company business . . . I always knew you had what it takes to run the trading side, but I didn't anticipate either the need or the ability to manage a manufacturing start-up, the way you have. To learn your only surviving cousin was dead—and now that she's alive—I'm sure it's been a shock."

Grief had receded, but it didn't feel like joy, not yet. At least it was no longer pain.

"So . . . what is my assignment?" Stella asked.

"You don't believe Ky is dead, in spite of any rumors that show up. If the Moscoe government decides to admit she's dead, you are shocked and grieving, almost refusing to believe it."

"What about other—I mean, does Nexus know the truth?"

"No. They refused to join the alliance, you recall.

They're out of the loop. I don't know whether they think she's dead or not—depends on whether they queried Moray for any reason. They did know the fleet was headed there."

"Will Ky come swooping out of nowhere, like the *deus ex machina* in those old plays?"

"We hope so. But I must tell you, Stella, that the odds aren't good. Turek got away with almost half the ships ready at Moray. His fleet's larger than Ky's, and more of it is real warships. That's why it's critical that Turek continue to think she's dead."

"We could be attacked here. At Cascadia."

"Yes, but we expect him to hit Nexus."

That was nowhere near as comforting as Grace probably meant it to be. But Ky was alive. At least, had been alive the last time Grace had word of her.

"I hope you understand why Ky didn't—"

"Yes. I'm glad you told me, though. If I'd thought she was just leaving me in the dark again, the way she did before, I'd have been furious. We're partners—well, maybe not exactly, but she's family, the closest I have in my own generation. She's got to trust me."

Moray System, Aboard Vanguard II

Ky was just heading for the personnel lifts on the Environmental level when the doors slid open and Master Sergeant Pitt appeared.

"Thought you might be on this deck," Pitt said. "Message from Slotter Key on the CCC ansible."

Ky's stomach clenched. She followed Pitt into the lift tube and pressed the control. This *Vanguard* had a CCC designed into it from scratch—larger than the other one and centrally located on the command deck. Unsealed as it was now, it looked like a simple mirror of the bridge forward: the 3-D tank display, the curving double row of control stations, the command chair in its gimbels. The communications tech at the ansible station stood up and saluted. "Urgent request to speak directly to the admiral, ma'am. Sorry. It's from the Rector of Defense; I thought I should pass it on."

"Quite right," Ky said. She sat in the station's chair instead of the command seat, engaged the privacy screen, and tapped the code she and Grace had agreed on into the board. Grace's face came up at once.

"You're on your way, then," Grace said.

"How'd you know that?"

"Your face. You've got that look. I've got a large packet of data to send you—and no, I didn't need to bother you personally for that. But I had to tell Stella you were alive, and you need to know that. You were right: Turek's agents are spreading the tale of your death, and it was going to interfere with Stella's work . . . and with family. Also, I need your voiceprinted authorization for her to vote your shares— or me, or Helen. We have a situation here at Vatta headquarters. Young Maxim, who's acting CEO here, is also an Osman bastard, adopted by the Termanian family—the same family as one of the ISC Board members backing Parmina."

"He's a traitor?" Ky said.

"I don't think so. Not that I can prove, anyway. But he's a scientist, not a businessman, and he's making mistakes Stella wouldn't make. He's being stubborn about turning things over to Stella and going back to his lab. MacRobert thinks it's because of an office romance, not anything more sinister. We need to get him out, and someone else in locally to manage while Stella's on Cascadia."

"Makes sense," Ky said. "And you need my shares to vote?"

"Yes. Your parents had filed their wills, and you're the remaining heir—so you've actually got a very large interest. However, the bylaws state that any vote of shares more than five percent must be voiceprinted."

"That's going to reveal I'm alive," Ky said.

"No. We don't have to reveal the time stamp, for one thing—only the voiceprint compared with your reference voice, which I have. And we can backdate it. You could have done the voiceprint before you left Cascadia."

Ky had her doubts, but though the business was important, other things were more urgent. "Just tell me what to do and I'll do it."

"Read this aloud; you can change Stella to Grace or Helen if you want to." Grace held up a sheet of paper stating that Kylara Evangeline Vatta authorized "my close relative Stella Maria Vatta, presently residing on Cascadia Station" to vote her shares in the next election of Vatta's officers, and stating her preference for Stella Maria Vatta as overall CEO.

Ky read it out aloud, then pressed both hands flat against the plate beside the screen. That would transmit her handprints and further verify that she was who she claimed to be.

"That's very helpful," Grace said. Then she held up her left arm. "Look—it's almost grown. Soon I'll be out of the wraps."

It looked grotesque to Ky—the wrong size, the wrong color, a child's arm stuck on an old woman's body—but that was not something she could say.

"Ky—what I really want to ask—it's—you've been through a lot. Lost a lot of friends. I know what that can be like."

"Aunt Grace, it's all right. I went into treatment at Moray. They have a rapid-cycle post-trauma treatment for military personnel."

Grace scowled. "You sure it did the job?"

"We'll find out, won't we?" Ky said. "But I think so. They took my implant, stripped a lot of stuff out of it into external storage, soaked me in one set of neuro-chemicals after another, dragged me through talk sessions, recalibrated the implant's control functions, and told me I can't put the externally stored things back in for a least a year."

"Oh, my—I'm sorry, Ky. That's my fault. I didn't think to run a check on your father's implant—it had all his recordings of that day, didn't it?"

"Yes," Ky said.

"It was so chaotic," Grace said. "I should have—but I had to get Stella away safely, I knew you needed his command set, and so much was happening—I just didn't think of that—"

"It's all right," Ky said. "I'm fine, now."

"It makes me wonder if I am," Grace said. "My brain, I mean."

Ky had never seen Grace as anything but the indomitable old lady with no doubts at all that she was perfectly right in all circumstances; she wasn't sure she wanted an Aunt Grace with vulnerability. "It's all right now—"

"Oh, I know that. But even an old bat can express regret for a mistake. Your job is to say Thank you, Aunt Grace, and I'm fine now Aunt Grace, and Good-bye, Aunt Grace."

Ky laughed. This was the Grace she remembered. "Thank you, Aunt Grace; I'm fine now; good-bye and take care. I hope to get back to Slotter Key and see you in person again."

"Do that," Grace said. "But not before you've dealt with that so-and-so."

ISC Headquarters, Nexus II

"This is a mess," Rafe said, staring down at ISC's front entrance. Police cars. News vans. Helicopters hovering around trying to get pictures through the windows, not that they could. "We have a real threat that might wipe out the whole system in another tenday or so, and instead of dealing with that, they want my head for something I didn't do."

"Would it be better to *be* a murderer?" Gary asked.

"I was, according to some," Rafe said. The news notes had painted him as the blackest villain, vicious from childhood, since only a truly vicious child could have killed two trained adults. Unrepentant after years in a reformatory. Exiled from home for years. Supposedly—given a nasty emphasis by the talking heads—returned to help his family escape from abductors, but where was the proof that he had not been colluding with Parmina all along?

"They're sure it was poison? And administered by someone else?"

"So they say. Some metabolic thing to mimic a heart attack. Could be absorbed through the skin. I didn't touch the man. I didn't hand him anything. There should be surveillance tapes proving that, but they claim the tapes are fogged. I can't prove they aren't."

"Do you think Isaacs was one of Turek's agents?"

"No. I think he was lazy, greedy, and perfectly willing to take money from Parmina to ignore ISC's deficiencies. Corrupt, but not a traitor."

"Didn't you tell me that Turek's agents—or some of

them—had an implanted suicide code of some kind? When you were with that Vatta woman, didn't someone die?"

"Yes, but he was a low-level crook—someone's henchman in a criminal gang. Under interrogation he started to say Turek's name and that released the poison— a metabolic decoupler—" Rafe frowned, trying to remember if the man's symptoms had been like Isaacs'. "It was faster, I think. And Isaacs wasn't trying to say anything like that."

"Did you see anyone hand him anything—did he pick up anything on his desk?"

Rafe thought back. "When I was let in, Malendy and a secretary came in, too. The secretary put a packet of data cubes on his desk. Nothing was passed hand-to-hand." He paused, trying to re-see everything that had happened. "Isaacs didn't—wait—he did. He started fidgeting, picking things on his desk up and laying them down. A letter opener. He—he opened the folder, fumbled with several of the data cubes, just running them through his fingers as he talked. I was reading that as agitation about our conversation—"

"It probably was, but it suggests how a contact poison might have gotten to him."

"But the secretary must've put those cubes into the folder—"

"So maybe the secretary's the murderer. Or maybe Isaacs knew they were poisoned, and chose that method of suicide, to cast suspicion on you even as he died. Or someone else gave the packet to the secretary. Wonder if anyone's tested those things, or if they've been lost, perhaps by intention."

"I suppose I should tell them that," Rafe said.

"Yeah, but the question is how," Gary said. "I don't

want you leaving this place. Once they have the proven bad boy in custody they aren't likely to listen, and like you said there are far more serious things to worry about than a dead Secretary of Defense. You need them to listen—and by the way, which of your armchair admirals are you going to nominate to run the defense? Or do you think you can do it?"

"Jaime Driskill's done the best so far—his ships were in better shape overall than anyone else's, despite the budget cuts, and he responded quickly to my original suggestions. I have no idea how competent he is as a combat commander, though."

"If you could get an experienced merc commander to talk to him?"

"That would help, certainly. But that all depends on the government agreeing to do something, not just scream at me."

"Where's Driskill now?"

"On his way here, with the best ships he has. I've also ordered the best of the other ISC units here. They should arrive insystem in four or five days."

"Rafe—what's going on?" Penny came into the office; she nodded politely to Gary. "And don't try telling me it's nothing for me to worry about when there are flashing lights, helicopters, and people switch off their screens and look away when I ask them."

Rafe sighed. "You're going to have to stay here at least overnight, Penny—"

"Answer my question," Penny said.

Rafe looked at her. She had changed a lot in the past half year—no longer the frightened waif he'd rescued from abductors, or the grieving, depressed widow—but what he saw now surprised him. She looked—completely adult, completely competent, and completely determined to have her way. Like Stella, in fact, or Ky. He had never imagined her that way, as other than his little sister.

"When your party was interrupted last night," he said, "it was to tell me that Turek's fleet had attacked a military shipyard at Moray—a system about twenty days' FTL flight from here. The Moscoe–Slotter Key allied fleet drove them off, but Admiral Vatta was . . . was killed."

Penny paled. "You didn't tell me!"

"No. I didn't want to spoil your evening and I couldn't—couldn't talk about it then anyway." He couldn't talk about it now, either. He had no time for private feelings. "I was also warned that the Moray government believes Nexus will be Turek's next target. This morning I had to meet with the Secretary of Defense. You know that I'd previously warned him about the deficiencies in ISC's fleet, that we did not have the ships or weapons to defend this system. We were discussing options—he said the government wanted ISC to hire and pay for mercs to do the job we weren't doing—when he suddenly collapsed, and subsequently died." Rafe paused, not sure how to say the next bit.

"How awful," Penny said. She was looking out the window, then her eyes widened and she turned to him. "Rafe—do they think *you* killed him—did something to him? Is that why—"

"Apparently," Rafe said, "he died of poison, and yes, they think I did it. That's why the media's starting to paint me as the permanent blackest sheep in Nexus history. You might as well know—they're even suggesting that I was involved with Parmina in your abduction and staged the whole thing just to gain power, killing Parmina to hide the evidence."

"That's ridiculous!" Penny said.

"It would be, if there weren't all those official cars out

there. Thank any god you care to that ISC territory is officially not Nexus territory, or they'd have special-security
teams running down the corridors and I'd be dead in minutes."

"You're not giving up," Penny said.

"Not giving up, but not sure what to do, either," Rafe
said. "I could tell them that they should be looking for
contact poison on the data cubes Isaacs was fiddling with,
but they won't believe me. They say the surveillance tapes
from his office are fogged and they think I did that, too,
so even if they found and tested the cubes, and the poison
was still there, they'd think I put it on them." He sighed.
"And I have messages from a majority of the Board, who
want an emergency meeting. The only reason they're not
having one is that all that mess—" He waved at the
window. "—won't let them in. Another lucky break is that
our charter specifies all binding Board votes must be taken
on ISC territory."

"What about Ser Box?"

"Ser Box is highly annoyed with me. I'm not sure he'd
vote against me, but he's not helping. And Emil's father
has already suggested that my resignation might be a good
idea."

"You wouldn't do that," Penny said. Then, more doubt-
fully, "Would you?"

"Not planning to," Rafe said. Though he wished that
some miraculous storybook hero would come sailing in,
take over, and tell him he could go back to a life that
involved nothing more dangerous than the occasional
assassination attempt. But that wouldn't happen. "For one
thing, who would succeed me? Nobody, including Vaclav,
on the Board is really capable of doing what we need now.
I can see it, but so far I haven't gotten it across to them."

"Well, I understand it," Penny said. "And not just

because I'm your sister. All that digging into the records you asked for . . . and the courses I've been taking—"

"You're taking courses?"

She flushed a little. "My therapist suggested it, a way to keep busy in the evenings. And really, it's fascinating . . . the way everything fits together. Dad never talked about business at home, and Mother was always talking music. She didn't want him to talk business. Jared—" She didn't even wince now saying her dead husband's name. "—Jared just assumed I wouldn't be interested, I think. We had other interests, we talked by the hour, but not about the company. So I never knew . . ."

Rafe could hardly believe this was the same Penny; not just from last fall and the rescue, but the same Penny he'd known all his life. Or not known, he realized. Now, eyes alight, voice eager, she looked like someone who had found the right place to be.

"Um . . . so you see yourself staying with ISC?" he said.

"Unless you fire me. I know you meant it to be just a temporary thing, Rafe, a way to get me out of that horrible house, but really—I want to stay here. In fact—" Her voice took on a mischievous tone. "—someday I may challenge you for that corner office."

Penny as CEO? That was something he'd never imagined.

"Not yet, of course," she went on. "I need more education; I need more experience. Not to mention age, because the Board certainly wouldn't accept me now. They probably think of me as you do, just Rafe's little sister, poor thing. But I can see, just as you can, what needs to be done to keep us afloat. More than afloat, in fact."

Both Gary and Emil looked as startled as he felt. Rafe tried to think of the right thing to say, and found nothing coherent. "I guess," he said finally, "I needed a good smack on the head where you were concerned. You just delivered it."

"I didn't mean to hurt you," she said quickly.

"No. I'm not hurt. Surprised, startled, amazed, all of those. But if you do aspire to the corner office someday, do you have any suggestions for how to handle this?" A wave of the hand toward the windows and the mess outside.

"Actually, I do," she said. "But you're not going to like it."

Rafe had the uneasy feeling she was right. "What, then?"

"I'll talk to them. They'll be sure I'm the little sister dazzled by your—" She looked him up and down. "—handsome face and slick manner, but remember that I'm the one who found the skeletons in the financial closets."

"You wouldn't—"

"Of course I would. Isaacs is dead. Can't hurt him to explain why he might've committed suicide. Once they have something more juicy than old lies about you—and I will certainly be asking where they got that information, since it must've been passed on by someone other than Parmina—the pressure should come off. Besides, I'll look good on camera. Just you wait and see."

"I don't think it's wise—" Rafe began. Penny interrupted.

"I am of age, Rafe. And it's my decision." The grin she gave him then might have come out of his own mirror, in those days when he still led the life of a rogue. "Watch me, big brother."

Penny swept out. Emil's jaw had dropped; Gary merely looked rueful.

"I'm beginning to think you have a very strange effect on women," he said. "That young lady had victim written all over her last fall and now—now she's gone the way of

your—" He stopped abruptly. "Sorry. I forget she had . . .
um . . ."

"Died," Rafe said. Misery landed on him, a thick suf-
focating weight. "And now Penny—"

"Won't," Gary said. "Stay here; I'll be back." And he
was gone, no doubt to provide coverage for Penny, back
and front and side.

"Food," Emil said, unexpectedly. "I'll order some in.
You're looking pale."

"I'm looking dumbfounded," Rafe said. Misery receded
a centimeter. Emil showing more initiative. Penny turning
into—whatever she was turning into. Something extraordinary. Perhaps he, Rafe, wasn't *that* bad an influence.

NINETEEN

Slotter Key

"I want to go," Grace said, for the twentieth time.

"You can't go," MacRobert said. "You're the Rector; you're not in the military, and you have a half-grown arm." He had said that before, with the usual effect people had when trying to talk Grace Vatta out of what she wanted to do: none. This time he went on. "And you could very well get Ky killed."

She scowled at him. "How?"

"No one is going to ignore what the Rector of Defense says. But you have no more experience fighting a space battle than I have making fruitcakes. I know you—you can no more stay in your cabin and keep your mouth shut than you could knock me out with your short arm—"

"I could try."

"Grace. Listen this time. I'm not playing protect-the-sweet-old-lady. I'm not treating you like a child or a fragile flower of womanhood. I am treating you the way I would treat any fellow professional who wanted to be part of a mission. You are not qualified. You are not capable. You need to stay here and be sure we get the support the fleet needs—and incidentally ensure that any more of Turek's agents hiding out are found and eliminated. What if Turek decides to make a side trip to wipe out Ky's home world?"

"But *you're* going." He heard the surrender in her voice and did not try to force more out of her.

"I'm going because Slotter Key needs a military person who has a direct connection to Ky and knows she's alive, someone she will recognize and—hopefully—trust. Our ambassador at Cascadia can't do that. The privateer captains and their military advisers can't do that, because Spaceforce won't necessarily trust them. I'm the one person who can do that."

"You get all the fun," Grace said. "I need some compensation for all the work I put in getting those ships loose and committed to this joint operation."

"I'm leaving in four hours," MacRobert said. "Let's get started on that compensation."

Eight hours later, settling into his compartment aboard *Mandan Reef,* one of the heavy cruisers, MacRobert remembered his own first cruise on *Paleologus,* commanded by the man who was now Commandant of the Academy. Instead of a first-shift slot in the crowded crew quarters between missile tubes five and six, now he had a small cabin to himself, as the Rector's personal assistant and liaison to the allied fleet. He had no shipboard duties—he would not be scrubbing latrines to a mirror shine or swabbing the environmental section deck when a culture leaked or washing dishes. And he had no stripes; he wore civilian attire, which felt completely alien aboard ship.

"Master Sergeant—" That was a junior enlisted, a mere Skinny with the narrow band around the cuff of his shirt and FENTON on his name tag.

"Yes?" MacRobert said. The youngster almost jumped backward. "I don't bite," he added.

"The—the first officer wanted me to—to invite you to the bridge. Sir."

He was neither a sir nor, any longer, a master sergeant, but the youngster was doing his best to be polite and was probably scared out of any wits he had ever possessed. MacRobert closed the case he'd been unpacking and stowed it, latching the cabinet properly. "Coming," he said then.

All the way upship, he met men and women who knew who he was. "Good to see you, Master Sergeant MacRobert," and "Master Sergeant—good to have you aboard." Some of them he recognized—officers he'd harassed and guided when they were cadets, other enlisted who'd been assigned to Spaceforce Academy while he was there. Nobody called him Ser MacRobert here, as some now did in government offices; he was apparently still a master sergeant in the eyes of Spaceforce personnel.

Mandan Reef's first officer was Lieutenant Commander Dale; MacRobert remembered him as a brash young man who had required some firm handling, but turned out well, in the top fifth of his class. "Captain's in with the admiral," he said now, extending his hand. "Suggested I show you the bridge, Master Sergeant. It's been awhile."

"That it has, Commander," MacRobert said. He glanced around. "Been with *Mandy* long?"

"Year and a half. Commander Seristhan brought me along from *Firewort*." Dale introduced MacRobert to the rest of the bridge crew. "Captain said you'd be welcome up here anytime, 'cept of course in combat—"

"I'll try not to wear out my welcome, Commander," MacRobert said.

"And as a—I guess you are a civilian, officially—you're welcome to mess with either officers or enlisted."

"Um. I haven't been an official civilian that long,

Commander. If it won't offend anyone, I'd rather leave the officers to their wardroom and mess, and me where I'm comfortable."

Dale chuckled. "Master Sergeant, I have the feeling you're comfortable anywhere from the pink palace on down, but suit yourself. Captain said to ask."

MacRobert made it back to his quarters, finished his interrupted unpacking, and wondered how Grace was doing. He had gotten used to being her counterweight, and her being his, a relationship more of working partners than anything else, though the intervals of pleasure were . . . pleasurable. He had arranged additional security for her; she was as accurate with her weaponry as ever, but until that arm was full-grown and up to strength, he still worried. They'd found four more of Turek's people . . . he doubted that was all.

He ate his first meal aboard at a table of senior NCOs, most of whom he knew; they shared stories of past cruises and adventures. *Mandan Reef,* steady as the planet itself by feel, gave no sense of motion along any axis. MacRobert hadn't been in space, other than brief trips to Slotter Key's orbital stations, in several years; he hadn't been aboard one of the heavy cruisers in a decade at least.

The first days of the trip were unremarkable; Admiral Padhjan asked him for his analysis of the effect on tactics of onboard ansibles and MacRobert spent two work shifts writing it out, revising it, then revising it again. He presented his data cubes—text and visuals—to the admiral's staff, and went back to his own pursuits for another four days. With no assigned duties, he used the time in the gym and onboard weapons range, as well as chatting with enlisted personnel, all of them openly curious about his life after retirement and the Slotter Key commander of a new joint force who had once been a Spaceforce cadet.

They wanted to hear marvels, he knew. They wanted to hear that she was the smartest, the bravest, the best, of all he'd known, his favorite—someone worth trusting, someone who would not waste their lives doing something stupid.

This far from Grace, he could admit—to himself—that Ky had not been his favorite of all the cadets he'd known. Very good, yes. Everything her marks and evaluations promised. But he had pegged her as too upright, too humorless, too conventional a product of a merchant family. His favorite of all time had been a witty rakehell, an admiral's son who escaped trouble by the skin of his teeth time after time, and still topped the charts. Nasim had died fifteen years before, no fault of his own, when his ship, exploring a new route, had downjumped into a large mass. Nasim would not have fallen for the Miznarii's sob story; he'd had political sense from the first day. But then, Ky had never jumped blind and run into a rock.

What really irked MacRobert about Ky, he had to admit, was that he had not seen all her potential when she was right there under his eye. He had seen the dedication, the courage, the integrity, but he'd missed the killer Grace had seen. He hadn't even looked for it in a merchant's daughter. He'd thought of the letter of marque more as a way of keeping contact with someone who might be able to supply useful intelligence—who had enough military training to know what might be worth sharing—than as taking the leash off a born combat commander.

He told the enlisted men and women most of what they wanted to hear—it couldn't hurt—and when two days from downjump the admiral and staff called him in to ask much the same thing, he told them, too.

"You've got her dossier, Admiral. You know what the

Commandant thought of her. She had a lock on being honor graduate, until then."

"She fell for some young man—" Admiral Padhjan's expression edged on contempt.

"No, sir. She was his assigned mentor; she believed he was in distress; she tried to find him appropriate religious counsel. She should have come to me, or to one of the instructors, yes. But she did not see it as a political problem, and she did not think approaching a religious person, a cleric, would cause the trouble it did cause."

"But if she makes mistakes like that, how can we be sure—" Clearly, orders to put his squadrons under the command of someone he'd never met—someone who was not even an Academy graduate—were fraying in the admiral's memory.

"Sir, if she still made mistakes like that she wouldn't be alive." MacRobert put on his most familiar persona, the senior NCO who, perfectly respectful, nonetheless steers his seniors around the potholes they are unable or unwilling to see. "Cadets, you know, do make mistakes. Sometimes serious ones. Sometimes in class, sometimes in barracks, sometimes on the drill field . . ." He paused; Admiral Padhjan acquired a faint flush. "That's how they learn," MacRobert went on, ignoring it. They both knew what Padhjan's mistake had been, and he hadn't repeated it, which was the point.

"And you think she's really competent to command large forces in combat?" Admiral Padhjan said. "A mixed force like this?"

"She's the only person on our side who's done it," MacRobert said. "And she's survived. So it's the Rector's judgment that she's capable, and I concur."

"The Rector is her relative," the admiral said. "That suggests her judgment might be less than impartial."

"The Rector is a combat veteran herself," MacRobert said. It took an effort to keep his voice even, but he'd had years of practice.

"A long time ago." Padhjan sighed. "All right. I take your point. The Rector isn't just a political appointee; Ky Vatta isn't just an impressionable girl. I hope you're right."

MacRobert hoped so, too. Ky had exceeded his expectations; she had exceeded everyone's expectations so far, but at some point she would run into her limits.

"Let's get to the details. I've looked over what you supplied, and what little information we've had direct from Admiral Vatta. I've had some thoughts I'd like to discuss with all of you—" He glanced around the compartment.

MacRobert was relieved that Padhjan finally used Ky's rank. Maybe that particular hurdle was past.

"If there is time to train together, of course we will do that," Padhjan said. "But the Moscoe and Moray governments both think an attack will come soon, possibly immediately on our arrival or, if we are unlucky, before we arrive. We must have plans in place for all those, in case we do not get to talk to Admiral Vatta before we're engaged."

"Does she know we're coming?" Captain Seristhan asked.

"We're not sure. The Moscoe government knows, but she was maintaining communications lockdown—could receive but would not send. The timing was close—she may have already jumped when the word came through Moscoe."

"I see . . . so she might shoot us herself—"

"She knew negotiations were ongoing," MacRobert put in. "I wouldn't expect her to fire at anything with a Slotter Key beacon ID."

"Was sure her relative would come through, eh?" Seristhan said.

MacRobert put on his bland look again. "In my experience, Captain, the Rector is uncommonly effective at getting done what she thinks needs doing."

Seristhan nodded. "She got us a full load-out of missiles and a new set of coils for number four faster than I'd ever seen Supply hustle. I like that kind of effectiveness."

"It was with great difficulty I dissuaded her from coming along," MacRobert said. He enjoyed the horrified looks that resulted. "She is, after all, a war veteran, as she reminded me, and she felt that her presence might be . . . helpful . . . in dealing with other governments." MacRobert paused again. Grace's reputation had not lessened in her time at the head of the Defense Department. No one thought of her as a potential diplomat.

"But the President wouldn't have let—" began Captain Seristhan, then stopped. Clearly all remembered what had happened to the former President, and the rumors about Grace at that time. "And you—changed her mind?"

"In a manner of speaking," MacRobert said. "She's very dedicated to the welfare and safety of Slotter Key, and she finally saw that her place was there, guarding the rear, as it were. I pity the pirate who tries to get past her."

Nexus II

Penelope Dunbarger—she had taken back her maiden name for business use, and insisted that the media use it—looked perfectly at ease in the chair placed for her by a solicitous host on the main news program. Rafe could hardly believe this was happening. She had left the building not by the underground route he would have recommended, but by the front entrance, smiling and waving at the astonished police and news reporters as if she were a vid star. After disappearing into a crowd of uniforms and cameras, she had reemerged and entered the rear door of a long, sleek vehicle that looked suspiciously like his own, and he had heard nothing from her for hours. Five minutes before, Gary had walked into his office and turned on the main screen without comment.

Now here she was, about to be the first news item interview, by all appearances.

"You've made extraordinary accusations, Sera Dunbarger," the host said. "You must realize that defending your brother—a known criminal—by attacking a senior government official could be interpreted as . . . as, well, more family loyalty than anything else."

Penny produced what sounded like an artless gurgle of amusement. "Come now, Stan," she said, patting the man's arm; he looked startled. "Everyone knows that sisters know brothers' faults. We aren't dazzled by them; we've seen them with their pants down. Literally. When they were knobby-kneed little boys."

"She's good," Gary said, as if he were evaluating a prospective hire.

"You've got people—" Rafe began.

"Of course. She's covered. She said to get back here and make sure you saw this. She said it's payback time."

"Payback?"

Gary chuckled. "Rafe, I know you're having a bad day, and I'm truly sorry about Ky Vatta. But with this one, you did something extraordinary. You may not be able to appreciate it now, but you should. You freed the genie from the bottle."

On screen, the host was attempting an avuncular tone and only managed to sound condescending. "In other words, you're saying you're not blind to his faults—"

"Gracious no!" Penny shook her head. "I'd be the first to tell you that Rafe snores so loud you can hear him three doors away—"

"I do not," Rafe muttered.

"Doesn't matter," Gary said. "It makes you human." Rafe gave him a sharp look. "And you did snore in the dormitory, back at that place, about the time your voice was breaking."

"You told her?"

"She asked for something harmless. Snoring is something innocent, like farting, only that's low-class, and snoring happens in the best-regulated families."

The host glanced at his notes and went on. "But when your brother was here before—"

"He was young and wild, yes," Penny said.

"He killed two men—" the host said, looking severe.

"Saving my life," Penny said, now leaning forward, all earnestness. "My family wanted to spare me the trauma— a lot was hushed up that should not have been, because Rafe saved my life that night. Men broke in, killed the house staff, and were going to kill or abduct us—"

"Are you sure it's not just an excuse he made, something he told you?"

"I wasn't a baby," Penny said. Rafe had to admire her voice control; she placed every word and every tone for maximum effect. "I was in school, Tolver Junior Girls. I remember it very clearly indeed. The man had grabbed me out of bed, half smothered me in the duvet, and was carrying me away when Rafe shot him."

"Playing him like a violin," Gary murmured. "Now she has me wondering how often she's played *me*."

The host almost stuttered, caught himself. "But—we obtained the official records and it says Rafe—your brother—hit you—"

"When I saw the cook's body downstairs, I started screaming; I couldn't stop. Rafe slapped me so I would stop. I don't mind that; he hadn't done it before and he never did it again."

"So it's your contention that his killing those men was in self-defense?"

"Not contention. Fact. Completely self-defense."

"Then why was he sent to the Gardner Facility?"

"Lew Parmina," Penny said. Now her voice was cold, chips of winter granite, all sharp edges. "He told my parents where to send us for post-trauma therapy, and then got the therapist to say that Rafe was dangerous. I don't think he'd ever have done those other things he did, if he hadn't been locked up there."

"Wouldn't have had the contacts to get her out, if I hadn't," Rafe said, with a sharp look at Gary. "Not that I appreciated that at the time."

"She's doing a perfect job," Gary said. "I could use someone like that in my organization."

Rafe nearly choked. "She wants my job, Gary, not yours. Luckily for you."

The interview went on, the interviewer doing his best to present Penny as the besotted little sister of a dastard, but Penny neither wavered nor lost her amiable composure. Finally, with the perfect timing that was impressing Rafe more every moment, she took control.

"What you have to understand," she said, "is that I'm the one, not Rafe, who's been looking into the financial details of deals cut between individuals in ISC and the Nexus government. Rafe gave me a temporary job to keep me busy while I mourned my husband's death; he thought I would just sit there doing data entry, but instead—" She pulled out a data cube. "—I found myself fascinated with the number of people who had their noses in the same money stream. The late Secretary Isaacs, for instance, had been taking in tens of thousands of credits a year—money I can trace to Ser Parmina by way of the former enforcement chief at ISC. Money allocated by ISC's Board of Directors for maintenance of ISC's fleet—which as you know is a major component of the System Defense—was going everywhere *but* the fleet."

The data cube glittered in the light as she rolled it in her fingers and the camera zoomed in. The news anchor stared at it avidly. "That's—do you have proof? Is that it?"

Penny smiled at him, the fond smile of an indulgent mother for a rather backward child. "Of course I have proof. *I'm* not in the habit of making false accusations. This is your copy—" She handed it over. "And there are many more, of course. I had not had time to tell Rafe about all I found. He's had one crisis after another to deal with."

"Now, you've made comments about Secretary Isaacs—"

"That he was involved in cheating the government, yes. And that he had reason to think someone might be on to his misdeeds, and thus might well have considered a suicide that implicated my brother and ISC as a way out."

"But your brother was there—"

"Of course he was. It helps to get the person you wish to frame at the right place at the right time, doesn't it?" She smiled at him, nodded as if he'd agreed, and went on. "Isaacs' secretary ushered my brother in, and laid a packet of data cubes—just like that one—on his desk. Then he started fiddling with one of the cubes, the way you're doing—" The man dropped the cube as if it were hot suddenly. "—and collapsed," Penny said. "It would have been easy to put contact poison on the data cubes and have them—or one of them—ready in case of need."

"Do you know if the cubes have been tested?"

"No," Penny said. "I did suggest that to the police, of course. They weren't aware that the cubes hadn't been there all along, that they had been brought in just when Rafe was meeting the Secretary."

"It could mean that Secretary Isaacs was murdered by someone else—even if the cubes are found, and are contaminated, that doesn't mean he committed suicide." The host was doing his best to regain control, and before Penny could answer he went on with another quick glance at his notes. "Now—there have been suggestions that the incident in which your husband was killed and you and your parents were abducted was in fact organized by your brother, in league with Lew Parmina, to disable your father and then, by apparently rescuing you, be enabled to take over ISC. Lew Parmina, the only person who might incriminate your brother, is conveniently dead at his hand, without trial for his alleged crimes—" The host finally had to pause for breath.

"In a word, no," Penny said. She was smiling, but now it was a cold smile. "It was Lew Parmina who told my parents what therapist to send Rafe and me to after the home invasion. It was Lew Parmina who ingratiated himself with our father, became his right-hand man, and—to prevent being displaced by my brother Rafe—engineered his commitment to the Gardner Facility. It was Lew Parmina who doled out his allowance, introduced him to prostitutes, encouraged his vices—"

"Do you have any proof?"

"Yes, but that proof is not with me today. I was at work, as you know, and had available only those matters pertaining to ISC–government relations." Penny's smile warmed again. "I will of course be glad to provide it—"

The host glanced, with some desperation, to the side.

"Begging for the producer to signal a break," Gary said. "But they're all too interested . . ."

Penny wasted no airtime. "There's a far more serious problem," she said. "You recall I said that Parmina had squandered on bribes money meant to keep ISC's fleets in repair—well, there's imminent threat, and Rafe needs to talk to the Premier, but the Premier won't talk to him because he believes what he was told, that Rafe killed Secretary Isaacs."

"Wha—er—that's not—" The host jerked his head around to gape at Penny.

"So I wanted to make this public appeal," Penny said. "Rafe didn't kill the Secretary, but he might be able to help save us all if he gets to talk to the Premier and they work together. If he's under arrest or the Premier won't listen to him, he can't. He has a pretty good record of pulling off rescues—as I should know—" Penny chuckled here; she did have, as Rafe knew, an infectious smile. "And we need to give him a chance to do his best for all of us." She turned back to the host. "Thank you so much, Stan, for having me on your show—"

"Er—uh—you're welcome, Sera Dunbarger, and—I guess that's all our time—"

"I give it less than a minute," Gary said.

"A minute to what?"

"The phone call from the Premier's office, suggesting that you should come over there. Don't. Invite him here. Tell him there's data you can only access here, which is partly true at least."

"I don't think—" Rafe heard the buzz from Emil's desk just outside. Gary grinned and spread his hands.

"I should have asked you to bet on it," he said.

"And you'd have won. If that's the Premier."

"Premier on the line," Emil said, as if on cue.

"She's going to make a great CEO," Gary said, "if she doesn't decide to go into politics."

"Huh?" Emil looked confused.

"Penny," Rafe said. "I'll take the call in here, Emil." Gary followed Emil out; Rafe made sure the recorder was running before he picked up the headset. For this one he wanted a reliable record.

"Did you put her up to that?" the Premier said as soon as Rafe switched the headset on.

"No," Rafe said. "This was all her idea."

"She's younger than you—"

"She's a grown woman who's already told me she wants my job," Rafe said. "I thought I was giving her busywork to take her mind off her losses, and she was burrowing into the archives learning the business."

"She . . . she what?"

"You're not more surprised by this than I am," Rafe said. "She walked out of here this morning without asking my permission, having told me to stay in my office and keep out of it, and the next thing I knew she was on that news show."

"She flabbergasted Stan. I've interviewed with him; he's not easy to shake. Are you sure this is the same Penny I remember swimming with my younger children? Sweet little Penny?"

"This is sweet little Penny grown up," Rafe said. "The kind of trauma she's been through crumbles some people, but apparently not her."

"She's on her way over to meet with me. If I'm convinced by her that she's really behind this, I'll get you out of your pickle and we'll talk."

"Bring her back over with you," Rafe said. "I have data, ISC data, you need to see."

"Concerning—"

"Concerning the mess we're in, militarily and financially."

There was a moment during which Rafe listened to the Premier's breaths, four of them, and then the Premier grunted. "Well. You know I'll have to bring my own security."

"Of course."

"They tell me your sister's car is almost here. Do you suppose her driver would know how to disappear the way you did this morning?"

"I have no idea," Rafe said. "But it would be best for everyone if—should Penny satisfy you—you either came with her to the main entrance or came in your own car the same way. There's been far too much secrecy. We need to be seen to be honest men." Whether or not they were. Rafe waited through another pause.

"All right then," the Premier said. "If I come, that's what we'll do. Open and aboveboard." He said that last almost like a curse. "And I've already instructed the investigators to look for those data cubes and examine the entire executive floor over there. If it was murder, we need to find out who did it and why. Suicide—well, I'm sorry for the family."

When the Premier had closed the connection, Rafe sat and squeezed his eyes shut, trying to think what he should say, do, plan to have ready . . . he was usually the one driving events, pushing the pace, but now he felt sluggish, tumbled in a rushing stream . . .

His door clicked; he opened his eyes and realized that sluggish or not, his reflexes still worked: he had his Rossi-Smith out and his other hand on the alarm button. Emil was ushering in a woman with a meal cart. The food Emil had mentioned before. "I did food," Emil said.

"So you did. Smells good. Join me? You and Gary both?"

As he'd expected, there was enough for all of them; they moved into the office suite's small dining room. The attendant unfolded the meal cart's several serving areas, set places at the table, and withdrew at Rafe's nod.

"So," Gary said, pouring himself a glass of water. "Are you off the hook?"

"Probably," Rafe said. "Penny's going over there to talk to him in person. Assuming she succeeds—and after that performance I imagine she will—he'll be coming here." He stared at the food cart. He'd skipped breakfast . . . he should eat . . .

"Soup," Gary said firmly just as Emil said the same thing.

"Some CEO I am," Rafe said, filling a bowl with soup and sitting down. "Can't even decide what to eat."

"If the Premier's coming here for a briefing," Emil said, "we'll need the big briefing room. I'll call down, make sure it's clear, have a security sweep—" He left the room, a stuffed roll in hand.

"He wasn't that smart when you took over," Gary said, brows raised. "What about him and Penny?"

"Nothing so far as I know," Rafe said. Even a few spoonfuls of soup had revived him. "But then, I'm beginning to wonder how much I know."

"Beginning of wisdom," Gary said. "Wisdom's fine, as long as it doesn't slow your gun hand."

Rafe laughed. "So . . . are you coaching Penny in marksmanship?"

"Doesn't need much coaching," Gary said. "Didn't know that, did you?"

"No," Rafe said, taking a slice of roast lamb and some potatoes onto his plate.

"Her husband had started her on it; your parents didn't. He gave her a lady's pistol but the thugs took it; it was in her purse, across the room. If you really want to get on her good side, Rafe, you'll take her shopping and get her what she needs. She's been using one of the range loaners."

"I still find this difficult," Rafe said, through a mouthful of lamb and gravy. "She's my little sister, dammit. Penny with a weapon—"

"Will be safer. Your admiral carried—"

"It didn't keep her alive." Lunch turned to stone in his belly.

"You're sure—" Gary began. Rafe held up his hand.

"I don't want to be sure," he said. "But that's all the evidence I have." His skullphone pinged; he turned it on and activated the visual and recording.

"It's me, Rafe," Penny said. "I'm at the Residence."

"I'm eating lunch," Rafe said. "I missed breakfast."

"I'm bringing the Premier over, unless you're going to need the car this afternoon—or he can bring his own."

Rafe forced a chuckle. "I've got enough work to keep me here well into the evening, Penny. By all means use our car."

"He's asked me to lunch first, though—I'm thinking we'll be an hour, maybe two. I know it's urgent, but is that all right?"

"Penny—" He wanted to say more than he could possibly fit into this kind of conversation. "It's fine," he said finally. "But you don't need to ask me. Your judgment is good enough."

"It's with lemon-lime pie," Penny said, sounding almost girlish. "And he says he has the same cook as before, back at their house—I remember that pie." And she was being the perfect guest, attaching all those memory-hooks to the sweet-girl-Penny the Premier remembered splashing in the pool.

"Enjoy it," Rafe said. "I hope the rest is as good."

"Baked fish stuffed with crab and shrimp," Penny said. "I'm sure it will be. See you after lunch."

Emil came back in as Penny's call ended. "Are you going to want archival material? And when do you think they'll arrive."

"My brilliant sister," Rafe said, "got herself invited to lunch over there, ensuring that we have a couple of hours." He was hungry again, to his own surprise. "As soon as I finish, I'll tell you what I think we need. Gary, the Premier will arrive with his own security. Make sure we have tags ready, code-locked to his so they can't roam around. Emil, make sure we have the VIP reception team rested and fed and ready to go." He eyed the rest of the offerings on the cart and decided to skip dessert. It would not hurt him to look lean and hungry.

TWENTY

Aboard Vanguard II, En Route from Moray

Ky rode out the downjump of *Vanguard II* in the CCC along with its specialists and her senior staff. The days in FTL flight had been nerve racking . . . what was Turek doing? Had the Spaceforce fleet left Slotter Key yet? Had the Nexus government come to its senses and asked its former allies for help? It was a relief to have the waiting over.

The beacons of the forward scouts showed up almost immediately, right where they should have been. Ky knew that an automatic arrival message had been shot to the Moray government as soon as their onboard unit detected normal space conditions again. Other than that, down-jump turbulence obscured scan briefly, then cleared.

"There's Ransome," the CCC senior scan tech said. "And . . . a few light-hours' scan lag . . . some unidentified—"

"Good thing I warned him we'd be coming in with some velocity on us," Ky said, watching her own heads-up display. "We could have run right over him." As planned, their formation executed a maneuver to clear space for ships following; she watched the ship icons seem to skid along the surface of her display.

"Contact with Ransome."

"Transfer," Ky said. Teddy Ransome's face came up on the screen, and he did not look nearly as happy as she expected.

"They've gone."

"Gone?"

"Went into FTL eight hours ago, about. Once I located them, and contacted you, I shifted around to find a better vantage point that wouldn't be in your way if you followed the same path. A lot of com chatter, ships moving around. There's some kind of installation there but I didn't dare close in, just in case. A couple of days ago, standard, a good-sized ship arrived. Either no weapons, or weapons locked down. I'm guessing supplies, because there was a cloud of little stuff zipping back and forth, and when that ended there was a long transmission—I copied it for you—and then they moved into formations and boosted for jump."

"Did all the ships leave?" Ky asked. "We're picking up some presence, but several hours' lag out."

"No, there are still a few, maybe ten or twenty. But I haven't picked up any chatter and none of those have hot weapons. I'll send you scan history—" A light came on the data-only channel.

"Did you get an exit vector?" It might help identify Turek's destination, though Ky felt she knew . . . it had to be Nexus.

"Better than that," Ransome said. "They're headed for Nexus, and they're planning an eight-day hop. I couldn't understand a lot, but I understood that much. I did transmit to Moray's government, and they may have passed it on to the others."

"How many?"

"I don't have an exact count, but somewhere over three hundred."

Ky's mouth went dry for a moment. "Three hundred?"

"Yes." Teddy didn't sound ebullient at all now. "It's mixed—the Moray ships he got are the biggest. But from somewhere he's got seventy-two of the same size as the Bissonet cruisers, though not all the same design. He must've raided other systems."

"No doubt," Ky said. "Send us what data you have." Three hundred. More than three hundred. More than three hundred anything was far more than she had.

"Any word from Captain Baskerville?" Ky asked.

Ransome shook his head. "I'm afraid he may have had a malfunction in FTL flight," he said. "Or something went wrong on downjump."

That was the most likely answer, Ky knew. "I hope he turns up," she said. "But given the hazards on that route, I'm afraid you're right."

On scan, two of the icons moved, followed by short broad acceleration cones—low boost.

"Did you pick up any of his stealthed observers?" Ky asked.

"No . . . I was trying not to be noticed myself."

"Contact Captain Yamini," Ky said. "See if he's seen anything." Her senior communications tech nodded, but even as she reached for the controls, Yamini called in.

"Two watchdogs, system relative coordinates as follows—" Icons came up on the screen, translated from the coordinates he sent. "They just told their base you were here, and to lure you in—they've got fixed emplacements in something—big rocks I guess—"

"Let's not take that bait," Ky said. The CCC crew chuckled. "Captain Ransome, you'll be part of the forward scout unit; you should be receiving updated navigational data. Move into position. There's no green route from here to Nexus; all ships but medium and heavy cruisers should be aware of the effects of the mapped hazards that may affect fleet formations and the downjump exit location. Be prepared to make immediate adjustments. All ships: remember orders per rest period prior to downjump. We expect to come into trouble; we need to be ready for it."

Nexus II

"They found the pirates' base, and Nexus is definitely the target," the Premier said, handing the hardcopy of the message to Rafe. In the days since Isaacs' death and Penny's intervention, the Premier had shown himself more competent than Rafe had expected, if not as swift in action as he'd hoped. He seemed more interested in finding out how Isaacs had died and investigating the connections between Parmina and various individuals in Defense than in prodding the government to do anything about the inevitable invasion. The pirates might attack Cascadia instead . . . that was the argument. Now he looked two shades paler than usual. "The Moray government says the enemy had left a staging area eight hours before their fleet arrived, but they had sent an advance scout . . . somebody named Ransome . . . who located the base days ago."

Rafe grunted.

"You know this person?"

"Teddy Ransome. Yes. I met him on Cascadia Station. Flamboyant character, but capable." Teddy Ransome had been glued to Ky Vatta's side at that formal reception and dinner. Rafe was reasonably sure she wasn't falling for him, but it had been painful to watch and now that she was gone forever, more painful to remember.

"The Moray government waited to inform us until the fleet arrived and confirmed Ransome's report—apparently they weren't convinced he was reliable—so we have ten or eleven days' less warning than we might have had—"

"We're fortunate they warned us at all," Rafe said. "Did they say how many, and where they are—?"

"Over three hundred, ranging from the new Moray-built heavy cruisers to armed converted merchanters. Estimated that about twenty of the ships are resupply, but they may be troopships. And supposedly only an eight-day FTL transit."

"Three hundred!" Even at his most pessimistic, he had never imagined Turek having that many ships. The fleet in Moray, even if it came directly to Nexus System, was hours behind and at most a third that size. And eight days? He had been lulled, he realized, by the same assumptions as the Premier. Moray was twenty days' FTL . . . when twenty days had passed without an attack, he had imagined the pirates being still twenty days away . . . or at least ten. Rafe thought of the time wasted in investigation, consultation, discussion—days they could not get back now, when they needed them most. "You have notified the Moscoe Confederation?"

"Of course. Moray had already told them. And I requested assistance. They reminded me that we had refused to ally with them in this matter and said the ships they could spare were with the fleet coming from Moray, at least until reinforcements from Slotter Key arrive."

"They're getting more privateers from Slotter Key?"

"Spaceforce, this time, apparently. I've tried to contact Slotter Key's Rector of Defense, but I'm told she'll be unavailable for some hours. Their President says he would prefer to have the Rector communicate with me. I understand that's another Vatta."

"Grace Lane Vatta," Rafe said. "I heard a lot about her from . . . the Vattas I met who knew her."

"Is she likely to help us? Surely she'll understand the importance of Nexus—"

"She's said to be touchy," Rafe said. "And as you may recall, both Secretary Isaacs and our ambassador said some harsh things about the Vatta family and my connection with it. And since her niece—great-niece, I think it is—Ky Vatta was killed, I suspect she may be touchier than usual."

"Surely she wouldn't let that influence her, with so much at stake—"

"We can hope," Rafe said. "Any luck with Mackensee?"

"They have ships on the way, they said. But from the Mackensee home base, and those ships are not equipped with onboard ansibles, any more than the ISC fleet or our home guard ships are. Do you think Turek had enough to equip his whole fleet?"

"Maybe. It's impossible to know," Rafe said. "If not, he'll probably cluster his ships, no more than a half-light-sec distance between those without and one with the onboard. Otherwise, he has too much lightlag for accurate control." Rafe considered. "He probably has already sent stealthed observer/controller ships into our systems. You need to have someone go over the deep-space scans very carefully—"

"Nothing unusual has come through the jump points," the Premier said. "I did think of that."

"They won't come in by the regular jump points," Rafe said. How could someone get to be Premier and not understand even that much about war? "I'll get our best people on this, too—they're going to be hard to find. Ky—Admiral Vatta—told me how they operated in the Boxtop incident. She didn't know how far in advance these ships were emplaced, but was sure they were there prior to the main attack. The stealthed observers will definitely have their own ansibles, and can serve as relay stations for conventional communications if necessary."

"Eight days," the Premier said. "Three hundred of them. Do you think we have any chance?"

"Not if we sit here doing nothing," Rafe said. "Let's get busy, instead."

"Right." The Premier stood. "I just—this isn't really in my area of expertise . . ."

The Premier's areas of expertise, Rafe thought sourly, lay in posing for photographs, shaking hands, and behind-the-scenes arm twisting of government opponents. "Nor mine," Rafe said. "But we do have some competent military commanders, even if our resources are less than we could wish."

"What about the civilian population? What can we do for—for the people out there?"

Not a thing, really, Rafe knew. From the evidence of a few past wars, the civilians might be killed even if the home fleet won. All an enemy had to do was throw large rocks at a planet to cause catastrophic damage, and the larger beam weapons could deliver deadly force through atmosphere. But it would not do to say so.

"Your emergency management personnel should know that . . . I'd hesitate to say. I need to get my people busy on looking for Turek's advance ships, so if you'll excuse me—"

"Of course. Go ahead."

Rafe glanced up at the soft blue sky as he headed for his car. A lovely spring day, the scent of new-mown grass and the first of the roses, the very fragrant old white rambler trained up one side of the Premier's residence, the fresh green of new leaves on the trees that edged the lawn, the low border of purple star-shaped flowers whose name he didn't know, a bird's call, the hum of distant traffic . . . it seemed unreal that somewhere out there three hundred hostile ships were coming to destroy all this. That this blue sky could be stained with fire and smoke, the grass blackened, the trees—

But that was as real as this. It had happened elsewhere; it could happen here. If things went badly enough, not only Nexus, but all the systems that depended on Nexus could be destroyed. Billions of people.

He looked out the window on the way back to ISC headquarters, trying to fix each scene in his mind—the streets, the buildings, the individual people walking or riding or standing, the trees and flowers of the median . . . and yet how did that help? If his worst fears came true, he would be one of those killed, and no memory of his would help.

Inside ISC, tense faces seemed to relax as he entered. Idiots. Fools. He was not a miracle worker; he could do nothing to stop what was coming. Rafe called Enforcement, gave them the bad news, and told them to set up a search pattern for the stealth ships he expected were in place or would arrive.

"And make sure you do full visual and instrumented inspections of all the system ansibles every four hours, with different teams," Rafe said. He had said this before, but like the Premier they found it difficult to believe anyone really would attack Nexus. Now their expressions registered the shock they should have felt long before. "We're very likely to have infiltration by Turek's agents, possibly set in place years ago, ready to sabotage the system ansibles on his command or at a set time. You've got my information on the kinds of damage I found in other systems."

"But we have six platforms—we can't cover them all on that schedule."

"I'm releasing Repair and Maintenance teams to this mission, as we've discussed," Rafe said. He would have done that before, but the platforms had limited space and life support; they could not be triple-crewed for long. "We must keep the platforms up and running. They're vulnerable to space-based physical attack, but the more likely danger is that Turek will use his moles just before or as the invasion fleet arrives. If we're cut off—well, you know what that means."

Denny Cuthen's replacement, Arturo Valencia, nodded.

"So don't let us be cut off," Rafe said. "You can have as many people from R and M as you need. It's better if they're dispersed anyway. You have priority for all ISC shuttle service until your people are in place. Let me know when you have an estimate of that time, and then when they've arrived." For the most distant platforms, that would take a minimum of eight days . . . probably not enough time, but he had to try.

"Yes, sir."

Rafe switched off. "Emil, please get Penny and other section heads except Enforcement tipped in. I need to do a briefing. After this briefing, I'll do another for the Board, so you might as well give them a heads-up."

"Right away," Emil said.

On the screens in Rafe's office, faces began to appear. When they were all in place, Rafe turned his own video pickup on.

"Most of you are aware that there has been a threat of hostile invasion of this system for some time," he said. "And most of you, if not all of you, know that our own ISC fleet is obsolete, badly maintained, and incapable of providing a viable defensive force. I have now been informed that an enemy fleet—a very large enemy fleet—is on its way here and expected to arrive insystem in less than eight standard days."

The faces on screen showed every shade of shock, fear, and horror that someone like Turek could hope for.

"So far, these details have not been made public, but the Premier is planning to make an announcement within the next few hours. Our job, in this time of crisis, is to keep ISC equipment working. The better the communications, the better our chances. I have released all Repair and Maintenance personnel and all ISC-owned transport vessels to Enforcement. They will transfer to our ansible platforms and be ready to deal quickly with any problems that may arise. All ISC fleet vessels and their personnel have been deployed under the command of Jaime Driskill, who has been in charge of upgrading the fleet since I discovered its deficiencies and authorized funding for this effort. Nexus' own space defense forces have been seconded to Admiral Driskill as well. We are expecting reinforcements from other systems, but the exact timing of their arrival—as of the enemy's arrival—is not known. Questions?"

"Does Driskill have any kind of plan?" That was the latest head of Procurement.

"I'm sure he does," Rafe said. "However, neither you nor I have a need to know what it is."

"Do you anticipate a need for sudden generation of more power either here at headquarters or on the ansible platforms?" The head of Repair and Maintenance, this time, Minvier Grobb.

"I don't know," Rafe said. "Would that change your release of personnel to the ansible platforms?"

"No, sir, but it might change how the teams are organized. Right now, and what Enforcement asked for, is that personnel start moving to the shuttle fields and just load and go, first come, first taken, with the first shuttle heading for the most distant platform. But if you think the attack might target power source and power transfer, either here or aloft, then we should include a minimum of five specialists in power for each destination." From the tone, Grobb thought Rafe should have asked him first; Rafe could understand the man's frustration.

"That's an excellent point," he said. "In the organization and procedures I've seen, Enforcement would be in charge, with R and M folded in, but this is a unique situation and I should have consulted you simultaneously." To Emil, he said, "Get Valencia in on this; we have a procedural problem."

Valencia's face came up, shifting one row sideways. "Ser?"

Rafe explained the situation, assigned the two section heads to work it out between them, and asked if the others had any more questions. No one seemed to, but Penny stayed connected as the others left.

"What about the others?" she asked.

"Who?"

"Mother and Dad. Should we tell them?"

The last person Rafe wanted to tell about the coming crisis was his father. And if worse came to worst, there would be no safe place anyway.

"I don't think so," he said.

"Now that I've made myself so very popular—" She winced dramatically. "—I'm wondering what you want me to do. I can keep digging in the figures, of course, but if we're all going to be blown away, I'd rather not have my last memory be of a page in the account books."

"Liaison," Rafe said promptly. "I need an ISC mouthpiece to Moscoe Confederation, to Vatta Enterprises, to Moray, and to our own government. If I do it, that's all I'll do. And I should be staying on top of ISC functions. But only if you're willing."

Penny grinned. "I can do that." No hesitation, no shakes.

"I'll tell them all—we'll tell them—that you're speaking for me. I'll tell you what resources we have and don't have—you know most of it anyway—so just don't promise anything we can't deliver."

"Right."

From that moment, the next days passed in a blur of activity. Rafe snatched a few hours' sleep when he could but spent every waking moment dealing with myriad large and small crises, from the failure of a supply ship to deliver enough food to one of the ansible platforms to the cook in the employees' dining hall who suddenly went berserk and started throwing pans of hot food over the serving line, screaming "Aliens are eating the chairs!" All the usual problems, and all the additional ones brought on by the stress of longer hours and the fear of invasion.

Penny appeared on the news at least once a day to explain what ISC was doing or why it wasn't doing what someone thought it should, and she handled all the foreign communications with the aplomb he now expected. He came into his office the third day to find her arguing with Stella Vatta.

"—the entire production run is already sold out," Stella was saying. "We're at maximum, we have back orders . . ."

"And we have an invasion now two days away," Penny said. "I believe our need is more pressing . . ."

Rafe had warned her that Stella would not release any of the onboard ansibles, but Penny must have decided to tackle the problem herself. He paused just inside the door, outside video pickup range, and watched.

"Even if we released some, the shipping time is too long—they wouldn't arrive in time—" Stella said.

"I'm willing to take that chance," Penny said. "Why aren't you?"

"Because I don't want them falling into Turek's hands, that's why. If your government hadn't refused to work with us, you'd have some—but it did, and the governments that agreed got them instead. It's not my fault that your government got its tail in a knot about Vattas." Stella had the expression Rafe knew well, and for a moment he thought there might be a battle over family honor, but Penny laughed instead, that warm, happy laugh that had disarmed so many.

"I know," Penny said. "And I shouldn't laugh, but really—that whole so-called chain of evidence about a Vatta conspiracy—it's ridiculous. Rafe would have known, if there'd been one. And for our government to keep him away from your cousin Ky—"

Stella arched her brows. "Your government wasn't the only one."

"What do you mean? Who else would care?"

Stella sat perfectly still a moment; Rafe held his breath. How would she say it? Her voice softened a little. "Sera Dunbarger . . . your brother . . . was never the right man for Ky."

Now it was Penny's turn to show anger; Rafe saw the flush on the back of her neck. "I hope you aren't saying what I think—"

"I told Rafe to stay away from her," Stella said. "Look— I knew Rafe years ago. You probably don't know this but he . . . was not a man who was . . . who did—"

"If you mean he was wild in his youth and had flings with young women, I know that," Penny said coldly. "Everybody knows that. But that was Rafe then; that is not Rafe now, and Rafe now—"

"Said he loved her. I know. But I don't believe he knows what that means. I'm not blaming him; I realize he had a horrible time. But she's—she was—my cousin, and I didn't want her hurt."

Rafe edged along the wall to where he could just see Penny's profile. She looked as angry as she'd sounded. Time to intervene. He stepped into pickup range. "Sorry to interrupt," he said. "But there's a situation. Stella, do you know anything about those reinforcements from Slotter Key? I've got questions from our commanders and I was going to ask Penny to ask you—"

"All I know is that they're in FTL flight, their arrival time is uncertain, and Aunt Grace isn't willing to say any more this close to the blowup we all expect. Rafe, if you heard what I said about you, I am sorry if it hurt your feelings . . ." She looked as beautiful as ever but worn. Ky's death, he knew, must be affecting her even more than it had him.

"I have more to worry about than my feelings," he said. "Please pass on to the Rector my concern that without a list of ship IDs, our people might shoot the wrong icons. We need some kind of recognition code."

Stella frowned. "I forwarded that when the fleet left Slotter Key."

"I never got it." Rafe struggled through the chaos in his mind to remember what day that might have been. "Sorry— when did you send it? I've got too many details—"

"I'll send it again," Stella said. "Now. Of course you need that."

"If we've got another traitor," Rafe began.

"I sent it to your Defense Department," Stella said.

"Send it to me, this time. We've had some problems— but I'll see the information gets to our ships. You know our government's asked for help from Cascadia—"

She nodded. "And I know they won't release ships from here; they still fear that Cascadia may be the real target. But you've got the fleet coming from Moray." Her expression changed as she said it; he felt the same—the combined fleet Ky had pushed for, organized, commanded . . . and now it was someone else's, and she was gone.

"Hours behind Turek, at least," he said, forcing himself away from that thought as he had many times a day since he first knew. "And no idea if any of the others will get here in time."

"Rafe, I hope—I hope you—"

"Make it? Me, too. But I had better get back to juggling what few options we have."

When he broke the connection, he turned to Penny. "And how are you holding up? It's been a big help having you running interference."

"It wasn't very nice of her," Penny said.

"About Ky?" Rafe looked away, then back. "Her relative, Penny."

"Still. Now that Ky's . . . gone, there's no need to be insulting about you. And I don't think she's all that beautiful."

"Penny," he said and stopped. He found he was growing warm. "Stella didn't just know me some years back. She *knew* me. She even fancied herself in love with me."

"Did you love her?"

"Stella? No. She was fun . . . fun to talk to, fun to impress, fun to fool. I had her convinced I had bootstrapped my way up from the dregs of society—not very nice, but we were both pretending to be not very nice people, at the time. A pair of corporate spies, one slightly more experienced than the other. But love wasn't in it. When I saw she was beginning to slide that way, I pulled out."

"And that's why she thinks you didn't love Ky?"

"Probably. Look, Penny, I'm sorry but I really don't want to talk about any of that now. I have to go on; I have to do things; if I think about Ky and all that . . . I can't."

Penny nodded; Rafe left the office, checking with Emil

for any messages. Stella had sent the data on Slotter Key's
ships. He routed that to Admiral Driskill.

Mandan Reef, in FTL Transit from Slotter Key

Admiral Padhjan raised an eyebrow. "Master Sergeant, why
are you suggesting we drop out of FTL at the next jump
transit?"

"Orders from the Rector, Admiral," MacRobert said.
"We need to make a contact; that will determine our destination."

"My orders say Moscoe Confederation," the admiral
said.

"With all due respect," MacRobert said, "the admiral
might want to review this data cube." He pulled it out
and handed it over. The look Padhjan gave him was not
quite a glare, but very close. MacRobert had been glared
at many times before, by people of higher rank than
Padhjan, and knew he presented the blank impenetrable
expression of experience.

Padhjan put the cube into a reader. "Is it going to self-
destruct and destroy my reader as well?"

"Not at all," MacRobert said. "But the Rector wanted
it hand-delivered after we entered FTL flight and before
we arrived at this next jump transition."

Padhjan read the text, mouth thinning as he read. "I'm
not sure I like this, MacRobert." It was the first time he
hadn't used MacRobert's old rank. "I was specifically told,
more than once, that I was to place myself under the command of Ky Vatta and Ky Vatta only. Now—"

"In war, people die," MacRobert said. "She was certainly alive the last time the Rector spoke to her, shortly
before we left Slotter Key—"

"You're sure of that."

"I saw her myself, on the screen. Ansible contact, responsive conversation—and I know her, so I know for sure that was Ky Vatta. If she has been killed before we get where we're going—"

"You know where that is, do you?"

"I know that making ansible contact when we come out of jump will tell us. We have the code for her onboard ansible, and the codes for the Moscoe Confederation and Nexus governments." And Stella Vatta, and the Mackensee home planet, though MacRobert didn't think the admiral needed to know that.

"So—we could be diverted from Cascadia, go into a battle without these fancy new ansibles—"

"That's right, Admiral."

"That sounds really stupid to me." Padhjan's tone bordered on belligerence.

"It's usually best to think of the Rector's strategy as densely layered," MacRobert said.

Padhjan opened his mouth to answer, then made an obvious change of direction. "And you understand it all?"

"I don't try to understand it all," MacRobert said with serene dishonesty. It was better for them all if Padhjan continued to see MacRobert as the simple errand boy of a scheming old woman.

"Fine," Padhjan said. "We'll all drop out at the next transition point and waste however much time it takes to retrieve a message. Does this transition jump even have a relay ansible in the same system?"

"The onboard unit can access both onboard and system ansible networks," MacRobert said. Though most of the ships in the fleet had none, Grace had insisted that the flagship have one—over Padhjan's objections.

Six hours later, the fleet dropped out of FTL space.

MacRobert, with Admiral Padhjan glowering at his back, turned on the onboard ansible and called Slotter Key. As he expected, despite the local time there, Grace was at the console.

"Admiral Padhjan, MacRobert," she said. "Ky's in FTL on the way to Nexus, following Turek's fleet. Estimates of his fleet size give over three hundred ships. She anticipates an attack on Nexus fairly quickly after his down-jump, which should be no sooner than thirty-six standard hours from now, relative time—but could of course be later. You will go to Nexus System; she will command all allied forces. Nexus has formally requested alliance aid, and has the ID data for your ships."

"I understand," Padhjan said. He glanced over at the displays. "But it will take us a minimum of thirty standard hours to reach the charted Nexus jump point. Not much margin."

Grace grinned at him, the wicked grin MacRobert knew so well. "Ah, but Turek doesn't know you're coming. We've told everyone you're going to Cascadia. Pure nepotism— the Rector sending Spaceforce to the aid of her niece just to protect Vatta interests. There's a good bit of noise about it in the media just now."

"Oh . . ."

"Your margin, Admiral Padhjan, is his ignorance. Don't waste it." And she was gone, with Grace-like decisiveness.

"You could have told me sooner," Padhjan said to MacRobert.

"I could. But of the two of you, I'd rather have you mad at me than her, even though you're closer."

Padhjan, for a wonder, chuckled at that. Then, with efficiency MacRobert admired, he gave the series of orders that shifted the fleet into assault formations, and they were back in FTL flight within two hours.

TWENTY-ONE

"It's not that hard to knock out an ansible platform," Rafe said. "They're big; they're fragile; they can't be jumped around like a ship. And Turek's attacked ansibles before."

"Not as easy to hit as a planet, though," Gary said. "They do move some, and they're easier to miss, at their size. A ship would have to get pretty close to just lob a rock at one and hope to hit it. We, on the other hand—"

Rafe had not, previously, paid much attention to the many ways someone in space could inflict severe damage on a planet. Nor had many in Nexus Defense, though it should have been their job. Now, with a vast volume of space to protect with minimal resources, the gaping holes in Nexus II's ability to keep the planet from being hit by any of a number of weapons were all too obvious. He had convened a small dinner meeting of experts both inside and outside ISC. Dinner over, they were tackling the hard questions.

"It would take time . . . the planet's orbit is predictable and it's large enough, but it would take weeks to get one of the chunks of rocks up there to an interception."

"Or months," someone else said. "Depends how fast you want the attack to be . . ."

"Ten to the seven chunks big enough to cause catastrophic damage, at least, you said." Rafe shook his head. "Nobody's mapped them; there's no way to know if someone strapped a space drive onto one of them a month ago—"

"That we do know," said an astronomer with System Survey. "We have the scans; we know none of the big ones is on an intercept course right now."

"What's the fastest unconventional nasty thing they could do?"

The woman with the mane of frizzy pale hair spoke up. "Install FTL drives and a nav computer on several large-enough rocks, microjump them into atmosphere, and then turn on the drives again. The downjump would produce a massive electromagnetic pulse; the attempt to jump out would vaporize the rocks . . . it's the combined-mass thing."

"That could be done?" Rafe asked.

"Theoretically. Practically speaking, we don't know the integrity of those rocks. Taking one through an upjump transition might convert it to pebbles right there."

"So we may have rocks, but we definitely have a large fleet—I think we'll stick to realities for the time being," Rafe said. He looked at the holo display set up in the conference room. Depending on which vector Turek came in on, he should quickly see a large fleet, which he would know to be weaker than it looked. With any luck at all, he would not see those elements of the fleet that were not as weak as they had been. Five squadrons now operated on AI control, programs hastily adapted from those used on targeting drones. The sixth—the sixth was Rafe's one hope for effective action by ISC ships. Still near obsolete, still mounted with older weapons, but with repairs and upgrades as complete as possible in the time they'd had since Boxtop. Nexus' own fixed defenses, mounted on "rocks" in the outer system, were positioned primarily to guard the usual traffic lanes. Nexus' insystem ship defenses now lingered close to Nexus I, the planet first settled and still mostly agricultural. It had a moon large enough to offer concealment without too great a gravity well.

If all went well—

"We've lost Number Four!"

Rafe had seen it almost that fast. Platform Four wasn't transmitting. Three light-hours out from the planet—they wouldn't find out what happened until then. "Warn the others. Double staffing on all positions. It was probably sabotage."

Moments later Platform Three reported in. Someone on regular assignment there had tried to cut off power, had been observed by backup crew. The other platforms reported similar acts of attempted sabotage—over the next hour, several from each. Four came back up, reported in, then went down again, only to come back.

"Redundancy is so useful," Rafe said, trying for a tone he hoped would dispel the tension. "And no sign of Turek yet, but I'll bet within a few hours—" The lights went out. As others exclaimed in various tones of alarm or surprise, Rafe dropped to the floor and crawled quickly to the nearest wall, setting his back against it. He stood cautiously. He could just see out the window; instead of the city center lights, he saw only the pulse of emergency beacons on the tops of buildings, their timing proving they were on backup power.

"Ser Dunbarger!"

"Rafe!"

Rafe did not answer. He pulled the hood of his personal armor out from under his collar and over his head, slipped on the goggles that let him see more than natural vision could, shrugged off his jacket and eased it silently to the floor, took off his shirt, then set his armor to black. He checked all his weapons and equipment, unholstered his pistol, and loosened his knives in their sheaths. People near the table were holding each other, clustered, beginning to move toward the window. His security detail and Penny's both had weapons out and were pulling on goggles like his. He could reassure them, or he could—what *could* he do?

Across the boulevard, lights came on in the Mercer Building, floor by floor, as emergency generators kicked in. Now light from the window was bright enough to see expressions as well as bodies. Far across the city, lights were still on; their glow lit the sky. Only the area around ISC's headquarters was dark.

All at once he knew what the purpose of this dark patch was, besides alarming the populace. ISC's headquarters, like every other building on the planet, could be watched from one of the satellites orbiting the planet, and for that reason had been built with confusion in mind and a very sophisticated stealth shield . . . from space, it did not look like what it was. But the stealthing required power. ISC had its own multi-redundant backup power system that should have switched on instantly, preserving their disguise as well as their connection to the ansible system. Yet here they were, in the middle of a big black patch, radiating in all the ways unstealthed buildings and machinery and transmissions did radiate—an ideal target, obvious to anyone who stripped the satellites of their data, even hours from now.

Someone here had to have done that. Someone in the building. ISC, even under Parmina, had not neglected its power security, and Rafe had insisted on daily checks of the system, checks he himself had overseen only the day before. Someone who had obtained codes to the satellites.

Someone, moreover, who knew exactly when to do it, who knew—who must know—when Turek was entering the system.

Someone who had an ansible . . . one of the onboard ansibles.

"He's in the building," he said, from his position by the wall. The others turned to him. "And he has an ansible, and right now he's busy telling Turek that the big black spot in the middle of the city is us. He could be anywhere in headquarters complex, and we have to find him."

"Near the backups—" someone said.

"He could have turned those off hours ago," Rafe said. "I would have, if I'd been doing this. But by all means, we need someone down there turning them back on. Penny, you must stay here, with Security. I'm the only one who knows what one of these things looks like; I have to go, and we need someone at the top able to answer the calls that will come in when power's restored."

"The satellite he'll be wanting to work with isn't geo-synchronous," Gary said. "It'll be overhead in about twenty minutes."

"Others could take the pictures," Rafe said.

"Yes, but that's the best for what Turek'll want, and if we can get the shield back up before it gets a good picture—"

"Good, then you take charge of that. I'm going—Gary, as you find Security have them spread out and look for a box about this size—" He gestured, knowing that Gary's goggles were giving him enough light to see the size he meant.

"You're not going alone—"

"We don't have time," Rafe said. He was already on his way, knowing that only those with low-light goggles could see him as more than a shadow in shadows. "I have an idea." He had seen the ansible, he realized. He had seen it on an equipment rack in a corridor . . . and he had seen it again, on an equipment rack tucked into the corner of a workroom. It had been positioned backside-out every time, and he'd seen an ISC logo and serial number plate, but—it was exactly the right size, just a little deeper than the rack, and a slightly darker gray than ISC standard. Yet no one noticed those details—*he* had not noticed those details.

He kicked off his shoes before he was halfway to the stairs, pulling out the padded, grippy footwear he had favored for adventures in his rogue days. Up here, no one else was in the corridor, but he heard voices from below, bewildered and worried voices. Which of the workshops had that been? Not on this side of the building, he was sure of that. He tried to think what else had been in that workshop, what distinguished it. When had he seen that ansible and its cart last?

The day the Secretary of Defense had died, when he had rushed through less familiar corridors. Someone—a man wearing a Technical Services blue overtunic—had hastily pushed it aside as Rafe had hurried past. Now Rafe queried his implant, but the remembered face found no match. ISC HQ had too many employees; he had not loaded a complete database. He could, however, find the place again. Left here, down a flight of stairs, pitch black without even a glimmer of light but for the ghostly imprint of feet and hands that had warmed the treads and handrail just enough for his goggles to register. Out the door, patched with handprints brighter than the footprints. Right along here, right again at a T-intersection . . .

Light flared around him; his goggles damped quickly. Someone had turned the emergency power on; the light was weaker than usual, from tiny bulbs in a line along the ceiling. Ahead, a scatter of objects in the corridor—something someone had stumbled over during a panicky run out of an office? No . . . as he came closer, Rafe saw that they were placed to cause a stumble, not as the result of one. Fallen boxes would not have landed with a glass full of spoons balanced on top of them. Beyond them—and a cross-corridor—was another similar barrier. Someone wanted to know if anyone came down that corridor in the dark.

Rafe pulled out his long-handled mirror and extended it past the corner—sure enough, similar barriers on the cross-corridor, but farther from the intersection. One door in either direction was open; light spilled out of one. The other was dark. Rafe's skin tingled. Definitely not an innocent construction. He should call in, let his people know what he'd found . . . but whoever it was might hear. From the darker open door came the sound of a flushing toilet. Rafe pulled his mirror back, slid it into its pocket, and flattened himself against the wall, crouching behind one of the boxes with a glass on top.

Footsteps. A door closing. Footsteps approached in the cross-corridor, certainly headed for the other open door. Would whoever it was stop to check the corridor and his traps? But they continued without a pause; Rafe got a glimpse of an ordinary Technical Services tunic with the ISC logo on the back. He waited until the footsteps faded into that room, then stood. The quality of light changed as whoever it was almost closed that door.

He really should call in. Gary would be furious if he didn't. But this was too much fun, and it had been too long.

Penny had her own weapon out; the specialists who'd been called in for the briefing backed up, eyes wide. "Just take your seats," Penny said. "You'll be safest in here with me. If Rafe is right and there's someone in the building committing sabotage, we don't want to get in the line of fire."

"But—" one of them said.

"We'll just wait," Penny said. She had no special goggles, like her escorts, but with the slow return of emergency lighting in buildings across the boulevard, she could see well enough. She didn't tell them to be quiet—she didn't care if they talked—but they just sat there as if frozen in place. One of her escorts went out, and came back with a set of goggles he handed to her. His weapon was out; she set hers down and put on the goggles. Now she could see the little pile of Rafe's jacket and shirt by the wall.

Her skullphone pinged. She tongued it to internal only, and a tinny voice spoke. "All the auxiliary power's down. We're working on it. External security will go up first, but we should have emergency lighting in the next fifteen minutes. No need to answer." She didn't. It hadn't been Rafe or Gary. Outside, she heard sirens in the distance.

When the lights came back, dimmer than usual, Penny removed the goggles and smiled down the table at the others. "Well, that was exciting," she said. "I would offer something to settle your nerves but I suspect kitchen service isn't back up yet."

"Aren't you scared, Sera Dunbarger?" asked the woman with the frizzy hair.

Penny shook her head. "Not after my other adventures," she said. "Though I don't recommend them as a preparation for a power outage."

"But if there's someone in the building—they could shoot us or blow us up or—"

"Or we could be hit by a rock someone sent this way

weeks ago," Penny said. "I don't see any of that as reason to panic."

"When can we leave?"

"When my brother gets back," Penny said.

Rafe eased past the amateurish barriers that might have been an effective warning system if he'd been in the dark without goggles. His suit warning pinged. Some surveillance system had picked him up. It might be ISC's internal system, which should be functional again. Or it might be something the traitor had set up. Rafe didn't care. He was happy as he had not been happy since he first came back to Nexus.

Lightly, silently, he moved across the corridor and eased along the wall to that almost-closed door. Someone was in there—he didn't hear more than one, even when he boosted the implant's audio. The man—it was a man's voice—was muttering to himself. "Come on, come on . . . stupid piece of garbage . . ."

Rafe pivoted around the door frame, pointing his weapon at the man bent over the ansible, prodding its controls.

"Need help?" he asked silkily.

The man whirled, nearly falling over, mouth open. He reached toward his pocket.

"Oh, don't do that," Rafe said. "You really, really don't want to do that."

"I . . . don't?" The man's voice squeaked.

"No," Rafe said. "Because then, when I shot your hand off, I might damage that piece of . . . garbage, did you say?"

The man said nothing.

"What is that, by the way?" Rafe pushed the door shut behind him, moved a waste container in front of it. "That thing you can't get to work?"

"Er . . . nothing," the man said. "I mean . . . it's a . . . a machine. You wouldn't understand. Look, I'm an employee, I'm not an intruder. I'm supposed to be here." He pointed to the ID card hanging from its chain, the ISC logo on his tunic.

"An employee," Rafe said. He hitched a hip onto a low counter beside the door. "I see. And your name?"

"Olin. Olin Zennarthos. TS-3." Zennarthos sounded more confident now. He could soon find out how mistaken he was. "I guess you're from Security—something happened and the lights went out and you're checking things?"

"You might say that," Rafe said. "What's your emergency station, Olin Zennarthos?"

"Why, it's—it's—" He looked around the room as if he expected to find the yellow square with its big black number somewhere on the walls. "It's here."

"Oh, Mr. Zennarthos," Rafe said, shaking his head. "I do believe you just told a lie. Do you know what happens to people who tell lies to . . . to Security?"

Zennarthos glanced from side to side, then his wavering glance came back to Rafe. "I—I was scared. It was . . . dark?"

"Dark, yes. And you put those boxes out there, with glasses and forks and spoons in them, so if the bogeyman came down the dark, the very dark corridors, you would be warned, is that it?"

Zennarthos completely missed the implications in Rafe's tone, and nodded. "Yes. Yes, I was scared, I thought—with the invasion coming—it might be somebody bad coming."

"It was," Rafe said. He would not have the chance to kill the man who had killed Ky, not personally, but this one—this one who worked for the man who killed Ky—would do.

"Uh?" Zennarthos stared at him, confused and scared and not understanding. Rafe wanted him to understand.

"I mean, I am somebody bad. For you." He stood up again, and took a step forward, then another. "I know what that is, you see. That's an ansible. That's a portable ansible. And the only way you, Olin Zennarthos, could have a portable ansible is if you were sent it by our enemies—because our friends don't have any to share."

His gaze held Zennarthos immobile until he was almost within reach, but then the man broke, scrambling back to put the ansible between himself and Rafe. "I—I didn't— don't—"

Rafe vaulted over the ansible and grabbed Zennarthos by the tunic neck, swinging him around and shoving him back hard against the ansible case. He laid the muzzle of his pistol against Zennarthos' cheek. The man's eyes rolled, struggling to see it, and his breath came in ragged gasps. "You are in trouble, laddy, and any more lies will cost you blood."

"I—I didn't . . . I don't . . . don't hurt me . . ."

Rafe stepped back, yanking Zennarthos forward to meet the pistol with his nose. "Don't *hurt* you? Are you giving me orders?"

"No . . . no . . . I—"

Rafe swung the pistol as if to hit Zennarthos again; as the man flinched away, Rafe used that movement to swing him farther, then kicked the side of the man's knee and let go of his tunic. Zennarthos fell on his side against the cabinets on that wall. Before he could get up, Rafe grabbed a shelving unit stuffed with heavy-looking boxes labeled with parts numbers, and pulled it over on Zennarthos' legs; the man screamed. "My legs!"

"Your legs are safe for the moment," Rafe said. "I can't shoot them without breaking something more valuable."

"Who *are* you?" Zennarthos whimpered. "You're not Security—"

"I'm your worst nightmare," Rafe said, intentionally copying the wording and tone of a vid-cube villain. He'd found it effective before. "The one where you dream you're about to die . . . and you are." He moved around the mess on the floor and crouched behind Zennarthos' head. The man tipped his head back. "Don't move your arms," Rafe said. "Unless you want me to shoot your head off right now. You picked the wrong employer. If you'd been loyal to me—"

Zennarthos finally caught on. "You're—you're Chairman Dunbarger?"

"I am indeed," Rafe said, and tapped Zennarthos' forehead with the muzzle. "Maybe you do have something inside that skull after all. We'll find out later. For now—have you contacted Turek yet?"

"I—I didn't know—"

Rafe slipped the smallest of his knives out of its sheath into his left hand. He moved it into Zennarthos' range of vision. "Do you know what this is?"

"A—a knife?"

"Yes. A very, very sharp knife. Now, if you tell me the truth when I ask questions, without making excuses, things will go marginally better for you. If you don't . . . I will use this knife in ways you may find very unpleasant."

"But—but you're a rich man—you wear a suit!"

Rafe chuckled. "Olin, you have some very wrong ideas about rich men. Enough time wasting. Who have you contacted with this ansible today?"

"I—I don't know his name . . . *OW!*" Rafe had yanked one of the man's arms up, bent his hand, and parted the finger web. Zennarthos stared at his hand, where blood dripped from between his fingers.

"Put it back down," Rafe said. Zennarthos obeyed, trembling. "That answer was not responsive," Rafe said. "If you do not know a name, give me a location and as much as you do know."

"He—he is on a ship. A kind of spy ship, I think. I don't know for sure where it is—I don't—I think it's in this system but I don't know . . ." His voice trailed away in a wail as Rafe touched the knife to his lips.

"Next question," Rafe said. "When did you get this ansible?"

"About three years ago," Zennarthos said. "It was shipped in; I was supposed to watch for it, take care of it—"

"And use it?" Rafe asked.

"Well . . . yes."

"Were you given access numbers to load into it, or were they stored when you were contacted?"

"I—I had a list of numbers. A file. But it wasn't supposed to be loaded until I got a signal. That was nine days ago."

"So all the access numbers are in it now?"

"Yes. And they use this funny code—that's in there, too."

Rafe grinned. "So I don't need you at all, do I, Olin Zennarthos?"

"But—but you can't just shoot me!"

"Wrong again," Rafe said.

"But I told you everything you asked—I cooperated—"

"You did," Rafe said. "And that saved you a great deal of pain, but here's the thing: the man you chose to work with killed the woman I love, and since I can't kill him—yet, anyway—you will have to do."

Zennarthos moaned. Rafe ignored him and considered his options. The pistol would make a lot of noise and mess this close, and there might be damage to the ansible. He put the pistol away, aware of Zennarthos watching avidly, and pulled out the needler. Quiet, less messy.

"If you believe in a deity, this would be a good time to pray," he said. "And if you believe in reincarnation, remember to be good next time."

Zennarthos jerked as the poison-tipped needles, a full load, entered his body. It was a quicker death than he deserved. Rafe stood, letting himself enjoy that moment before working his way back around the fallen shelf to the ansible. Zennarthos, in a rush, had tried to stuff the power supply's prongs in backward, and luckily had not succeeded. Rafe gathered up the power cord and pushed the unit toward the door. When he opened it, he could hear voices down the corridor.

Gary had already told Penny, on her skullphone, that Rafe was safe and had found the traitor. She had not expected that Rafe would reappear in a perfectly tailored suit, all signs of the rogue-Rafe once more concealed, or that Gary, with him, would look quite so grim. Rafe had the portable ansible on a wheeled frame and a smug grin.

"Stella can sue me later," he said, "but we're going to use this. The fellow who had it loaded it with the access codes for all Turek's ansibles and Turek's codebook or the equivalent." His diamond-bright gaze challenged them to ask unnecessary questions . . . and regret it. "I need to fiddle with it a bit, make sure we don't transmit on one of Turek's channels by accident."

"Where's the traitor?" asked the astrophysicist.

"Dead," Rafe said, as if that should have been obvious. He pulled the cart over near a power outlet. Almost on cue, the lights brightened. "Ah. We're back on main power, I gather. Good. Penny, our guests may wish to leave; if you could take care of that and any incoming calls, I can tinker with this."

"Rafe—" Penny began, then subsided and did as he asked.

"How's it feel now?" Gary asked, after the others had left the room.

"Satisfying," Rafe said. "If I can't get Turek—"

"That's not what I meant and you know it. I saw the body."

"He's got one small mark on him, is all," Rafe said. "And to answer the question you intended, it felt lousy. I've apparently been contaminated by upper-class squeamishness again. That's what you used to call it."

"Or her," Gary said. "You know she wouldn't like it."

"She's dead," Rafe said. "She wouldn't know."

"Ah, but you would. Actually . . . aside from wanting to wring your neck for chasing off alone and not calling in your location . . . you did well."

"Yeah, well, that was a mere snippet. There's the rest of the war. Speaking of which, I need some tools. That fake china cabinet over there—second drawer on the right."

TWENTY-TWO

Aboard Vanguard II, in FTL Flight

"It's time, Admiral."

Ky opened her eyes to the smell of breakfast and the chime as the compartment door closed. Time. They would be dropping out of FTL into Nexus System in forty-five minutes; most of the crew would have been up just a half hour longer. She had insisted on arriving rested, at peak, because the most dangerous time was that downjump insertion. They had no way of knowing where Turek was, how he had arranged his fleet, or even if Nexus still existed.

Now she rolled out of bed, her implant picking up the timing and bringing her to full alertness. Shower, dress, eat. She was in the CCC, in her seat, fifteen minutes before transition, feeling the knot in her stomach familiar from every downjump transition—had the drives functioned properly, were they reasonably close to where they meant to be?—familiar yet always a little different, because no one could see past the wall of uncertainty. Here, where they came into an inhabited, busy system but not at its mapped jump point, and into the near certainty of hostility, the uncertainty reached unity.

"Thirty-second warning," came over the ship com. "All

personnel take downjump precautions. Weapons hot—
confirm all stations." Ky's display showed the confirming
blinks from each of *Vanguard II*'s weapons stations. She,
like others in the CCC, wore her protective suit, helmet
in ready position on its mounting rack.

"Fifteen-second warning. Scan positions ready." Screens
flicked from clean blue or green to the swirling multicol-
ored hash that was all scan provided in FTL flight. From
across the CCC, Pitt gave Ky a thumbs-up.

"Ten . . . nine . . . eight . . ." Ky checked all her hookups
again, and lowered the command canopy; the sound of
voices and hiss of air from the ventilators fell away, and
the final countdown continued.

"Two . . . one . . . downjump transition . . . successful . . ."

Ky let out a breath she didn't realize she'd been holding.
Scan looked dark, which was good, with wobbly streaks
of light—downjump turbulence.

"Ansible contact, Admiral!"

"Patch it," Ky said. She listened as the five forerunner
ships—Ransome and four other fast, smaller ships—
reported in and transferred clearer scan data to *Vanguard*
and the others in that formation. Red blurs sprang up on
the displays—enemy ships, weapons hot, their positions
inexact, shown by fuzzy ovals. Smaller green blurs: ISC
and Nexus Defense ships, many fewer of them.

"System ansible in operation. Third formation downjump successful, ship-ansible contact confirmed—" That
from the bridge, but she could see it on the CCC screens
as well. Moment by moment, their movement and the
decrease in downjump turbulence combined to produce
better data, more accurate positions. Ky had tried to come
in well off the ecliptic, avoiding the big rocks and the most
traveled traffic lanes, but even with good charts that was

difficult to do when not using mapped routes. They were only eleven degrees off, not the seventeen she'd tried for, but they looked to be a comfortable three light-hours from any of the enemy icons—or where the enemy had been when those images reached them.

Ships had drifted out of alignment during the days in FTL flight; Ky listened as the group commanders chivvied them back into place and locked their chronometers.

"Ready, Admiral," she heard from one and then another.

"Scouts two, Formations primary five," she said. The battle plan had defined concentric spheres around Nexus and its primary, with jump maneuvers to shift from one to another. First the scouts—Ransome, Yamini, and the others—microjumped into place fairly close in—the second sphere, and then the fleet—the tiny fleet, compared with Turek's—split up, microjumped to form a vast globe eight light-hours across, centered on Nexus' sun. From there, each jumped out another light-hour.

"That should confuse somebody," Pitt said. "We came, we danced around, we ran away."

"He's not going to think we ran away, but his scan techs will be struggling," Ky said. "Ah—here comes something we want—" Scan data relayed from the scout ships began to come in, data only a few minutes old.

"He's changed his formations," the Moray liaison said. "It looks like clusters."

"If he doesn't have enough ansibles, he'll cluster for command and control," Ky said. "If we can figure out which of them has the ansible—how many clusters, do you think?"

"I can't tell yet."

Yamini's voice came in. "They've knocked out one system ansible platform; Nexus has—had—six. There've been missile launches at the planet itself, apparently targeting urban areas; they've already knocked out a couple of satellites. Minimal damage so far onplanet, but one of the orbital stations has heavy damage."

Ky imagined terrified civilians on the orbital station— there would be families, not just adult workers. Fires, decompression, death . . . she pushed that aside.

Yamini went on. "There are boosters all over the place, so communication's really good, but collisions are taking out the boosters. I'm in contact with an ISC admiral . . . two-second lightlag. He's just squirted me some data you'll want—oh, damn. They've hit the main ISC formation near Platform Two."

Ky left analysis of the data squirt to the techs for the time being and directed her ships out-sun of Platform Two to microjump in and engage the ten enemy ships that had just savaged the ISC formation. Ransome, the nearest of her scout ships, provided current position data on the enemy. *Victory* and *Guardian,* two of the new Moray heavy cruisers, and three lighter craft caught the enemy clusters in the flank. Two converted merchanters blew at once; the stolen military craft returned fire that splashed off shields without causing damage.

"They're converging on the fight," Yamini reported. "Just as you thought they might."

"Polson Three, execute Backdoor." Her third formation, high above the ecliptic, was best placed to run up the rear of Turek's massive fleet. She watched as they microjumped into position and struck; the rear clusters of Turek's fleet disintegrated as captains microjumped their ships into diverging vectors.

"Bissonet Two, disengage. Number four, rabbit-hunt." Formation four consisted of the boldest of the privateers, those who had been most impatient with Ky's planning sessions. *Termagant* blinked offscan at once, reappearing briefly as Merced popped out to fire at one of the scattered ships then jumped back out. That ship's shields flared but did not give. *Polygony,* on a slightly different vector, was a precise two seconds behind and hit the same ship; this time its shields did go, and apparently damaged its inspace drive. As it drifted past the moon of Nexus I, one of the fixed installations there blew it to bits.

Once, Ransome's Rangers would have been among these, but not anymore. Teddy Ransome was exactly where Ky had asked him to be, onstation and staying out of trouble. Now she contacted him directly. "Watch the clusters re-form," Ky said. "Maybe we can figure out which ships have the ansibles, so we can target those."

"They're splitting," Yamini said suddenly. "Looks like five separate formations, dispersing—they may be coming after you—"

"They shouldn't have us yet," Ky said. "Have you located their observer?"

"No, haven't had time. They may have somebody far enough out to give a real-time position on one of our formations."

"We're jumping to ring three," Ky said. Just as she gave the order to the fleet, Yamini was reporting the disappearance of most of Turek's ships. *Vanguard II* and the others reappeared closer in; if Turek's stealthed observer had reported their true position, he would have overjumped them and been nine hours out . . . and probably furious.

The ships Turek had left behind still seemed intent on attacking Platform Two.

"Somebody's gotten stubborn," Ky said. "Or there's something about that ansible platform that we don't understand."

"Or it's a trap . . . they'd like to lure you into showing the size of your whole force."

"That, too. Ransome, Yamini, see anything?"

"It's the platform closest to the primary mapped point, entry to the usual inbound lane. Fixed defenses along the lane—"

"I'll bet they want to mine the jump point," the Moray liaison said. "They don't want a functioning ansible there able to tell someone where the mines are."

"They may be laying mines now."

"Well, we don't want them blowing that platform. There's what—three or four thousand people on it?" She looked at the various readouts. "*Angelhair, Greeneyes, Hawkwing,* and *Guidon,* you need to get them away from that platform. If you run into mine drifts, call on *Bluebells.*" Her two minesweepers were far in reserve, but to save a platform she'd risk them.

Platform Two was far enough from her observers that Ky had to depend on reports from the attack force; she would not get lightspeed reports for several hours. But Turek's ships jumped out the instant her ships appeared on their screens; *Angelhair* had programmed to fire immediately out of jump, and those missiles sped away, part of the dangerous debris of a space battle. The other ships withheld fire, and quickly returned to their stations.

"I was afraid they wouldn't stay stupid," Ky said. "And that bunch coordinated very well . . . I wonder if he left ships that all had ansibles."

"Twenty ships, six clusters, near Platform Three," Yamini said.

"Formation five," Ky said. Turek had plenty of ships for a strong attack on each platform if he chose . . . and it was his habit to knock out ansible communication first. Why wasn't he doing it that way? She watched scan from *Cobani,* the nearest observer ship to Platform Three; a ten-minute delay was better than hours, but still too long for planning.

The enemy appeared suddenly on scan, along with flares from the platform's defensive weaponry. Enemy weapons detonated on the platform's shields. The clusters moved as one, but independent of other clusters. Then their formation five appeared, and scan data for the exchange went current.

"Tobados Yards was so right, putting in all those extra screens," Ky said. The Moray liaison grinned. On the old *Vanguard*, they'd lacked the capacity to display data from separate scan inputs, let alone integrate them with the right time delays.

The ships exchanged fire, Turek's force proving slightly less accurate, but all shields were flaring. The Platform Three ansible suddenly went off—possibly debris damage, possibly something else . . . but there were still people to protect.

"Another attack group, Platform Four." Ransome called that in. Ky sent her third formation after it, and looked at what she had left. She had lost only one ship so far, the privateer *Lady Gina*, but the smaller Moray ships, *Rothes* and *Kyle*, had taken damage. With the numerical advantage Turek had, the damage she'd inflicted so far merely nibbled at his force's strength.

"We'd better be very smart mosquitoes," she said, unaware she'd spoken aloud until several people turned to look at her. "Dancing with the bear, people. It'll take us awhile to suck him dry, so we'd better be really smart."

"Any idea when the Slotter Key contingent will arrive?"

"Any time now would be good," Ky said. "But no, I don't know." She looked at the chronometer. Hours had passed that felt like crowded minutes . . . she didn't feel tired yet, but the time would come—and more for her force than Turek's—when exhaustion would slow reflexes, perhaps fatally. Turek could send part of his force out far enough to be safe and rest them, and still keep hers busy trying to protect the critical targets.

"Ansible contact from Cascadia, for the commanding officer. Does the admiral want it?"

"I'll take it," Ky said. It was too late for the Moscoe government to send help; even if they were willing, by the time they arrived the battle would be over, one way or the other. She could, however, tell them what was going on.

But instead of someone in Moscoe Defense, it was Stella's voice. Ky had an instant to wonder how furious Stella would be, then her cousin said, "Ky—thanks for having Grace tell me about you. You need to know that Moray didn't tell Moscoe about Turek's target until after you'd confirmed it, and then they dithered a day or so—so there are Moscoe ships on the way, should be arriving anytime."

"Why are you telling me, instead of Moscoe's military?" Ky asked, only realizing once it was out of her mouth how ungracious that sounded.

"Because I had to hear your voice for myself," Stella said. "But don't let me interrupt your day—" She sounded considerably annoyed.

"Battle," Ky said. "So far it's more battle than day."

"You're fighting *now*?" Stella said. "I thought you'd go in and wait for the others to show up—"

"Nothing so civilized," Ky said. "Turek was over eight hours ahead of us; we arrived in a mess and it's not improving much. Any specifics on when those Moscoe ships might arrive? And what their IDs are?"

"Er . . . no," Stella said.

"Then I'm afraid I have to go, Stella . . . we're outnumbered more than three to one—"

"Vatta forever!" Stella said before the connection broke. Ky snorted. Stella was the perfect CEO for the new Vatta— she couldn't see beyond it.

She put Stella out of mind; she had more immediate problems. Graphic displays kept her apprised of the weapons status of all her ships, individually and in the formations as a whole. She'd told her captains to fire only on ideal solutions, but given the reality of battle, hitting a target with every missile was impossible. Now 20 percent of her ships had expended 30 percent or more of their load. Half of those were privateers, which didn't have the capacity of the military ships, but it was time to pull them back. Her transports, ten light-hours out, had additional munitions, but reloading in space, in combat conditions, defined highly risky. Especially if Turek figured out where ships that disappeared for a few hours were.

"*Termagant,*" she said. "You're running low. Take a break." She could depend on Merced to make the transfer as fast as possible—the woman was almost as bold as Ransome had been, and that without a Romantic attitude.

"We could fight a little longer—" Merced said, predictably.

"I know that. But then you'd have to go, possibly right when you're most needed. Go."

Next—the enemy could probably figure out where her spotters were—at least their distance from Nexus II, if not their exact location. Ky ordered them out, to see if they could find where Turek had taken the bulk of his fleet—it wasn't showing up on her scan yet, and it had been an hour. Then she switched to one of the alternative plans she and her staff had come up with, in case of just this situation: if Turek repeatedly sent in multiple small-but-substantial attack groups to diverse targets.

Contact with the insystem defense forces had been sporadic, handled captain-to-captain as ships came close enough for lightspeed communications. As the booster units were knocked out by debris and collision with ships or weapons, as the ansible platforms one by one went out of service, the possibility of organized communication and action faded.

A twenty-ship contingent of Turek's force appeared at low-orbital distance above Nexus II and launched a missile attack on the planet. "Light cruisers and above only," Ky reminded her commanders as she ordered a pursuit. "Mass issues . . . if we take the heavies in, we can't jump out at that distance. Heavies stay out at jump radius—" *Vanguard II* shifted this time, with six other Moray heavy cruisers, in the hope of pinning the enemy in the gravity well. Her smaller ships were pounding Turek's but not breaching the shields with missiles. Ky ordered her ships to switch to beam weapons.

ISC Headquarters

With the first missile strikes, just after dawn, Rafe had everyone move down to the reinforced sub-basement parking area. It might not help, but it gave an illusion of safety, and a better space to work in. He had the pirates' ansible out of its casing, and had been struggling with it for hours. He could listen to any all-ships transmissions or tune to individual ships using the list Zennarthos had downloaded. He could even understand some of the pirate jargon. But so far he had not been able to find or create a channel on which he could contact the system ansibles or the fleet from Moray.

A tech who'd never worked on ansibles before had been able to give Ky secure channels on one of these things and he couldn't do it—ridiculous. And Toby, a mere boy, had outsmarted ISC's lockout from the system ansibles. He'd taught Toby—if the boy had extrapolated from what Rafe taught him, then Rafe, surely, should be able to figure it out.

He'd have asked the local technicians to help except he'd sent the entire ansible repair and maintenance section out to the ansible platforms. He stared at the uncommunicative guts of the ansible and wished he could express his feelings and smash it to atoms. It seemed emblematic of his life . . . promises not kept, hopes not fulfilled, great effort that ended in great anguish.

Emil had been monitoring ansible activity until this last wave, when the last two communications satellites within range died. The irony of being the head of the greatest communications network in the history of humankind— and yet unable to call his family a mere thousand miles away, let alone get a line offplanet—was not lost on Rafe, but he was in no mood to laugh, even bitterly.

"That's the end of it," he said, sitting cross-legged beside the ansible. "We existed because we delivered what we promised—communication anywhere, instantly."

"All the platforms may not be down," Penny said.

"They don't do us any good if we can't communicate with them," Rafe said.

"It'll be easier to rebuild if we don't have to start from scratch," Penny said.

Rafe blinked. She had slept for a few hours while he continued to work on the ansible, and now sounded far more hopeful than he felt.

"You're right," he said. "I'll try to remember that."

"You might try to sleep," she said. "You've been up most of the last week."

Rafe looked around the area. Over half the people there were asleep, huddled under emergency blankets. Penny had snatched pillows and blankets from the visitor's quarters where she'd first stayed; now she pushed an armful at Rafe. "All right," he said. "But I don't think I can actually sleep."

He woke to a vile stench and a movement of the floor beneath him, as if someone had picked up and dropped the whole building . . . he never could tell, then or later, which had come first. The overhead lights flickered, then steadied again. Penny had her hand on his shoulder.

"How long have I—"

"Three hours."

His eyes still burned, but he felt more awake. "What's that awful smell?"

"What smell?"

"You don't—oh." The cranial ansible. Had the concussion that shook the building shaken his head, made it come on? It couldn't be anyone calling . . . Parmina had gotten the code from his father, but Parmina was dead. Only Ky, and she was dead, too.

The stench intensified. What if Ky wasn't dead? But where were his cables? He hadn't had them for days . . . he remembered then that he'd pulled them from his pocket and dropped them in the bottom left drawer of his desk, thinking them useless.

"I have to go upstairs," he said.

"You can't—what if it's not there—if there are more explosions?"

The building shuddered again. "I need a power cable," he said. "For an implant jack."

She stared at him. "Why?"

"I can't tell you. I just do."

"Is something wrong with your implant?"

"No. I just need an external power source." The smell was nauseating now. He scrabbled in the tool and supply kits he'd brought down to use on the ansible . . . there. It wasn't the custom one, but it should do. Ansiblecompatible power supply jack . . . but the other end was meant for a low-voltage battery, none of which were in the toolbox. A transformer, then—a universal adapter to mate the noncompliant plugs and sockets—and now to find an outlet. "Penny, don't let anyone disturb me for a bit. I'm going to be fairly incoherent."

He tested the output of the transformer first, dialed it down to the correct voltage, and hooked up the lines. Just as he plugged it into his socket, he wondered if this was really such a good idea. Penny stared at him, unspeaking but clearly worried.

Ky was there. Like coming out of dark into light, out of storm into peace . . . the voice he had never thought to hear again. "Rafe! You're alive!" She even sounded happy about that.

"I'm definitely alive. What's going on?" That was a stupid question, slipping out before he could frame it better.

"We're outnumbered," Ky said. "We can't stop all the attacks. Which ansible platform's the most critical?"

"Are any of them still up?"

"Three are, but one of them's up and down. Only one is gone completely, Six. If we can only save one, which—"

"Pick the easiest," Rafe said. "They're all fully redundant. Do the attacks on the platforms stop if the ansible goes down?"

"Yes, though I don't know if that's just until they knock them all out."

"I thought you were dead," Rafe said. "They said— Moray said—you were dead."

"Yes, well . . . it was supposed to give Turek false confidence and delay his attack on you. Unfortunately, with over three hundred ships, he has reason for plenty of confidence. You have a captured pirate ansible down there, don't you?"

The abrupt change of topic caught him off guard. "Er . . . yes. But I can't use it; I can't get it onto whatever channel you use, and I don't know your access codes."

"I'm squirting you a conversion set, including codes; when you have it up and running, use that to communicate with us. We're having problems coordinating with your people."

"Jaime Driskill? That's our commander."

"On an ISC ship or one with a Nexus System beacon?"

"ISC. *Raging Torrent*, I think it is. I grabbed the best ships we had left, put him in charge, and we upgraded as much as we could in the time we had. But we have no shipboard ansibles and depend on booster units."

"Well, most of your fleet's pretty well destroyed, as at Boxtop—"

"Most of them were uncrewed, on AI control. Decoys we hoped Turek would spend munitions on."

"And he did. Just not enough. I'm guessing Driskill's commanding those ships over by Nexus I?"

"Right."

"What I'd like to do is pair his ships with ours—we could use more firepower, and he needs the communications. But so far he hasn't agreed. If you get that pirate ansible working, we can relay you through that to him, and maybe he'll listen to you."

"Dammit, I told him to cooperate—"

"Well, fix that ansible and you can tell him again. I can't court-martial him for failure to obey orders when he doesn't think I'm his commander," Ky said.

"I'll do that," Rafe said. "Anything else?"

"I'm glad you're alive," Ky said.

"Likewise," Rafe said. His throat closed on everything

else he wanted to say, and before he could get it out, Ky had closed her end of the connection, and he had another set of smells to deal with. He closed the internal switch and opened his eyes to find Penny sitting right in front of him, Gary behind her shielding him from the view of others. "What—did I twitch?"

"You were talking to yourself," Penny said. "And I'm thinking that's a kind of skullphone, only it's not just a skullphone."

"It's something that doesn't exist," Rafe said. "And we never mention it."

Penny's brows went up. "I've seen you, remember? And heard you? And in addition to that, why are you suddenly happy?"

"Happy?" He tried to scowl, but couldn't. Ky was alive. They might both be dead soon but right now, this moment, she was alive and he had heard her voice.

"Happy," Penny said. "You know something good, and you're refusing to share. That's not very cooperative."

"I can't discuss it now," Rafe said. "But I know how to fix that ansible, and I need to do it now."

Penny gave him a dirty look as he unplugged and coiled all the cables and moved back to the ansible. He shook his head when he looked at it. "I should've seen this last night. I was just too tired." The new information in his implant enhanced his moves, but he could see it for himself. This—this here—reverse this—add this—and it would have three times the channels. He plugged it in again, entered the access codes Ky had given him, unfolded the viewscreen, and made his first call.

Not Ky, but a broad-faced young woman seated at a console—the video pickup also included objects behind her, including an enclosed egg-shaped object with someone inside—Ky? He couldn't see it clearly.

"New node," the young woman said. "This is Nexus II planetside ISC?"

"Yes," Rafe said. "I'm Rafe Dunbarger."

Ky watched Rafe's image on screen through the canopy of her chair. Still alive and much more the Rafe she remembered so clearly from those early days—but it was not the time for reunions.

"Downjump turbulence, something big, relayed from *Prufrock*. Coordinates: plus forty-seven point three, sixty-two point four. No tags yet."

"Number?"

"Unsure."

"New ansible node! Identifying as Slotter Key Spaceforce, Admiral Padhjan, commanding, for Admiral Vatta."

"Here," Ky said. Then, "Admiral Padhjan, this is Kylara Vatta, Space Defense Force."

The man facing her in the familiar uniform of Slotter Key Spaceforce looked every centimeter an admiral; he might have come off a publicity brochure. He also looked angry. "My orders are to place this force under your command, Admiral Vatta. What is the situation, and what are your orders?"

Now came the moment she had both wanted and feared. Could she possibly gain Padhjan's trust, and his captains' trust, in the few moments available? On one side of her display, the familiar ship names came up as their beacons registered: the *Reef*-class heavy cruisers *Mandan*, *Bailey's*, *Seegan*, and *Adelie*. Medium and light cruisers *Rapier*, *Arbalest*, *Trebuchet*, *Warhammer*, *Scimitar* . . . names she had learned that first year, when they'd had to recite them during PT, every ship on the books.

She had struggled to come up with a plan that used

Slotter Key's traditional strengths, but melded them with the new reality of onboard ansibles. And instead of trying it out in training—or even in a dry simulation in a conference—they were in the midst of a battle.

"You're a welcome sight, Admiral," Ky said. "In brief, we have roughly three hundred enemy ships insystem, combat in progress. Situation report follows on data channel. Are all your ships capable of precision micro-jumps up to two light-hours?" Spaceforce training concentrated on shorter distances.

"Er . . . no, Admiral, not really precision, at that distance."

"We need to get your ships out far enough that we can pair them with those carrying ansibles. We operate dispersed, in pairs or clusters—"

"That's very unorthodox—how do you control—" His face changed. "Oh. You're used to this."

"Yes, Admiral, I am. You should have received the situation data—"

"Yes—"

"I'm now squirting you the orders for your formations; you will be met by Space Defense ships there, with either that beacon, Moray, or Cascadia." On her display, *Vanguard II*'s forward beams stabbed out at an enemy cruiser in a series of timed bursts, shields snapping shut between them. The enemy fired back, but their own shields held. "Captain Argelos, *Sharra's Gift II*, will be your liaison; we're presently engaged."

"You're fighting now? Which?"

"*Vanguard II*," Ky said. "If your scans have cleared, I suggest you get to the coordinates on those orders immediately. Turek has plenty of ships; he can jump in thirty or forty on you at any time."

The *Mandan Reef* ansible snapped off; she hoped that

meant they'd jumped as she directed, but there was nothing she could do about it if they didn't. If nothing else, the arrival of another force should shake Turek up. He had run before when he found force building against him.

She had other calls waiting—the ISC commander, Driskill, with a patch through an ansible platform and boosters, had accepted Rafe's order, and was now willing to cooperate fully. His ships, however, were incapable of keeping up with hers in rapid maneuver, even without the lightlag problem . . . her original plan, to twin them with her ansible-bearing ships, would not work.

"I've been watching on scan," he said. "Your jump precision and your gunnery—brilliant. We'd slow you down."

"What about your weapons?"

"Old," he said. "But we do have fresh munitions and plenty of them. Chairman Dunbarger got us the funds."

"I'll shift one of our ansible-equipped ships to you for communications," Ky said. One of the slower, less able privateer ships would do. "If you're within three thousand kilometers, the lightlag in communications will hardly be noticeable, so that's your maneuver envelope. If an enemy attack formation is in range, and you can hit them in the flank, do it . . . but if they're not in range, don't go looking for them unless I say so. Now, what about Nexus Defense?"

"I'm in command of that, too. It's all small ships, fast and agile but small. Lightly armed."

"Small, agile, and fast is perfect," Ky said. "But you'll be busy. I need a separate commander for that."

"Senior Commander Stanson. Shall I patch for you?"

"Yes," Ky said. Moments later she was telling Stanson what she needed from him. "—And if you find any of the stealthed observers, hit them with everything you have."

"Found the main fleet." Yamini gave the coordinates.

"I don't think I was spotted; some of them may not realize we captured this ship at Boxtop."

"How close are you?"

"Just out of my missile range. Inside the range for you, but it's a long shot. If you want to land on top of them . . . even this bunch outnumbers you; it'll be risky."

"They're resting, we're fighting," Ky said. "If I can distract them while Argelos pairs the Spaceforce ships with ours, it's worth trying. Do you have a range on them? And do you know which ship is Turek's?"

"Yes, I have a range—coordinates transmitted. There's apparently a command cluster, and I think Turek's ship is the one tagged *Bloodblade*."

"It would be," Ky said. "Fits his style."

"By its mass and weapons signature, it may be one of the new Moray-built heavy cruisers," Yamini said.

Bloodblade's position, according to Yamini, was nestled in the middle of the enemy ships, but Turek had arranged them in an oval disk not nearly as deep as it was wide. Clusters of three to five were within a kilometer of one another, and separated by only five to ten kilometers. Ky brought her attack group of heavy cruisers in above the center, only a kilometer out. At that distance, there would be no scan lag—and no room for error.

Vanguard II emerged exactly on target; its preprogrammed weapons sequences locked on to targets and fired within a hundredth of a second, faster than human reflexes. Fourteen heavy cruisers, point-blank into the enemy ships, sustained fire that ruptured five of the enemy at once, spalling off debris that impacted shields on ships farther away. The formation loosened but only a few ships blinked out, having jumped somewhere. Past the closest ships, the outer guard, *Bloodblade*'s beacon showed briefly, then other ships intervened. Then the preprogrammed jump whisked them all ten light-seconds away, and none had taken damage.

"Good shooting," Ky said. "Yamini, have you tracked *Bloodblade*?"

"They're re-forming—you shook them up, but they're still functional—there they go, fifty or sixty. All into jump at once—should be an attack force . . ."

"Three attack forces," Ransome reported. "All three remaining ansible platforms. The Nexus ships are harassing them."

Argelos had the Spaceforce ships organized by now; Ky sent them out, also in separate groups, to jump in on the attackers. Spaceforce ships, she noticed at once, caught on quickly and did what they were told. Their gunnery was outstanding compared with the privateers she'd started with. Each enemy attack group lost ships and fled before doing much damage to the platforms.

Yamini reported that Turek had dispersed his large formation. "At least three more ships blew after you jumped out; I couldn't tell if it was debris strikes or their attempt to return fire hitting some of their own ships. Some of the uptransitions showed wobble—I think several have damage to their FTL engines. I'll keep looking for them."

"Found a stealthed observer," Ransome called in. He gave the coordinates. "You want me to take it out, don't you?" Ky had an idea.

"Let's see if the pirate ansible onplanet can contact that ship and distract it with a demand for information—then you'd be safer coming in behind it." She contacted Rafe and explained what she wanted. "If you have enough of their code," she added.

"Their local agent wasn't the brightest star in the sky," Rafe said. "I should be able to fake something, and I do have that access code. What do you want me to tell them to do?"

"Anything that focuses their attention—tell them you heard there's another relief force coming in, from Cascadia, say, and you just want them to know it."

"Right. And then I'll do a dramatic cutoff that makes them think I've been spotted, how's that?"

"If you think it's necessary," Ky said. It was a Ransome-ish sort of idea, and she had never imagined Rafe as a Romantic.

"Craft," Rafe said. "It's all about craft. You do realize that your ships could be giving false data to the enemy if you had their specific access codes and enough of their jargon, don't you?"

Ky had not thought of that. "You mean, Ransome could blow their observer, then report that he'd blown one of ours?"

"His ship-chip would give him away . . . but only when their scan picked him up. It's not part of the ansible's transmission."

"That's a brilliant idea," Ky said.

"In fact, I could do that from here; ansible signals are only slightly directional and in the midst of a battle with ships jumping all over the place, no one really notices if the signal comes from the ship—other than originating and access codes. Which I have."

Fifteen minutes later, Ransome was able to ease *Glorious* near enough to the observer that he blew it with his first salvo. Then, using the codes Rafe had transmitted, he reported that he'd blown an intruder.

Meanwhile, Rafe began transmitting from a variety of shipcodes, copying *Vanguard II* so Ky's staff would know what the enemy were being told. She herself followed the flow of battle, redirecting her forces as it shifted, a corner of her mind aware how different this was from the days when she'd blundered her way through her first fight. Layer after layer of data, complexity on complexity—never complete, never the same from instant to instant—yet she felt—she knew—she was sensing the shifts correctly, making the best decisions anyone could.

Attacks . . . counterattacks . . . skirmishes between Nexus Defense's tiny cutters and any enemy ship unlucky enough to be found far enough from help. Their weak shields made close attack suicidal, but their weapons were only accurate close in. Two of them sneaked through Turek's guardian escorts to fire directly on *Bloodblade.* Once inside that cordon, the escorts could not fire without risking a hit on *Bloodblade,* and Turek's own defensive fire was inhibited by the escorts' positions. But *Bloodblade*'s shields held and both the cutters blew as Turek's return fire caught them.

"That was Stanson," Ky's communications senior reported. "Next in line would be Woodward." But Woodward did not answer a hail, and four more cutters immediately wove their way through murderous fire—one blown ten thousand kilometers out by one of the escorts— to attack *Bloodblade.* Ky shook her head. If every cutter attacked Turek's ship at once, they could not possibly over- whelm his defenses. At most, they could distract one of his scan techs and—

Even as she thought that, she spotted what the cutters were doing now. Not merely distraction, but temptation. Tempting little fish in a barrel . . . tempting Turek's weapons crews to drop the shields long enough to burn them with the stern beam. One after another, as if crazed with rage at their commander's death, they moved in to attack *Bloodblade*'s stern, firing their own puny beams. *Out of missiles,* that would signal.

One after another died, vaporized . . . until Turek's gunner, enticed by the easy kills, left the beam on long enough for one to approach at a different vector and launch a full load of missiles into *Bloodblade*'s unprotected stern.

"Damage!" Ky's scan senior reported. Ky could see it herself, the telltale burst of radiation across the spectrum.

"Would be nice if it just blew," she muttered to herself. Next to getting the kill for *Vanguard II,* she wanted to see Turek blown apart by anyone, and the Nexus cutters deserved it—they had lost nine in the attempt. But *Bloodblade*'s stern shields came back up, and whatever damage the missiles had done clearly wasn't fatal. Well—a chance still for *Vanguard II.*

Turek's clusters unraveled as Rafe's fake transmissions, supposedly from their ansible-equipped companions, sent them to coordinates where they had only lightspeed communications until they could jump back. Ky's force inflicted more damage than it took, but every ship lost was a larger fraction of her total force. Admiral Padhjan's Spaceforce contingent had saved them for a time—and Ky wondered in a fleeting moment what her former Academy classmates thought of her command—but even they were wearing down.

More and more volume of space filled with deadly debris: the remains of blown and damaged ships and platforms, weapons that had missed their targets. Ky's scan showed expanding and overlapping red zones, where only the most powerful of shields might allow a ship to go.

Still . . . they were gaining. She had no accurate count of Turek's fleet now, but she felt a lessening of the pressure, a softening of the attacks, as more and more of his ships simply vanished. But even the heavy cruisers were down to less than 50 percent of their munitions load. Her own people must feel as worn as she felt.

Then the Moscoe fleet—small but fresh, and all supplied with the latest ansible improvements—jumped in just as a contingent of Mackensee ships came in on the far side of the primary.

"Admiral Vatta, this is Admiral Pollack, Moscoe Defense—sorry we were delayed—what are your orders?"

"Glad you're here," Ky said. Her pulse quickened; she felt a burst of renewed energy. Her mind raced, putting together the current situation with the new assets, new possibilities.

"Admiral, the Mackensee commander wants to speak with you—"

"I'll squirt you the current integrated situation report," Ky said to Pollack. She signaled her senior communications tech, who nodded. "I'm patching into the Mackensee commander so you'll both get this. Please switch to channel forty-three." All that time spent making contingency plans was about to pay off.

"Mackensee's here? Oh—yes—" Admiral Pollack must have taken a look at the situation squirt.

Ky welcomed the Mackensee commander, Colonel Baxter, then Pollack came in on the same channel.

"You need to jump in to a one-hour lag," she told Colonel Baxter. "We can feed you real-time data there, through ansible. How many of your ships are ansible-supplied?"

"About ten," he said. Mackensee had sent fifty, far more than she'd expected.

"Excellent. Half your ships above the ecliptic, half below: you're the cat by the mouse hole escaping mice want to reach. They need to see you and panic."

"And our ships?" Pollack asked.

"*Bloodblade* is Turek's ship. Built on Moray, new, only hit once that we know of, and we can't tell how much if any damage. It's still maneuverable. Go after that. His escort ships include another Moray-built heavy cruiser and several Bissonet-built. You should also know we have someone on their channel giving them false reports and orders."

"A spy?"

"Sort of," Ky said. "When Turek's people notice you, I expect more will flee. Some may be decoys. Pursue at will, but if they jump they might be jumping back here, so don't lose contact. His Bissonet and Moray ships—and maybe others—have that precision. However, we don't want his fleet to escape and re-form."

She was watching the holo simulator as she spoke, and already some of the Moray units seemed to be withdrawing, breaking off attacks to move away from the conflict zone as the Moscoe and Mackensee forces jumped in closer.

"They're starting more general withdrawal," Ky said to both. "Colonel Baxter, I'm switching you to channel forty-two; my comtech will be relaying any change in orders, but basically—go get 'em."

Suddenly a burst of chatter came from the pirate channel, and the enemy ships all broke off and fled— jumping immediately if they could, wherever they were, or making abortive attempts. Scan showed the character- istic flutter of damaged FTL units or incomplete shield formation that would prevent uptransition.

Bloodblade itself did not jump; its emissions flared, died, flared again. Turek had only three escorts left—two had fled—and Ky felt a surge of savage glee. He couldn't run, and she had plenty of firepower to deal with three enemy ships, no matter how powerful. He was hers.

"He can wait," she said. "Get all the other cripples. Let the bastard watch his so-called empire go up in flames. And by then, some of the mess in there will have cleared out. Then I want him myself."

Vanguard II stayed out of the chase; Moscoe Defense and Mackensee ships, the freshest, picked off the other ships in Turek's force that could not make jump, while Ky stretched, closed her eyes for a few seconds. She told the CCC crew to take a break; most of them stood up, stretching.

"He's broadcasting! And *Bloodblade*'s changed course!"

The CCC crew were back at their stations in an instant; Ky punched in for general ansible transmission and also enlarged the scan screen for Turek's ship.

His maroon-and-black uniform was rumpled; his eyes red-rimmed; his left eyelid twitched. He stared at the video pickup for a long moment, then spoke.

"You think you've won, bitch. I know you're watching, or you'll see this later. I don't care. You haven't won. I won. Your family's dead. And you haven't saved Nexus and anyone you care about down there. You can't stop me now!"

He was heading for Nexus II itself, and Ky had no doubt he was heading for its capital, for ISC's headquarters. Three of Moray's heavy cruisers, coming in like old-fashioned planetary weapons . . . they could vaporize the city and surrounding territory, just as an impact of that much mass at that velocity. They could do worse, if he sent off all his remaining munitions to collide with the planet. She had to blow him before he did—if he hadn't already.

"Argelos—Pettygrew—" They had been with her from the first; they deserved a chance at the final kill, and she knew exactly how fast they could react. Turek expected this, she was sure, expected her to come dashing in, and had something planned. But she was all admiral now, not the rash Ky of her first encounters nor the uncertain Ky of the flight from defeat . . . she could outthink Turek. She had been doing that all along.

She gave her orders crisply, and in moments the ships she'd chosen appeared where she'd ordered. Ahead of *Bloodblade,* Argelos in *Sharra's Gift II,* painting a swath with his stern beam that detonated the cloud of weapons and debris Turek had sent toward the planet, then jumping a quarter second to blast Turek's escort. Pettygrew in *Bassoon,* much smaller than the others engaged, drew fire from Turek's second escort, distracting it until the Moray-crewed *Bannockburn* poured enough ordnance into it, and it blew messily, debris impacting *Bloodblade's* shields until they flared a little.

"Power's iffy there," the senior scan tech said.

"So I see," Ky said. "Two down, one—" but the third escort accelerated away from *Bloodblade* and jumped abruptly, just escaping a fusillade from another of the Moray cruisers, *Mameluke.*

"Now," Ky said to her flag captain. "Now we attack. The rest of you, give us the first shot then join in."

Vanguard II launched its remaining missiles, then the beam stabbed out, first sparkling on *Bloodblade's* shields, then flaring them. Ky punched in to transmit on Turek's own channel, using visual at her end.

"You haven't won," she said. "You're dead; I'm alive. Slotter Key is alive. *Vatta* is alive and we will remember you only as an unpleasant interlude in our long and very successful history."

"You—" A burst of what must be profanity in his native language; the visual from him was blurry and flickering. Then it blanked.

"It's blown! It's gone! Turek's gone!" came from several stations in the CCC. Cheers rang through *Vanguard II's* CCC, and Ky knew they were being echoed throughout the ship, in other ships. She felt a visceral surge of glee, almost as powerful as when she had killed Osman. She had done it. She had avenged her family; she had saved many others.

Ky's moment of jubilation faded over the next hours as exhaustion rolled back over her and the damage Turek had inflicted became clear. Ships had blown or taken damage; crew had died or suffered injury. The death toll on ansible platforms, on Nexus II's ruined main orbital station, continued to rise as search and rescue teams went to work. And they had not destroyed every one of the enemy. They might have fled in disorder, but they'd fled in whole ships, with weapons and ansibles. Bissonet and other systems were still—as far as anyone knew—in enemy hands. She knew she had to let her people celebrate, but she also had to get them thinking about the future.

But not now. Now she could rest for a while, knowing what she had accomplished, knowing she had earned the rank she now held. Admiral Vatta signed out of the CCC and made her way back to her quarters through the passages lined with applauding crew.

TWENTY-THREE

The formal celebration of victory came later, when the last of the enemy had been scoured from the system, when five of the six ansible platforms were back in service and the sixth was being rebuilt. Nexus' government had allied with the other governments, but Nexus no longer centered human space in the minds of most, for even ISC formally agreed its monopoly on ansible communication was broken. The Space Defense Force had the support of nearly all governments from Lastway to Sybilla, four systems hubward from Moray. Bissonet was already free, its ansible back in operation; without Turek's influence, his associates had fled with what wealth they could. Only the anti-humod worlds refused to join.

Now the main celebration, on Cascadia in the Moscoe Confederation, would be mirrored elsewhere—victory parades, speeches, award ceremonies, dinners. Rafe, leaving Penny behind on Nexus, had come to Cascadia to take part in the negotiations that would determine ISC's place in the new order. And tonight was the opportunity he had most wanted—a grand reception in honor of Ky Vatta and all the militaries that had combined in what was now known as the Battle of Nexus.

Rafe went down to the car in a mood he himself knew

was dangerous. The reception honoring Admiral Vatta and the forces under her command was no place for intimate conversation; if he saw Ky and shook her hand, it would be the most he could hope for—in that direction. In another direction, the evening promised to afford him an opportunity to indulge himself as he had not done for far too long, something even better than killing Zennarthos. Someone richly deserved a hiding and someone—his thoughts halted abruptly, as he saw who was in the car, waiting.

"You're up to something," Gary said. "And it's not good. I'm assigning myself as your bodyguard at the reception tonight."

"You're not," Rafe said. "You quit, remember?"

"I haven't left yet," Gary said. He signaled the driver, and they set off for Government House. "Consider this my last night of duty. If you behave yourself, I'll be on the flight home tomorrow. And trust me, you don't want to disappoint my wife; she's expecting me for Hannah's birthday party."

"I don't need a bodyguard inside with me," Rafe said. He didn't want anyone inside with him, not for this event. He checked his appearance in the mirror on the front of the passenger compartment: the formal shirt with its elaborate silk tie, the formal coat with its wider satin lapels and gold buttons, the silk vest, the right pale gray gloves, shoes polished to perfection. Under it he wore light armor, as always, but the clothes were tailored to conceal that. "It's a reception, for pity's sake. Military personnel, government—"

"Snakes, most of them," Gary said. "And you're wearing your protection, aren't you?"

"Of course; I feel naked without it. But they're not going to attack the head of ISC in front of everyone while swilling champagne, raiding the buffet, and bragging about their exploits." Rafe put on his most beguiling smile and beamed at Gary. "No problems, and no reason for you to accompany me at all, let alone inside. And I didn't put in for a badge for you, in any case."

"But you're up to something and you want to cause trouble. Don't bother to lie, sonny; I can read you like a book." This, Rafe knew, was unfortunately true. "The war's over; the company's crawling back into the black; I hear from my sources that the Board is now in the palm of your hand. But you're lit up like a marker beacon. Is it something your lady would approve of?"

The car slowed to a crawl, behind others making their way up the driveway of Government House.

"I don't know what you're talking about," Rafe said. He knew Gary wasn't fooled. "But I'm not going to appear so fearful that I need a bodyguard in there—" He tipped his head toward the entrance. "You've had your chance to put in surveillance equipment; that will have to do."

"Boyo, I don't know what it is, but you're in a killing mood and I'm not the only one who will read it that way. Whatever it is, don't do it."

Rafe allowed himself to subside into his ISC identity, all civilian CEO and business. "I am in the mood to celebrate a victory. The champagne is in there, and I am out here."

Gary eyed him. "You may fool eighty percent of them, but you won't fool them all. Where should I station the reserves, for when the blood starts flying?"

Rafe smiled. "There will be no blood." And then, as Gary continued to give him the same challenging look, "There is more than one way to kill."

"Money, family, or that woman?"

Rafe shook his head. Gary touched his, in a brief salute.

"She is worth it, I will say that," Gary said, before taking his station in the foyer of the ballrooms.

Rafe presented his ID and invitation to the liveried servants at the door—guards, he noted, and armed as well as decorative—and went into the first of the linked rooms. He passed through the receiving line, polite handshakes, nods, murmurs of conventional courtesy. Ky's smile seemed genuine; he bent to kiss her hand and she flushed a little, but as he'd expected they had no time for more as the line behind him stretched to the door and beyond. Good. She should be stuck there long enough; with any luck he'd be able to complete his other mission and get back to her before she had reason to wonder where he was.

Somewhere in this crowd, Rafe knew, he would find the Slotter Key junior officer he most wanted to find. With consummate skill, he had extracted the crew list from each Slotter Key ship as it arrived . . . and on one, he had seen the name. Hal Coughlin, once a classmate of Ky's, now a sub-lieutenant on *Bailey's Reef. That* Hal. He'd obtained an image of the man's face by means circuitous even for him and it was now in his implant, easy to compare with every face he saw.

He was sure that Ky would not approve of what he intended, which meant he could not ask openly about the man: someone would be certain to tell her anything the head of ISC seemed to find of interest. On his search, he spoke politely to admirals and colonels and ship captains by the dozen, nodded politely to others from Nexus, Cascadia, Moray, Sabine, Slotter Key. The rooms were large, crowded, and interconnected so that the crowd could circulate . . . new arrivals coming in by one entrance, wandering past the cluster of dignitaries and most senior military to the long tables loaded with food and drink, and then on to the other two ballrooms.

Junior officers, he suspected, would hang around the serving tables and then find corners where they could talk without being overheard by their seniors. Hal might be the kind of suck-up toady who'd stick near his boss, but Rafe had eyed the name tag of every such youngster he'd seen near a senior rank and hadn't found him.

In the first corner he investigated, he found Teddy Ransome holding court for an admiring throng of juniors from Cascadia. Rafe eyed the dashing Teddy without enthusiasm; he would like to have despised him for being all flash, but Ransome had performed well. The next looked more promising, an almost solid phalanx of Slotter Key Spaceforce uniforms.

Rafe paused a safe distance away, pretending to sip his drink while looking for the face matching the image in his implant. But it was not until he spotted a young officer edging along the wall, clearly making for the exit, that he found him.

Years of experience moved Rafe through the crowd faster than the young man; he caught up with him in the least crowded room near the exit.

"You're Hal Coughlin, aren't you?"

"Yes, sir." He was tall, square-jawed, conventionally good looking, the sort Rafe categorized as "a young girl's fantasy prince." Much like Teddy Ransome, for that matter, though dark-haired. Rafe himself had been good looking, had even played on such fantasies—something he abhorred now—but he had no tolerance for it in other young men. Especially not in young men who had mistreated Ky. The young man smiled, a little tentatively. "You're—you're Ser Dunbarger, head of ISC, aren't you?"

"That's right, yes," Rafe smiled. The young man didn't flinch, which meant he was projecting what he meant to: older man-of-the-world politely interested in a younger one. "You're from Slotter Key, are you not? I believe I am right in recognizing that uniform?"

"Yes, sir." Hal straightened slightly, the young officer aware of his duty to make a good impression for his service.

"Good," Rafe said. "I had heard that you knew Admiral Vatta back on Slotter Key . . ."

Hal flushed. "Well . . . we were at Spaceforce Academy at the same time, but I can't say we . . . er . . . knew each other."

"Oh." Rafe let Elder Authority weight his tone; Hal's color faded a little. Rafe cocked his head. "Really. I find that interesting, since she certainly told me about you." A lie, but this young lout wouldn't realize that. "In fact, I understand that you were in the same class—"

"Well, yes, but—"

"And exchanged class rings. Unless, of course, you wish to accuse Admiral Vatta of lying—"

Hal's eyes wavered back and forth, but no escape route appeared. Behind him, one or two uniformed men had slowed, paused, to see what was going on. Rafe let himself smile his most dangerous smile, and Hal stepped back a half pace. "Er . . . no," Hal said. "No, she's not lying, it's just that . . . that . . . we were very young then."

"And you, my boy, are very young still," Rafe said, still smiling. He pitched his voice to carry to the men behind Hal. "It never occurred to you, did it, that she might be your commanding officer someday? When you sent that rather . . . how shall I put it? . . . disgusting missive discarding her like soiled tissue?"

"I—I didn't mean it that way," Hal said. Rafe watched the pulse now pounding in Hal's throat, the sheen of moisture on his brow, with clinical interest. Beyond Hal, more men and women had slowed to listen.

"Really," Rafe said. He dropped his gaze to his fingernails, as if fascinated by them. Beyond, though out of focus, he could see the tremor of Hal's trouser leg. It pleased him; he let his voice go silky but he knew it would carry. "The phrase *deliberate attempt to sabotage not only my career but the honor of the service* was not intended to be just a wee bit negative?"

"Well, I mean, I had to kind of . . . you know . . . distance myself . . . after she got in such trouble."

Rafe looked up and pinned Hal's wavering glance with his own steady gaze. "You had to cover your cowardly ass, you mean? You had to lick the right boots, kiss the right cheeks until your nose was brown to your earlobes? Because the woman you claimed to love—oh, yes, I know about that—had her confidence abused by a politically motivated slimeball, you had to abuse her yourself, insulting her motives, defacing her Academy ring? Just to make sure everyone knew how pure and innocent you were?" With every phrase, the silence around them spread, so that Rafe didn't need to raise his voice. He could see the shock, and then disgust, on the faces of those eavesdropping.

Hal was white now, shaking with what Rafe hoped was rage enough to inspire an aggressive move. Just one. Just one little twitch, to give an excuse for the fist that itched to smash Hal's nose, the arm that wanted to flash out in that blow, the eyes that wanted to see that spurt of blood.

"I—I didn't know," Hal said, his voice shaking. "I didn't expect—I mean—it was just—"

It was the white of fear, not rage, the tremor of near panic, not impending attack. Rafe felt the first shading of pity, and resisted it. He didn't want to pity this coward; he wanted to rip Hal to shreds for what he had done to Ky.

He looked Hal up and down, hoping his expression held all the contempt he felt. "You," he said, "did not

deserve her friendship. You are not fit for anyone's friendship. You are not fit to hold a commission . . . you lack
the fundamental qualities—courage, integrity, decency,
loyalty—that friendship demands."

Now Hal flushed again, slightly, and glanced around,
as if for support . . . but the faces staring at him were all
closed. Some, Rafe assumed, were just like Hal himself,
willing to condemn anyone condemned by the powerful—
and he himself, as the known head of ISC, was more powerful than most. Others might actually agree, might
actually grasp that Hal had done something wrong. Rafe
didn't really care.

"There you are!" Behind Hal, the crowd parted now,
shuffling quickly away from the one person Rafe did not
want to have witness what he was about. Ky, grinning widely,
swept toward him, flanked by two of her aides. Hal turned
brick red, and started to step aside, but it was too late. She
was abreast of him now, looking at Rafe. "Rafe, you know
the Premier wanted to meet you—why didn't you stay in
the main ballroom? You'll have to come back inside—"

And then she glanced, as anyone might, at the person
beside her, and he saw recognition on her face, and the
instant control that changed her expression to the cool,
guarded gaze of the professional commander.

"As you see," Rafe said, "I have been having a little chat
with Sub-lieutenant Coughlin."

"How interesting," she said in a colorless voice.

"But I would be delighted to come meet the Premier,"
Rafe said. "I'm sure the sub-lieutenant will excuse us."

"Ky, I—" Hal began. Rafe subtracted another hundred
points from the man's estimated intelligence.

Ky turned and faced him directly. "You had something
to say, Sub-lieutenant?" Her voice remained perfectly
steady, perfectly cool, admiral–to–sub-lieutenant.

"Er . . . no, ma'am. Just . . . I'm sorry . . ."

"It is of no consequence," Ky said, each word uttered like a flake off a flint core. She looked back at Rafe, her eyes now as hard as that core. "If you please, Ser Dunbarger. The Premier is waiting."

Rafe bowed slightly. "Of course, Admiral. At your service." He brushed past Hal without saying anything more; she had already turned on her heel and started back to the ballrooms without looking back. The crowd melted before them, silent until they had passed, when a rising murmur suggested what they discussed.

"I will smack Stella silly," Ky said once they were inside. "I can't believe *you* would have rifled my desk."

"Stella," Rafe said with some care, "warned me off you, for your own good."

"She had no right," Ky said. She shot a glance back at him, and he saw, not surprised, that she was angry with him, as well as with Stella. "And you—you had no right to parade my—that—here—"

"I wanted him dead," Rafe said. "He hurt you."

"I'm over it."

"Oh, really." Rafe touched her arm and she swung around; her aides stiffened and closed in, ready, he saw, to take him down. "That's not what Stella thinks. Or I think."

"We are not having this conversation." Ky turned again and strode off toward the first ballroom and the receiving line. "Not here, not now, and hopefully not ever."

"Not here, not now, but definitely sometime," Rafe said to her retreating back. For a short woman, she walked remarkably fast, the crowd opening a lane for her as if she were royalty. Considering what she'd done, she might as well have been.

But then they were in the first ballroom again, and he

was engulfed in the elaborate courtesies of rank and station, and Ky, at his side in body only—or so it felt—kept up a murmur of introductions and polite comments that irritated him as much as he admired her poise. He bowed, he shook hands, he chatted with the Premier of this government, the President of that, the Prime Minister, this admiral, that general, a Minister of this and a Secretary of that, being, as best he could, the urbane senior executive while on the inside he felt alternating waves of fury at Hal and fear that Ky would never speak to him again.

Two hours later it was over . . . though a cluster of ranking officers and politicians still surrounded them, chatting and exchanging contact information and casual invitations, the lights had blinked three times and attendants were clearing the serving tables onto carts. The group moved toward the ballroom doors without breaking up. Gary, waiting there for Rafe, gave him a minute head shake . . . so evidently the story had spread outside the ballrooms already.

Rafe lagged behind the group, wondering if Ky would be occupied all the way back to her flagship—or if she was staying downside tonight. He had to see her, explain, even apologize if she insisted . . .

"That was a cruel thing to do," Gary murmured as Rafe came through the door and Gary took up position beside him.

"Not half as cruel as what he did," Rafe said, in the same quiet tone. He was not really surprised that Gary knew what had happened, not with the kind of surveillance Gary normally set up.

"Youngsters dump youngsters; it's human nature. They can grow out of it."

"It was more than dump," Rafe said. "It was battery and dump."

"Youngsters have no sense," Gary said.

"You think I should have let it go?"

"Do you really think it will help you with her?" The question was serious, no mockery at all in the tone.

"I don't know," Rafe said. He felt bone-deep tiredness now. Ky was angry with him . . . maybe seriously angry, not just a little annoyed, and now that his adrenaline was lower, he could see that airing her former heartache might not seem to her the protective act he'd convinced himself it was. "I wanted to kill him," he said to Gary.

"That was obvious. Might've caused less trouble if you had."

"And I couldn't even hit him. He was such a . . . a self-serving little twit."

"Yeah, that's what that fellow on Slotter Key said—"

"What!" Rafe's voice came up and someone at the back of the group glanced at them. He lowered it again. "Who are you talking to on Slotter Key?"

"Security stuff, boyo. Fellow who was at the Academy, now in the Defense Department with the admiral's aunt. Knew this Hal when he was just a cadet—knew the commander as well, for that matter. Arrived with the Slotter Key Spaceforce, the Rector of Defense's emissary."

It must be the legendary Master Sergeant MacRobert, Rafe thought. Now apparently Ky's aunt's assistant.

"Said he was a bright-enough cadet, more polish than substance maybe, but not from breeding. Riding the admiral's coattails."

"I suppose," Rafe said, climbing into the car again. "You think I was an idiot."

"Something like that, yes," Gary said. He tapped on the partition, and the driver set off. "But men like you, if they ever do love anyone, are apt to do stupid things. I certainly did."

"She will forgive me," Rafe said, with more hope than confidence.

"Keep the hope," Gary said. "I'm off home tomorrow, whatever. I need a break from all this drama . . . but if you ask me, which you haven't yet, the best thing you can do is just tell her."

"I still say he deserved it," Rafe said.

"Maybe. But I'm not sure he deserves what he's going to get in the end."

"Disgrace? Maybe discharge? You don't think he deserves that?"

Gary sighed. "Rafe, after all this time there are still things you don't understand. You've got a lot more power than you realize. ISC may be less than it used to be, but it's still the single more powerful corporation anywhere. Every word you say carries more weight, sets off more tremors. If that boy only loses his commission he'll be lucky."

Master Sergeant Cally Pitt had no part in the festivities going on at Government House, but had come to the hotel bar across the street to meet the renowned Master Sergeant MacRobert (ret.) in person.

"So, how did you personally meet Admiral Vatta?" he asked after the first introductions. He had insisted on buying her drink because, he said, he was now a loafing REMF and she still worked for a living. She knew better; he might not be in uniform, but he was far from retired, and she doubted that his assignment to Slotter Key's Defense Department would keep him out of uniform for long.

"I damn near blew her head off," Pitt said, sipping her drink.

"That sounds . . . like an interesting introduction," MacRobert said. Pitt was aware of something dangerous in his tone.

"You know most of it," Pitt said. "We were in Sabine System. She was on that little unarmed freighter—you knew that. We were supposed to check out every ship in the system—including hers—pick one to stow commanders of ships on, one to use as a courier—the usual."

"My experience has not, heretofore, included system invasions," MacRobert said. "I'm presuming you were hired for this?"

"We were hired, supposedly, by a legitimate government to pressure Sabine into something—I wasn't clear on what. Seize the main space stations, seize shipping and hold it. At any rate, it was a routine boarding—and I was impressed that she was being as by-the-book as we were—until an idiot crewman tried to ambush us. I did try to push her out of the way, but—" Pitt shrugged. "Instinct takes over. She took damage; the other fellow died. We got her back to our surgeons, and they fixed her up." Pitt did not want to detail the injuries, not to someone who looked so twitchy. She hadn't expected this reaction, exactly. He knew what she—and Mackensee—thought of Ky Vatta. They hadn't intended to hurt her; it had been an accident. Surely he understood that. He looked to be a good ten years older than she was, but that meant little if he had the skills.

"An odd beginning . . . I understand you requested this assignment, to be with her."

Pitt shrugged again. "I did. She's—she was remarkable, in several ways. You've heard about the rest of the Sabine thing? How she handled a mutiny of the prisoners we put aboard her ship? I thought she'd make a great officer in our company and told my CO that. He said try to recruit her. I wasn't surprised to find out she'd had military training."

"Yes, I knew about that." MacRobert sipped his drink.

"What I don't quite understand—and forgive me if this is too blunt—is why she wanted anything to do with you."

"I don't get it, either," Pitt said. "Usually when you almost kill someone, either they go all appeasing and clingy, or they want you dead. She decided to be grateful we'd saved her, held no grudge for the incident—and I don't think she'd know how to be clingy if you gave her a college course in it."

MacRobert snorted. "No. She wasn't one of those isolated kids, when she came in, but she wasn't always looking for someone to follow, either. That's what made it so infuriating when we—they—had to cut her loose." He shook his head sharply. "Sorry, Cally. I didn't mean to go all protective and prickly. You've been straight with us so far, and I'm sure you did what you could. But with all that happened to her—and her family—"

"No worries," Pitt said. "She was angry enough with me, when she found I'd told you she was alive after that battle at Moray."

"Um. Gathered that from what she sent Grace."

Pitt noticed he didn't refer to the Rector of Defense by her title, which was out of character for someone with his background. She asked no questions, but came to her own conclusions, and also that they were of no military significance. "My round," she said, lifting an eyebrow at him; he nodded, smiling, and she gave the order to the bartender. "My CO wants me to stay in touch with you," she said next.

"I have no objection," MacRobert said. "As long as it's fine with my seniors—and right now it is."

"What do you think of Cascadia so far?" Pitt asked.

"Not enough fly-fishing streams in range," MacRobert said. "Otherwise, a nice-enough place to visit. What about you?"

They discussed vacation spots for the next hour or so, watching as the line of arrivals across the street died away and then the shiny green cars began to line up once more, to take the guests away. Pitt had long since decided that MacRobert was charming and deadly, a combination she liked very much.

Now he cocked his head. "I think the celebration's breaking up over there. Are you on escort duty, or would you like another round?"

"I should get back," Pitt said. "My boss wants a written report on the evening and I need to debrief a few people, so I should catch the next shuttle up."

"I hope to see you again, then. You're welcome to stop by, if your duties take you to Slotter Key. Grace would love to meet you."

"As duty takes me," Pitt said. She was not at all sure she wanted to meet Grace Vatta.

"As duty takes all of us," MacRobert murmured, standing politely as she slid out of her seat and turned away.

TWENTY-FOUR

Master Sergeant Cally Pitt had enough rank to get a seat in the forward compartment of the shuttle, since all the officers who'd gone downside to attend the reception were staying overnight. She could have stayed—would have stayed, if a certain other senior NCO hadn't been so obviously not looking for company. But better to get back aboard and sleep in her own bunk, if no more was to be gained. The chatter in the shuttle's lounge area, juicy as it was—Rafe Dunbarger had attacked Ky Vatta's former boyfriend in public, at the reception—seemed too far-fetched to be of interest. She overheard four different versions of it, from a mild rebuke (well, maybe) to both participants having screamed obscenities at each other until separated by Security (unlikely). Whatever had happened, she was sure, was none of her business, and the facts of what had happened would show up eventually in the official report of someone who had been there. She dozed lightly on the way up and waited until the troops and civs in the rear compartment—some slightly boozy— had exited before she left. With luck, she wouldn't have to notice any of them; their respective shore patrols would pick them up before she got there.

From the shuttle dock, Pitt moved briskly toward the

Mackensee docking area, out at the tip of one of the lower branches—stupid design for a space station, but she didn't have to live here.

Then she saw a too-familiar movement in the huddle ahead of her, across the corridor. The uniforms weren't Mackensee, which meant it wasn't technically her business, a mix of USD and Slotter Key and Cascadian and Nexan . . . none of whose own security forces seemed to be in the area.

"Here!" she said loudly. The back row turned, stared at her a moment, and then edged away. "What's going on?"

"Nothing to concern you," one rash youngster said, then took another look at the rack of medals on her dress uniform, the stripes up her sleeve, and shut his mouth. Pitt gave him a humorless grin.

"Disorder concerns me," she said. "As guests on Cascadia Main Station, where by Cascadian law rudeness is punishable, it should concern you as well. Now: what's going on?" She walked up to them as if she owned the place; they moved aside reluctantly. In a heap on the deck lay a man in a Slotter Key dress uniform, with the pips of a sub-lieutenant on his shoulder, a *Bailey's Reef* ship patch, a single narrow stripe on his sleeve, and entirely too much blood on the deck under his head. He stirred slightly; at least he was breathing.

"Well," Pitt said. "I'd say you lot have something to answer for. Names and ships, if you please." One on the far side took off running, but the others, now shamefaced and shuffling their feet, mumbled names and ship assignments into her recorder. "And why, precisely, should I not immediately call Station Security and have you arrested?" Pitt asked.

"He deserved it," said one, a thickset young woman in Bissonet's lighter blue. "Bastard trashed the commander."

"Commander . . . ?"

"Admiral Vatta. I was there when that ISC man told him off. Worthless pile of trash—" She made to nudge the fallen man with the toe of her boot; Pitt stopped her with a look.

"They were friends," another Slotter Key sub-lieutenant said. "I was at the Academy with them; I knew that, and then he turned against her after she left. I didn't know about the letter and the ring, though, until tonight."

Pitt sighed. She'd hoped she'd left the gossip behind her but clearly not. Someone probably called Cascadia Station from the planet, and of course the story had grown with each repetition. Junior officers left behind on Cascadia Station—bored, possibly drunk—had leapt on it with enthusiasm and come to meet the shuttle. She suspected that the story now included much that never happened, though she wondered what letter and what ring he was talking about.

"Admiral Vatta put whatever happened behind her," Pitt said, certain that was true. "If she isn't pursuing it, you shouldn't, either. It dishonors her, to have people who claim to admire her brawling in the station corridors."

"I don't want him on my—our—ship," the Slotter Key sub-lieutenant said. He, too, had a *Bailey's Reef* ship patch.

Stubbornness, Pitt thought, seemed to be a Slotter Key trait. She fixed him with her best senior-NCO glare. "Sub-lieutenant, with all due respect, until you command your own ship, you will serve with anyone your commander accepts, and treat your fellow crewmembers with the respect due them as your shipmates. Or you are not worthy of a commission, whether he is or not."

His jaw dropped a little; clearly that thought had never occurred to him.

"You're not one of us," began someone else. Pitt looked that one straight in the eye as well.

"I am not in your chain of command, no. But I suggest you consider how your chain of command will regard this breach of discipline. However your commanders may regard this unfortunate individual—" She glanced down at Hal, who was now moving a little, and groaned as if for punctuation. "—they are unlikely to agree that you had a right to corner him in the corridor and assault him. Discipline, not self-righteous, self-indulgent rage, is what enables military success, ladies and gentlemen." That was almost word for word the lecture she had gotten as a youngster, one time when she and her fellow privates had ganged up on the fellow they suspected of being the barracks thief.

"What's going on here?" came a call from down the corridor. Pitt recognized the tone of reinforcements with some relief.

"We need a Slotter Key Spaceforce medical team," she said, without taking her eyes off the group in case they bolted. "And shore patrol from the following ships . . ." She read the names off.

"Trouble?" But that was followed by a murmur as whoever it was called for assistance; then he came up beside her, looked down at Hal, and whistled. "Well, this is a fine mess." He was also in Slotter Key colors, and also had a *Bailey's Reef* ship patch and as many hashmarks on his sleeve as Pitt.

He glared at the nearest Slotter Key sub-lieutenant. "Tell me you had nothing to do with this . . ." But the bruised knuckles told their own tale. He sighed. "Captain Angard is going to have your hide," he said. "You know what she said at Orders this morning."

"I was just so angry," the sub-lieutenant said. "After all

he did . . . and they weren't even going to do anything about it . . ."

"With all due respect, sir, you were just so effing stupid." He glanced at Pitt. "Excuse my language, Master Sergeant."

"I've used worse," Pitt said.

"I've called for medics and shore patrol. Captain says she's on the way." The sub-lieutenant looked scared now. Behind him, down the corridor, a unit of the Slotter Key shore patrol jogged around the bend, their armbands bright.

In just a few minutes, all the assailants were standing in a row against the bulkhead waiting for the arrival of their relevant officers, and a team of medics had turned Hal over, revealing the unlovely result of a multiperson beating . . . the flattened nose, the black eyes, the split lips, the lumps of bruises already darkening, and that was only what showed. Two bloody teeth lay on the deck; one of the medics scooped them into a jar and tucked it into his pocket. Under the uniform, Pitt knew, would be other injuries. He regained consciousness as they cut away his uniform, peering through the slits the swelling black eyes left him.

"What happened, sir?" asked one of the medics.

"Feh dowah ladduh," Hal said, his speech slurred. Pitt gave him a point for that, at least.

"A ladder with a lot of people on it?" asked the other medic, grinning.

"Juth feh." The missing teeth robbed him of the sibilant.

"Well, we're taking you to sick bay . . ." The medics loaded him onto a gurney, and the gurney onto a scooter, then climbed on and eased away, tires humming softly on the deck. Pitt glanced at the *Bailey's Reef* NCO, who was staring at the bloodstains on the deck, sucking his teeth.

"If you don't need me—" she began.

"Captain'd like to speak to you," he said. "She said if you would—"

"Of course," Pitt said. "But I need to report in myself." Easy enough by skullphone; she called her ship, explained that there'd been a little disturbance on the dockside, and she'd stopped it, but would need to wait for someone else's CO to interview her.

"Is this something Admiral Vatta needs to know about?" the duty officer asked. "Trouble with the Cascadians, an alliance problem?"

"Not that," Pitt said carefully. "But in the end, yes, she needs to know it. I'd rather deliver that report in person, sir."

"Very well. Call if you need me."

Ky Vatta maintained appropriate decorum, pleasantly refusing invitations to come to this or that home for a nightcap and insisting that she really did need to get back to her quarters. She said nothing to her aides on the way back to her suite. She knew they knew she was upset about something; she knew they would find out what it was all too soon, if they hadn't heard already, and that was an additional humiliation. If Rafe had been there, she could have torn a strip off him . . . but he had not tried to catch up with her. Just as well. The person she really wanted to eviscerate was Stella, and Stella was an inconvenient distance away.

She acknowledged the salutes from the few uniformed personnel in the hotel corridors as she headed for the lifts.

"Would the admiral like anything—?" one of her aides said as the lift stopped.

"No thanks," Ky said, summoning a smile. "I just have a few things to do before bed." The aides stayed on the lift; Ky nodded to the guard at the door of her suite and entered, closing it carefully behind her, closing the second door that shut off the little entrance foyer.

Even then she did not do what she felt like doing, which was screaming and smashing something. Jaw clenched to keep from the screaming part, she undressed carefully, hanging her evening dress uniform on the rack provided, where she could push it into the antechamber for the cleaners to take care of.

Damn Rafe. Damn, damn, *damn* Rafe. How dare he? How dare Stella talk to Rafe? How dare Stella read that letter, which she herself had so carefully forgotten? How dare anyone remind her . . . and to see Hal again, in that context, with everyone around. She yanked the pillow off her bed and threw it at the mattress, a trick she'd learned as a child—it made no sound or mess. She showered, brushed her teeth . . . she was still too angry to rest. She went into the suite's office area.

Unlike either the bridge or the CCC, it had no shipboard ansible . . . she'd forgotten that. It did have a terminal for normal ansibles, though, and that was all she really needed. She put through the call to Stella's office up on the station, managing a pleasant tone as Stella's assistant answered and until she had Stella on a full-visual link.

"So how was the reception, Ky?" asked Stella. She looked relaxed, happy, and completely unaware of the trouble she'd caused.

"You disgusting, nosy, interfering bitch!"

"What?" Stella stared, eyes wide. "What do you think I've done?"

"Don't play innocent! You poked around in my desk is what you did. You found the letter . . . you found the *ring*! And you couldn't even keep quiet about it. You told him—you told *Rafe,* of all people, and probably everyone else—"

"I did not," Stella said, coloring. "I told Rafe, yes, but he was the only one—"

"You had no *right!*" Ky's head throbbed; she felt like throwing up and smashing the screen and bursting into tears, and she must not do any of those. "You had no right to tell him—to tell anyone—least of all him—"

"It was for your own good, Ky," Stella said. "He's . . . he's not safe. He's not the right man for you. He needed to know that you'd been hurt, and I didn't want you hurt again—"

"I am not a fragile blown-glass flower," Ky said. "And it's none of your business who I like, or who I choose to be with—and anyway, maybe it's just that you want him back. Maybe it just stuck in your throat that for once beautiful Stella didn't get what she wanted and Ky did—or would have if you hadn't ruined it."

Stella paled again. "That is ridiculous! And unfair. I am not after Rafe; I do not want Rafe; if I didn't think he was bad for you, dangerous for you, I wouldn't care if the two of you spent the next twenty years in bed."

"Which we will never have a chance to do, thanks to you!"

"I don't know what you're talking about," Stella said.

"Because of you, because you told him about . . . about Hal, tonight at the reception—the formal reception, in front of everyone in the universe—he buttonholed Hal and ripped him a new one—"

"What! Rafe?"

"Yes, Rafe. Publicly. So everyone knows the whole story now. I'm sure the entire fleet and the governments of at least four planets are having a nice juicy gossip about my first love affair and what they think is my second . . ."

"I can't believe he would—"

"Believe it. He did. Made me the laughingstock of . . . of everyone. And it's because of you, and your interference—"

"Ky, I'm sorry, but I never meant—"

"It doesn't matter what you *meant*. What matters is that you've completely ruined my reputation and my authority—".

"Don't be so melodramatic—"

"Don't tell me what to be!"

Stella opened her mouth, then shut it. Ky could see the pulse beating in her throat. Good.

"Ky, I'm sorry," Stella said then. "I did not mean to hurt you. I did not mean to embarrass you. When I read it, it was an accident—"

Ky huffed but said nothing.

"And yes, it was a time when I was annoyed with you, and yes, that may have colored my judgment. When I read it, I wanted to—I wanted to make it go away, so I didn't tell you I had. And when Rafe came, and told me he was—was in love with you, I didn't believe him—"

"Because little cousin Ky couldn't possibly have someone in love with her," Ky muttered.

"Oh, stop it!" Stella leaned forward. "Ky, I have an adolescent love-crazed girl living with me now, and I also remember what it was like. Of course you could have someone in love with you; of course you could love someone. But consider this: the last time I'd seen you, you didn't show any signs of caring about Rafe. With his past, I didn't believe he really cared about you, except as another of his conquests. I thought, if he knew that you'd had a bad experience, he'd go pester someone else, particularly in a political situation where showing interest in you would harm his interests."

She paused; Ky said nothing. "And I did what I thought was best for you at the time, and . . . I had no idea he'd go off his rocker and make an embarrassing scene at your reception." Another pause. "What exactly did he do?"

She said it again, slowly and distinctly. "He went and found Hal. I don't know how he found him, but it is Rafe, after all. Somehow he found him, and—I didn't hear it all, but knowing Rafe I imagine he introduced himself and started in slowly. I knew Rafe had come in—he'd passed through the receiving line—he looked better than he had on Cascadia Station, before—" He had looked like the old Rafe, fully alive, an edged weapon looking for blood; she had felt her pulse quicken. "—and the Premier wanted to talk to him. I said I'd go find him. I was trying to get away from a terminally boring district superintendent from someplace on Cascadia, who wanted to tell me all about the genealogy of trees or something."

"There's one at every business party," Stella said, with feeling.

"So I spotted Rafe, but didn't recognize Hal from behind, and got there just in time to hear Rafe quoting . . . one of the more scathing bits of Hal's letter . . ."

"That *idiot!*" Stella said. "What was he thinking?"

"And by then people had seen me; I had to just go on, and I didn't know—well, not for sure—that it was Hal until I saw his face. And there was Rafe, and Hal, and all those people staring to see what I'd do . . ." Suddenly, unexpectedly, it seemed funny. She felt the laughter bubbling up, uncontrollable as the rage had been, and struggled to hold it down. She was not ready for it to be funny; she had a right to be angry. But the laughter came anyway. "Oh, Stella. If you could have seen their faces—and probably mine—it was horrible—but it must have been funny, too—"

"What did you do?" Stella said.

"What could I do? I'm the Great Admiral Vatta; I'm not allowed to have vapors or girlish feelings. I was coolly polite to both of them and led Rafe back to the Premier. Then I had to be gracious and polite to fifty more people, when what I wanted to do was disembowel someone. Rafe. You. Anyone. I did glare at the district superintendent until he backed off." She could not help the chuckle that escaped.

"You did better than I would have," Stella said. "I would have killed him. Them. Both of them. At least."

"You wouldn't—" But now something heard and not registered caught up with her, something that had generated the bubble of humor. "Did you say—did you actually say—Rafe told you he was in love with me?"

"Yes. I didn't believe him; if I had—"

"But he said it. You think that was why—"

"Oh, Ky, for pity's sake! I get enough of this with Zori! Of *course* it was why. Of course he meant it. Now would you please either go stick a knife in him for embarrassing you, or go tell him you love him, and let me get on with this beastly audit?"

"But—what about you?"

"What *about* me? I'm buried in paperwork, that's what about me. I would much rather have been at the reception, but I couldn't spare the time."

"And you don't . . . you're not . . ."

Stella looked ready to explode, but instead burst out laughing. "Ky, you and I are both idiots, but in different ways. Listen carefully, cousin. I do not want Rafe. I do not need Rafe. I don't, I've realized, need any man. I think I may turn out rather like Aunt Grace—"

"Who has MacRobert."

"Good for her. In her—I dare not say dotage; she'll

come through the ansible and whap me with a fruitcake—
in her golden years, let's say, she's enjoying herself. But
for much of her life she ran solo."

Ky laughed again. She didn't feel angry anymore, or not
very. "What does your mother say?"

A long silence. Stella sighed. "We've talked. This thing
with Zori—I realized I have to get over—"

Ky's door chime binged. Startled, she looked at the
clock, an antique-styled confection on the fake mantel-
piece. Late. Later than late. More than halfway to morning.
"Stella, I've got to go—I'll call you later." She closed the
ansible down and spoke to the guard at the door. "Yes?"

"There's a gentleman to see you, Admiral."

"At this hour?"

"I told him—but you did say you had work to do; I
thought you might be still up."

Up, but not dressed. "Who is it?"

"Ser—Ser Dunbarger."

Not again, was her first thought. Wasn't it enough that
he'd ruined her reputation in front of everyone at the
reception—now he was coming to her suite in the middle
of the night? Her heart thundered, drowning out the prudent voice in her head.

"A moment," she said. She raced to the bedroom, flung
off the robe, snatched her uniform from the rack, and put
it on. Snarling at her fingers as she fumbled for buttons.
Cursing the day anyone invented formal footwear. Jabbing
at the deskcomp's controls to bring up an impressive
screen full of obviously military data. Knowing the whole
time that the snarling and cursing and complaining were
covering up something else.

She opened the inner door, and signaled the guard to
open the outer one.

Rafe was still in impeccable evening dress, holding a

bouquet so large it almost hid his face. "In honor of your stellar performance this evening," he said. One eyebrow lifted just a bit. "I had foolishly left it behind earlier—"

Drops of water sparkled on the shoulders of his jacket; his hair was shining not just with its natural gloss but with water.

"You're wet," she said.

"Well . . . I had to find a flower market. And it's started raining . . ."

"You'd better come in and dry off—" Her voice was cool, contained. "I'm working on—" She waved toward the desk. He came past her.

"Where's your guard—Gary?"

"Gone. He took the last shuttle up, to catch a ship back to Nexus tomorrow. Today, maybe. I'm not sure what time it is on the station. Do you have a vase? I'm sure the hotel—"

"That one, on the mantel." She closed the inner door, fully aware of all implications.

Rafe unwrapped the paper around the stems, not looking at her; she watched his hands as he flicked the paper loose at last and eased the stems into the vase. "I was an idiot," he said, still not looking at her, pushing the flowers this way and that in the vase. A blue one flopped over sideways, and he prodded it upright. "Gary told me . . . I should have known—"

"That making it clear to all the world I'd been dumped by a third-rate coward wasn't the way to enhance my reputation? Yes, you should have—and if you think you've improved it by showing up at my suite in the middle of the night—"

But now he was looking at her, the look she remembered; her voice disappeared to somewhere south of her navel. Head slightly cocked, eyebrow raised high, corner of his mouth twitching a little. "You didn't have that uniform on five minutes ago."

"I certainly did!" Ky said.

"Did not. You were undressed . . . probably in that robe I can just see half on the bed in the other room—"

She should have shut the door. She'd meant to shut the door.

"And the way I can tell, before you ask, is the buttons. Admiral Vatta never in her life buttoned her tunic crooked. So either Admiral Vatta wasn't wearing that uniform five minutes ago or . . . you are someone else. Maybe not the Admiral Vatta I embarrassed over there across the street, but—"

Ky glanced down at her tunic. He was right, damn him. It was crooked. If the guard had seen—and guards always saw everything—he, too, would know she had not been at work, still dressed.

"I was talking to Stella," she said. He flinched. "She told me how you knew. The pair of you—I was—am—furious with you both."

"Yes," he said. "I understand that. I'm sorry. Truly."

"And back before I left for Moray—the way you were then—"

He closed his eyes a moment; his mouth thinned. Then he gave her a challenging look. "I think your not letting me know you were alive, after Moray, was as bad."

For a moment she glared back, the anger rising again. But it was no use. All the old clichés ran through her mind: in for a penny, in for a pound; might as well be hung for a sheep as a lamb. She moved to the desk and shut down the deskcomp, then went to the suite's bar, crouching to look into the cooler.

"What's this—?" Rafe began. But she had found what she was looking for, and stood up again, holding a pair of limes.

"You showed me once," she said, "the way you peel a lime."

His face shifted from confusion to disbelief to delight. A rakish, wicked delight. "So I did."

"Perhaps," she said, as coolly as she could, "you would like to show me again . . ."

"You might be more comfortable with the demonstration if that tunic were buttoned properly . . ."

"Or," Ky said, "if it were not buttoned at all." She opened the top button. "Peel me a lime, Rafe."

TWENTY-FIVE

Sub-lieutenant Hal Coughlin was awake when Master Sergeant Pitt arrived, staring up at the ceiling with his one mostly open eye. Pitt tapped on the door; he barely glanced at her and stared up again.

"Want to talk to you," she said. "You may not remember me, and anyway we didn't get a chance for introductions. I'm Master Sergeant Cally Pitt, Mackensee Military Assistance Corporation, and we're interested in you."

"Huwh?"

"How? As a possible recruit. We do take people who are . . . how shall I say . . . not happy in their current organization, if we think they have potential . . ."

"You ought to be recruiting *her*," he said, his voice blurred by the injuries and repairs.

"Oh, I tried," Pitt said. "Tried for quite a while, more than once. Ky Vatta had better things to do, I think was what it came down to. You, on the other hand, don't."

He appeared to ruminate on that for a few moments, then asked, "How do you know I'm any good?"

Pitt ticked off points on her fingers. "You were an honor graduate of your Academy. That means you're not stupid. You've had good to excellent fitness reports since. That means you're not obviously lazy, dishonest, or incompetent. Until recent events, your CO thought highly of you and considered you promising."

"She doesn't now," he said.

"Well . . . no. Not just because of what you're alleged to have done, but also because you've become a public relations nightmare and you've created a discipline problem in your own fleet." Pitt thought it amusing that the man who had dumped Ky Vatta for being a public relations nightmare was now himself a public relations nightmare. She doubted he appreciated the irony. "There's always been a place for men and women who needed a change of identity for perfectly legitimate reasons—people like you. We can solve your fleet's problem, and your problem."

Within a day, former Slotter Key sub-lieutenant Hal Coughlin had resigned his commission with the full consent of his commander, and had been moved aboard a Mackensee ship to continue medical treatment.

Once they were safely aboard *Ashford,* Lieutenant Colonel Parker nodded to Pitt. "Good job, Master Sergeant. This should do us good with Slotter Key, and our intel people should learn a lot. A triple win. How're you coming along with that fellow in their Defense Department? MacRobert, isn't it?"

Pitt shook her head. "He's as tough as I am or tougher, sir. Years of experience in spycraft, is my assessment, and not about to let out anything he doesn't want to. And no, sir, before you ask, I can't get him drunk."

"Just maintain a friendly contact, then. You know what we're after—"

"Yes, sir." Pitt knew she hadn't a chance of getting useful information out of MacRobert, but she was enjoying the time she spent with him. Still . . . he called the Slotter

Key Rector of Defense "Grace." However much she enjoyed the time, he was not for her.

Master Sergeant MacRobert (ret.) appeared on Admiral Vatta's list of morning appointments with a tiny question mark beside his name. Ky deleted the question mark. Of course she wanted to meet with MacRobert again. She had seen him from a distance, and they had nodded at each other in recognition, but this would be a chance to find out about the situation back home. Including whether MacRobert and Grace Vatta were more than co-workers.

Ky finished up the list of commendations for the Nexus commanders involved in the final battle, handed that to the Nexus Defense Department courier, and stretched before telling her secretary (seconded from Cascadia's Defense Ministry) that she was ready for MacRobert.

"Admiral Vatta," he said. "It's been a while."

"It has that," she said. "And I wasn't an admiral. Sit down, Master Sergeant. You've come with messages from the Rector, I imagine?"

"Your Aunt Grace, yes. Some from her as Rector and some from her as your aunt. Which would you like first?"

"Official business first," Ky said. She felt uncommonly good this morning.

"For hand delivery only," MacRobert said, pulling a packet out of his inner pocket. "The Rector's report to you on some pertinent bits of recent history."

"That's official?" Ky asked, taking the packet.

"It is now that she's in the government," MacRobert said. "Official, but not public. And I'm to answer any of your questions and make myself available until you're satisfied."

"My first question is, just exactly what was in that ship-model thing you gave me right before I left Slotter Key?"

"Oh, that. Well . . . it could have been the Slotter Key version of what your cousin's now manufacturing . . . if it had worked. We were trying to build a miniaturized ansible or semi-ansible. More of a booster unit, actually. And there were some access codes I thought you might find handy—whatever happened to it?"

"Cannibalized for parts for the ship's own communications," Ky said, "when the mutineers had control of the ship for a time."

"Ah. Well, that's probably for the best."

"I do know Aunt Grace lost an arm, and that the old government fell. I presume those were related?"

"Yes. The whole story's in those data cubes, but basically Grace figured out early on—before the government imposed sanctions against Vattas—that someone high up had been bought out. Blackmailed, it turns out. I don't know how much you knew about her position in Vatta Transport—"

"Not much," Ky said.

"Nobody was supposed to, except your father and Stella's. She headed corporate security—including threat assessment—and she knew the only way the plot against your family could have gotten past her was with government support."

"But why?" Ky asked.

"We think that was your infamous relative Osman, but given that he's dead I doubt we'll ever know the whole story. Grace said he had a serious grudge against your father and Stella's because they were the ones who got him expelled from the family."

Grace. The man who had been a stickler for military courtesy as long as she'd known him called the Rector of Defense just plain Grace? And, as she looked at him, he was almost grinning at her, reading her reaction to that as he had once read cadets' faces.

"So," Ky said, yanking her mind firmly away from any consideration of Aunt Grace and MacRobert in the same situation as herself and Rafe, "what about the government connection?"

"That we did uncover. All governments have some level of corruption—power attracts those who want it, and if there's been a completely honest government in the history of humankind, no history book's ever mentioned it. So it was no surprise to find some shady stuff going on in Slotter Key—bribes offered and taken, evasions of tax laws and rules, and so on. And like all large societies, we had our organized crime, and it had its contacts with interstellar criminals. The former President had a choice, as he saw it, between exposure and prosecution for the illegalities of his time in office, or letting the Vatta family be attacked. For the tiny bit it's worth, I don't think he had any idea how big the attack would be, or what Turek's real goals were."

"And Aunt Grace—?"

He grinned openly now. "She managed to infiltrate all sorts of places the government thought were impregnable, including the President's private quarters. She had taps left over from the Cape Girond Rebellion, and she'd never stopped keeping them updated. She had agents of her own, non-Vatta people she'd used to acquire information on Vatta's competitors."

"How did you get involved?" Ky asked.

"We—Spaceforce that is—knew someone in government must have been complicit because of the form of attack on your family's Corleigh compound. The only way to land the kind of weapons used, and then clear away the evidence, was a shuttle landing—a shuttle landing that managed to go unrecorded. Someone in the government had to tell someone in Spaceforce when to shut off the satellite surveillance and fake the continuity of its data. With the attack coming so soon after the incident that got you in trouble . . . well, I saw connections. Grace worked out the way we could communicate unobtrusively—"

"Which was?"

"Fly-fishing. We met on a river—she'd moved Helen and Jo's children to a country place, and I'd rented a cabin a few kilometers away. She was planning on doing it all herself, but after she lost her arm when assassins tried for the children—"

Ky blinked. "Slow down. Tell me the whole thing."

MacRobert began with the layout of the country house and grounds, the security Grace had designed and planted around it, and the circumstances that had led up to that morning.

"We were going to meet on the river that afternoon; I'd started fishing early, as I usually did on our meeting days, checking both banks upstream and down for intruders or surveillance gear. I didn't see or hear anything unusual until the first shot—it was far enough out in the country that the assassins didn't bother with silencers. I went up the slope from the river as fast as I could without being obvious, and came out of the scrub just in time to see Grace shot. With the assassin between me and Grace and the child, I didn't risk a shot—I just stabbed him with my fish-gutting knife."

"So if she was minus an arm, I'm guessing she didn't kill the President—did you?"

"He killed himself," MacRobert said. "When Grace let me access her network of agents, their data plus what we in Spaceforce had been able to compile was enough to bring down the government. The Commandant, I believe, visited the President and at some point the President decided that it would be preferable to end his own life

rather than face the kind of charges he would have faced."
MacRobert paused, then went on. "By the way, the
Commandant sent his personal congratulations to you. He
always thought a lot of you, and said to tell you he's not
surprised at your successes."

"I have been," Ky said.

"You Vattas are remarkable," MacRobert continued.
"Your enemies wanted you destroyed, but those of you
not actually killed just would not give up."

"Speaking of those not actually killed," Ky said, "we
learned yesterday that Toby's parents are still alive on
Elmendorf. Their ansible's been down, but they're fine.
They want him to come home and finish school. With
that dog, of course. Stella says he's a nice boy but it'll be
a relief to have a place to herself again. A teenage boy and
a dog are really not her idea of interior décor."

"Isn't he smitten with that girl whose father was—"

"One of Turek's agents, yes. Nice girl," Ky said. She still
wasn't sure what she'd said that helped Zori. "Toby's parents are helping her and her mother relocate to
Elmendorf—apparently the mother's not welcome here
with her own family due to the scandal. I expect those
two, if they stick together, will end up running the manufacturing end someday."

MacRobert nodded. "Nothing will surprise me about
your family, after the last few years."

It was not their first night together, but it might be their
last. Any night might be their last and they made the most
of this one. Still, the approach of separation led to talk of
the future.

"How do you define when the war is over?" Rafe asked.
"Vatta's won, but what about you?"

"How do you define when your job is done at ISC?"

Rafe ran a finger down her face. "A fair question. We both won, but different things. I can't leave ISC yet; there's too much to do, too many people who depend on me. And Stella was right about one thing—you aren't meant to be an executive's wife. Your fleet needs you as much as my people need me."

"I don't want to leave this," Ky murmured.

"Nor I. But we both know we will."

"But not tonight," Ky said. "And there are plenty of limes in the cooler."

Rafe looked at her. "My dear admiral . . . you've never seen what I can do with a *pear* . . ."

EXTRAS

www.orbitbooks.net

About the Author

Former marine **Elizabeth Moon** is the author of many science fiction and fantasy novels, including Nebula Award winner *The Speed of Dark*, and *Remnant Population*, a Hugo Award finalist. Elizabeth has earned degrees in both history and biology, run for public office and been a columnist on her local newspaper. She now lives with her husband near Austin, Texas and you can visit her website at www.elizabethmoon.com

To find out more about Elizabeth and our other Orbit authors, register for the free monthly newsletter at www.orbitbooks.net

If you enjoyed
VICTORY CONDITIONS
look out for

DARK SPACE

Book 1 of the Sentients of Orion

by

Marianne de Pierres

MIRA

I've heard you are beautiful.

Insignia was whispering to her again. This time the words were lucid. It was not always that way: mostly the voice in her mind was a mere hum, punctuated by peaks and troughs of half-formed words, as though the effort required to shape them into something she could understand was too great.

Could Insignia hear her replies? She did not know really, but still she spoke to it – it had been her only companion here when there had been no other.

Tonight is graduation, she explained.

Insignia sighed and Mira Fedor felt it as a pressure in her chest, a slight involuntary lift of her shoulders.

I have been alone for a long time . . .

Since my father died, said Mira.

She hoped her words might prompt it to say more but the biozoon's presence subsided back into an irregular drone.

As always, Mira felt its withdrawal keenly, and yet today would be the last time.

She inspected herself in the gilded mirror. Today, for graduation, she wore her familia's traditional five-thousand-gold-thread fellala with its blood-jewelled silk velum. The velum's rubies burned under the chandeliers. Faja had sent it to Mira from their villa in Loisa as a sign of her sisterly pride – for only one ceremonial robe remained in their familia now. It was heavy and stiff, and restricted her movement, but it gave her belief.

Smoothing loose tendrils of her dark hair under the headdress, Mira allowed excitement to twist her lips into a smile. It was said that for Fedors, first *union* with a biozoon was like a wedding night. The moment of her life's purpose had finally come, and it was not too soon, for dark, impulsive thoughts lurked near.

Her need for *union* with the Cipriano Clan's organic pilot ship had become a craving, a hunger in her mouth that she could not satisfy, an ungovernable heat in her lower belly. Such feelings were improper for a Baronessa – but then, a Baronessa had never harboured the Inborn pilot gene before: indeed, a *woman* had not.

The Studium bells tolled, jolting Mira from her reverie: the formal ceremony was beginning. She gave her room the barest of glances despite knowing that she would not return. Her years here had been at best disagreeable. She had detested the sly behaviour of the other aristos and the way they hung off the young Principe, Trin Pellegrini, as if he granted meaning to their lives.

'You *are* different,' Cochetta Silvio had drawled loudly enough for all at one dreary patrizio soirée to hear. 'So sombre, Baronessa. So *thin*.'

And, of course, there was the unspoken thing, the thing Cochetta was too refined to mention but which stood between her and the other aristos in the way that an infectious sickness created its own distance – her hereditary talent.

'Different? Si, thank Crux,' Mira had replied. But the sting of the snub stayed with her.

She dragged the heavy doors of her room closed with two hands and stepped out into the vast portico. The nano-filtered baroque arches lent Mount Pell a soft, almost benign appearance – so deceptive when the real Araldis sweltered under intolerably dry heat.

Mira let the view down to the Studium menagerie calm her: *All their taunts will mean nothing after today.* Straightening her shoulders, she sealed her velum and set the filter to hide everything but her eyes. Then she descended the central helicoidal staircase to the grand ante-room.

The entire Studium attended graduation, even the untitled Nobile. Now, as she entered, they jostled for position alongside the patricians like a gaggle of ornately feathered birds. Threading her way between them, Mira took her place on the dais to the side and a step behind the young Principe, Trinder Pellegrini, and his cousin Duca Raldo Silvio.

'Bonjourno, Baronessa,' said Raldo. He stroked his stiff moustache with practised affectation and gave her a smirking sideways glance.

'Duca,' she acknowledged with suspicion and the barest curtsy. Since when did Raldo Silvio use his guile on her?

On her other side Trinder Pellegrini dipped his head – enough to satisfy courtesy – but did not speak. In fact, he had not spoken to her for months now, not since . . .

'*Patrizios,* please be seated.' The Principe's maestro appeared at the edge of the dais. The ante-room's smart acoustics dispersed his command as if it were a whisper spoken directly into each person's ear. When satisfied that the audience was settled, he announced simply, 'The Principe.'